P9-CQF-723

LOST AND FOUND

ORSON SCOTT CARD

LOST AND FOUND

BLACK STONE
PUBLISHING

Copyright © 2019 by Orson Scott Card
Published in 2019 by Blackstone Publishing
Cover and book design by Djamika Smith

Printed in the United States of America

First edition: 2019
ISBN 978-1-9826-1341-9
Young Adult Fiction / Fantasy

1 3 5 7 9 10 8 6 4 2

CIP data for this book is available
from the Library of Congress

Blackstone Publishing
31 Mistletoe Rd.
Ashland, OR 97520

www.BlackstonePublishing.com

To Geoffrey, Emily, and Zina
Safe so far,
And never so lost
That you can't be found.

1

Ezekiel Blast liked to walk to school alone. Not that he liked anything about going to school. But since he had to go there, and the transportation choices were (1) crowded schoolbus, (2) Dad driving him, and (3) his feet, he chose walking. And since nobody came near him, walking meant walking alone, and he was fine with that.

So he was not thrilled when the short grade-school girl started shadowing him. Apparently one of the routes he took passed near her house, and because (apparently) nobody loved her, she had to walk that last mile on her short legs, taking two steps for every step of his.

She didn't call out for him to wait up. She didn't try to catch up—or if she did, she failed. But each day in that second week of Ezekiel's freshman year at Downy Soft High School, she was waiting on the corner of Blynken and Nod till he passed her. Then she fell in step behind him, each time starting out just a little closer.

This last mile was the part of the daily commute where Ezekiel had no choice of route—between the high-fenced railroad tracks and the Haw Haw River, you could only walk or drive on Winkle Road. This meant that all the walking dead from east of the school had to pass along the road at roughly the same time, and they began to bunch up and greet each other and talk and all those other things that brain-sucking high school students do.

Except Ezekiel. At least twenty yards ahead of him and twenty yards behind him, there was nobody. If it looked to the kids ahead of him like he might be catching up, they'd cross the street. And since they usually made it a point to glare at him as they did it, he could not "chalk it up to coincidence, you narcissistic bonehead," as Dad suggested when this all began back in fifth grade.

"They've all forgotten, so let it go," Dad said. Dad declared with utter certitude so many false things that Ezekiel had stopped trying to point out that since Dad had never seen how they treated Ezekiel, perhaps Ezekiel was the world's foremost expert on Ezekiel Bliss's continuing pariah status, and Dad might temper his conclusions in light of the data he received from the world's foremost expert. As Dad always said, "An expert is just an idiot who used to be pert."

On Monday of week three of the eighth circle of hell, Short Grade-School Girl stepped out just before he reached her lurking spot and fell into step beside him.

That lasted about four seconds, because Ezekiel picked up his pace and she was immediately left behind.

And about ten seconds later, here she was again, only now she was jogging. "I'm actually a pretty good long-distance runner," she said. "And there's almost nothing in my backpack because I do all my homework in the library at school before I walk home. So unless you run, which will make you sweaty and stinky, I can keep up this pace the whole way there."

"Thanks for the warning," said Ezekiel.

He realized at once that this was a mistake. By answering her, he had turned this into a conversation. Why couldn't she have been silent like the rest of the walking dead?

"I have one question," she said.

"The answer is, buzz off," said Ezekiel.

"Are you really a thief?"

He lengthened his stride until he was loping. Again he left her behind. And again, only a few seconds later, she was beside him, flat-out running. "Everybody says you're a thief and that's why they won't have anything to do with you. Is it true?"

"Yes," he said.

"That was a lie," she said.

"It's true that everybody says I'm a thief and that's why they won't have anything to do with me."

"But are they right? Are you a thief?"

Ezekiel abruptly stopped loping and settled down to a normal walking pace. Short Grade-School Girl slowed down, too, and was soon beside him again. She was the first kid who had actually asked him, to his face, and so she had earned an answer. "I never stole anything in my life," said Ezekiel.

"OK, that's the truth," she said. "And it's kind of what I figured, because if *everybody* says something it's almost always wrong."

"You must have real trouble with gravity."

"Everybody talks about gravity, but nobody knows what it is or how it works, so it's just an empty word."

"I don't talk about gravity," said Ezekiel.

"Because you don't talk to anybody about anything," said Short Grade-School Girl. "I hope you didn't mind my asking you about that."

Ezekiel didn't answer.

"OK, you *do* mind. You think I was incredibly rude to just blurt it out."

Ezekiel shook his head. He hated it when people assumed they knew what he was thinking. Especially when they got it completely wrong.

"Yeah, OK, *I* think I was incredibly rude to blurt it out, too. But tell me this, Mister Manners, how else was I going to find out the truth, except by asking the world's foremost expert on whether Ezekiel Bliss is a thief or not?"

World's foremost expert. The very words Ezekiel had used the last time he bothered having an argument with his father. Was he happy that he and Short Grade-School Girl talked alike? That would take some thought. Though he was unlikely to be able to have any thoughts until she stopped talking.

"Wouldn't you rather have me ask *you*," she said, "than listen to what the idiots are saying?"

"Why do you care whether I'm a thief or not?"

"Because I don't own much, but if I lose any of it, I can't afford to replace it. So if I'm going to walk to school with you, I had to know if I was in danger of you stealing from me."

"Don't walk to school with me."

"You don't own the road."

"I like to walk alone."

"You've already explained that to everybody else and that's why they clear the road for you."

"The walking dead can cross the street to avoid me or not. Since they don't exist, I don't care what they do."

"The walking dead," said Short Grade-School Girl. "I like that. Much better to call them 'the walking dead' than 'idiots.'"

"Are you stupid or what?" asked Ezekiel.

"Hard choice, but I'll take 'what,'" she answered.

"You know that I'm the school leper. Why would you walk with me?"

"I'm not walking *with* you. I'm walking inside your shunning bubble."

"Yet you seem to be here *talking* to me whether I like it or not."

"I'm just relieved to know you speak English," she said.

"Why do you want to share my exile?" he asked.

"Oh come on," she answered. "Are you blind?"

"So you ask questions, but you don't answer them."

"Look at me, Ezekiel Bliss. Who do you think is the biggest target for bullies at Downy High School?"

Ezekiel thought about that. "You'd think they'd be ashamed to pick on somebody your size."

"They're *proud* to think of new short jokes and new names to call me. And no, I'm not going to list them. Plus, tripping me is great fun because when I hit the ground I make such a tiny little sprawl. And shoving me into the lockers is something even the chess geeks are strong enough to do."

Ezekiel thought for another moment and then slowed down his pace. "All right, you can walk with me."

She also slowed down. "Thank you," she said.

"Am I going too slow now?" he asked.

"No, this is a comfortable speed."

"How about this," said Ezekiel. "You walk inside my 'shunning bubble' and I walk slowly enough that you don't have to run or jog to keep up. But you don't say anything."

"*Ever?*" she asked.

"You got it."

"Starting when?"

"Yesterday," said Ezekiel.

"If I had a time machine I wouldn't need *you*."

Ezekiel said nothing.

"Ezekiel Bliss, why do you think you have a right to control me?"

"I don't," said Ezekiel. "But I have a right to tell you what I *wish* you would do."

"I'm not your fairy godmother, Ezekiel Bliss."

"If you're going to talk to me—since you have no respect for my deepest, most heartfelt wishes— then please have the decency never to call me by that name."

"What, then? Zeke? Zek? Kiel? Easc? Easy?"

"Ezekiel is fine. But not Bliss."

She was silent for a moment. Ezekiel knew that it was too good to last.

"So you have a happy last name, but you don't like it," she said.

"My true last name," said Ezekiel, "is 'Blast.'"

"Ezekiel Blast, I'm glad to know you," she said. "Do you want to know my name?"

"What good would that do me?"

"None," she said. "But I'd rather you think of me by a name than as 'the short girl,' which is what you've *been* thinking of me as."

"I've *been* thinking of you as Short Grade-School Girl."

"I'm in tenth grade," she said.

"Give me a break," said Ezekiel. "I would have noticed you in middle school."

"You must have overlooked me," she said, but with a snotty tone that told him it was a joke.

"You transferred in?"

"My mom's job got her assigned here. Managing the Downy branch of Haw River Bank."

"It has branches?"

"Branch. There's the main bank in Haw River, and there's the Downy branch."

"So your mother is, like, a big deal."

"A big deal in the least significant bank in America," said Short Grade-School Girl.

"All right, tell me your name," said Ezekiel.

"Look me up."

"They don't sort the school records by height," said Ezekiel.

"I'm Betty Sorenson, and stop right now, before you make any jokes that involve mispronouncing my name as 'Bitty' or 'Itty-bitty' or 'Biddy' or 'Beddy' or 'Buddy' or 'Bidet.'"

"Wasn't going to use any of those, but thanks for the list."

"Like I told my mom, naming me Betty instead of Elizabeth was the second worst trick she ever played on me."

Ezekiel almost asked what the worst trick was but realized that it probably had something to do with her genes.

"Thanks for letting me walk with you, Ezekiel Blast. I promise I'll say only half the things I think of."

"My guess is that that will still result in a continuous monologue from the corner of Blynken and Nod till we get to the school."

"I'll stop to breathe now and then."

"Not as often and not as long, now that I'm not making you run."

"Very kind of you," she said. "Your scorn is preferable to the public shaming I would be subjected to every day on the school bus."

"You're really in tenth grade?"

"I don't lie."

"Are you *old* enough for tenth grade?"

"I'm smart enough for college but my mother decided not to push my luck. She needs a few more promotions before she can afford to send me to college."

"Community college is free, isn't it?"

"More than twelve hundred dollars a semester, plus it's too far for me to walk, and even if I were old enough to drive and rich enough to buy a car, I can't reach the pedals or see over the dashboard, so my mom would have to hire, or *be*, my chauffeur."

"So what's your deal?" asked Ezekiel. "You're incredibly short, but you don't have any of the disproportions that usually go with dwarfism."

She stopped cold.

Ezekiel paused for a moment, then kept on walking.

He thought she had given up on the whole project, but then he heard the pitter patter of little feet.

"You're a jerk," she said.

"Wow, it's worth running really fast in hot weather to tell me something I already know."

"I'm a proportionate dwarf, if it matters so much to you. I don't have achondroplasia, I have growth hormone deficiency and a metabolic disorder so I'll never be a giant but I also will never be fat and if I ever buy a bra bigger than triple-A cup I'll have to stuff it with kleenex."

"You don't know that," said Ezekiel.

"I know what kind of luck I have," she said.

"How old are you?"

"I'm almost fourteen."

"That's old enough to know that if you can ask *me* a rude question because I'm the world's foremost expert on the topic, I can ask you any damn thing I want about subjects on which *you're* the world's foremost expert."

"There are dozens of experts who know way more about dwarfism than I do. I met them all one at a time when they examined me."

"And you know more about your body than any of them ever will," said Ezekiel. "You want me to call you Betty?"

"Beth," she said. "If Betty can be a nickname for Elizabeth, then Beth can be a nickname for Betty."

"Beth Sorenson, I'm the thief you chose to walk to school with. And you're the proportionate dwarf that I choose to walk to school with."

She seemed to digest that for a few moments.

"So we're friends?"

Ezekiel shook his head. "Nothing's ever good enough for you, is it."

"All right, I won't try to eat lunch with you," she said. "Or help you with your homework."

"Really tenth grade," said Ezekiel, shaking his head.

Beth set her face and kept walking in silence.

"So you're some kind of genius," said Ezekiel.

"I'm very good at the subjects they teach in school. Including P.E., which consists of running from one end of the football field to the other. I usually finish first because I actually care about running."

"Meaning that you have nobody to talk with along the way," said Ezekiel.

"I say what I mean," she said icily.

Silence for a dozen more steps.

"That's right, nobody talks to me, and the really nasty girls say things that would make me cry if I were a real live girl instead of a wooden puppet."

"I'm glad you're sticking with your policy of telling the truth."

"And you hate it that nobody will talk to you except the pathetic short thirteen-year-old tenth-grade girl."

"No, I hate it that the pathetic short thirteen-year-old tenth-grade girl won't stop talking."

A longer silence than before.

"Those were your words, not mine," said Ezekiel.

Still silence.

"If we're going to be friends," said Ezekiel, "you have to deal with the things I say, just like I have to deal with the things you say."

"I liked you better as a thief," she said.

"Yeah, I get it," he answered. "But you're the one who decided to travel inside my shunning bubble."

Beth brushed her sleeve across her eyes. "What name do you use on Facebook?" she asked.

Ezekiel looked askance at her.

"OK, right, not on Facebook. Or Twitter or Snapchat or—"

"Not on anything," said Ezekiel.

"No computer access?"

"Of course I have computer access. How else am I going to plagiarize my papers for school?"

"Are you poor, or is your dad working class, or what?"

"My dad's a butcher at the Food Lion here in Downy."

"And your mom?" she asked.

"Dead," said Ezekiel.

"Cancer?" asked Beth.

"Bad driving," said Ezekiel. "Not hers. Guy who hit her got six months in jail. I was four."

"Were you in the car?"

"She wasn't in a car," said Ezekiel. "What about your dad?"

"He's probably alive. Somewhere. Couldn't deal with how tall I wasn't at the age of eight. Or else he found somebody he liked better than Mom. If I ever see him again, I'll ask."

"Now we have shared our deepest pain," said Ezekiel. "Can we please shut up now? For the last fifty yards before we enter Downy Soft High School?"

Beth gave him a chuckle. Which he appreciated because this was the first time he had ever told anybody his private name for the school. Or, for that matter, his true last name. Or what happened to his mother. Or what his dad did for a living. Or anything.

He mostly hated that now he was going to have company—chatty company—every day on the way to school.

But he was also partly looking forward to tomorrow. Because he hadn't realized until this morning how many words he had stored up inside, waiting for somebody to say them to.

Also, because she was talking to him, he hadn't obsessed over all the lost objects he passed today. Seventy-four that had been there every day since the start of school, most of them girls' scrunchies, which apparently fell off their heads at an alarming rate. And three new lost items: a single toddler-size shoe, a hand towel, and a Hot Wheels Batmobile. Without

Beth's chatter—and his own decision to respond and even ask questions of his own—he would have spent the walk thinking about how the shoe belonged to a child in a really poor family, who would have a hard time replacing it, and where he could possibly take it so that they would have a chance of getting it back. And imagining how a hand towel might fly out the window of a car, or get ripped off a backyard clothesline by the wind, or get used to pick up a dying pet from the street. And thinking of a child looking and looking for his coolest Hot Wheels, all through the house, all through the yard, never knowing that somehow it ended up in the gutter on Winkle Street a quarter mile from the shared campus of Downy High, Downy Middle, and Howard Coble Elementary.

Of course, he had still thought about all those things, between the bits of chat. But because of his conversation with Beth, he wasn't *anxious* about them. This was starting out to be a pretty good day.

2

Ezekiel Blast was called out of second period and followed the hall monitor to the office. He knew that he had done nothing wrong. There was no excuse for this, not even ignorance. How could he possibly be in trouble?

It was Short Tenth-grade Girl. Beth Sorenson. Somebody had seen them together this morning and accused him of bullying her. What else could they think? Why would anybody walk with him voluntarily? He must have forced her, intimidated her. It wasn't enough to pointedly shun him, they had to find ways to make him suffer, perhaps even to get him expelled, because when the judgment has been passed, the punishment pronounced, no glimmer of light or hope could be allowed. No *friend* could be tolerated.

I never should have spoken to her. When we got to school, I should have pushed her into a locker or made her sprawl and scatter her books. If I really had bullied her in exactly the way other kids did, then how could they accuse me of it? Only by being innocent was I vulnerable to their false accusations.

He stood at the counter, looking at the new school secretary. The nameplate on her desk said Mrs. Nussbaum. His brain immediately kicked into gear. Mrs. Nuts-Bomb. Mrs. Nice-Bum. Mrs. Newsboy. Mrs. Sonic-Boom. He almost smiled, but knew that her name would be Nuts-Bomb. It was usually the first one he thought of that lasted. And since it was only in his head that the game was played, it's not as if he could lose, no matter what he chose.

Or maybe he'd tell it to Beth.

Nuts-Bomb looked up and saw him. "Oh," she said. "How can I help you?"

"You can send me back to class," said Ezekiel.

"What's your name?"

He wanted to answer, My real name? Or should I just call myself the school thief and scapegoat?

"Wait, are you Ezekiel Blast?"

She didn't really say Blast. He just chose to hear it that way.

"I am," he said truthfully.

"Then you weren't supposed to come here."

"I came where I was led."

"Mistakes happen," said Nuts-Bomb. "I hope you'll forgive the error."

He assumed the statement was rhetorical. Yet she seemed to be waiting for an answer.

"May I return to class now?" he asked.

She seemed to startle out of a reverie. "Ms. Banerjee wanted to see you."

Banner-Jeep. Banshee. Band-Orgy.

"Can you tell me where I might find her?" asked Ezekiel, in his best fake-sophisticated suck-up voice.

"She's the new school occupational counselor."

As if that were some kind of answer to the question of location. Still, the job-title sounded evocative. As if ninth-graders were going to be recruited heavily by corporate headhunters.

"Ah. So she'll be in the Occupational Counseling Center," said Ezekiel, nodding.

"Now you're making fun of me," said Nuts-Bomb. "There's no such center." A pause. "Is there?" Then she rolled her eyes and smiled. "You asked where she is. I'm new here, and it takes me a moment to think of exactly ..."

"One of the offices on Counselors Row?" Ezekiel prompted her.

"Counselors Row?" Then Nuts-Bomb smiled. "So you kids have a name for it. Of course. Yes, the alcove where the counselors have their tiny, tiny offices. Be careful when you turn around in there, somebody could get hurt." She laughed at her own little joke.

Normally Ezekiel ignored adult attempts at humor, except his dad's, but her laugh was so contagious—so generous and self-effacing—that he gave her a smile. A civilized human being who hadn't yet realized that Ezekiel was not to be spoken to civilly.

He didn't wait to find out which of the counselors' offices he was looking for, because it didn't matter. They all had little windows in the doors so that students couldn't claim they were molested or abused by a counselor—it's all about risk management, Dad told him—and he could look in until he saw a woman who looked like she belonged with the name Banerjee. If "Ms." stood for "Miss," and Banerjee was her birth name, then she'd look Indian or Paki or Bangladeshi. And if she was married to someone named Banerjee, then she'd either look Indian or not, and he'd play it by ear.

She looked Bangladeshi. Because as soon as he opened the door, before even saying who he was, he asked. "Hindi, Pakistani, or Bangladeshi?"

She looked up, eyebrows raised. "Athens, Georgia, where my father is a professor of geology. But the *name* is Bangladeshi. The 'jee' part of my name is derived from 'jha,' which means 'teacher.' My father loves explaining that to people. I'm so glad we could have this chat about etymology."

"So you're not married," said Ezekiel.

"I have the same surname as my father and have not changed it," she replied. Her accent was gently southern, not like the movie *Gandhi* at all. "I'm assuming you're the student I sent for?"

"The monitor took me to the main office and Nuts-Bomb told me to come here."

Banerjee nodded sagely. "What nickname have you chosen for me?"

"It's kind of short notice. I didn't know you existed until now."

"You've already thought of several, though, right?"

"Jee-Threepio," said Ezekiel. "Baner-jeewok."

"*Star Wars* was all you could come up with?" she asked.

"Banshee. Banner-jeep."

"*Star Wars* was better," she said.

"Well, now that that's settled." Ezekiel put his hand on the doorknob.

"Not yet," she said. "Please sit down."

Ezekiel kept his hand on the doorknob and remained standing. "School has barely started. I haven't done anything."

"Yet," she said.

"Ever," he answered.

"Please have a seat."

"I'd like to have my lawyer present," said Ezekiel.

"You seem to be skeptical of the reasons why I might have called you in for a conversation."

"You've read my file," said Ezekiel.

"I have."

"Did you see some wonderful occupational future awaiting me? Pre-law? Dentistry?"

"My title has to do with occupations, but I'm still a regular school counselor and I can talk to students about anything."

"Anything school-related," said Ezekiel. "You are *not* a licensed therapist and if you start trying to act like one, you'll lose your job."

"Will I?" she asked, again with the raised eyebrow.

"Fourth grade and seventh grade," said Ezekiel. "Apparently they didn't put in my file the fact that my father knows how to write letters to the school board, citing the relevant statutes."

"'Relevant statutes,'" she said.

"I memorized all the legal talk," said Ezekiel. "In case some new clown dragged me in for more fake therapy."

"I see that you've already decided everything about me," said Banshee.

"And I didn't even have a file to help me," said Ezekiel.

"So we're going to be adversaries?"

"What else could we be?" asked Ezekiel.

"Two human beings having a conversation."

"So if I send a hall monitor to fetch you, you'll drop everything and meekly come where I am?" said Ezekiel.

She inclined her head. "You're right. It would be false if I pretended our levels of authority here were somehow equivalent."

"You can make my life as hard as you want," said Ezekiel, "but only for a while."

"How long do I have?"

"That'll be between my dad and the district. And my dad promised me that if I get any more crap, he'll change jobs and move if that's what it takes."

"You don't like it when people look at your file and judge you," said Banshee.

"Wow. You sure are good at therapy-talk."

"At least the file I looked at had your name on it. What did you find out from the Banerjee file that made you feel entitled to judge me?"

"Why would you be different?"

"Different from what?"

Ezekiel realized that he had blown it. He had gone on the attack before she actually said or did anything outrageous.

So he let go of the doorknob and sat down in the one chair there was room for in the tiny office.

She didn't thank him, or comment in any way. She began as if he had sat down the first time she asked. "I usually read through all the student files before the school year begins, and several piqued my interest." She raised one hand slightly from the desk surface. "No, I didn't believe for a moment that you were stealing any of the things you turned in to Lost and Found back in elementary school."

That was the first time anybody but Dad had ever said such a thing. "Why not?" asked Ezekiel. "Don't you know how unlikely it is for one person to keep *finding* so many things, day after day, week after week?"

"I assume that's a quote from …"

"Everybody," Ezekiel answered.

"Well, how foolish of them. Because I also looked at your grades. When you're not being harassed and suspended by idiots, your grades are quite good, and your standardized tests are … way above standard. Also, no matter how you were provoked, you never raised a hand in violence, not even to protect yourself. I quickly realized that you were … what—"

"A wimp," suggested Ezekiel.

"A civilized human being and a very smart boy. How stupid would you have to be to steal things and then keep trying to return them to the *same* Lost and Found?"

"A line of reasoning I've suggested several times, but it only seemed to make people more suspicious."

"The police were brought in twice and yet you were never charged."

"They wanted to—such a hungry look in their eyes—but my dad got a lawyer to point out to them the complete lack of evidence that I stole anything."

"I like you," said Banshee.

"That was quick," said Ezekiel. "But that wasn't a therapy-ish thing to say, so … I'm not sure how to interpret it."

"I don't think there's anything about you that requires therapy. You have a thick protective wall, but judging from this ridiculous file, you had no choice but to build one. A couple of teachers told me that you're a pariah—"

"My word is 'leper,' but 'pariah' will do."

"Outcast, persona non grata, undesirable, expatriate," she listed.

"Exile," said Ezekiel.

"Friendless," she offered.

"Will you be my friend?" he asked, his eyes all innocence and hope.

"Oh, you are so *good* at irony," she said. "I may very well be somewhat useful or helpful to you during the coming year, but no, we're not going to go to the movies together and I don't want you showing up on my Facebook feed."

"I didn't ask."

"Then you catch my drift."

"I'm not friendless," said Ezekiel.

She waited.

"That's what therapists do, wait for me to get anxious and fill the dead air."

"And it worked, because you filled the dead air by saying 'That's what therapists do,' et cetera."

"I made a friend this morning on the way to school," said Ezekiel.

"And if someone asked him if you're friends, would he say yes?"

"I don't know who you're talking about," said Ezekiel.

Instead of getting frustrated or ticked off at him, she took a moment to think, and said, "So, not a boy. A girl."

"Not a *girlfriend*. A friend. Who's a girl."

"Well, that's very nice. So you have someone to go to the movies with."

"Always did," said Ezekiel. "My dad."

"And this girl?"

"Walked beside me to school today. Conversed with me."

"Are you walking home with her after school?"

"I don't know. If she decides we're walking home together, then we will, whether I like it or not. So I'm not friendless."

"A major change in your social status, according to your file," said Banshee.

"Till I find something she lost," said Ezekiel.

"You still find stuff?" asked Banshee.

"Not anymore," said Ezekiel. He stood up. "This therapy session didn't suck as bad as all the ones before, Ms. Banshee. But it's also our last one, don't you think?"

"It wasn't therapy," said Banshee. "My name is Banerjee. And we *will* meet again to figure out what career a talent for finding things might lead you to."

"Ex-convict," said Ezekiel. "I've already been told that many times, by experts. And in order to train for the job, all it takes is several years as a convict, with full tuition and room-and-board at the expense of the state."

"Well, then, my work here is done," said Banshee, nodding to him gravely.

"You're not bad at irony, yourself," said Ezekiel.

She looked at him blankly. "Irony?"

He opened the door and left. She didn't try to stop him.

This year was going to be different. Already *was* different. Beth was annoying, but Banshee was scary. Which, when he thought about it, was pretty much a banshee's whole job description.

3

Ezekiel Blast tried to avoid making plans because any plan he made, something would come up to break it.

Father would plan things, of course, because he had to get to work every day, save money to pay for car insurance and repairs, mow the lawn and keep a decent-looking yard, and make sure there was time to shop for food. He had planned well enough that when Ezekiel needed new clothes this fall—having grown so much last year that his pants were a full four inches from the tops of his shoes by the end of summer—Father paid for what he needed with cash. Nothing fancy. Nothing with a label anyone would recognize. But decent, serviceable clothing, all from the men's department and nothing from Walmart. Because Father was a provider, and providers have to be planners.

Ezekiel didn't know what he was, or what he would become, or how many choices he would have in his life. But he knew that it was futile for him to plan anything. His talent for finding things, his obsessive hunger to return things to their owners, had owned him before he had language. Mother told him stories about how he returned to her anything she dropped, even when he was still crawling or toddling with a sagging diaper. It was as if he had been born with this mission in life: to see that all lost things were returned.

But when he lost Mother, he couldn't find her. He couldn't return to himself the most precious thing he owned.

As he got older he began to realize that Mother was not, had never been a "thing." In all his finding of lost objects, none of them had ever been alive, except as a raw material. He could find a scrunchy, and even caught some glimmer of information about the girl whose hair had worked its way free of the scrunchy's tight embrace. He could find Mother's purse, thrown even farther than her body had flown when the car hit her. But Mother herself stayed gone. He had no inkling where to look for her.

Mother had planned the whole day. What she and he would do together every hour. "And we meet Father when he comes home from work," she said, "because his labor pays for all we have. He needs to remember why he works so hard, so there we'll be when he gets out of his car. We don't run to him because he likes to be silent and still for a while when he gets home. He's weary and he isn't ready to be his cheerful happy self. He's been cutting meat all day, and he needs to get used to the idea of seeing a living human face and listening to what it says. So, Ezekiel, my dear, we stand there and smile at him, and then open the door of the house for him, and then you come into the kitchen and help me with dinner while Father rests in the den and thinks all his thoughts. And when he's ready, he comes in and joins us in the kitchen, and helps us, and then he eats with us. That's how this happy day will end."

It was a speech she spoke to him often, the words and sentences changing each time, but the gist of it the same: Here is our plan. This is what will happen. And every day it did happen, until the day that it did not.

Father didn't come home, or if he did, Ezekiel wasn't there to see him. Instead Father came to the police station and took Ezekiel from the woman who had let him sit in her office. She gave him some baby toys to play with, but she wouldn't let him "play with the books" because she wouldn't believe that he could read. "You haven't even been to school yet," she said, and that was true, except that Mother said, "Our home is a school, every bit of it, and every day we learn." That plan, also, was fulfilled every day until the day it wasn't.

"Hey, Zeke," said Father. "We need to go get some dinner."

"It's too early for you to be home from work," said Ezekiel.

"I took the rest of the day off. The store manager said I could go, so don't you worry." Father knew how Ezekiel worried when things went wrong, when plans weren't followed.

Ezekiel wanted to remind Father that Mother already had dinner planned. But before he said it, he remembered: Mother wasn't home fixing dinner.

"Where is Mother?" asked Ezekiel.

Father didn't understand the question. "The car that hit her broke her body very badly, Zeke. It doesn't work anymore."

"Not at all?" asked Ezekiel. "Can't be fixed?"

"She won't be coming home. She won't make dinner for us ever again. That's how it is."

But Ezekiel had assumed as much. And that wasn't really the answer that he was looking for. "Where *is* Mother?" Ezekiel asked again.

Father took a deep breath, and talked about how we didn't know much about heaven but some part of us lived on after death yadda yadda. Ezekiel had listened when Mother took him to church so he was familiar with the idea, and that was *not* what he was asking.

Ezekiel got up onto his chair and put his hands on both of Father's cheeks. "Father," he said, more insistently. "*Where is Mother?*"

Father blinked and looked at him a little longer. Then he tipped his head a tiny bit to one side and gave Ezekiel a kind of sad smile. "Sorry, Zeke," he said. "Mother's body is still at the hospital. They really did try to fix her, but she died before I got there. They sent her body down to the morgue. The people from the funeral home will go there to pick it up. Pick her up. Some of the women from church will go to the funeral home to dress her and do her hair so she'll look nice in the casket."

Ezekiel nodded at that. Mother would never go outside the house without making sure she looked nice. "Let's thank them for doing that," said Ezekiel.

"I have already thanked them, the ones I talked to, and I'll be thanking them and many other people who loved your mother for the many kind things they plan to do for her and for us."

"I can make dinner now," said Ezekiel. "So you don't have to come home and make dinner for us."

"You're four years old, Zeke," said Father. "You don't have to take your mother's place."

"I've been fixing dinner for my whole life, Father," said Ezekiel.

"Have you ever fixed a whole dinner by yourself?" Father asked.

"I've fixed every part of dinner, even turning on the stove and turning it off again. I've baked two cakes where all Mother did was plug in the mixer, and I've iced one cake that she made, with icing I made myself. She never let me handle the big knife, though. She said she was out of spare fingers so until she got some more, I couldn't use the knife."

When Ezekiel said that, Father burst out laughing, just a couple of laughs, and then he sat down on the chair beside Ezekiel in the policewoman's office and he cried. Ezekiel wasn't sure what to do, because Father had never cried before, but he figured that this was probably something Father wanted to do alone. Ezekiel started to leave, but Father caught his arm and pulled him back and held him close and cried into his hair.

When Father stopped shaking and let go of Ezekiel a little, Ezekiel said only one thing, because he had been thinking of it the whole time Father talked to him. "Mother never calls me Zeke," he said. "Mother always calls me Ezekiel."

Father nodded gravely. "Then so will I," he said. "Names are very important, and that's one thing I know that I'll get right from now on." And it was true: Father never called him anything but Ezekiel after that.

Ever since that day, Ezekiel was skeptical of anyone who said, "We'll do this," or "That's what'll happen," or "At nine-thirty in the morning," or anything else that sounded like a plan or a promise. He knew that nobody else but him felt the need to add a silent, "If you're not killed by a car first."

Now Ezekiel was in high school and he never made plans. He allowed himself to think of what-ifs—what if I go to college, what if I join the Navy like Father did, what if I blow some of the grocery money on a cake mix just for no reason at all—but he never allowed any of the what-ifs to become a plan, because he knew that absolutely nothing was under his control.

That's why he wasn't surprised that after Father left for work one

Thursday morning, about three weeks after Beth had become his annoyingly relentless friend, the doorbell rang just before Ezekiel had to leave for school, and it was a cop standing there.

Not a uniformed cop. But Ezekiel knew the look and besides, the man showed him a badge as soon as Ezekiel opened the door.

"My father isn't home, he's at work, and you can't take me anywhere without his permission unless you're arresting me."

The cop pushed past Ezekiel and walked straight to the kitchen table as he said, "I don't want to take you anywhere."

"You can't just walk in here," said Ezekiel.

The cop sat down at the table and pulled out a chair so Ezekiel could sit across the corner of the table from him. "My uninvited entry means that even if I *were* investigating you, which I'm not, anything I found out would be inadmissable, so my rude and unconstitutional action makes you safer."

Ezekiel sat down in the offered chair. "My father works at Food Lion in the meat department so if you want to talk to him about something—"

"Don't need to talk to your father, I just need to talk to you."

"I have to leave for school in five minutes."

"Somebody's picking you up?"

"No."

"Forget the bus, I'll drive you there."

"You can't drive me because I walk to school and that's hard to do inside a car," said Ezekiel.

The cop grinned, but he also looked kind of quizzical, because maybe he wasn't sure whether Ezekiel was joking. "So today I can save you a few steps," said the cop.

"I meet a friend partway and we walk together. She'll be worried if I don't meet her."

He could see a little smile start to play about the cop's lips and Ezekiel headed him off. "No smarmy jokes about my having a girlfriend, please. She's one grade ahead of me and we are really truly friends." Only as he said it did Ezekiel finally admit to himself that yes, Beth was his friend. He also didn't tell the cop her name because it was none of his business.

"I need to talk to you," said the cop.

"Whatever it is, I didn't steal it," said Ezekiel.

"I know you didn't. Believe me, I went through your whole file before I came over here, and as far as I can tell, you never stole anything in your life."

Ezekiel tried not to show any emotion at that, but it was hard to hide his feelings because his eyes got a little swimmy. That was the first time a cop had ever said any such thing. All those other times they left Ezekiel feeling pretty sure that they still believed Ezekiel was a thief and they were annoyed that he had gotten away with it again.

"What do you want?" asked Ezekiel.

"You have this talent," said the cop. "And we've got a missing girl."

Ezekiel shook his head.

"Please hear me out. She's been missing for weeks and the chief wants me to move her to cold cases because everybody pretty much assumes that she's either dead already or she's been taken out of our jurisdiction, but I wanted to try one more—"

"Did you notice me shaking my head the whole time you've been talking?" asked Ezekiel.

"I saw that, yes," said the cop.

"Do you know what that means?"

"It usually means no."

"Well, then, aren't you a little slow on the uptake, sir?" asked Ezekiel. He always added "sir" when he was being deliberately rude. He also made sure to sound very humble and sincere while saying rude things. Adults had no idea how to respond to that because if they got mad, it made them look like idiots.

"I was hoping you could listen to me while shaking your head," said the cop, "because with most people, shaking their head doesn't make their ears stop working."

"You thought I'd hear you mention that missing girl and I'd get all worried about her and tell you where she is."

"That was the plan, more or less," said the cop.

"If you really read my whole file," said Ezekiel, "you'd realize I'm saying 'no' because never once in my whole life have I ever found a living thing, not a puppy, not a person. That's not part of my talent."

"So you can find a missing bike and you know who it belongs to, but you can't find a missing child?"

"I don't make the rules. When the wind blows the leaves move. When the wind doesn't blow, the leaves just hang there."

"Ninth grade," said the cop.

"Getting good grades in our fine educational system has been my whole reason for living for the past month," said Ezekiel. "I haven't turned in a single thing to any lost-and-found anywhere in the world during my time as a ninth-grader. I kind of hoped that would mean that the police would leave me alone."

"She was a very sweet girl and her parents—"

"You know who was sweet? My mother was very sweet," said Ezekiel, "so when you find her and bring her back, I'll start looking for that sweet girl. How's about that?" Ezekiel didn't even feel guilty about bringing up his dead mother and using her that way, because it didn't make her any deader, but it *did* make adults extremely uncomfortable because they thought Ezekiel was about to go psycho on them or something.

But this cop didn't look ashamed or embarrassed. "You're fourteen, you know your mother's dead, so cut the crap," he said.

"I don't owe you anything," said Ezekiel. "I'm going to school now." Ezekiel got up from the table and headed for the door.

"Did you forget your lunch?" asked the cop, following him.

"Dad pays ahead for school lunch and I've got three days left on it, so no, I didn't forget my lunch. The cafeteria threatened us with seriously crappy meat loaf today, so I'm gonna see if they have the guts to carry out their threat." He started to pull the front door closed behind him. "Make sure to turn off the lights and lock up when you leave," he said over his shoulder.

The cop pulled the door back open. "Come on, we need to …" If he tried to grab Ezekiel by the arm, he missed.

A minute later, the cop caught up with him. Ezekiel was jogging, because the cop had already made him late to meet Beth. "I get it, you don't find living things, but could you find her if she's dead?"

"Humans and animals aren't lost," said Ezekiel. "When people put up signs because they're looking for a lost dog, it just shows they're dumb about animals. If the dog is dead, it isn't lost, it's dead. If it's alive, it *still* isn't lost because dogs always know exactly where they are, and so do cats."

"Come on," said the cop, breathing a little heavily as he sort of half-jogged, half-walked to keep up.

"A dog or a cat always knows exactly where he is," said Ezekiel. "He's *right there.*"

"What?" asked the cop.

"Wherever he is, that's where he is, right *there,*" said Ezekiel. "He may not know where his slavemaster is, or where the house is, but he always knows where *he* is. He's not *lost.*"

"Well, the girl we're looking for—"

"If she's still alive," said Ezekiel, "then she also knows exactly where she is, she's right there. And if she isn't alive, then she isn't lost because she's *dead.* People talk as if having somebody die is like they just mislaid them somewhere. 'Oh, did you lose your mother, you poor thing?' 'No, ma'am, I did not "lose" my mother, she's *dead.*' And then they get all huffy and go away, but it's just the simple truth. What I find are lost *things,* not people that wandered off or got kidnapped or died."

"I guess you've got this all figured out."

"You've got a long walk back to your car and you're breathing pretty heavily, sir."

"Is that your girlfrien—I mean your friend?"

It was just a random girl waiting at the bus stop or for some carpool to pick her up. "No," said Ezekiel.

"I can see that you're kind of bitter about the police," said the cop.

"*If* you read my file, you know that it fills an entire box," said Ezekiel, "and every file folder in that box means hours of being questioned and called a liar and threatened with juvie starting when I was only *six* years old because I insisted on telling the truth when all they wanted was for me to confess to something I didn't do, and I wouldn't do it."

"I'm sorry, but I'm not those guys."

"Yes you are," said Ezekiel, "because you won't believe me when I say *no.*"

"I get it," said the cop.

"If you got it, you'd be in your car way back to the station instead of harassing me on the way to school."

"The exercise is good for me," said the cop.

Ezekiel stopped jogging. The cop took a moment to react and come back.

"Even if I *could* find lost children or pets," said Ezekiel, "I wouldn't do it. Because as soon as I said, 'She's right over there buried in those roses,' you or some other cop would say, 'You knew she was there because you put her there,' and then it starts all over only this time it's *murder* and I'm not playing that game again, not ever. I will *never* find anything, living or dead, for the police or anybody else. Do you get that? Nod your head and say yes."

The cop shook his head, of course, instead of nodding—he couldn't be seen obeying a ninth grader, could he?—but he did say, "Yes."

"Now go back to your car and don't *ever* come see me again unless you have actual evidence that I've committed an actual crime, because Buddy, I promise you, I will never, *never*, never do anything to help the police in any way, ever. Did I say enough nevers and evers in there for you to understand me?"

"Wow," said the cop. "You're seriously pissed off."

"And you're seriously stalking a fourteen-year-old boy on his way to school."

"I apologize for my actions today and all the actions of all the cops before me."

"Not the lady cop who tried to take care of me while my father was at the hospital arranging for my mother's funeral. She was completely incompetent about it, but she was *trying* to do me some good. She also didn't accuse me of killing my mother by pushing her in front of the car, so she's pretty much the only cop who *didn't* accuse me of anything."

The cop stood there, looking at him.

"And right now," said Ezekiel, "you're actually thinking, 'Did he, as a four-year-old, really push his mother in front of a car?'"

"I was not," said the cop.

"Liar," said Ezekiel.

The cop pulled out a card and handed it to Ezekiel.

Ezekiel ripped it up. "Notice that I'm putting the fragments in my pocket so you can't cite me for littering."

"I'm really sorry. I was so focused on that lost girl, and I only just now got it that we lost *you* a long time ago."

Ezekiel pointed to himself. "Not lost. I'm right here. I'm going to school now. If you follow me another step, I'll go on Facebook and tell everybody about the cop who followed me to school and tried to touch me inappropriately."

"You're not even *on* Facebook," said the cop. But as he said it, he turned and started walking back toward Ezekiel's house.

Ezekiel had a pretty good memory, so he was able to tell Beth all about what happened with the cop, and whenever he didn't remember things exactly, Ezekiel gave himself much smarter things to say than he had actually said. But he also admitted that to Beth whenever he did it, calling it the shoulda-been version, and she laughed even more at the stuff he hadn't really said at the time, so it was cool.

And then he spent second period putting together the fragments of the cop's card and memorizing it. He was Detective Lieutenant R. P. Shank. Ezekiel tried to think of a way to change his last name but he finally gave up because "Shank" was better than anything else Ezekiel could think of. Shark? Shrink? Shame? Stink? Stank? Silly childish names. "Shank" was just the sort of name a detective would make up for himself, if detectives made up their names. For all he knew maybe they did.

When he'd memorized everything, including Shank's phone number, he dribbled the fragments of the card into the wastebasket on the way out of class.

4

Ezekiel Blast figured that Beth must spend some serious time thinking up semi-startling things to say first off when they met in the morning.

"I'm writing a young adult novel," she said.

Ezekiel was trying to respond to these conversational come-ons with silence, mostly because he assumed they were designed to set him up for some kind of zinger.

"What civilized people say at this point is something like, 'How interesting,' or 'I suppose somebody has to write them,' or 'Why don't you wait until you're actually a young adult yourself,'" said Beth.

"It's *not* interesting, and the other answers are rude," said Ezekiel.

"But it is interesting if you ask me what my novel is about."

"So you're actually writing it?"

"I'm going to write it because I thought of a bestselling title. It's—"

"No, you can't tell me," said Ezekiel, "because it'll be so brilliant I'll blab it around and it will get to some famous young-adult writer and they'll get the title into print and you'll be left there weeping over your wasted pages."

"That's a pretty good plot and I may steal that for the sequel. Here's the bestselling title: *The Girl Who Was Smart Enough Not to Go Chasing After the Cat When There Was a Murderer Loose in the House.*"

Ezekiel had to confess his admiration. "It has that 'Girl Who' opening. Very smart."

"And look how it references the cat in every horror movie including *Alien*."

"The cat can just die," said Ezekiel. "Every cat owner knows that if the cat can't get itself out of a bad situation, there's nothing *you* can do about it."

"Cat owners call the fire department to get tree-climbing cats out of trees," said Beth. "That's like calling the Coast Guard because a walrus got itself trapped in the ocean."

"Another plot that's worth using, I think," said Ezekiel.

"So you agree that *The Girl Who Was Smart Enough Not to Go Chasing After the Cat When There Was a Murderer Loose in the House* is a surefire bestseller."

"I think you're too smart to write the kind of book that would please the kind of reader who would buy a book with that title."

"No, no, the title is obviously ironic, Ezekiel Blast, so it will be an exceptionally smart readership and I'm well-qualified to write for *them*."

"But that's a very, very, very small readership so you can kiss all those big bestseller bucks good-bye," said Ezekiel. "You're still gonna have to make do with the allowance from your parents."

"Books aimed at exceptionally smart people also sell to people who want to *seem* to be smart," said Beth.

"OK, you're rich again," said Ezekiel. And then they were at school.

* * *

To Ezekiel's surprise, his father was standing just inside the main entrance of the school. The principal was beside him. Since Ezekiel knew that he was fine, and Father's presence here was proof that *he* was fine, Ezekiel couldn't imagine what was happening.

Well, he could *imagine*. The school had decided to expel him. Or they called Dad in because they needed his permission in order to allow Ezekiel to skip this year of school and go straight to tenth grade. Or college, with a full scholarship to Duke. That was it.

None of the above. The principal ushered them into his office and then explained that a Dr. Withunga, a psychology professor at Deverell University in Danville, Virginia, had invited Ezekiel to take part in a study.

"I don't want to be studied," said Ezekiel. "Not even in Virginia."

"They aren't going to study *you*," said the principal.

Dad cut in. "I've been looking into this for the past week, Ezekiel."

"Without breathing a word to *me*?"

"I'm breathing a word to you *now*. I wasn't going to bring it up with you until I was sure that it was legitimate, that it wasn't some government thing, that it wasn't a therapy group or some attempt to 'cure' you of something."

"But it's about me finding stuff," said Ezekiel.

"Believe it or not," said Dad, "the name of this study is 'Group of Rare and Useless Talents.' What does that make you think?"

"That somebody isn't really serious," said Ezekiel. The initials of the main words would spell GRUT. Even with the first letters of the unimportant words, it would be GORAUT. Either way, cool.

"I've checked out Dr. Withunga's credentials," said the principal, "and—"

Father interrupted him. "Excuse me, sir, but I've got this."

The principal looked offended—what, a mere *butcher* preempting the words of a man with a doctorate? But after one brief sputter, he leaned back in his chair and let Father proceed. After all, thought Ezekiel, the man's doctorate was only an EdD, not a PhD. No language requirement. Ezekiel figured it was the educational equivalent of a Certificate of Participation.

"The group meets once a week after school," said Father. "You'll get picked up in a van and the van will bring you home."

"A white panel truck or a black SUV?" asked Ezekiel.

"A. Van." Father looked askance at him. "Not *Men in Black*."

Ezekiel got the hint. But he still had to put the worst possible spin on it. "If I go to this thing, then everybody can tell themselves they've done something to help me."

The principal looked uncomfortable. Father just shook his head. "You can spend your life hiding this thing you do, trying to ignore it."

"That's the plan," said Ezekiel.

"Or you can find out about it and see if you can use it," said Dad. "Control it."

That took Ezekiel by surprise. Using his ability to find things would be a lot better than trying to live with the anxiety.

What kind of a name was Withunga? It made Ezekiel think of the name of the River Withywindle in *Lord of the Rings*. He could maybe do something with "hung," or …

Father was talking again. "This is the first time somebody has offered to treat your talent as something other than a disorder."

"Or a crime," said Ezekiel.

The principal seemed to want to interject something at this point, but Father pointedly spoke louder to preempt any attempt at joining in. "This Dr. Withunga thinks that talents like yours are just like any other ability. Like being really good at language. Reading, writing, speaking, understanding. You just take it for granted."

Yes, Ezekiel knew he scored high on all the language aptitude tests. And he took it for granted. But he also got good grades because of that ability. So far nobody gave him good grades for finding lost stuff.

"Some people hide their talent for language, so that other kids won't call them a nerd or a geek or something," said Dad. "But other kids work hard and try to improve their talent at language. Find out what their skills and strengths *are*, then use them to build a career."

"What if I want to be a butcher?" said Ezekiel.

He knew he was being bratty by saying that. He knew that, as a kid, Father always meant to go to college. Instead he got married, and working at grocery stores was the only way he could earn a living right then. He worked hard and got training, and grocery store butchers can make a living. But thirty thousand a year is not a *good* living, as Dad had pointed out before.

Right now Father didn't even bother to answer him. "I had to bring the school into this because the cost of the van comes out of a school accessibility budget, and because I had to authorize them to let someone other than me or a school bus pick you up from school."

"And because it was probably the school counselor who arranged all this," said Ezekiel. "Which you're trying to conceal from me or she would have been here for this."

"She's a floater," said the principal. "She's at another school this morning."

"So when do I start putting in my ten thousand hours?" asked Ezekiel.

"The ten-thousand-hour thing is deliberate practice, not just sitting in a circle talking," said Dad. "Maybe this group will give you something *to* practice."

"I'll do it. I'll try it, anyway. If I can quit whenever I want." Then he thought of something. "Wait," he said. "This means once a week, Beth has to walk home from school alone."

Dad and the principal looked at each other.

"Not his girlfriend," said Father.

"She started walking to and from school with me in order to fend off the crap other kids gave her," said Ezekiel. "I can't just decide to drop her one day a week."

"Well, she can ride the bus," said the principal.

"The sadistic kids are as likely to be on the bus as on the street," said Ezekiel. "And if you think the bus drivers actually protect kids from bullying you're crazy."

Dad shot him a glare.

"Sorry," said Ezekiel. "I mean if you think that, you're a complete lunatic, sir."

The principal made a placating gesture toward Father. "Don't worry, I already have an understanding with Zeke."

Ezekiel wondered what that understanding might be, since he'd never heard of it.

Meanwhile, Father said, "It's not much of an understanding if you think that anyone, ever, calls him 'Zeke.'"

The principal gave a wan smile and a slight shrug.

"Can Beth come with me?" asked Ezekiel. "I mean she might not want to, what with driving to Virginia and back. But if she wants to, can she come?"

They both looked as if this request was too weird to consider.

So Ezekiel played the crazy-kid card. "This is all making me so anxious, having a friend with me might be better."

Anxious was the key word here, and the principal was all, "We'll see what we can do," and Dad was all, "As long as she knows you're still not her boyfriend."

Ezekiel, for his part, wasn't sure whether he hoped Beth would say yes or not. If there were other kids in the van, then yes, he wanted her there so that he didn't feel their shunning so painfully. That's right, adult persons, I really do use Beth to protect me as much as she uses me to protect her. But he said nothing.

* * *

"We really do have to change the name of our group," said Dr. Withunga.

Ezekiel and Beth rolled their eyes at each other. They both liked calling it GRUT.

"We've changed the name of the study to 'Micropower Uses and Limitations,' so why not call this the Micropower Group?"

Ezekiel rolled the word around in his head for a few moments. Micropowers as opposed to superpowers. It didn't have the irony of Group of Rare and Useless Talents, but it kept the self-deprecation. He raised his eyebrows at Beth, and she gave a microshrug to say that she didn't mind either way.

"Since we have a couple of new members today," said Dr. Withunga, "I'm going to take a couple of minutes to re-explain our purpose here. This isn't therapy and the *last* thing we want to do is interfere with anybody's, uh, micropower."

Ezekiel memorized this so that on the way home, he could say to Beth, "I'd rather be in a group where the *last* thing we want to do is have everybody get ripped to shreds and tubes and hair by a herd of feral cats." And then she'd tell him three better collective nouns for cats than *herd*.

"I think we've lost Ezekiel," said Dr. Withunga.

"I didn't go far," said Ezekiel.

"He was storing up what you just said in order to make fun of it later," said Beth.

Since it was true, Ezekiel only stared blankly at Dr. Withunga.

"Well, you're free to take notes, if you want, Ezekiel," Dr. Withunga said.

"Not right now," said Ezekiel.

"Imagine someone coming here with a truly trivial power. Let's say she could tell, with fully clothed people, whether their navel was an innie or an outie."

Everyone sat there blankly.

"It would be hard to think of a more useless power," said Beth. "But it's better than mine."

"Because you think you don't have one at all," said Dr. Withunga.

Beth shrugged.

"But I just saw you read Ezekiel's mind with perfect accuracy," said Dr. Withunga.

"You don't know she was accurate," said Ezekiel.

"You didn't contradict her," said Dr. Withunga. "I think you would not have let an error stand."

"I can't read his mind," said Beth.

"Excellent," said Dr. Withunga. "Because mind-reading is kind of over the line into the realm of 'superpowers,' and then we'd have to kick you out of the group."

"Belly buttons," said Ezekiel. "Innies and outies."

"Yes, let's turn analytical eyes toward this micropower," said Dr. Withunga. "How far away does the power extend? Twenty feet? Twenty yards? Could she watch a basketball game on television and discern their various innies and outies? The TV is two meters away, but the players are hundreds or thousands of miles."

"That would be too intimate a knowledge to aspire to," said Beth.

"With Olympic beach volleyball, *anybody* can tell innies from outies," said Ezekiel.

"Let's suppose that it doesn't work over the airwaves at all, for navels concealed by clothing. In fact, it only extends about thirty meters. But then further questioning and thinking in this meeting reveals that the gift is not limited to the people she looks at. Quite the contrary, she has always known the innies and outies of people in the same room as her before she actually took notice of them. Including people who were behind her and therefore out of her line of sight."

"So she knew they were there before she saw them," said Ezekiel, "because she knew their navel status."

"Exactly," said Dr. Withunga. "No one who possessed a navel could sneak up on her from behind."

"It would make her murder-proof!" blurted Beth.

Ezekiel gave her an intentionally irritating smile. "You're forgetting sniper rifles. And poison. And arson."

"But *you* remembered them, you sweet boy," said Beth.

Dr. Withunga chuckled. "You seem to be such good friends, or you really detest each other, or both."

"Good job," said Ezekiel. "All bases covered, so you can't help but be right."

"There are more bases than that," said Beth.

"I admire your scientific skepticism," said Dr. Withunga.

"But now my micropower tells me that you've lost something," said Ezekiel.

"Have I?" asked Dr. Withunga.

"Your story," said Ezekiel. "It's now drifting about without its proper connection with you."

Withunga raised an eyebrow. "What story is that?"

"You're the one who knows innies from outies," said Ezekiel. "You're the one who can't be snuck up on."

"Sneaked," corrected Beth.

"Snatched," said Ezekiel.

Then silence in the group, with the others looking at Dr. Withunga with wide eyes. They must have heard the story before without realizing it was true.

"I have a question for you now, Ezekiel," said Dr. Withunga. "Was that a guess, or was it really your micropower that gave you this knowledge?"

At first Ezekiel started trying to think of what answer would give him the best advantage. Then he realized that if Dr. Withunga really needed to know the truth in order to train him to use his micropower, which might benefit him in the future, it was a good idea not to lie *too* outrageously.

"I think it was my micropower," said Ezekiel. "It came into my head the same way. I got this sense of abandonment about your story, because you tossed it out there without claiming ownership of it. I had to return it."

"So why don't you see your own lies that way?" asked Beth. "I mean, your last name isn't Blast."

"Yes it is," said Dr. Withunga.

"You *have* his records," said Beth with disgust.

"I do," said Dr. Withunga. "That's the official name. But this isn't an official meeting. I'm not grading him. I'm not reporting anything about him. And if he presents himself here as Ezekiel Blast, then that's his name, in this room, on this day, among these people." She addressed the others. "Anybody need any name other than Ezekiel Blast?"

Ezekiel shook his head. "You just stole it," he said.

"Stole what?" asked Dr. Withunga.

"You just *bestowed* the name on me."

"I did nothing of the kind," said Dr. Withunga. "I *recognized* it."

"How is it still mine?"

Beth touched his wrist where he rested it on the desktop. "Because you made it up and made everybody call you that. You tore up whatever name was on the birth certificate."

Ezekiel sat back, pulling his arm away. But not violently, not rudely, because he liked the fact that somebody touched him. It had been a long time. Not that he had *any* romantic interest in Beth. But he liked the lingering feeling on his skin.

Her touch had kept him from really blowing up at Dr. Withunga. It had kept him from walking out of the meeting. But it also made him completely forget what he had been arguing about.

Oh. Right. His name and how she had pretty much performed a christening on him, bestowing his own name.

"Pick another name," said Dr. Withunga. "I promise not to take possession of it by encouraging other people to accept it."

"Dr. Withunga," said Ezekiel. "What Beth just did, touching my arm and sucking all the anger out of me. Is that a micropower?"

"Yes," said Dr. Withunga. "But pretty much all girls have it, when they touch a boy, and they always have."

"So … not recent, not *evolving*," said Ezekiel.

"I'm not saying *that*," said Dr. Withunga. "Maybe she only has power over people who are already her friends. People who are kind to her."

"Or you're in love with me," said Beth.

"I'm definitely not her friend," said Ezekiel.

"Too late," said Beth. "Already locked in. Now you're under my magical girlspell. Look—it's making your eyes roll."

They had been friends long enough for Ezekiel to know better than to try to think of some kind of devastating retort. Because if it was anything less than devastating, she'd top him. And if it really *was* devastating, then she'd look so hurt that he'd feel like an aardvark turd for the rest of the day. They had already agreed it was the most disgusting kind of turd because it was full of ants.

"Nobody has observed your micropower more than you have, Ezekiel," said Dr. Withunga. "So at this moment, you're the world's leading expert on the micropower called 'finding.'"

"If I'm the expert, why am I here?" asked Ezekiel.

"To help you find out what you already know."

"If I already know it, why do I need—"

"Come now, Ezekiel," said Dr. Withunga. "I was told that you're quite bright."

"Who fed you an aardvark turd like that?" asked Beth.

One of the other kids, a lanky boy considerably taller than Ezekiel, spoke up. "We all know things that we don't know that we know. Asking the right questions brings our secret knowledge out into the open."

"What's *your* thing?" asked Ezekiel, surprised at the tone of challenge in his own voice.

"I stink," said the boy.

The girl next to him rolled her eyes. The boy on the other side tittered.

"Well, not right *now*," the boy said.

In Ezekiel's mind, the boy had just received the permanent name Skunk.

"She'll ask you questions," said Skunk. "We'll *all* ask you questions, and if you know the answer, great, and if you don't, I promise you'll think of nothing else for at least a week."

"I don't know if I want to answer questions," said Ezekiel. "Not yet, anyway."

"What are you waiting for?" asked Dr. Withunga. "I don't mean that as a challenge. Merely so we can know what we must strive for. Or even if the goal is possible. Yours is a potentially useful micropower, Ezekiel. Unlike my truly useless one. Yet mine could be studied, *was* studied, and we found ways to make it … somewhat useful. Usefulish."

"Then tell me about one that's *more* useful." Ezekiel could not help but look at Skunk then, because to Ezekiel, Skunk seemed to have the kind of cockiness that came from knowing he amounted to something in the world. Ezekiel wanted to see if Skunk was judging him.

But Dr. Withunga took it another way. "So you want to know about Lanny. About his micropower."

"No he doesn't," said Skunk. "Nobody does."

"I do," said Beth. "Because your stink can't be *much* if people are willing to sit by you."

"I think this will be a good example, Lanny. Is it OK with you?"

"The short kid won't give me any peace unless I do," said Lanny.

"My name is Beth," said Beth. "And damn right I won't."

Ezekiel was glad he had insisted on bringing her. She was saying things that Ezekiel might well have said, only even when Beth was being obnoxiously insistent, he could see now that there was something endearing about her. Something that made you want to tell her what she asked.

Like I did on that first day we walked together. I think I know her micropower. If there really are such things.

Out loud, Ezekiel said, "Maybe we could start with Dr. Withunga telling me whether I'm an innie or an outie."

"Innie," said Dr. Withunga instantly. "But most people are. Beth, now, she's *both* an innie and an outie."

"Not fair," said Skunk. "You can't have it both ways."

"But she does have it both ways. A deep innie, but rising out of the center of it is a veritable mountain of a navel that reaches exactly to the level of the surrounding skin."

Beth laughed and raised her shirt a little, exposing exactly the naval that Dr. Withunga had described.

"And you saw that how?" asked Ezekiel.

"I didn't *see* it at all. I simply knew it. Now, Lanny, tell him your tale."

Lanny shifted on his seat. "My body gives off every odor you can imagine. But not all the time."

"That's true of practically everybody," said Ezekiel.

"It doesn't come from my butt," said Lanny. "It comes from my skin. I sense whatever the prevailing odor is, and then up from my skin there comes a counter-smell. So that after I've been in a room for a while, there is no discernible odor at all."

Naturally, Ezekiel had to take a deep breath through his nose, as did Beth.

"So we're smelling nothing, but … doesn't that just mean this room doesn't smell?"

The other group members laughed or chuckled or smirked. "Just wait till the first time you get here *before* Lanny," said a girl who looked like she might be a college student. "This place kind of reeks."

"So you're an air freshener," said Beth.

"I can be," said Lanny. "But here are some rules we've learned, by questions and experiments. First, the stronger the original odor, the more it exhausts me to counter it. And I mean it makes me really tired *and* my ability to deal with the next smell is weaker."

"So you walk into a bathroom where somebody just laid a reeking loaf," said Ezekiel, "and you make that odor go away, but when the next person farts you can't handle it."

"No, farts are pretty much alike," said Lanny, "except for a few regular variations based on diet. So my original countermeasures continue to cope with it because my body's already producing the counterstink."

"You make farting sound like science class," said Ezekiel.

"Just like science class," said Dr. Withunga. "Because we learned a great deal more than that."

"See, when I *leave* the bathroom that I've just been de-reeking and come out into the civilized world," said Lanny, "if I'm tired my body isn't resilient. It takes maybe ten or fifteen minutes before I can switch to a new countersmell, and in the meantime I'm still giving off my anti-fart odor mix."

"And *that* can be vile," said College Girl.

"What does it smell like? Another fart?" asked Beth.

"No," said Dr. Withunga. "It's a completely unidentifiable odor, because nature doesn't produce anti-farts, so there's nothing in our experience that Lanny's counterodors smell *like*."

"But my nose *hated* it," said College Girl.

"It made me throw up," said a high school boy, "and I never throw up."

"And let me guess," said Beth. "Lanny was exhausted so he couldn't deal with your vomit smell."

"No," said Dr. Withunga, "because by the time Mitch threw up, we had already learned how to replenish Lanny's strength."

"Gatorade?" asked Beth.

"Almost," said Dr. Withunga. "Or rather, not *just* Gatorade, though a few swallows of it are a good foundation. It takes a real fruit juice—grape works best—plus a few bites of a Pepperidge Farm butterfly cracker."

"Oh come on," said Ezekiel. "That's pretty specific. He just *likes* butterfly crackers."

"I had never had them before. I knew I was hungry for something and we kept trying stuff and then Jannis had a Pepperidge Farm cracker assortment—"

"I was on my way to a party," said College Girl. "I don't normally carry around—"

"Nobody thought you did," said Dr. Withunga, "but you're preempting again, my dear."

"*I* thought she did," murmured Beth.

"I tried the others, plus a taste of whatever else anybody had, but the butterflies did the trick," said Lanny. "So I munched a butterfly cracker and took a shot of Gatorade and just like that, the vomit smell was gone *and* so was any trace of my anti-fart smell."

"So your great scientific breakthrough was snack crackers," said Ezekiel.

"Your tone of ridicule doesn't fit in with our mutually supportive culture here," said Dr. Withunga. "But we'll put up with it if you really need to be snotty."

"He doesn't," said Beth. "He can be really nice. I'm the one who needs to be snotty, like, always."

"What Lanny hasn't explained," said Dr. Withunga, "is that none of this was ever under his conscious control. It began when he was a baby— he really was an infant whose poo didn't stink, even after he started in on vegetables and fruits. We have that from his parents, of course. But poor Lanny couldn't actually *smell* anything wrong."

"I can't smell anything at all," said Lanny. "I have vague memories of smelling things as a child. When I was three, I got a whiff of soft-boiled egg and it still haunts my nightmares. But most of the time, I don't smell anything. Not even Mitch's puke. My skin senses the ambient smell, and then my skin replies to it. All out of my conscious control. Though I did learn to avoid places likely to have bad, exhausting odors. I had worked that out before joining GRUT. Not really scientifically, I just didn't *like* to go into places where I'd been worn out before. I thought of them as bad places. I didn't think of them as stinky places."

"I thought you said Lanny's micropower was more useful than belly-button-omancy," said Beth.

"So her micropower is word coining," said a kid; Ezekiel didn't notice who.

"Let's say you want to administer a poison with a strong odor," said Lanny.

"Enough with the poisons," said College Girl, alias Jannis.

"Lanny's imagination runs toward the macabre," said Dr. Withunga, "but yes, his micropower could mask—no, *does* mask—some pretty strong odors. Including the smell they add to natural gas so people will notice if there's a leak."

"Oh," said Ezekiel. "That's dangerous. Has anybody been hurt?"

"Not yet," said Lanny. "But on the good side, if somebody bakes something delicious while I'm in the room, nobody else catches a whiff and wanders in. More for me."

"The ability to manufacture counter odors is something a lot of corporate chemists would like to study. And copy, if they can. And there are physiologists who would be stunned that Lanny's skin can sense odors and respond to them without any intervention from his brain."

"So if you, like, wore a spandex suit like Spider-Man," said Beth.

Lanny finished the thought for her: "It would seriously interfere with my micropower."

"What do you think, Ezekiel Blast?" asked Dr. Withunga. "Is this something you'd like to do? Approaching your micropower scientifically to see whether you can control it or enhance it or overcome it or whatever you want?"

"Next time," said Ezekiel. "I've got to think about it some more and see what I actually know about it *before* I hand it over."

"Perfectly understandable," said Dr. Withunga. "Last time, we spent most of the session working on Dahlia's ability to make other people yawn."

"Please no more this time!" said College Girl. "I yawned until I *cried*."

"Or we could start quizzing Beth here," said Dr. Withunga, "to see if she even *has* a micropower."

"I hope I do," said Beth.

"Only because you're insane," said Skunk, alias Lanny. "These suckers can deform your whole life."

Ezekiel looked at him and realized that having a power you couldn't *help* but use could be way worse than one like Ezekiel's, which he could conceal by simply *not* trying to return things to their owners. Though that was a rule right there, because when Ezekiel *didn't* return things, he got so anxious he could barely function.

If they could help him control the anxiety, then it would be worth it.

All the way home from the session, Beth kept going on about what her own micropower might be—they had touched on several possibilities in the session, though Ezekiel thought they were all just normal human abilities. But Ezekiel didn't try to argue with her or even respond. He couldn't stop thinking about his own experiences, trying to find some kind of system, some set of rules about how his finding worked.

5

To Father's credit, he didn't ask about GRUT. He didn't ask if Ezekiel "liked" it, he didn't ask if it was "helping," he didn't even ask Ezekiel if he actually stayed and took part or just hitched a ride home.

What Father *said* at dinner was, "How would you feel about going to the beach this summer?"

That came out of nowhere. "Dad, it's October. I'm still deciding whether maybe this year I'll go trick-or-treating."

"Totally your call," said Dad. "Till you're sixteen, and then it's just disgusting to go begging for candy."

"Didn't know that rule, Dad," said Ezekiel. "Now trick-or-treating at sixteen sounds really enticing."

"Your call," said Father. "Look like a pathetic, greedy teenage moron if you want, but only if you actually dress in a full-fledged costume so it looks like you *tried*."

"I'm in pretty good shape," said Ezekiel, "what with all the walking. So I think I could rock Spider-Man spandex."

"The beach is something we have to decide together," said Father. Clearly he wasn't going to take the spandex bait. "We have to decide kind of now, because the places we can afford but that we don't have to share with rats and roaches get spoken for pretty quickly."

"And you'll have to save pretty hard to pay for it." For Ezekiel, that was reason enough not to go.

"Hence the need to decide now," said Father, "before the cheap-but-good places are all gone."

Ezekiel thought for a moment. The word "beach" had already done its damage. Memories of Mom and Dad together, all three of them together, swimming, body surfing, sitting behind one or the other of them on a jet ski, holding on for dear life. Bringing them shells he found. Sand-castle building. All of that was just there in his head, instantly, at the word "beach."

"What you're really asking," said Ezekiel, "is do we go to Cherry Grove or Myrtle Beach like we used to, or the Outer Banks like we did that one time when somebody from church invited us to use their 'cabin' there."

Father smiled at the word *cabin*. "If that was a cabin, this house is a hut. A shanty."

"I've always wondered what a shanty was," said Ezekiel, looking around at all the stuff it was his job to keep dusted. "And now I find out that all I had to do was click my heels together and say, 'There's no place like shanty.'"

"What I was really asking," Father said, "was whether you could enjoy going to the beach without your mom. It's been nine years since we lost her, and—"

By reflex Ezekiel got a little angry and said what he always said when people talked about "losing" someone. "If we had lost her, Dad, I would have found her by now. She isn't lost, she's—"

Father cut him off. "Stop being a language nazi," he said. "What if I can't bear to say the word 'dead'? What if that word is a knife in my heart? What's wrong with my joining the entire English language and saying that she's *lost*? Just because you have this talent for finding *things* doesn't mean that this wonderful woman isn't lost *to me*."

Ezekiel put his hand over his mouth.

"I didn't mean you should stop talking," said Father. "I just meant you should stop trying to shape the way I talk about my *dead* wife."

Ezekiel nodded. But he couldn't take his hand away from his mouth because that was the gesture he always used to keep himself from crying. He didn't know why it worked, but he had found out, when he was five, that covering his eyes didn't work, turning his back didn't work, looking away and trying to think of something else didn't work. But for some reason covering his mouth made it so tears didn't come to his eyes, and if he waited long enough, he could talk without his voice getting all high and whimpery.

"Dad, you can say whatever you want," Ezekiel finally said—mostly behind his hand. "I'm sorry."

"It's fine, Son. I'm sorry I snapped at you."

"But Dad, you *never* talk about your *lost* wife."

"Don't I?" asked Father. "I thought I talked about her way too much."

"Not to me," said Ezekiel.

"Well, if I don't talk about her with you, then I guess I don't talk about her at all."

"I don't talk about her either," said Ezekiel.

"You've told Beth about her," said Father. It was actually more of a question, though he said it as a statement.

"Yes," said Ezekiel. "She asked about my family and I told her that I had you, but Mother was dead. I wasn't good at explaining because I've never talked about it with anybody, either. I told her it was a car accident, so she assumed Mom was driving and I was in the car. It was weird to me that she just assumed that, but then I realized I hadn't said it clearly. My fault."

"People assume that 'car accident' means two cars," said Father. "Explaining it is the reason I just don't tell people. Nowadays if somebody asks if I'm married, and sometimes they do, then if I'm in a decent mood I say, 'Yes, but she's not alive,' and if I just don't want to talk about her at all, I say, 'I can't think why you would need to know that information,' and I walk away."

"In case you didn't know," said Ezekiel, "that's actually rude."

"So is asking a middle-aged stranger if he's married. Your mother and I read a Miss Manners book when you were just a baby, and *she* says that if people ask rude questions, you don't have to answer or explain or get mad or anything. You just ask them, 'I wonder why you think you need to know that,' and then change the subject or, you know, walk away."

"Wear your ring," said Ezekiel helpfully.

"Butchers with rings get them covered in blood. Or they take them off and lose them. Or the ring gets snagged on something and they lose a finger. And yes, I know that they know *exactly* where their finger is, but it's a figure of speech."

"I don't really know that much about Mom," said Ezekiel.

"Come on," said Dad. "You know everything that matters."

"I have to look at her picture to remember her face," said Ezekiel.

"You know that she was kind. That other people adored her. You know that she was always helping other people—people from church, total strangers. She was always generous, always gentle, always funny without ever being mean. Everybody wanted to be her best friend but they never could be, though, because that position was taken."

"You," said Ezekiel.

"No, stupid child. You," said Dad, smiling.

"She never used to let you say 'stupid.'"

"True. I had to call stupid people 'differently abled' in a really sarcastic voice."

"And then she'd hit you anyway."

"Not very hard, though," said Dad. His face looked funny, just for a moment. Then he took a deep breath.

That deep breath, thought Ezekiel. That was Dad's hand over his mouth.

"If you want to talk about your mother," said Father, "then I'm happy to help you remember anything you want."

Ezekiel didn't have a list of questions. He didn't know what he had forgotten. How could he ask about stuff he couldn't remember?

So he mentioned something he had noticed for a long time. "You never say her name," Ezekiel said.

Father did that deep breath thing again. "I haven't forgotten it."

"I didn't think you had," said Ezekiel.

Father nodded. "And when I say, 'your mother,' are you ever confused about who I'm talking about?"

Ezekiel shook his head.

"What *do* you remember about your mother?" asked Father.

Ezekiel thought of the clothes still hanging in the closet in the master bedroom, which he used to go into a lot when he was younger. To just lose himself among the skirts and blouses and trousers and dresses and sweaters, tripping over her shoes but always putting everything back exactly the way she had arranged them. He hadn't done that in years. Well, weeks.

What he said was, "I know she believed in God."

Dad nodded. "So do I," he said.

Ezekiel wasn't buying it. "You never went to church with her. You don't go now."

"I'm not good with people in large groups. Or small groups. What I'm good with is cold dead animal carcasses, and I can *almost* tolerate one butcher or one customer at a time. Church doesn't work that way, you have to be nice to everybody who talks to you, so I stopped going. But I believe in God."

Ezekiel had never drawn a line in his mind between belief in God and going to church. If Father really believed, then he'd suck it up and go to church anyway, and since he didn't, it was hard to take his claim seriously. "Which amounts to what, exactly?" Ezekiel asked. "An opinion?"

Father looked kind of nonplussed, as if he didn't know what to say.

"If you don't go to church," said Ezekiel, "what does it matter if you have an opinion that God exists? I mean, so what?"

"I believe in life after death," said Father. "I believe the soul goes on."

Ezekiel stopped himself from saying, So what you mean is that you believe in Mother.

"But you're asking what I *do* instead of what I *think*," said Father. "It's not a long list, but I do it every day. I keep the commandments I know about. The ones that mattered to your mother."

Ezekiel tried to think what commandments he might mean. No idols? No killing? Smaller stuff: Not cheating people. Not hitting people.

Not hitting *me*. Not even getting angry at me. Or at anybody, not even at work, where customers come in crowd form all the time. "You're a good guy, Dad. You'd do that anyway."

Dad just gave his head a tiny shake. Then he added to the list. "I also pray."

That was just too much. After Mother was killed, they even stopped praying at mealtime. "You never," said Ezekiel.

"Just because I don't kneel down and you don't see my lips move doesn't mean I'm not praying. I pray all the time."

Ezekiel wasn't trying to be snotty, but "all the time" was too big a provocation. "You mean you're praying right now?"

Father's face got kind of firm. Ezekiel realized that maybe this conversation was too hard for him, especially with Ezekiel in brat mode. It was hard for Ezekiel, too. But they were both strong guys. If either of them ducked out of this conversation now, they'd never have it again.

Dad answered after only a momentary pause. "If your definition of prayer includes showing God the yearning of my soul, then yes, I'm praying right now."

"And what are you yearning for in a prayerlike way?" For a moment Ezekiel feared that because of his tone of voice, Dad was going to back away.

But then Father said, softly, "I'm yearning for you to find a way to be happy. And I'm thanking God for all the progress you've made."

Ezekiel gave a bark of a laugh, without even meaning to. "What progress?"

"You have a friend," said Dad.

Oh, right, Beth. "An annoyance, you mean," said Ezekiel.

"You aren't annoyed *now*, Ezekiel, and I think you never were. From the first time you walked to school with Beth, you've changed."

"Lost weight? Less acne?"

"You don't get up so angry every morning. You aren't so lonely. I've seen you smile."

"I'm not in love, Dad."

"You look forward to something every day. You have somebody to talk to."

"*You've* always listened to me."

"Yeah, but she gives you crap all the time, and you need that."

"You could do that, too, if that's what I need."

"From a friend you need to take crap. But I'm not your friend. I'm your father. And nobody needs to take crap from their father."

"And you think God did that?"

"Did *you* choose Beth as a friend? Did I find her for you and take you on play dates? Was she given a school assignment to find some lonely, quiet kid and make him walk her to and from school?"

Ezekiel realized something then. "You're really trying to be a good dad."

Dad just sat there looking at him.

"Not just *trying*," Ezekiel corrected. "You *are* a good dad. But, like, you *mean* to be. You think about it."

"That's mostly what I pray about," said Father. "I mean, I pray about other things. For nobody to lose any body parts while cutting meat. For the strength to not be as snotty with customers as you are with me. And no, that wasn't a criticism, I admire your skill at snottiness, it's a real talent and I'm happy to let you practice on me."

Ezekiel gave him a little laugh about that. "I didn't know I was *practicing*."

"You never draw blood," said Father. "No knockout blows. So I've always assumed we were sparring."

"So," said Ezekiel, "you pray for the willpower not to kill customers, for nobody to cut off any body parts, but mostly you pray for God to explain what's wrong with me."

"I'm not trying to figure you out because, hey, I can't even figure out myself, and I know *everything* I'm really thinking. But just … I just ask for help knowing what I should *do*."

"Did you ever get any answers?"

"Mostly in the negative, but yes," said Father. "Every time I think of doing something really stupid, I get a very strong feeling that says, 'Wow, that's stupid, don't do that.'"

"Is that why I'm not in therapy? Assuming this GRUT thing isn't therapy in disguise."

"That plus I couldn't afford any therapist worth going to."

Something occurred to Ezekiel for the first time. "Are you, like, *not* dating anybody because of me?"

Father laughed and shook his head. "You don't get over a woman like your mother in a mere nine years."

"Especially not when you spend all your time either working or looking after a kid."

"Ezekiel," said Dad. "Earning a living for us and spending time with you isn't keeping me from *anything* I want to do."

"I think it is," said Ezekiel.

"OK, yes, it is," said Dad. "It's keeping me from despair."

"Oh, so I'm, like, your therapist?"

"Ezekiel," said Dad, "you're my *purpose*. That day in the hospital, I lost your mother, but I still had this boy, this strange and wonderful, injured, broken boy."

"I didn't have a scratch on me, Dad. The car took her and left me there beside the road. Untouched."

"The woman who had devoted her whole life to you, from the moment she knew you were inside her, that woman was torn out of your hands. Your body showed no injury that the doctors could treat, but I knew it was there, I knew that it shattered you, you were maimed, you were crippled that day, and there was nothing I could do, I couldn't replace her, I couldn't change my whole character and *become* that vibrant, happy, loving, chattering, kind and generous person in whose circle of light you had spent your entire life. She was gone, and you were broken."

And at that moment, as tears streamed down Father's face for the first time in, like, ever, Ezekiel understood something that had never really crossed his mind before. "You're broken, too," Ezekiel said.

"Maybe," said Father, pulling himself together. "But mostly, Son, I'm lost."

6

Ezekiel Blast's life continued in the regular, boring rut of a high school kid: Get up, pee, wash hands, eat, walk to school with a friend, sit through classes, eat when told to, go home afterward, then continue to perform slave labor for the school by doing homework, see a parent before bed, go to bed, fall asleep later than you should, so you can wake up next morning earlier than you wish.

Yet Ezekiel could feel a sense of impending ... well, not *doom*, exactly. But things were coming to a head. There was a crisis looming. He had no idea what it was. Another round of accusations and police questioning? Some kind of crisis with his fellow wackos at GRUT? A violent incident at the school? Something awful happening to Father?

None of this would be preventable, but Ezekiel did watch his father more closely, looking for signs of stress, ill health, anxiety—something that might lead to that one more unbearable loss that would make Ezekiel's life unimaginably horrible. Once Father had shown Ezekiel his vulnerability, Ezekiel could only worry about him more.

That level of dread was not really sustainable, on top of all the suppressed anxiety about found objects that Ezekiel ignored. Since his path through the world mostly consisted of the walk to and from school, he kept noticing the same lost objects, and, trivial as they were, the fact that he had done nothing about getting them to their owners sometimes made him almost frantic.

"So pick some up and take them to Lost and Found at school," said Beth.

"That means giving them to Mrs. Dollahite."

"Fine. She's nice."

"She's nice to *you*. To you she doesn't say, 'Nobody wants these. Why don't you just throw them away?'"

"Why don't you?" asked Beth. "Throw them away, I mean."

"If I could do *that*, I could leave them where they are."

"You have. For weeks. Left them I mean. Why can't you just change your mental state and instead of seeing them as lost, see them as stuff you found and then threw away, right where they already were on the street."

Ezekiel realized that this was one of the rules that Dr. Withunga was always looking for. "There's a connection with the owner," said Ezekiel. "I don't have the *right* to throw them away."

"Then you, my friend, are screwed," said Beth. "Because even I can see that for the past couple of weeks you've been practically crawling out of your skin over these things."

That was exactly what it felt like. "You have a way with words. And if I *could* crawl out of my skin, I'd do it."

"You don't like being you," said Beth.

"Not much."

"Welcome to the club. But like the bumper sticker says, you gotta be yourself, everybody else is taken."

Ezekiel chuckled. "If you fit all that on a bumper sticker, it would have to be in a typeface so small that anybody who tried to read it would end up rear-ending you."

"Always looking on the bright side, aren't we, Mr. Blast," said Beth.

"I just know that this experiment in trying to curb my finding is a failure. Seeing the same things every day and just walking by …"

"We could take a different route to school," said Beth.

"There *is* no different route that doesn't involve a two-mile detour."

"I'm not afraid of distance but you're right, that would chew up a lot of time in our day. So that leaves only one thing to do. We'll gather up the crap you've found, every speck of it, into one bag, and *I'll* turn it in to

Mrs. Dollahite. She'll know it's from you, because everybody knows that you're the only human who's willing to admit to being my friend."

"And vice versa."

"But if she says anything stupid, you won't have to hear it," said Beth.

"So this is the big displacement experiment," said Ezekiel. "We find out if I can delegate the lost-and-found step to you."

"Based on trust. You trust that I'll actually do it instead of just getting some tall person to heave the bag into a dumpster for me."

For a moment, those words caused a surge of anxiety, but then it passed, and Ezekiel felt relieved. He realized that he really *had* feared that she'd just trash his findings, even though it hadn't become a conscious thought yet. But now that she had addressed the matter, and promised not to fail him, the anxiety eased. He really did trust her.

How did that happen? Ezekiel wondered. How did this short human female skip from annoying him—which still happened, a lot—to being a person he trusted so deeply that his need-to-return-stuff responded to her promise?

On the way home from school, Beth drew out of her purse two large, clear plastic garbage bags that she had begged from the janitor. "We can't fill them too full or they'll tear," said Beth, "because they're meant to line plastic trash cans, where the can bears the stress of containing things with edges and corners."

"Don't get all physics on me."

"That's geometry and chemistry but you know that," said Beth.

It was a long, slow walk home, but not as long and slow as Ezekiel had expected, because unbeknownst to him, he had a complete mental list of every single object he had been studiously ignoring for weeks. There were hundreds of separate things.

"And these are all *lost*?" asked Beth. "Because I think a lot of this might have been thrown away."

"Stuff that's thrown away doesn't keep any connection with the owner," said Ezekiel. "Notice we have no gum wrappers and no gum in our collection. If somebody spits it out, they didn't lose it, they threw it away."

"So what *is* the connection?" asked Beth. "Is it in the object itself, or are you sensing it from some remote person who used to own the thing? Is there any distance limitation? I mean, what if some tourist family from Florida or California drives down this street and a mean brother throws his sister's stuffed animal out the window and nobody else in the car notices until they're way gone. Once they're back in California—or Taiwan, or Kathmandu—you *still* feel the connection between the stuffed animal and the girl who lost it?"

"First," said Ezekiel, "I don't know if 'stolen and thrown away' qualifies as 'lost' in the first place. But second, I don't know where the owners of this stuff might be. If I knew, I could return it directly."

Beth pantomimed knocking on a door. "Yes, ma'am, I believe you have a daughter and this scrunchy belongs to her."

Ezekiel rolled his eyes. "They'd want me on the sex offender registry for stalking their daughter."

"So once again, my friend, you're screwed," said Beth.

"I'd rather be suspected of petty larceny or manic garbage collection than some kind of perverted interest in girls who can't keep their scrunchies in their hair."

"If that's the menu that you have to choose from, I'd agree that 'pervert' is the least attractive option."

And finally they were done. Soon enough that it still wasn't dark in mid-October. Soon enough that neither of them would be late for dinner.

"All it cost us was our homework time," said Beth.

"Let's be rebels and refuse to do our homework today."

"A homework strike?"

"Shall we carry placards?" asked Ezekiel. "March around the school chanting 'homework is slavery'?"

"If you and I tried to start an anti-homework movement," said Beth, "the only result would be that all the other kids would suddenly find that they *liked* homework."

"We could make homework popular for the first time in history," said Ezekiel. "It would change the world."

"Making it even crappier than before," said Beth. "No placards."

"OK, but we still don't do our homework. We're both pretty much perfect on homework up to now, right? So they can't get all urgent about it if we miss one night."

"The dog ate my homework?" asked Beth. "Since that's always a lie, we don't have to actually own dogs to use it."

"No excuses," said Ezekiel. "No comment. If asked, we say, 'I didn't do it, so I couldn't turn it in.' And if asked why we didn't do it, we say, 'I chose not to.' And if they bluster and threaten, *we* say, 'You may do as you choose. But try to keep it in perspective. I'm not going to be denied the Nobel Prize because on one night of my life in high school I chose not to do my homework.' And if they start talking about makeup assignments, we say, 'I won't do makeup work for an assignment I chose not to do. Why not wait and see how I do on the test, and if missing the assignment didn't harm my honestly scored test, why penalize me for taking a night off from the endless meaningless round of homework that is stealing my childhood from me?'"

"Got it. I'll memorize your script and use it faithfully," said Beth.

"You'll be true to your character. You'll do your homework and turn it in on time," said Ezekiel.

"Well, yes, probably."

"Definitely."

"There's a *high* probability. But maybe I'll have a relapse of my West Nile Virus tonight."

"You can't have a relapse when you never had the disease," said Ezekiel. "But I may use that myself, because people believe *any* weird story about me."

Ezekiel walked her to her front door because he was carrying both bags. She would have dragged them on the ground and the friction would have torn open the bags.

Ezekiel saw no obvious explanation for her never having brought him to her house before, but apparently nothing had changed because she didn't invite him in and said a hasty good-bye after he set the bags in the front hall. The house didn't seem particularly rich or poor. It was right in line with the neighborhood, which is what zoning laws were designed to achieve. But if she didn't want him inside, it wasn't any of his business. Wherever she drew the line, it was fine with him.

Except that whatever Ezekiel was shut out of, he became much more curious about.

No, she was a private person, that was all, and speculating about this was a kind of invasion of her privacy too.

* * *

In GRUT, Dr. Withunga was pleased with their methodical information gathering.

"It's not scientific yet, of course, because the sample size is too small," she said.

"Two full bags is too small a sample size?" asked Ezekiel.

"One *finder* of random lost stuff is too small a sample size," said Beth. "And there's no control—stuff 'found' by people who don't have Ezekiel's particular micropower."

"How is your sample different from just picking up all the garbage on the road?" asked College Girl.

"Because Ezekiel can tell you all the stuff that was there but didn't feel lost to him," said Beth.

"No I can't," said Ezekiel. "I don't *notice* stuff that isn't lost."

"So maybe your finding is really just noticing," said Dahlia. "Whatever you notice, you think you 'found.'"

"Ignoring the snottiness of Dahlia's tone," said Dr. Withunga, "I think that may be a good question. Do you have any independent verification that the things you found are lost, and the things you didn't notice were thrown away deliberately?"

"I'm more interested in the most important question," said Skunk.

"Which is?" asked Ezekiel.

"People. Can you find lost people?"

Ezekiel shook his head. "I've thought about that a lot since I started coming here. And before that. I had the power of rational thought plus curiosity before coming to GRUT."

College Girl said, "I thought we were all on board with Micropower—"

"I'm not," said Ezekiel. "I may be new, but I have a vote, so stop rolling your eyes and listen."

"Why does Ezekiel's micropower dominate our discussions week after week?" asked Dahlia.

"Because he's new," said Dr. Withunga, "so his micropower is only beginning to be explored."

"Because finding lost things is a lot more important and useful than making people yawn," said Beth. Which meant that Ezekiel didn't have to say it, so he was grateful.

"Why is *she* here?" asked College Girl. "She doesn't even have a micropower."

"She has the micropower of seeing up people's noses," said Dahlia.

"Enough," said Dr. Withunga. "This is way too personal. Beth is here as Ezekiel's companion animal. But as long as she's here, she has a right to speak and be heard."

"Companion animal?" asked Beth softly.

"If you bite and snarl," said Dr. Withunga, "are you civilized?"

"You mean domesticated?" asked Beth, even more softly.

"Take a joke, Beth," said Dr. Withunga.

"I will when you make one," said Beth. She rose to her feet. As she headed toward the door, she told Ezekiel, "I'll meet you at the van afterward."

Ezekiel stood up. "If Beth and I aren't full members, both of us, as people and not animal test subjects, then we're wasting our time."

"Both of you grow a pair and sit down and let's get down to business," said Dr. Withunga.

"I can't believe that *you* called her a companion animal," said Ezekiel.

"I'm not a therapist and I'm not paid to be nice," said Dr. Withunga. "I don't do reflective listening and nobody here is on a couch. We're doing research, and every single project is based on a sample of one, so *none* of our research will ever rise to the level of statistical significance. Now get back to your chair, Beth, don't tell me you haven't been called worse than a companion animal. Besides, that wasn't a slam at you, that was a slam at Mr. I'm So Important That I Come With An Entourage."

"Slam noted," said Ezekiel. He watched Beth.

She came back to her seat. Still looking pissed off, but then, she usually did.

Skunk resumed the discussion. "We were talking about whether you can find—"

"People," said Beth.

"*Lost* people," said Ezekiel, "and that's a problem. When we say that a person is lost, what we mean is, either *they* don't know where they are, or other people who think they have a right to know, don't know where they are. Two very different meanings."

Dr. Withunga nodded. "When you see a thing on the ground, it knows right where it is: in that spot, on the ground."

Beth immediately chimed in, "It doesn't *know* any—"

"We are allowed to use metaphors and anthropomorphisms in order to explain concepts, and we try to understand each other's meanings rather than picking apart their wording," said Dr. Withunga.

Beth closed her mouth and regarded Ezekiel with her very, very slight smile.

"Dr. Withunga is right," said Ezekiel. "Things don't lose themselves, like a kid who wanders away from his parents and can't find them again. But if the kid is lost because he can't find a way back to his parents or back to his home, and the parents *also* don't know where he is, then is he lost in both senses? Like a scrunchy that worked its way out of some girl's hair?"

Mitch spoke up. "So a dementia patient in a care center, who doesn't know who anybody is or where his home is, he's lost, but because his children and spouse and other relatives and friends know *exactly* where he is, he also *isn't* lost?"

"Nobody's lost in that first sense," said Beth.

"When they can't find their way home—" said Ezekiel.

"Then they *have* lost their home, but they know exactly where *they* are, because everybody, even that dementia patient, everybody is always *right there*."

Skunk got it at once. "They always know where they are, they just don't know where other stuff is."

College Girl, whose official name was Jannis, wasn't having it. "Come on, we all know what it means when somebody says, 'I'm lost, can you tell me how to get to, like, Mulberry Street?'"

"Mitch, what's your micropower? I don't even know everybody else's micropower yet," said Ezekiel.

Mitch was about to answer, but Dr. Withunga interrupted. "One thing at a time. We're finally getting somewhere and you want to change the subject?"

"But we're only walking down well-trodden paths," said Ezekiel.

"Trodden by who?" asked Jannis.

"Whom," said Beth.

"An archaic word with few remaining uses, *not* including this one," said Ezekiel. A recurring argument. "And, 'trodden' by me. Or, if I feel like it, 'I.'"

"Trodden by I," muttered Beth. "Mad world."

Ezekiel spoke at once, to regain control. "Mitch, please."

"I always know where the spiders are," said Mitch.

Everybody fell silent.

"There are always dozens of spiders within a hundred yards. I'm actually aware of spiders *much* farther off, but it's more vague." Mitch shrugged. "I'm not scared of them, and most of them are completely harmless to people, so I ask you not to squish any around here, because I feel it every time."

"I should have mentioned," Dr. Withunga said. "This is a spider safety zone."

"I'll try," said Ezekiel. "But I don't always notice."

"That's incidental spider death," said Mitch. "It doesn't hurt me nearly as bad as deliberate spider death."

Somebody else started talking about something else, or maybe something else again. Ezekiel had heard something in what Mitch said that resonated with him. "Advertence," he said. The others kept talking. "Advertence," Ezekiel said more loudly. "Advertency."

"What are you talking about, Zeeeeke?" asked Jannis.

"Advertising," said Dahlia.

"What I'm talking about is motive, Juh-anus," said Ezekiel.

"Let's call each other by our authorized names," said Dr. Withunga.

Oh please. As if nobody else ever thought of her as "Anus" with a "J" in front. And she had pointedly called him Zeke, so turnabout and all that. "Motive," said Ezekiel. "Mitch can tell the difference between when somebody kills a spider accidently, never knowing that it's there, and when they deliberately stomp it or crush it with something, right?"

Mitch agreed.

"And he doesn't necessarily even see the spider crusher, right? He's not reading their mind or looking at their demeanor. He doesn't see a light of fiendish glee at spider-assassination, or happy-go-lucky innocence when it's accidental. But he knows."

"And that's how you know something's lost and not discarded," said Beth. "You and Mitch both know whether it's inadvertent or deliberate, and that's the difference between lost and not-lost."

"Of course we have no idea about the mechanism," said Skunk. "Do Ezekiel's objects and Mitch's spiders have an aura?"

"A penumbra," offered Beth.

"A very delicate stink," said Skunk.

"But we have a rule in common," said Ezekiel. "Mitch and I both know the motive behind somebody's action. Killing a spider, dropping a scrunchy."

"On purpose or by accident," said Mitch.

"Good," said Dr. Withunga. "Not the question we were asking, but ..."

"It's one of the questions *I* was asking," said Ezekiel. "But it applies to maybe finding humans. Hansel and Gretel. Their mom sent them out into the woods, *hoping* they'd 'get lost.' Or get eaten by wolves, or whatever."

"So they didn't know how to get home," said Beth, "but the mother didn't regard them as lost, because she was discarding them."

"It was their stepmother," said Dahlia. "Mothers wouldn't—"

"It was the mother in the original stories," said Beth. "The Grimm brothers cleaned them up to be stepmothers. But in the original old wives tales, they knew what mothers can be like."

"Enough with the fairy-tale origin stories," said Dr. Withunga.

"So when the police want you to look for a lost child," said Beth, "maybe you can't sort through the confusion of motives. If the child ran away on purpose, is she lost? If the parents in some way wanted the kid to get lost, then it was discarded, not lost at all, right?"

"Maybe that's why I've never looked at a person and felt that lostness," said Ezekiel.

"But it doesn't mean that it could never happen," said Dr. Withunga.

"Hasn't so far," said Ezekiel.

"Because you haven't walked near a graveyard, apparently," said Dahlia. "Those people are *all* lost. Like a bunch of buried scrunchies."

"That's sick," said Skunk.

"The bodies are *not* lost," said Beth. "They've just passed from being people into being things. Nobody's yearning for the *bodies* or wishing they could get them back, because the mind is gone and we want all our walking dead to be on TV."

"Or the soul has wandered to loftier spheres," said Skunk. "No religious or anti-religious assertions in the group."

"But the bodies are generally right where they were buried," said Beth, "so ... not lost."

"Graverobbers?" asked Mitch.

"Another causal question," said Ezekiel. "If somebody deliberately stole a thing, is it lost?"

"To the owner," said College Girl. "It isn't where they put it and they don't know where it went."

"But it was the result of a deliberate act," said Mitch. "So ... not *lost* but taken."

"Not the *owner's* motive, though," said Ezekiel. He was thinking of the lost girl that Lt. Shank wanted him to look for. "Stolen, but the owner doesn't know where and the owner is still connected to it, never deliberately broke the connection."

"All right," said Dr. Withunga. "That's a good starting point."

"Then why does it sound like you're wrapping it up?" asked Beth.

"A starting point for research and verification," said Dr. Withunga. "But one last question, Ezekiel. Have you ever found something that was stolen?"

"Yes," said Ezekiel immediately. "One of the worst ones. A bike that somebody stole out of a kid's yard. New bike, birthday present. I found it and it was still pretty shiny *and* I knew right where it belonged because the connection was still so strong. Took it back and got the crap beat out of me *and* the cops were called and they *didn't* charge the kid or his dad for the beating I got *and* I got taken to the station and threatened with everything short of capital punishment or deportation if I didn't lie and admit that I stole it."

"Wow," said Skunk.

"That's bogus," said Mitch.

"Nobody says 'bogus' anymore," said Dahlia.

"I do," said Mitch.

"Like I said," said Dahlia.

"I think that we are at an end of all productive discussion today. Dahlia, how is your experiment with expectoration going?"

"People have to be choking before I can try to yawn them into a self-Heimlich," she said.

"They don't have to be choking for you to get them to yawn food out of their throat. Just wait till they swallow," said Dr. Withunga.

"So GRUT is also a kind of prank show?" asked Beth.

"No cameras," said Dr. Withunga, "so, no. But several experiments that cause other people momentary discomfort and embarrassment. So, yes."

"And what's my experiment, Dr. Withunga?" asked Ezekiel.

"See if you can find something you're actually looking for, instead of just happening to find things that somebody lost," she said.

"That's the big one," said Ezekiel. "How about if I just try to find the difference between lost and stolen? Or prove that there isn't a difference to me?"

"That's no easier, but no harder either. And Beth, *your* assignment is to find your micropower."

"If I have one," said Beth.

"Oh, you have one," said Dr. Withunga.

"Meaning that you think everybody has one?" asked Beth.

"Meaning that you have one, and it will be interesting to watch you discover it."

"You sound more and more like a psychic every time you open your mouth, Dr. Withunga," said Beth.

"But I'm not one," said Dr. Withunga, "though I do wonder why that's where your imagination immediately led you. Psychic. Fortunetelling. Magic."

"Just want to see you in a swami outfit, Dr. Withunga," said Beth.

Ezekiel looked at Withunga's concentration-camp scrawniness and imagined her wearing something like the costume in *I Dream of Jeannie*. He thought, Not me.

"What a good idea," said Dr. Withunga. "And with Halloween only a week or so away."

7

Ezekiel was still in bed the next morning when Dad came in and woke him.

"There's someone at the front door for you," said Dad.

Ezekiel squinted to see his bedside clock through bleary eyes. "Dad, *God* doesn't wake up this early on a Saturday."

"Yes he does," said Dad. "And he's up with the owls all night, as well."

Ezekiel staggered to the bathroom and peed, because whoever was at the door wasn't more important than that. And then, whoever they were, they wanted him to wash his hands, and put on pants.

When he finally got to the door it was Beth, and she had one of the big transparent bags of found items. Ezekiel was instantly angry that she hadn't turned them in to Lost and Found, but curbed the impulse to slam the door or yell at her about how he trusted her and she let him down.

"I know you think I broke our trust," said Beth, "but hear me out. I sorted both bags into significant and worthless items. No girl is ever going to put a street scrunchy back in her hair even if it used to belong to her. Stuff that even the owners couldn't possibly want, all of that I took to Mrs. Dollahite."

"And this is what you're donating to the Louvre?" asked Ezekiel.

"Please invite me inside," said Beth, "the way polite people do, even when they're pissed off."

Ezekiel did not point out the irony of how she had given him the bum's rush when he stepped inside *her* sacred domicile the evening before. Instead he bowed and gestured her into the house. In the living room, Beth opened the bag wide and held up a couple of items. An action figure from a movie, a plastic cement mixer truck.

"Now, *these* you can imagine might have some value to the owner. Some kid whose set of action figures is no longer complete. A kid to whom trucks are important, and this cement mixer was his favorite."

"Why would you think these are the favorites? Obviously somebody was careless enough to lose them."

"Obviously somebody liked them well enough to take them *with* when they left their house."

"OK, maybe, why not," said Ezekiel. "So what?"

"That stolen bike," said Beth. "How did you know who the owner was? Where he lived?"

"I don't try to return anything directly now," said Ezekiel. "My reward was getting beaten up and arrested."

"Detained," said Father from the kitchen, where he was making breakfast. "No arrest record."

"They've got files on all of it, so there's a record," said Ezekiel loudly enough for Father to hear.

"Right," said Beth. "You've stopped looking for the owners, and for good reason. What I'm saying is, start looking again."

"I don't want to," said Ezekiel.

"For science," said Beth. "If the location of the owner was inherent in the objects before, why would that information disappear today?"

"I don't want to," said Ezekiel again.

Beth regarded him for a long moment. "You already know who owns everything in this bag, don't you," she said.

Ezekiel didn't want to answer. But what was the point of resistance? When Beth knew something, it was known. "Of course I do," he said. "It isn't found if I don't know where it goes."

"So taking stuff to the Lost and Found …"

"Self-protection. Anonymity. If they want it, they can check the Lost and Found for it. They can't accuse me of stealing it just because I brought it back, if I don't actually bring it back."

Beth grinned. "So you know which girl each scrunchy should have gone back to."

"Nothing says 'scary stalker' like bringing a girl a filthy scrunchy you found in the road."

"Picking up her handkerchief used to work fine," said Beth.

"But picking up a filthy snotrag that's been run over by three cars doesn't have as strong a record of success," said Ezekiel.

"This cement mixer, then," said Beth. "Where does it go?"

"I don't know the address, but I know where it is. Where the kid lives."

"So let's go and test your accuracy," said Beth.

"I already know I'm accurate," said Ezekiel.

"But science doesn't know it. We'll keep a notebook of items successfully returned."

"I don't want to," said Ezekiel.

"Why *not* keep a record? That way we have something scientific we can report to GRUT."

"I don't want to return things," said Ezekiel. "Because the fact that I know where the owner lives is used as proof that I know where I stole it from."

Beth looked surprised. "Didn't think of that."

"'I found this toy truck in the road. No identifying marks on it, no address, no name, but I just *know* it belongs to your child.'"

"OK, yeah, I'd probably think of calling the cops, too," said Beth.

"So for the past five years I've pretended that I lost the ability to know where the owner is. I've mastered the art of saying 'I have no idea' to policemen."

"But you do have an idea," said Beth.

"I've been ignoring it for years, but yeah, I guess I get kind of a lot of information about the owner from the object."

"Including their location?" She looked at him with expectation. She had something in mind. Ezekiel could feel another experiment coming on.

But even though he hated acting out anyone else's script, he was curious. "What are you after here, Beth?"

"Do you know their location?"

"I already told you I do," said Ezekiel.

"We're defining terms now," said Beth. "*Current* location, or just domicile?"

Ezekiel startled at that. "Never thought about it."

"If the owner is off on a school field trip," asked Beth, "would you see their location as the building that contains their underwear drawer, or the place where their body is currently standing or sitting?"

"It hasn't come up," said Ezekiel.

"Impossible," said Beth. "But maybe you only go to their domicile when you unconsciously sense that they're home."

"If I could do that, then I could go to their house when I know they're *not* home and return things with zero face-to-face," said Ezekiel.

"So it would be useful to find out if you can fine-tune your location skills, wouldn't it?" said Beth.

"This is a micropower we're talking about here," said Ezekiel. "Not a geographical ouija board."

"GPS, not ouija," said Beth. "No spirits involved."

Ezekiel held the action figure in his hand and tried to get a feeling from it. Trying to get a feeling worked about as well as trying *not* feel something. Totally out of his control. He said so.

"Out of your control so far," she said. "You have to *have* the feeling first, I think, and *then* see if you understand what's happening."

"Well, good. That really helps. I'm still left here staring at … what movie is this from?"

"Not a movie, a videogame," said Beth.

"Which one?"

"Can't remember," said Beth.

"In other words, you're embarrassed that you know this game so well that you can identify an action figure from it."

"You should be embarrassed that you don't know it, because every human being under eighteen knows who that is," said Beth.

"A statement whose falsity I demonstrate before your very eyes."

Beth just smirked.

"Oh, I see, you're saying, 'Not human.' Very cute."

"Micropowers! The next hominin species!"

"Thanks for hominin instead of hominid. I think."

Sympathetically, Beth replied, "I thought 'humanoid' might really hurt your feelings."

"I know where this guy goes," said Ezekiel, "and I know who it belongs to, but weirdly enough I can't picture the kid's face or think of his name."

"So it might be a 'her'?"

"No, the kid is male."

"No name, no face, but you know whether he has testicles or ovaries."

Ezekiel shrugged. "And maybe I'm wrong," he said.

"Have you ever been?"

"Perhaps you missed the part where I haven't returned anything directly to the owner in years," said Ezekiel. "I have no idea if I'm always right. I think I always *was* right, but I was a child."

"Unlike now."

"Now I am an efflorescent adolescent."

Beth whooped in delight. "Efflorescent adolescent," she repeated. Then her lips moved as she subvocalized it several times. "Such a cool euphemism for acne."

"So you have to move your lips to memorize."

"Memory is more about sound than sight, and more about kinetics than optics," said Beth.

"You're such an intellectual, I'm surprised kids didn't put you in a locker *every* day."

"I can talk with *you* using my whole vocabulary," said Beth.

"Both real words and the ones you make up," said Ezekiel.

"I don't make up words," said Beth. "I *coin* them when I need them, and then they're real."

They continued the conversation as they walked—it wasn't far—to the action-figure house.

"So I memorized an online list of collective nouns for cats," said Beth.

"That's not weird at all," said Ezekiel.

"A 'clutter' of cats."

"I think it should be a clutter of Legos," said Ezekiel.

"A 'pounce' of cats," said Beth.

Ezekiel thought that one was pretty good, but they were at the house.

"Any feelings about the owner, before we see him?"

"It's not a feeling," said Ezekiel, "I just know. About nine years old, wearing a sweatshirt."

"Did you know this before you saw him right there in the front yard?"

"I don't know when I knew it," said Ezekiel. "When I actually saw him, I wasn't surprised."

"This is working out so well," said Beth.

"Get real here, Betty," said Ezekiel. "I can't watch myself to see the exact moment when I remember something or come to know it. It doesn't set off an alarm. It's just there when I look for it, even though a little while before, it wasn't."

"For every time you call me Betty, I call you Zeke a thousand times."

"Punching you in the arm a thousand times is going to make my arm tired."

"You can't hit me, I'm smaller than you so that makes you a bully, and I'm a girl so that makes you an abuser."

"He just saw us," said Ezekiel.

"How are you going to play this?" asked Beth.

"I don't know," said Ezekiel.

The kid walked to the sidewalk and stood at the curb. "What are you looking at?" he shouted.

"Come here and see," shouted Ezekiel.

The boy clearly wanted to, but he hesitated, teetering on the curb.

"You're not allowed to cross the street, are you," called Beth.

The boy didn't want to answer.

Ezekiel lobbed the action figure high over the kid's head so that it would land on the lawn and maybe not break.

It didn't. The detachable parts came free, but the kid could find them all, if he cared.

"The boy's name is Ronnie," said Ezekiel.

"Hey, Ronnie, thanks for letting us use it!" called Beth.

By now the boy was kneeling in the grass, picking up tiny plastic armor and weapons while holding the now-underequipped action figure in one hand. He looked at them quizzically and then in consternation, but they had walked far enough that he couldn't ask them how they knew his name or when it was that he lent them his toy.

"The weirdest one is a 'dout' of cats," said Beth. "But not 'doubt' with a 'B,' because cats aren't famous for being skeptical."

"Cats don't believe a thing you say," said Ezekiel.

"No, cats don't *care* what you say, so they don't believe *or* doubt."

"So, d-o-u-t dout?" asked Ezekiel.

"Look it up yourself," said Beth, "because it isn't my job to make your life easy."

"Good thing," said Ezekiel. "But since you ordinarily are *happy* to demonstrate your superior knowledge, I'm betting that you *forgot* what it means."

"Something to do with extinguishing something," said Beth, "but I couldn't see how it applied to cats."

"I think the best collective noun," said Ezekiel, "would be an 'internet' of cats. Plenty of visual evidence for *that*."

"We actually owned a cat for a while," said Beth, "so I think the best would be a 'vomit' of cats."

"That has power," said Ezekiel. "That sticks in your mind."

"Other real ones," said Beth, "are a 'nuisance' of cats, a 'glare' of cats, and a 'destruction' of cats. Or maybe that was feral cats."

"They're all feral whenever they get the chance," said Ezekiel.

"I've got it," said Beth. "An 'afternoon' of cats."

"Thinking of a cat asleep in a patch of sunlight," said Ezekiel.

"It's what they do," said Beth.

"So do snakes," said Ezekiel.

As they neared the house of the toy cement mixer, the conversation switched to the micropower experiment.

"With a truck it *has* to be a boy."

"It is," said Ezekiel.

"Got a name?" asked Beth.

"Diesel," said Ezekiel.

"Oh come on," said Beth. "That sounds like a name you just made up."

"I'm betting he was named for Vin Diesel. He's younger than the early *Fast and Furious* movies."

"*I'm* younger than the first one," said Beth.

"Did you know he was the voice of the *Iron Giant*?"

"Oh my suffering heart," said Beth. "You're a *fan*."

"The kid's name is Diesel," said Ezekiel, "which you have to admit is a cool first name, and he's five years old."

"What's he wearing?" asked Beth.

"He's out of diapers, so … not that."

"This is actually serious, Ezekiel," said Beth.

"I don't know what he's wearing," said Ezekiel.

"So … you don't always get that information."

"He's wearing nothing," said Ezekiel. "Because he's taking a bath."

"So I'm not going to be able to test anything you said," complained Beth.

"Is that your roundabout way of suggesting we knock on the door and ask whichever parent answers?"

"No," said Beth, "because I know you won't do that."

"But *you* could," said Ezekiel.

"While you watch from across the street?"

"I didn't say *now*," said Ezekiel.

"Oh, so I'm supposed to come back another time? It's *your* micropower we're testing, not mine."

"His name is Diesel Moon," said Ezekiel, "which is even weirder, but Moon is a real last name so … why not?"

"If somebody has a last name like Moon," said Beth, "they have a sacred duty to give their children safe and practical names."

"Like 'Sailor,'" said Ezekiel. "Come on, you were a fan."

"Still am," said Beth, "and not ashamed of it." She took the cement truck out of Ezekiel's hands and walked up to the front door of the house. She didn't ring the doorbell, she just set down the truck and walked away.

Someone inside must have seen her, because a fifteen-year-old girl in shorts and a t-shirt came out, nearly tripped over the truck, and yelled, "Hey! What's this for!"

Beth called back, "It's for Diesel Moon!" Then she kept walking.

When she got to Ezekiel he said, "What if she chased you?"

"For what?" asked Beth. "To give her brother's truck back to me?"

"*She* didn't play with it," said Ezekiel. "Why would she recognize it?"

"The kid leaves it out where it can get tripped over or, you know, *lost*. She knows that truck."

"Still, I wish you wouldn't do that. I should have a vote in this."

"She wasn't going to chase us," said Beth.

"Is that your micropower? To know who chases and who doesn't?"

"It's not a micropower, it's hearing my mom talk about stuff. The girl has huge boobs and she isn't wearing a bra. No *way* she's going to sprint barefoot down a sidewalk. She'd blacken her eyes and maybe break her nose within ten steps."

Ezekiel covered his face with his hands. "Please, God, take that picture out of my brain."

"It's never going to leave your brain. I've ruined big-breasted women for you forever."

"I don't care about women's breasts," said Ezekiel. "I don't look at them."

"You would have looked at these," said Beth. "Freakishly large. Her life must be hell. Boys hitting on her, taunting her, girls shunning her."

"So big boobs are like being short?" asked Ezekiel.

"Except for the part about boys hitting on her, kind of similar," said Beth. "If *I* had boobs like that, I'd fall over."

"Why?" asked Ezekiel. "Just get a toy shopping cart. It could hold your books *and* your—"

She punched him in the arm.

"No hitting," said Ezekiel.

"Sexist pig," said Beth.

"*I* didn't bring up the topic of huge boobs," said Ezekiel. "*I* didn't make a joke about them hitting her in the face when she runs."

"You're right," said Beth. "I just didn't like you combining my boob humor with your lame little short joke."

"I didn't make a short joke!"

"A *toy* shopping cart," she said.

Ezekiel fell silent. "I'm mortified," he said. "I wasn't even thinking about that, it just came out."

"It didn't 'just come out,'" said Beth. "You were picturing *me* with those boobs—"

"You're the one who said, 'If I had boobs like that I'd fall over,'" said Ezekiel.

"And so you needed a toy shopping cart to finish the image."

"You're right," said Ezekiel. "And if you had huge boobs like hers, you'd need a shopping cart, and it would have to be a toy one. Not the little plastic ones for three-year-olds, but the kind of small childsize carts they have in grocery stores."

"Are they hoping the kids will put things in their baskets and mom will just pay for them?" asked Beth.

"Until they implant RFID chips in children, and then their items will get charged separately."

"I'm changing the subject because I'm sick of it," said Beth. "Not because you were right about anything."

"I accept your apology," said Ezekiel, and then immediately topped her protest with, "What have we learned?"

"That even when you're relaxing at home, you should still wear a bra, because you never know when you're going to need to chase somebody."

"I'll remember that," said Ezekiel.

"You know where to return objects you find, though we still don't know if you know where the *owner* is or where he lives. You find out the name the closer you get to the owner, but you knew from the start whether it was a boy or a girl. You either know or pretend to know what they're wearing. And you got their age, though you could have guessed that or assumed it from the toys themselves."

"Can't guess it from scrunchies," said Ezekiel.

"Well, I got rid of all those because you're not going to return them," said Beth.

"We actually know quite a bit," said Ezekiel.

"No, *you* know quite a bit," said Beth. "From a lost item, you know some pretty incredible information."

Ezekiel took this, for a moment, as praise. But good feelings like that never lasted, because almost at once he thought of Lieutenant Shank and the little girl he was looking for. He stopped cold and looked down.

"What is it?" asked Beth. "Did you spot something lost?"

"I've passed about twenty lost objects along the way today," said Ezekiel. "But they don't matter because Lieutenant Shank wants me to help find that little girl."

"So you think you *can* find lost people?"

"It's not part of any scientific study," said Ezekiel. "Somebody took away their little girl, and if there's even a *chance* I can help, I have to try. Even if it lands me in another whirlpoo."

"Whirlpoo?" asked Beth. "And you complain that *I* make up words?"

"It's my dad's word. It's a replacement for 'shitstorm,' which was his first word for the mess I got into, getting beaten up and then the police getting involved. He used 'shitstorm' and then I started using it and he came up with 'whirlpoo' because nobody could take offense at it. I could say it and not get sent to the principal's office."

"Oh, so your dad's the clever one," said Beth.

Ezekiel noticed where they were. "Do you need me to walk you the rest of the way home? I mean, do you know the way?"

"Yes I know the way," said Beth, "and because it's about noon on this fine sunny autumn Saturday, and people will be out in their yards most of the way, I'll manage to do the forty-five minutes of walking all by myself without getting killed or kidnapped or hit by a ..." Her voice trailed off.

"It's OK to refer to being hit by a car," said Ezekiel. "I don't take it as a reference to my mother until somebody makes a big deal of not saying it."

"Car," said Beth. "I'll be safe. You go on to the police station."

"No, I'm walking you home. It's stupid for me to go to the police because I don't know when Shank's on duty. This *is* Saturday and maybe he has a life. I'll give him a call."

"Whatever you want," said Beth.

"Nothing ever goes the way I *want*," said Ezekiel.

"Not *nothing*," said Beth. "But if you really feel that way, I know a complete fix."

"Oh, really? For everything that doesn't go the way I want?"

"Right," said Beth. "Just decide you wanted things the way they went."

"Man, you not only come up with platitudes all the time, but they're also lame and impossible. Wanting is about the future, not the past."

Beth just started whistling as they walked on.

Ezekiel wanted to say something like, Well, now I know how to shut you up, all I have to do is be right.

But then he realized maybe she was whistling to cover up for the fact that she was hurt by his saying she came up with lame platitudes. That was a hurtful thing to say.

"I'm sorry," said Ezekiel. "Most of your platitudes are appropriate and the ones you make up are usually clever."

"I know," she said, and resumed whistling.

"Maybe we don't know each other well enough yet to be ragging on each other," said Ezekiel.

"I'm fine," said Beth. And resumed whistling.

"If you tell me what tune that is, we can whistle together," said Ezekiel.

"If you can't tell what tune it is without asking, then no, we can't whistle together, because you don't know the melody."

"I know the tune *now* because you've been whistling it over and over."

"It's the *Jeopardy!* theme and I can't believe you're in high school and you don't already know that tune."

"I know the theme music to *Tosh Point O*," said Ezekiel.

"And I can whistle *The Flight of the Bumblebee*," said Beth. "We're now forty minutes from my house. Let's go our separate ways and continue this insane discussion, um, never."

"Agreed," said Ezekiel. "Thanks again for putting in so much time on this."

"Have fun with the police," she said. And then she was striding off down the sidewalk, leaving him behind. When she was by herself, her shortness relative to other people wasn't so obvious, and her stride looked much longer, her pace much swifter. That girl can *move*, thought Ezekiel.

She also looks like an eight-year-old. Maybe a six-year-old. Heredity's a bitch.

Then, despite his expectation that Shank wouldn't be working today, Ezekiel headed for the police station anyway. What else was he going to do on a fine day like this?

8

Ezekiel Blast did not like police stations. He also disliked a lot of other places. Hospitals. Parking lots. Toy stores, especially Disney and Build-a-Bear, though he had no idea why. Parking garages. Car repair garages. Lube-job garages. Pretty much all garages, including the one attached to their house. He disliked the post office and any other mailing and shipping store. It's not that he threw a fit or had a panic attack or felt nauseated or anything like that when he had to go to those places. But if that's where Dad was going, Ezekiel would beg off the errand, even though he liked hanging out with Dad.

But Ezekiel's dislike of police stations was rooted in long hours of fear, hours of being bullied by people who refused to believe him, and he was ashamed of how many tears he had shed in police stations, though at the time he had been much younger. He was still ashamed of them, and angry at the injustices he had faced there, and at Dad's powerlessness to keep them from questioning him, at least at first, before Dad got a pro bono lawyer and found out that he didn't have to let the police question Ezekiel at all. There were things that Dad didn't know, and Ezekiel Blast found that out in police stations.

Yet here he was, walking in the front door, asking at the front desk for Lieutenant R. P. Shank.

"And your business is?" asked the desk sergeant.

"He wants to talk to me."

"He *asked* you to come in?"

Ezekiel wished he hadn't torn up Shank's card. It would have been nice to pull it out and show the guy. Though it probably wouldn't have made a difference, because this guy liked his authority, and in Ezekiel he saw somebody weak enough that he could push him around. If Ezekiel's micropower was the ability to give people sudden and sharp intestinal pain, followed by hours of diarrhea, he would have used it on this guy. But that wasn't his micropower, so he had to find a way around him.

Beth would know. Beth would put him in his place.

Got to do this on my own, thought Ezekiel.

"Sir," said Ezekiel, putting on his best humble voice. "I'm just doing what he asked. Why don't you find out from him if he wants to see me?"

"And who is 'me'?" asked the desk sergeant.

Ezekiel wasn't going to give him a name to put in the system and bring up all the files that were supposedly sealed but not really. "Tell him I'm the kid he walked halfway to school with a couple of months ago."

"So you're not going to tell me your name."

"Lieutenant Shank knows my name already, and he's the one I came to see."

"Do you know how far you're going to get in the world, being snotty to cops?" asked the desk sergeant.

"I just want to get to Lieutenant Shank. If I knew his extension I would have called first."

"Why don't I just take you to a holding cell and see what he wants to do with you?"

OK, thought Ezekiel. This had gone far enough. "Officer, what you're suggesting is the sequestration of a minor without his parents' consent. It's not quite a crime, but it puts a serious black mark on your record, and it will keep popping up every time your name is suggested for promotion, forever. Why don't you simplify everything, and get me out of your face, by simply picking up the phone and calling Lieutenant Shank and telling him the boy he walked with halfway to school is out here to see him?"

But it was too much for the desk sergeant to bear. Complying with Ezekiel's request would be tantamount to obeying him, to yielding, to surrendering. So instead the desk sergeant got up and left the room, muttering an admonition to keep his *ass* right where it was, followed by a string of epithets that were meant for Ezekiel to hear, but which he was pretty sure were not accurate descriptions of either him or his parents' status at the time of his birth.

The desk sergeant never came back. But after a while, Lieutenant Shank came in through the same door and greeted him cheerfully. "I'm betting Sergeant Glee gave you a hard time."

"He wanted to," said Ezekiel, "but my kind heart and cheerful manner won him over in the end."

That earned him a smile from Shank, who then turned and led him through the door into the inner sanctum. "I bet you made his day."

"As he made mine," said Ezekiel.

Shank had an actual office, which meant he was higher up the food chain than Ezekiel had supposed.

Shank settled down behind his desk. Ezekiel took a chair beside, not across from, the desk. He straddled it so he could put his arms on the top and rest his chin on his arms. He had gotten tall enough to do that only a few months ago, and he liked it.

"Ezekiel, I honestly can't guess why you showed up today. I'm usually not on duty on Saturdays, but I'm here because we have kind of a pressing situation that I—"

"I want to try looking for that girl," said Ezekiel.

Shank didn't ask what girl.

"I've been involved with a group that tries to help people with micropowers like mine to understand them and maybe even master them. I've only learned a little, and I have no real hope of doing anything useful, but to put it plainly, I realized that if I refuse to even try, just so I avoid complicating my own life, then I'm a selfish jerk."

"Or a kid who's been burned multiple times and wants to keep his hand out of the fire," said Shank. "I didn't condemn you, but I'm glad you're willing to try."

"I take it she still hasn't been found."

"She hasn't. Her name is—"

"Not yet," said Ezekiel. "Really. I'm not just being, like, weird. I want to see if her name comes up organically. The way the names of the owners of things come to my mind."

Shank looked at him a little sharply. "I didn't know that. You get names."

"I don't return things anymore," said Ezekiel. "I take them to Lost and Found so I can stay anonymous."

"But you know the name of the owner just from—what, handling the thing?"

"I only get the name when I'm trying to return it. I always get the location."

"Location of the owner," said Shank.

"Yes," said Ezekiel. "My friend and I—"

"Would this be your not-a-girlfriend?" asked Shank.

"She's the only friend I've got," said Ezekiel, "so she's an easy pick from the list."

Shank nodded. "You were saying something about location."

"She talked me into returning a couple of things I found—toys—to their owners. I told her the problem of me walking up to some kid's parents and saying, 'Look what I found. I just knew it belonged to you,' but she promised to do the actual delivery, and anyway, along the way she asked me if I knew the location of the actual person who owned the thing, or if I only knew their domicile. Place of residence."

Shank gave him a wan smile.

"Yes, I know you knew what 'domicile' meant," said Ezekiel, "but I get used to kind of apologizing for knowing rare words."

"Explaining the meaning of hard words when nobody asked you to isn't apologizing, it's condescending, and people resent it."

"Now who's talking down?" asked Ezekiel.

"But I'm a grownup, I have a badge, and I'm a little taller than you, so it's OK for me to talk down." Shank grinned.

"Is that sergeant's last name really 'Glee'?"

"Sometimes people are just like their name," said Shank. "Sometimes they're the opposite."

"I'm the opposite of mine," said Ezekiel.

"Which is why you went from Bliss to Blast," said Shank. "Ezekiel, here's the thing. You don't know if this will work, and I understand that. But I want to do anything I can to facilitate this. How do we start?"

"Since I've never actually *looked* for a particular lost object, and since I've never looked for a *person*, I don't have any kind of regular procedure," said Ezekiel.

"Take you to the place she was last seen?"

"I don't know what I'd do with that information," said Ezekiel. "I'm not a detective, I don't work from clues."

"I figured not, but I thought maybe you'd get a vibe from the place."

"But 'where she was last seen' isn't a *place*," said Ezekiel. "It's a coincidence, a random chance. Maybe if I went to a place that matters to her. A place where, if she isn't dead, she's wishing she could go."

"And that'll help?"

"I don't know if anything will help. Finding lost people isn't my thing."

"The reason I'm asking is, if I show up at the … at her parents' door, they're going to think I have some news. Instead I have a kid that … well, they're going to think that I'm going for psychics now. They're going to be—"

"Pissed off," said Ezekiel.

"No, they're good people, Ezekiel. They're going to take this as a sign of despair."

Ezekiel grinned. "Or they'll take it as proof that you still care about their little girl, that even if you're bringing a wacko kid in to look for her, at least you haven't given up."

"Or both," said Shank. "But not pissed off. For all those reasons."

"I didn't want to meet them," said Ezekiel. "But I think you're right. Even if I feel like an idiot, promising to do something I may not be *able* to do, meeting them may help me in some way. Or not. But if it's worth trying, why not go whole hog?"

"That's either optimism or desperation," said Shank, "but I think it's worth a shot. When can you do it?"

Ezekiel shook his head. "I'm a kid, Lieutenant Shank. I don't have an appointment calendar. What I have is school. I have this afternoon and I have tomorrow afternoon and then I'm back to school."

"They're most likely to be home in the evening."

"They don't get Saturdays off?"

Shank shrugged. "Maybe. I'll call their mobile phones and see if today works for them."

"If they aren't available till evening," said Ezekiel, "can I stay with you all day, Mr. Shank?"

Shank gave him a withering look. "If I didn't know your parents were married, I might start thinking Glee was on to something."

"I'm not a bastard, Lieutenant Shank," said Ezekiel. "I'm an orphan."

"Half orphan."

"No, according to the best dictionaries the death of one parent is enough for full orphanation," said Ezekiel. "I looked it up. If you lose both parents, then you're a double orphan."

"I'll take your word for it," said Shank.

"But people usually use 'orphan' for kids who have no living parents, or who've been abandoned by their parents."

"Your father isn't the abandoning kind," said Shank.

"Neither was my mom," said Ezekiel. "My mom had an appointment with me for every day of my life till I went off to college, but it's not her fault that she's missed every single one of them."

Shank looked at him oddly. "You can joke about that?"

"How was that a joke?" asked Ezekiel. "But yes, I can. It's been a long time. She keeps being dead every day, and it no longer takes me by surprise."

"And you don't like thinking of her as lost. It's better to think of her as, what, late for an appointment?"

"Really, really late," said Ezekiel. "I can sit here while you call the lost girl's parents, or I can leave the room."

"Because you don't want to hear her name."

Ezekiel shrugged. "Maybe it won't make any difference. But I think her name is Karen."

Shank regarded him steadily. "Why do you think that?"

"It just came to mind," said Ezekiel.

"Well, it isn't," said Shank.

"Ah," said Ezekiel. "But that's the name that comes to mind, so … maybe this whole thing is already a failure."

"Maybe. Want to cancel?"

"No. Still worth a try. The worst thing that can happen is that I fail completely and you're exactly where you were before."

"Unless her parents get their hopes up, and then they're disappointed," said Shank.

"Well don't *get* their hopes up," said Ezekiel.

"'Hi, I want to try something completely useless to find your daughter. It's doomed to fail, but would you mind meeting this child who has a way of finding lost things, even though he's sure he can't possibly do it?'"

"That's exactly right," said Ezekiel.

Shank shook his head. "Irony is wasted on you, kid."

Ezekiel gave him a half smile. "Everything's wasted on me, sir."

"Oh, hell. You're calling me 'sir' now?"

"My parents raised me right, sir," said Ezekiel.

Shank picked up the receiver on his desk phone.

"You want me to step out of the room?" asked Ezekiel.

"If you don't want to hear me say Karen's actual name. But it's your choice."

Ezekiel chose to stay. Without using the exact words, Shank tried to convey to the parents the utter hopelessness of this endeavor. Except that he couldn't keep the hope out of his tone of voice. And it was that hopeful tone, not his actual words, that would cause them to be disappointed when Ezekiel failed.

Her real name was Renee. With no accent mark. As Shank told him after the phone call, her parents had once explained, "We're not French. Americans don't do accent marks. We gave her the girl spelling with two *E*s at the end instead of the boy spelling, like Rene Russo has. But Rene Russo doesn't use an accent mark either because *we're not French*."

"You memorized that whole speech?" asked Ezekiel.

"*They* memorized the whole speech," said Shank. "I've heard them give it half a dozen times, including to reporters, so I've got it down. Word for word."

"I wonder what they do with the cedilla in façade," said Ezekiel.

"I think that, like almost every sane American, they never think about it, they almost never say it, and they certainly never write it down."

"Yes sir, that sounds about right," said Ezekiel. "By the way, that letter is called the 'cedilla.' I thought it should be pronounced 'cedeeya,' as it would be in both Spanish and French, but no, an online pronouncing dictionary says you say the Ls like in 'silly.'"

Shank regarded him in silence for a moment, and then said, "You don't converse with a lot of people, do you?"

Ezekiel realized that while his father would have been really interested in that, Lieutenant Shank wasn't.

Maybe Father wasn't, either, and just pretended so that Ezekiel would feel as if somebody cared what he was thinking about.

Beth would have cared. In fact, no matter how he pronounced "cedilla," she probably would have corrected him. Even if he got it right. Because she was Beth.

"You know what you are, kid?" asked Shank.

"A young goat?" asked Ezekiel.

"An intellectual. Not a pseudo-intellectual, not a scholar, not somebody trying to impress other people. You may not even be killer smart, though you sure sound like you are. You just think about stuff that nobody ever thinks about, but it actually turns out to be interesting. I'll forget what that weird-looking C is called in about a half hour, but right now, for this moment, I kind of like knowing that it has a name. Cedilla."

"You managed to turn calling me insane into a kind of compliment. I think."

"That was the intention."

"Because you think my insanity may be useful," said Ezekiel.

"I hope it is. But you're also a person, and even though you were a pain in the ass the first time we met—"

"I think there was a lot of ass-paining on both sides," Ezekiel interjected.

"Agreed. My point is, I don't know that I would want to spend hours conversing with you when this is all over, because I only got a bachelor's degree so I'm still pretty limited, intellectually. But I do like you, and more to the point, I respect you. You decided not to be a victim or a pushover, and that makes it hard to get you to do what I want, even when I wave my badge. But when you said you'd think about it, which usually is a polite form of 'hell no,' you actually thought about it and changed your mind."

"I didn't change my mind," said Ezekiel. "I learned a little more about what I can do and I began to think maybe I can help. It's not like I can test it out on somebody else first, though, because how many people have lost a child? So this *is* the test and I'm sorry if it doesn't work."

"Don't apologize until after you fail," said Shank. "It's a good rule. Because what if you don't fail? They'll still remember you apologizing. How does *that* help?"

9

When they got to the girl's house, Ezekiel hung back, sitting on a straight-back chair against the wall where he had a clear view of Shank and Mr. and Mrs. Delamare.

There was a franticness about them, even though they concealed it well. They sat calmly, didn't fidget much, and their voices didn't quaver as they asked Lieutenant Shank about the investigation. They were listening, and what they heard didn't make them any calmer.

Ezekiel noticed the room, noticed the things in it. This family had a little money—the neighborhood, the size of the house, what had he expected?—but the objects on display didn't seem to be there to say, We got us some money now. Everything seemed useful or, if it was there simply to be art, it was lovely. Delicate.

This is a breakable house, thought Ezekiel. But whatever else Renee Delamare might have lost, she still had a mother here. Still had a father. Just because she wasn't home right now and didn't know how to get here, perhaps, didn't mean that her home was lost. It was right where she left it.

No, no, he told himself. It's Renee who's lost. She's not the owner, she's the thing that needs to be found.

But did her parents "own" her? Was she like another delicate vase or porcelain figure?

Mrs. Delamare's voice seemed to be growing more agitated. "Please stop reassuring us about how the police are doing all they can."

Mr. Delamare tried to placate her. "We can't expect miracles, honey—"

"Why shouldn't we?" she insisted, then pointed at Shank. "*He* is."

Then she turned her gaze to Ezekiel. "You're the boy he talked about."

Ezekiel nodded, suddenly shy. He began to wish he had made Shank take him past Beth's house and pick her up. He hadn't realized how much he depended on her. Who was in whose bubble now? he wondered.

Mrs. Delamare stood up and walked toward him. She wasn't being overbearing—if anything, she looked like a supplicant. A beggar. O look kindly on us, thou magical being who can bring our daughter back. It was too much hope.

Ezekiel turned partly away from her and held up his hand. "It's not magic," he said. "I don't know what it is, and I don't know if it can even work, a person isn't a thing. I find things. I mean, I see things and I know which ones were lost and which ones were thrown away, and the lost ones, I know who the owner is, I know where they are. But that's *things*," he said. "Not people."

Mrs. Delamare stood where he had stopped her. "The Lieutenant, here, he specifically and carefully didn't promise anything. And we don't have any real expectation of success, because, well, the gift you describe is impossible. You're not a superhero, after all." She said this last with a kind of apologetic chuckle. But under that sad laugh, there was still that edge of desperation.

"Ma'am," said Ezekiel. "Whatever I thought I might find isn't in this room. Could I see Karen's—" He stopped himself. "I'm so sorry," he said. "Renee's room?"

The name Karen was still so loud in his head.

They led him up the stairs—stairs? A house with actual stairs, leading to a whole other house on the second floor? Of course Ezekiel had seen such houses in movies, but never in real life had he been on a stairway this wide, going up to a hall with so many doors in it.

They took him to a perfect little-girl bedroom, the bed neatly made, stuffed animals casually tossed on the bedspread up near the pillows.

"She loved all these stuffed animals, but her favorites were the Build-a-Bears she got on her fifth and sixth birthdays," said Mrs. Delamare.

Ezekiel had been to the Build-a-Bear Workshop in Greensboro, but that was when Mother was still alive. He had not let her buy him a bear because they creeped him out, being hollow and empty till you stuffed them. None of the animals on the bed looked like bears, anyway.

"Where are they?" asked Ezekiel.

"Well …" said Mrs. Delamare. "I don't exactly know."

"If her favorite animals aren't here, then this isn't really her room, is it?" asked Ezekiel.

Shank looked at him with consternation. "Ezekiel, we're not here to—"

"That's a very perceptive question," said Mr. Delamare. "This boy is no fool."

"We weren't trying to fool *anyone*," said his wife. "She slept here every night, *this is her room*."

Ezekiel remembered Beth's words. The domicile was the place that held her underwear drawer. But no, not really. It wasn't her underwear drawer that held the girl's heart. How did he know that? He just did.

"The center of her life," said Mr. Delamare, "was … *is* the screened-in back porch. Except on the coldest days of winter and the hottest days of summer, she was back there with her iPad—"

"We had *strict* limits on her screentime," said Mrs. Delamare.

Yes, you were good parents, thought Ezekiel. You made sure she knew that she was not free. "Could I go to that screened-in porch?" asked Ezekiel.

"Of course," said Mr. Delamare, immediately leading the way back down the stairs.

"The police have been over that room again and again," said Mrs. Delamare. "I don't know what clues you could hope to find."

"He doesn't look for clues," said Shank, saving Ezekiel from having to make a reply. "He's not a detective."

At least not a good one, thought Ezekiel.

And then there was a blast of sunlight as Mr. Delamare opened a door and they were on the back porch. The outside walls consisted of screens, floor to ceiling. There were a few old overstuffed sofas and chairs, and a toy chest overflowing with toys.

"Does Renee have brothers and sisters?" asked Ezekiel.

Shank rolled his eyes.

Oh, right. Shank had told him she was an only child.

But Mrs. Delamare's eyes flooded with tears. "She had a younger sister, born two years later. She lived three days, struggling to breathe the whole time, and then her heart gave out. But all Renee's life, whatever she did, I've imagined a younger girl, brown hair instead of blond, a little rough around the edges instead of delicate, tagging along after her big sister. I've even imagined them fighting the way I always did with my ..." Her voice trailed off as she grew too weepy to continue.

Mr. Delamare walked to her and pulled her close.

"What do you need to see here, Ezekiel?" asked Shank.

Ezekiel wanted to say, Keep your pants on for a minute, I don't know what I'm doing here but I'm damn sure *you* don't know how long it should take.

Instead, he said the thing that came to his mind, to his heart. "This porch feels sacred somehow," he said.

He didn't know why he chose that word. "Sacred." He could have said "holy" and it would also have been right.

"This is where the police think that Renee was when she was ... taken," said Mr. Delamare.

Shank explained. "The house has full security, but this back porch only has a screen door with a latch that could be raised with a credit card pushed through from outside."

"Not secure at all," said Delamare. "I already had a contractor ready to come and install some serious security, but as he said, there's no real security with screens that can be cut with a carpet knife."

"Were there any knives used to cut the screens, Walter?" asked Mrs. Delamare.

"If the door lock hadn't been so easy," said Mr. Delamare, "who knows what he might have done?"

"But the contractor never got your approval to *start*, did he, Walter?" And now Mrs. Delamare's voice was full of challenge.

Ezekiel turned away from the scene. Did his parents ever fight like that? He didn't remember any such scene. But then, *he* had never been kidnapped, leaving his parents to blame themselves and each other.

There were two bears half hidden behind a pillow and Ezekiel recognized them. To know they were Build-a-Bears was just a guess or logic—they had clothes, they looked added-to. But that wasn't what he was recognizing.

He heard a noise behind him, someone opening the screen door, but instead of turning immediately, he saw himself hiding the bears behind a pillow so they'd be safe from whoever this intruder was.

No. No, *he* didn't hear the noise. There was no noise right now. The door was still closed, but Shank and the Delamares had fallen silent. They were looking at him.

Why? Had he made a noise? Oh, maybe just a sharp little cry when he heard the door latch lift, the hinge creak.

Or maybe they were looking because he had piled two more pillows over the bears.

Ezekiel looked at Shank. "What?" he said.

"*That's* how we found this sofa," said Shank. "The ... photos."

Ezekiel guessed that what Shank had decided not to say was "crime scene photos."

"What do you mean?" asked Ezekiel.

"Three pillows hiding the bears," said Mr. Delamare. "You showed him the pictures?"

Shank didn't answer. Just kept looking at Ezekiel. And then, as if he was aware of the pressure that his gaze put on Ezekiel, Shank turned his head away.

"I thought I heard something, that's all," said Ezekiel. "I was wrong. Sorry if I startled you."

"You stopped us from stabbing each other with more blame, Ezekiel," said Mrs. Delamare. "We both know it's unfair, but sometimes it just—"

"He's not a therapist or a counselor, dear," said Mr. Delamare gently. "I don't know how much of our burdens he—"

"You heard the door open," said Mrs. Delamare. "As Renee must have heard it open when whoever-it-was came in. And your first action was what hers must have been. Protect the bears."

Ezekiel nodded. It was what he was thinking. Hoping, or maybe dreading. "Might be."

"Did you see anything?" asked Mrs. Delamare.

"No," said Ezekiel. "I mean, I saw the bears, I felt some urgency to hide them."

"As if you were channeling our—" began Mrs. Delamare.

"Channeling is for spirits," said Mr. Delamare, "if there's any reality to it at all. That would mean that Renee is—"

Ezekiel sank down onto the sofa at the opposite end from the bears. "I don't see anything," said Ezekiel. "I don't channel anything. Either I know stuff or I don't."

"Do you?" asked Shank quietly.

"I half-know," said Ezekiel.

"Like a word that's on the tip of your tongue," prompted Mrs. Delamare.

"Let the boy think, Evie," said Mr. Delamare.

"I thought," said Ezekiel. "I thought that we had to find a lost girl. But she isn't lost. She knows right where she is. What's lost is …"

They waited.

"Maybe the bears, but no. I mean they are, but no. What's *most* lost to her, what she owns but can't have and most *wants* to have is …"

It was too crazy just to say it.

"I find lost things, and then I learn things about the owner. I don't go the other way, from the owner to search for the lost thing. But she's not lost," said Ezekiel.

Again a pause, and then Mr. Delamare said it.

"*We* are."

Ezekiel nodded. "She's lost almost everything. Except herself. She's just barely holding on to herself."

Mrs. Delamare erupted with weeping. "She's alive? Are you saying she's alive?"

Both Shank and Mr. Delamare pulled her back from Ezekiel.

"When the owner's dead," said Ezekiel, citing a rule that he had only just realized was true, "then the object stops being lost. It's just … unowned." He spread his hands in a helpless shrug. "You're still lost. So yeah. I think she's alive?"

"Where?" demanded Delamare at once.

In answer, Ezekiel got up and walked to him. He tried to take the man's hand, but at first he shied away.

"What are you—"

"I don't know where the owner is, or who, or anything really," said Ezekiel, "till I'm holding the lost object with the plan of returning it."

"Returning it?" asked Mrs. Delamare through her snuffling.

Shank spoke up helpfully. "Returning *you*. To her."

"That's so backward," said Mr. Delamare, "but sure, I'll take that. However you say it." He was already clutching at Ezekiel's hand, then holding him by the shoulder, and it only scared Ezekiel. This was a strong man, and his grip was firm.

Ezekiel pulled away. "I said I had to hold the lost thing. I never had one hold *me*."

It took a moment for this to register, for Mr. Delamare to release Ezekiel from his grip. Then he held out a hand to Ezekiel, and Ezekiel took it between his hands, as if he were holding an object he had picked up from the street.

Blankety blankety blank. Nothing came to Ezekiel's mind.

Give it a minute.

OK, everybody's uncomfortable—especially me. Ezekiel let go of Mr. Delamare's hand.

"Try mine," said Mrs. Delamare.

Ezekiel looked above her proffered hand. "What if I get some information from *your* hand and not from his? What does that do to your marriage?"

Mr. Delamare gave a short bark of bitter amusement. "Even if it proves that Renee always loved Evie best, whatever brings her home."

Ezekiel took Mrs. Delamare's hand, wet from her tears and, Ezekiel immediately thought, probably her snot as well.

Again, nothing. No sense of place, nothing.

Ezekiel let go and went back to sit on the couch. "Sorry," he said. "I was afraid it wouldn't work."

"It did work," said Mr. Delamare. "Not fully, but what you did with the bears and pillows, what was that, random coincidence? Does *everybody* who sees two stuffed bears on a sofa immediately cover them with pillows?"

"And maybe she's alive," said Mrs. Delamare. "Didn't you say that?"

"Remember the 'maybe' part," said Ezekiel. "With found objects, I knew. No doubts, I just knew. But I don't *know* anything here."

"What if we try again?" asked Mrs. Delamare.

"Try *what*?" asked Mr. Delamare. "Walk onto the porch? The boy said that he doesn't *do* anything, it just happens. Or it doesn't."

"But surely there's something you control, Zeke, isn't there?" asked Mrs. Delamare.

Ezekiel felt himself build an instant shell to keep this soft-voiced iron-willed woman away from him. "Nobody calls me Zeke," he said softly.

Mrs. Delamare withdrew a step. "I'm sorry, I didn't mean …"

Ezekiel let her words dangle, looking at nobody, at nothing. Thinking of his mother, who called him Ezekiel and no other name. This woman was not his mother. She was nothing like his mother.

Except that she was a mother, there was that generic connection that perhaps binds all mothers together.

But sisterly solidarity wasn't like the bond between mother and child. That was indissoluble. And father and child, too. And parents with each other.

Only that bond *could* break. Ezekiel could always claim that his mother was his mother. But as years went by, it was becoming weird that Dad still claimed that Mom was his wife. She wasn't. Till death do you part. She was dead. That was a breakable bond.

"What she's lost," said Ezekiel, abruptly because it was only occurring to him as he spoke it. "What Renee has lost isn't either one of you."

Again a long pause, because the words he needed didn't come to Ezekiel.

"She's lost the two of us. The pair of us." The quiet voice of Mr. Delamare didn't like saying this, and he avoided his wife's eyes.

"I don't know anything about your marriage," said Ezekiel. "Heck, I don't know much about marriage, period. But even though Renee was taken from her home and lost everything familiar to her, that's not when she lost *you*, is it?"

Another long pause as the Delamares look long and hard at each other.

"I hope I'm not breaking off some vital stream of inspiration, Ezekiel," said Shank, "but I think that the Delamares will tell us when they're ready for you to return and, you know, try again."

"We know what we have to do," said Mr. Delamare. Mrs. Delamare nodded.

Ezekiel was glad to hear that, because he had no idea. How could they get back together when they were already both there?

Shank gently guided him to the screen door and they passed through it. Renee must have been dragged or led or carried or pushed through this very door. Ezekiel got no information from it. Maybe it had been too long. Maybe Renee was dead after all. Maybe Ezekiel's whole micropower was a crock. Maybe …

They were out in the back yard, skirting the pool and then moving through a sculpture garden. Though these weren't elegant statues, except for one lifesize bronze of a girl playing with a hula hoop, it still impressed Ezekiel that people could afford to put up statues in a place where almost nobody would see them. What was the point of art that nobody ever got to see?

They got to the car, saying nothing the whole way. But once Ezekiel was seated in the seat next to Shank, he couldn't hold it in for another second.

"I'm sorry I—" began Ezekiel.

"I'm sorry I made you—" began Shank.

Then the both laughed, or at least chuckled, at the coincidence. "I began to think it would work," said Ezekiel.

"Are you kidding?" asked Shank. "In what sense did you think this did *not* work?"

"I don't know where she is," said Ezekiel.

"Ezekiel," said Shank, "no way in *hell* you could know how we found those damn bears."

"OK, so maybe I … no, I really did get something there. It was like I *remembered* doing it, even though I was also partly acting it out."

"*Her* memory," said Shank.

"I hope so," said Ezekiel.

"What if they get their act together? What if they become again the couple they used to be, the partners, the *marriage* that Renee believed that she had lost?"

"I don't know any what-ifs," said Ezekiel. "I don't know what troubles they had or how Renee knew about them. So all I can do is worry about my Halloween costume while Beth makes fun of me for not going as a triple-A battery."

Shank barked his laugh. "She really has her heart set on that?"

"She doesn't care about Halloween, and neither do I," said Ezekiel. "I'm kind of thinking of a costume because Dad hinted that he thought I was too old."

"I'm not hinting," said Shank. "You're too old. If you go out asking for candy at strangers' doors, I'll have you arrested for begging without a license."

"On Halloween," said Ezekiel, unbelieving.

"You young hooligans," said Shank. "You come to people's doors, nearly fullsize adults already, and let's say it's a little old lady who answers the door. Even if you don't have a costume at all—no, especially if you just look like the lazy, slovenly teenager you are—she'll be terrified. You'll be lucky if she doesn't assume you're doing a front-porch mugging, slip a few twenties into your bag, and then call the police to tell about the pack of hooligans who extorted cash from her."

"Like that could happen."

"Twice last year. We didn't have enough evidence to prosecute, mostly because the old people—on man, one woman—didn't have good enough eyesight to make a positive identification."

"You have to be making this up. Cops arresting a trick-or-treater for begging? I would have read about it in the paper."

"They were released," said Shank. "And the names of minors aren't given out."

Ezekiel looked at the position of the sun in the sky. "Dad's only covering another guy's Saturday shift, he'll be home soon, if he isn't already. I'd just as soon he didn't see me pulling up in a police cruiser."

"Ah," said Shank. "You're right, you haven't exactly had a cozy relationship with—"

"Drop me at Beth's house," Ezekiel said. "She deserves a full report."

"Of what?" asked Shank. "Except for moving a couple of stuffed bears around, what exactly *did* you do that's worth reporting on?"

Startled at his suddenly negative words, Ezekiel looked at Shank's sober face. Until a smile cracked and Shank laughed a little. "Had you going, didn't I?"

Shank dropped him in front of Beth's house and drove off without waiting to see him go inside.

10

Nobody answered the doorbell. Not on the first ring, not on the second.

This didn't really surprise Ezekiel, though it disappointed him. It's Saturday, he told himself, and Beth already spent the whole morning with me. She doesn't owe me any more time.

Maybe she and her mom went someplace for dinner. Or they're out running errands. Or they drove to the big city—Greensboro or Danville, depending on how bored they wanted to be. Reidsville, if they didn't understand the meaning of the word "big."

Or Beth is sitting at the kitchen table fuming at the way that Ezekiel never seemed to get the message that Beth did not want him here, not ever, not for any reason.

What was the terrible secret she was hiding? That her mother was shacked up with some live-in boyfriend? That nobody ever cleaned the house? That her mother was a hoarder? There were holes in the living room carpet? That her mother had a large rat menagerie that was given free rein throughout the house? That Beth was the unwed mother of a huge baby that ate whatever it found, including the feet and ankles of visitors?

If Beth wasn't there, why didn't her mother answer the door? If Beth *was* there, why couldn't she come out on the porch to talk to him?

"Beth," he called out. "If I did something to offend you today, I'm sorry!"

Of course, if she wasn't there, who was he talking to? Voicemail he knew about, but he had never heard of a recording device for people who rang the doorbell. Bellmail? Doormail?

"I have to tell you what happened today. With the cops."

No reply. Not a sound of movement from inside the house.

No point in staying. Time to start walking home. Right now.

His hand was on the door handle, his thumb poised to press the lever.

Oh, good move, you're a *real* friend, to try her door just because she doesn't answer you when you yell at her.

He didn't press the lever. Probably locked anyway. But what if I knock with my hand?

He had heard the doorbell ring. No chance that they hadn't heard it.

He knocked. Loud. Louder. His knuckles hurt.

He slapped the door hard, pounded with the heel of his hand. Also painful after a few tries.

No response. He rang the doorbell again, because what if Beth's mom was asleep and it took a while for her to become aware that somebody outside her dream was knocking and ringing at her real door?

If she had been asleep, she remained asleep. Beth's mom must be a world champion sleeper.

Ezekiel walked down from the porch but instead of heading for the street like a sane person, he turned and started a circuit of the house. It was a fairly new development and only a handful of the houses had wooden plank fences. There was no barrier in the Sorensons' yard, just grass all the way around.

Weedy, clumpy grass which had been raggedly mown and not recently, either. Lawns in North Carolina were lousy, Dad always said, because *good* lawn grass, fescue instead of bluegrass, developed funguses in this moist climate and died. So any clump of weeds became a lawn, if you mowed it.

Well, this back yard was well on the way to becoming a meadow again. And, as Dad said, that meant all the windborne tree seeds, mostly maples, would propagate in the lawn and in five years it would be a stand of woods. That would look better than this lawn, thought Ezekiel, but it wouldn't meet the approval of the neighbors. The lawnmower business depended completely on the surly looks of neighbors, so that everybody had to keep mowing their useless grasspatches.

On the other side of the house, he came to the air conditioning compressor unit. It was silent and still. The fan blades weren't turning.

This was October. The day was warm, but not hot. It made sense that some people stopped using their air conditioning earlier than others.

But those people opened their windows. Let in the cooler night air, keep breezes blowing through the house. There *was* a breeze right now. There *should* be open windows.

None on this side. None in the back, none on the other side, and none in front. This house was sealed tight. That meant that all the sun's heat that pounded on the roof all day was sequestered in the house and it must be seriously hot in there.

So you're afraid of burglars *and* you can't afford to air condition the house when you're away. It might look like this. But it would sure be hell to come home to this *oven* and then try to sleep before the air conditioner could restore it to habitable temperatures.

Maybe Beth's mother had been caught embezzling from the Bank of Haw River and she had dragged Beth off to some haven. The Downy Branch of Haw River Bank being as small as it was, the total she stole couldn't be anywhere near enough to invest and then live on the interest. Mrs. Sorenson would have to get a job somewhere, and she'd have to get that job without being able to show references from her previous employer.

Maybe Mrs. Sorenson would put Beth out as a babysitter to make ends meet.

Almost, Ezekiel went to check the Sorensons' mailbox. But what would he learn? If it was full, it meant they hadn't picked up their mail yet today. If it was empty, it wouldn't mean they were traveling and stopped the mail; it might only mean that they already brought it in today, or that they had a neighbor picking it up for them, or that Mrs. Sorenson had never ordered anything by mail so she never got on any lists.

I've only known this girl for less than two months and she's so tightly woven into my life that I can't go a couple of hours without talking to her about everything that happened in my day. I'm not here to ask her about *her* day after we parted, because I'm not a good enough friend to *care* about what she does when she isn't with me. In fact, I'm actually a pretty lousy friend. I've never had a chance to develop those skills. I didn't have a mother around to teach me to have better manners than a crow. Though come to think of it, crows hung around with each other in flocks and gave each other warnings when there was danger and a come-here signal when there was food. So ... they have more social skills than I do.

Was Shank's original assumption right? Was Beth more than a friend? Was she a *girl*friend?

She's a smart, funny, compassionate, loyal, creative person. She isn't ugly, she's just short. She might even be pretty someday. All those things would put her completely out of my league. I should be so lucky as to have a girlfriend this cool.

Ezekiel walked home, brooding about whether he had romantic feelings ever about anyone, and also about whether you could be in love without actually knowing it and without having this uncontrollable desire to put your mouth on another person's mouth.

Father was home and preparing to grill some burgers in the back yard. True to form, Dad did *not* ask him about his day. It was up to Ezekiel to decide what he wanted to tell.

"I went to the cops," said Ezekiel.

"Were you ever behind a locked door?" asked Father mildly.

"No. I went to offer to try to help with that missing girl."

"Thought you couldn't find things you were looking for."

"I can't," said Ezekiel. "So far, at least. But Beth and I figured out that I actually know a lot about the owners when I pick up a lost object to return it to them."

"Such as?"

"It's not always the same."

"Name, address?"

"More like age, sex, size. And where they live. And where they are."

"Ah. So if you found the girl, you could take her home."

"That's why I only offered to *try* to help find her," said Ezekiel. "I told

Shank that it would be useless and we shouldn't get her parents' hopes up because—"

"Cops show up with a psychic—"

"I'm not a psychic."

"That's the category they'll slot you into," said Father. "Either they're going to despair because clearly the cops have given up all rational hope and they're clutching at straws, or they're going to get their heartbroken hopes up because that's what parents do."

"That's kind of how it went down. Except that I really did get some—guesses? Insights? It doesn't come at me like, you know, a psychic thing." He put on an oogly voice. "'I feel emanations from the world beyond.'"

Dad laughed, but he also shook his head. "Please don't *ever* get good at making that nonsense sound as if you meant it."

"I just think of something. But as I do, I get a sense of importance about it. It matters. So I tell them, let me see her room. Only we go there and it looks exactly the way their housekeeper would have left it. Complete with air freshener."

"Ick," said Dad.

"So then I asked, where is *her* room. Not where she sleeps, but where she plays, where she goes to be by herself. They told me it was the screened-in porch. Which turns out to be where she was when she was taken."

"And you got that how, exactly?"

"Just knowing how dead that fakey pastel little-girl room looked. It was like I had Beth with me, whispering in my ear, 'If this is really the way she likes her room to be, maybe she shouldn't be rescued.'"

"Is Beth really that mean?" asked Father.

"Verbally," said Ezekiel. "And then only to be funny."

"Then she must never have lost anybody in her life."

"Her father abandoned them years ago. She was old enough to remember him, old enough to assume it was because he couldn't cope with having a little person for a daughter."

"Not quite the same thing as a death."

"It's called gallows humor, Dad."

"Nothing is funny when it comes to a dead or missing child. I hope you never find that out."

"And how do you know?"

"By taking my experience with a dead wife and multiplying it by ten. Or my observations of *your* experience with a dead mother."

"I get it. I mean, I don't *really* get it because for pete's sake, I'm only almost fifteen. But I know that there's nothing more important than a lost child, or I wouldn't have gone to Shank, would I?"

"So you heard Beth's snotty little comment in your ear even though she wasn't there to say it—a very convenient kind of friend, I must say— and you went to the screened-in-porch."

"Where we found a cow carcass and a guy in a bloody white apron chopping off the rump and chuck."

"Ain't you cute," said Dad.

"I wish you'd teach me about the family business."

"It's Food Lion business, and what is this? You decided you didn't want to tell me?"

"I'm telling you something else first," said Ezekiel. "Because I realized that the parents hadn't 'lost' the girl as much as *she* lost *them*. Think about it. She knows right where *she* is, like the YOU-ARE-HERE arrow on the mall directory. But what is her most prized and beloved possession? Her parents. See?"

Dad nodded. "Makes sense. And then, if they're the lost objects, you can touch *them* and find their owner. The girl."

"That's what I thought. Maybe it would work. But first the dad tried to hold *my* hand, which *so* didn't work because, like, I *have* a dad, as you may know, and he was physically trying to control the situation. Not in a creepy way, just—dominating. That may have spoiled the whole experience, because I got nothing from taking hold of their hands after that."

"It was a clever idea, anyway."

"I think it still may be. Because they had been sniping at each other, sort of blaming each other for the girl being—for Renee-with-no-accent— being on a porch without a secure lock on the outside door. Like the father should have known that somebody would come after his daughter."

"He should have," said Father. "Speaking as a dad."

"Yeah, that attitude would keep a kid manacled to his bedframe."

"Just saying."

"Well, the dad thought so too, because he had already hired the guy to come make the screened porch secure."

"Has anybody investigated that guy? Or his company? Because if there was one group of people in the world who knew that the screened-in porch was *not* secure, it's them."

That made Ezekiel pace in a small tight circle there on the backyard grass. "Never thought of that. But the police must have, I'm sure that Shank—"

"Not sure until you ask. Then he'll say that your father should stick to butchery and leave the detecting to him."

"Probably but yes sir, you can be sure I'll ask him."

"OK, I put my burgers on about two minutes after yours, so mine is about perfect and yours is burnt."

"Well done but still juicy, the way meat is supposed to be," said Ezekiel. He knew that he was merely repeating what Mom used to say, but Dad didn't flinch or anything. It was just a family saying now. Even if Ezekiel was the only one who said it, because he was the only one left in the family who knew what "cooked" meant.

Dad put the meat on the four open buns and then they applied their assorted poisons. Father thought hamburger was supposed to taste like A-1 Steak Sauce, whereas steak was supposed to taste like Heinz 57. Ezekiel always made one burger with bright yellow mustard, thick ketchup, raw onion, a single slice of dill pickle, and a dash of vinegar. The other he sprinkled with Worcestershire sauce, mostly because he read once that it was from a recipe directly descended from the old Roman fermented-fish sauce, garum; then he layered it with cucumber slices and basically put a tossed green salad on top if it. The way Mom always made her burgers. Dad used to say, If you wanted a salad, why did you bother with the burger? And she'd say, Because you went to such care to cook it the way I like it.

"That's what was missing from the Delamares' marriage," said Ezekiel aloud.

Father, of course, had not heard Ezekiel's memory of Mom's and Dad's way of bantering and saying I love you in oblique ways. But apparently he didn't need to hear it. "Not everybody's marriage can be as good as your Mom's and mine. And you don't remember how impatient she sometimes got with me."

"And you with her," said Ezekiel. "I was little but I wasn't stupid. In fact I think little kids see more about their parents' marriage because they don't watch their tongues so much when a *little* kid is around."

"So we don't use bad words in front of the little ones, but we use all the others," said Dad. Then he bit down into his burger.

Ezekiel couldn't delay any longer. He bit into the sandwich he thought of as the Mommyburger and it tasted amazingly fresh and crisp, with the meat cooked just right and the bun getting soggy, not from meat-grease, but from the water clinging to and emanating from clean fresh vegetables.

"You're so healthy," said Dad with his mouth full.

"What?" asked Ezekiel. "Did you tell me to go to hell?"

Father swallowed. "I asked why you rang the bell."

Ezekiel took a bite and, with his mouth full, said, "Don't talk with your mouth full, please."

To which Father replied, "Did you ask why we don't have any cheese?"

Then both of them said, together, "If you wanted a cheese sandwich, why did the cow have to die?"

That was another family tradition—the complete rejection of the cheeseburger. Mother once explained that it was in respect to the prohibition in Leviticus or somewhere in the Old Testament, forbidding the Israelites to boil a calf in its mother's milk. But Father only scoffed at that. "Any relatives who kept kosher on *your* side of the family?" he asked, to which she replied, "Not even any Jews. I'm tref."

And Dad said, "We can't afford to outfit two separate kitchens, so here's why we don't have cheeseburgers, Zeke. A good cheese takes over and wrecks the taste of the meat. And a cheese that *doesn't* spoil the taste of the burger is so bland I wouldn't have it in my kitchen."

It was Mom who used to say she wouldn't have it in "my kitchen." And the bit about how they couldn't afford two separate kitchens, and the fact that Mother knew the word tref, even if she deliberately misapplied it to herself—that was as close as Ezekiel ever got to having his dad tell him anything about his ancestors. Apparently some of them on Dad's side were Jewish. Or not, and it was just a family joke.

No, a *married* joke.

"They didn't have jokes between them like you and Mom do," said Ezekiel.

"Nothing's funny when your daughter is missing," said Dad. "I thought we covered this."

"You and Mom looked at the world through the same set of binoculars," said Ezekiel.

"As much as that's possible, yes, we did," said Dad.

"Whereas they looked at each other with a microscope," said Ezekiel.

Dad stared at him for a long moment. "Very perceptive," he finally said.

"And what I realized was, little Renee didn't lose her individual parents—they still love her like crazy. Renee lost the married couple they used to be. And she lost that because *they* lost it, long before she was kidnapped."

"So you couldn't see who owned the parents because that couple disappeared."

"That's what I think," said Ezekiel. "I think what Renee is missing, the thing that would show me where she is, I think it doesn't exist anymore."

"I hope you didn't say this to them," said Dad. "Because they're likely to feel judged. They're likely to hate you for saying it."

"Even if it's true?" asked Ezekiel. And then, an instant later, he joined Father in answering: "Especially if it's true."

"But this is tough on Renee," said Dad. "None of this is her fault, but she still needs rescuing."

"I know," said Ezekiel. "And that's what I kind of left them with, a wish that they'd sort of make that marriage whole again."

"You don't undo years of damage in a few days or hours," said Dad.

"I know," said Ezekiel.

"So let me ask you, Ezekiel," said Father. "Since your micropower isn't about healing wounded marriages, is there something else you could use, something that maybe wasn't as important to Renee as her parents, but it would still give you her location?"

"I would have thought that her Build-a-Bears would do that," said Ezekiel. "She had all kinds of stuffed animals in her room, but they were just interior decorating. The Build-a-Bears probably came from a family outing—one bear from each parent—so when I saw those on the couch, I knew I had to cover them up. Isn't that weird? I put two pillows in front of them and Shank said that this was exactly how the couch was when they came to investigate the crime scene. So look, the girl hears somebody opening the screen door and she knows she's in danger, maybe she saw the guy approaching, but instead of running away, *she hides the bears*."

"Sounds like she loves them," said Dad.

"But I got nothing. Except when I realized that each of them reflects maybe the girl's relationship with one of her parents. There was the one she made with her mommy and the one she made with her daddy. That's how I first realized, these parents are way too separate. Karen wanted them together, which is why she never played with just one bear, she always played with both of them."

"When did her name become Karen?" asked Dad.

Ezekiel blushed and took a bite of the other burger, the mustard-and-ketchup one. He chewed as Father watched him with growing amusement.

"So is 'Karen' one of your made-up names, like Blast or Shank?" asked Dad.

"No," sputtered Ezekiel, trying not to spray too much of his burger on his lap. "Shank's name really is Shank. I tried to make one up for him, but I mean really, Dad, there *is* no substitute name even half as cool as Shank."

"And Karen?" asked Father.

"That's the name that came to me right off the bat. Before Shank ever told me her name. Maybe he was even testing me, I don't know. She was always the 'missing girl,' the 'lost girl.' But when I agreed to help—to *try* to help—this name, Karen, popped into my head, really insistently, like the names of owners come into my head as I'm getting nearer to them, close to their home."

"But it isn't her name."

"No. When Shank told me it was Renee I was swozzled. I've *never* been wrong with a name that came to me that strongly."

"I take it 'swozzled' is a Beth word?"

"No, it's an Ezekiel word that I just made up. Unless it already exists and I didn't know it."

"Karen," said Dad.

"Who knows why?" said Ezekiel. "But it makes me distrust everything about this situation. What do I think I'm doing when the very first thing that comes to me is wrong wrong wrong."

"No, it was only wrong once," said Dad.

"No *sir*," said Ezekiel. "I've referred to her as Karen several times since then, like just now, because the name won't go away. I'm thinking of the little girl and instead of her name, Renee Delamare, which I *know* is right, what comes out of my mouth is Karen. It's driving me crazy."

"We're all just a quick bike ride from crazy, Ezekiel," said Dad. "It almost never requires any driving."

"Dad, I carry crazy in my pocket all the time and keep taking it out to look at it. I'm saying, this Karen thing makes me wonder if it's *sanity* I keep in my pocket and it only looks like crazy because I'm already bonkers."

"As good a description of human life as I've ever heard," said Father. "I've been thinking about all the things you just told me, about what happened at the Delamare's house, the name, the parents, the porch door, the bears, the pillows, and I've been trying to visualize it all, and here's the question I keep coming back to."

Ezekiel waited.

"No, you probably already said, but I might as well ask, right?" asked Father.

"Yes sir," said Ezekiel. "But I probably did a crappy job of telling it so if there's a discrepancy—"

"I picture you going to the screened-in porch from inside the house, right? And you instantly take in the view of the back yard and all, but then your eye goes to that couch. Maybe it's your micropower, maybe it's the fact that they already told you about the Build-a-Bears, but it makes you look at those two stuffed animals. Then you walk over and pick up two pillows, right? And you cover the bears. Is that what happened?"

"Yes sir," said Ezekiel. "And then Shank said—"

"No, no, stay with that moment. Did you, at any time, actually *touch* those bears?"

Ezekiel knew immediately what Dad was asking. Like Ezekiel said, he had to touch the objects before he knew who lost them, which is why he tried touching the parents. But did he ever touch the bears?

Ezekiel shook his head.

"Did your hand even brush against one of them?" asked Dad.

"I don't think so. I kind of tossed one pillow in place and then set the other one on top so the bears were completely out of sight but by then my hand was up higher so it never came closer than a couple of inches from the higher bear."

"So maybe the parents aren't—"

"Dad, I've got to call Shank, I have to—"

"Finish your burgers and calm down," said Dad. "Be calm when you call, and be calm when you go back over to the parents' house. This might just be a huge mistake because I misinterpreted the way you told the story and—"

"No, Dad, you were right, I never—"

"This might just be confirmation bias, Ezekiel," said Dad. "Because I suggested that, maybe your memory unconsciously adjusted itself to fit."

"No, I—"

"Confirmation bias is unconscious, Ezekiel, and nobody is aware of whether they are or are not subject to it."

"What are you, a psychologist?"

"I was going to be, back when college still looked like it might happen," said Dad. "And I still read a lot in the field. But no, psychology gave me a name for it, but I already knew that people tend to see what they're told to see, and to remember what they're told to remember."

"All right, so I don't actually remember," said Ezekiel.

"You're missing the point. You might have remembered perfectly and that's why you gave me the completely correct impression that nothing you did involved actually touching the Build-a-Bears. See? It might be a completely reliable memory, or it might be a slightly tweaked memory, and I'm not saying either way, and because of confirmation bias *you* can't be sure either way."

"I feel like I'm circling and circling an airport that doesn't exist," said Ezekiel.

"I'm just saying that you need to stay very *tentative* in what you say to Detective Shank and to the Delamares."

"Oh, come on, Dad! I've already been so tentative that sometimes I wasn't even sure I was talking."

"Good," said Dad. "Because what I saw just now looked like certainty."

"Enthusiasm."

"I've never seen anyone be enthusiastically doubtful before," said Dad.

"First time for everything."

"And if there isn't a good outcome, Ezekiel, it's not your fault. It's the kidnapper's fault."

"Thanks for perfect burgers, Dad."

"Cutting meat doesn't mean you can cook it, but I try."

Ezekiel raised his burger in a kind of toast. Father raised his in reply.

* * *

"I have a life, you know," said Shank on the phone.

"Well, not really," said Ezekiel. "No more than I do."

Shank was silent for a long moment.

"It'll let the Delamares off the hook about trying to get their act together," said Ezekiel.

"Oh, you mean you *noticed* that you were triggering a downward spiral of self-doubt and self-blame in this very nice grief-stricken worry-ridden couple?"

"It wasn't my *plan*," said Ezekiel. "I don't have a—"

"Don't have a plan, I know," said Shank. "Just giving you a hard time. While trying to figure out why I thought I had a life."

"It's a common mistake," said Ezekiel. "But 'having a life' is what people do when nobody needs them."

"Ah," said Shank. "So now it's not completely an insult."

"It never was, not even a little," said Ezekiel. "So you'll come and pick me up?"

"You don't want to walk?"

"Kind of far," said Ezekiel. "Dad would let me ride one of his cows, but they're pretty dead."

"Butcher's children don't have any shoes," said Shank.

"What?"

"Old saying."

"No it's not, you're thinking of the cobbler's children."

"That makes no sense, Ezekiel. The cobbler's children are the only ones that *always* have shoes."

Ezekiel was about to explain irony to Shank, which might have taken a while, but Shank quickly said that he'd be right over and then the phone went dead. Was his one-year-old falling out of the high chair? Was the three-year-old on top of the fridge? Ezekiel had no idea about Shank's life or whether he had a family at all. Maybe he lived alone. Maybe he lived with his mother.

And why shouldn't a grown man live with his mother? Mothers were a rare and precious commodity and if you had one, why in the world would you leave her?

Ezekiel met Shank outside, with Father's admonition in his ears: "Take as long as it takes and try not to get killed by some serial killer kidnapper." Other kids got curfews. Ezekiel didn't mind having a weird father. It made Ezekiel feel as though his own weirdness was hereditary and inescapable.

As Ezekiel got into the car, Shank said, "You were about to explain irony to me, and I assure you, I not only understand it, but when I said the butcher's children got no shoes, I was being ironic and it sailed completely over your head."

"Got me," said Ezekiel.

It only took a few minutes to get to the Delamares' house, and Shank filled it with weird stationhouse gossip about people Ezekiel had never met and probably never would. "My point is," said Shank as they pulled to a stop, "if I *had* a life, that probably would *be* my life, so I'm just as happy not to have one."

"Yes sir," said Ezekiel. "But you're depriving all your coworkers of the chance to gossip about *you*."

They walked up to the door and it opened before they reached the porch. "Please come in," said Mr. Delamare.

"I told Walter that you left without really finishing," said Mrs. Delamare.

"She did," affirmed Walter. "Multiple times."

There it was, another little jab. But probably also the simple truth. They went right out to the porch. "I didn't touch anything since you left before," said Mrs. Delamare.

"It's probably nothing," said Ezekiel. "But I had the crazy thought— well, actually, my dad had the thought, and I realized it wasn't crazy."

"And what thought was that, Ezekiel?" asked Shank.

Ezekiel realized he was standing in front of the couch holding the two pillows. The Build-a-Bears were completely exposed.

"Nobody ever touched them," said Mr. Delamare. "If that matters. I remember that a crime scene guy picked up the pillows to see if there was anything behind them and there were only the bears. So he set the pillows down and then left everything else alone for the photographer to take his pictures and then that was it."

"We already had plenty of samples of Renee's hair," said Shank. "No reason to take the bears."

And Ezekiel understood the unspoken message: We were not going to take the missing girl's most beloved toys away from Mr. and Mrs. Delamare without a compelling reason.

Mrs. Delamare was about to say something at exactly the moment Ezekiel took one step closer to the bears. He could see Mr. Delamare raise his hand just a little to warn her not to speak, and Ezekiel was embarrassed all over again that everybody was taking his micropower so seriously when he didn't know whether it was worth anything or not.

As he reached for the nearer bear, he again felt the name Karen arise so strongly in his mind that he hesitated, not sure if this was a warning that he was about to make a mistake.

Or maybe the kidnapper had been a woman named Karen. Or …

Or or or or or.

Ezekiel touched the bear. He felt a wave of emotion wash over him and he trembled. He sank to his knees because he wasn't sure he could continue to stand. He took the other bear in his other hand. And then, on an impulse, he buried his face in one and then the other, and then he pressed them on both sides of his face, both bear bellies covering his cheeks but not his eyes. He could still see.

But what he saw was not the back of the couch. It was a concrete wall, streaky and damp. A child-sized bed, nicely made. A poster on the wall. And about a dozen Build-a-Bears. Or maybe fewer, because it was hard to count. They had been torn in pieces and somehow Ezekiel knew that the parts had been thrown as far as six-year-old arms could throw them and still they kept putting them back, putting them back, because she had to learn to take care of nice things and until she did she'd have to live with the consequences of her destructive actions, because nobody could afford to keep buying her the same things over and over. Only they obviously *could* afford it because they kept buying the same Build-a-Bears over and over but they were never the right ones and they never could be because the right ones were from Mommy and Daddy and not ...

"Got something?" asked Shank softly.

"She's alive," said Ezekiel.

He expected a sob or *some* response from Mrs. Delamare but there was silence. Then he pulled the bears away from his face and realized that they weren't there on the porch. It was just Shank and Ezekiel. "I sent them out," said Shank. "I thought it might help."

"Maybe it did," said Ezekiel.

"She's alive, but where?"

"She's inside, but the wall is concrete. Like a poured foundation."

"Poured?"

"Not cinderblock, just a solid piece. Streaky. Wet. Rain must leak bad. They've got a bed for her. Looks clean. Made. Stuffed animals. Kind of like they tried to replace these bears but she tore them in pieces and now the pieces are gathered on the bed."

"Ah," said Shank.

"I got the impression that they were making her sleep with the broken-up bears to teach her a lesson."

"As lessons from kidnappers go, it could have been worse."

Ezekiel could only agree.

"You say 'they.'"

"I don't know how many. I don't know gender. Didn't see them. Or him. Or her. Didn't see anybody. I usually don't *see* this much anyway."

"So the connection with the bears is clearer than usual."

"It's not like the address and phone number were written on the concrete wall."

"Anything else? A window, a door?"

"A door but it was closed and I had the idea it couldn't be opened from her side, at least not by somebody her size."

"No window."

"I wish. But you know that around here, all windows show the same thing."

"Trees," said Shank.

"That's the North Carolina view. There's the mountains, behind those trees. There's the river, behind those trees. There's the town of Downy, behind those trees."

"What I'm asking is, do you know where it is, the way you know where other lost things go?"

"Yes, I can lead you there."

"Oh, you're not going," said Shank.

"Yes I am," said Ezekiel. "I'm not being stubborn, I just can't *tell* you where it is. I can only show you."

"You can show me the outside, but you stay in the car."

"Come on," said Ezekiel. "For all we know it's inside an abandoned tobacco processing plant and you can spend all day searching for the exact spot."

"Ezekiel, I'm not putting you in harm's way."

"Then you absolutely *can't* leave me outside in a car. Especially one I can't get out of. Haven't you seen *any* movies?"

Shank barked out a laugh. "Yeah, the isolated kid is the one who dies first."

"So," said Ezekiel.

"Keep your mouth shut about what we're doing," said Shank. "Because I'm *not* taking the Delamares."

"No, you're not," said Mr. Delamare. Shank turned and Ezekiel could now see that they were back in the room. They probably hadn't gone far and were listening at the door. "Because we know we'd get in the way and if I actually see the kidnapper I might do something that gets me life in prison."

"Nobody would convict you," said Ezekiel.

"I'm afraid that he'd try," said Mrs. Delamare, "and the kidnapper would kill him."

"Thank you for waiting here," said Shank.

"Besides," said Ezekiel, "I'm probably wrong and why should you get your hopes up?"

They looked at him with contained skepticism. They knew he believed he could find their little girl. They knew he might be wrong. But nothing he could say right now would dampen their hopes. If he failed, they would be devastated.

If that happens, it's still not my fault, Ezekiel told himself. It's the kidnapper's fault.

"He'll do his best," said Mrs. Delamare. "If it can be done at all, he'll do it."

"No," said Ezekiel. "If I fail, that *doesn't* mean it can't be done at all. It only means that *I* couldn't do it."

"Got it," said Mr. Delamare.

As Shank pulled the car away from the curb, he sighed. "They're going to follow us," he said.

"You can't know that," said Ezekiel.

"I saw him show her the car keys when he said 'got it,'" said Shank. "And now in the rearview I can see their garage door opening."

"Great," said Ezekiel. "Are you going to, like, arrest them?"

"For driving their car on a street?"

"You know, like over-age trick-or-treaters."

"Oh, Ezekiel, we cops don't expect to be *obeyed* when our back is turned. Especially in the South where 'Oh I'd never' means 'Like you can stop me.'" Shank reached down to his radio microphone and said, "I need a car to intercept the very nice couple who are following me. They need to be stopped and contained in their own home until I say to let them out. They aren't guilty of anything, I just don't want them following me into harm's way."

"Got it," said the dispatcher. "And another car to back you up because, as you said, 'harm's way.'"

"Not yet. We aren't even sure where we're going yet. I'll call for backup, believe me. I'm not going to let an innocent child get injured because I tried to cowboy it."

"You mean—"

"Don't say names over the radio," said Shank. He clicked off.

"How many innocent children are you trying to find?" asked Ezekiel.

"I might have meant you."

"I'm leading myself into harm's way," said Ezekiel. "Come on, you might as well have said her name yourself."

"Yeah, I know, I screwed up first, but remember that most people listening to police radio are dumb as a brick so probably they won't add two and two."

"Most people listening to police radio are police," said Ezekiel.

"Like I said," Shank replied.

They drove for a while.

"You know that I have no idea where I'm going," said Shank.

"So far so good."

"We're getting closer?"

"I have no idea," said Ezekiel.

"I thought you—"

"It's not conscious," said Ezekiel. "It comes to me."

"I thought it already *came* to you. Back on the porch."

"It did," said Ezekiel. "But I don't 'know' it, I only have a sense of which way to go."

"Well, then, which way?"

"So far so good," said Ezekiel.

11

"This house," said Shank.

"No," said Ezekiel. "Definitely not this house."

"Then why are we here?" asked Shank impatiently.

"It kept being so far so good until now. Now, the car won't go where we need to go."

"Not this house, though."

"The water table is too high around here for a basement," said Ezekiel. "Look at it. There's a lattice surrounding the crawl space. You can't have a basement under a house that's sitting three feet off the ground."

Shank nodded. "Bet they have a rat problem under there."

"It's only a problem if you mind having rats," said Ezekiel.

"So what do we do now, if we're done with the car?" asked Shank.

"I'm not sure," said Ezekiel. "You do remember how this isn't an exact science, right?"

"This is October and the days are short. You do realize that if we're doing some kind of hike in the woods, we'll only have maybe a half hour of light to do it in."

"I don't want to park here," said Ezekiel. "What if the kidnapper has something to do with this house?"

"I wasn't planning to park here, Ezekiel," said Shank. This time his patience sounded more annoyed than his impatience had a few moments before. "But this road turns to gravel here and I wonder where I should go to cut the overland trek to a minimum."

"Straight on, I think," said Ezekiel. "Though I don't know where the road goes."

The road bent to the right and sloped downward. In a pretty short time it came to an end at the river. There were wooden pilings that looked more like the footings of a pier than any kind of bridge.

"What was this place?" asked Ezekiel.

"Remember the name of the road?"

"Old Ford Road." Ezekiel chuckled at himself. "I honestly thought it had something to do with a Model T."

"It was a crossing place for wagons and horseriders when water levels were normal, but it was a ferry when the water was higher. Dangerous, though."

"I didn't think this was much of a river. We're not that far from the source."

"You get a hurricane makes landfall anywhere from Myrtle to Manhattan, and the rain dumps here. This river can hit flood in a couple of hours, and these pilings won't even be visible above the water."

"Well, this is hurricane season, so …"

"Only hurricane on the radar right now is attacking Brownsville Texas," said Shank. "All we get here right now is regular rains, so the water's fast but a wagon could cross it."

"What about a car?"

"A car would get about halfway before the water wrecked everything and it became a bunch of metal to be recycled. Now, where are we going, Ezekiel Bliss?"

Ezekiel did not correct him. Not everybody was entitled to hear Ezekiel's Blast's true name.

"Downstream," said Ezekiel.

"A true country boy," said Shank. "You know which way is downstream."

"I can see the water flowing," said Ezekiel. "So what I am is 'not blind.'"

They began walking along the high bank because the stretch down close to the water looked muddy and treacherous. They knew they'd made the right choice when several times the river cut in close to the high bank and there wouldn't have been any place for them to walk lower down.

Ezekiel stepped into a patch of tall weeds on the uphill slope and reached down to pick up a scrunchy.

"Oh come on," said Shank.

"I don't pick up *every* scrunchy anymore," said Ezekiel. "But I thought this might be—"

"Of course it might be a clue. If we had one of the Delamares with us they could tell us if it's Renee's."

"Mothers put scrunchies on their daughters hundreds of times. You think they remember which one? And fathers never notice."

"There'll maybe be some hair in it," said Shank. "DNA."

"It'll only matter if we don't find her," said Ezekiel.

"When I said 'Oh come on' it was more about 'How did you even see that?'"

"It was lost," said Ezekiel. "I knew where it was."

"So these things call to you even before you see them."

"I saw it," said Ezekiel. "I just didn't pay attention to it till I caught a whiff of the owner."

"All right then," said Shank. "Is it hers?"

"So far so good," said Ezekiel.

"There are tracks here. Somebody's been riding a bike."

"Looks like a tricycle," said Ezekiel. "Look, there's always a track in the center and two equally spaced tracks to the side."

"Not a tricycle, though," said Shank. "Here, where it turns. It's a bicycle pulling a two-wheeled trailer."

"Or a motorcycle?" asked Ezekiel.

"Depends on how soft the ground has been. It's been through here about a half-dozen times since the last heavy rain. But the tracks aren't all that deep. So I'm thinking bicycle till I know otherwise."

They found out otherwise when they came to what looked like a mine entrance. Poured concrete, so Ezekiel was optimistic. He was about to say something when Shank touched a finger to Ezekiel's lips. Ezekiel understood. They didn't want to be heard by somebody inside, because what if they came out shooting? Or what if they panicked and killed Renee so she couldn't testify against them? All of Dad's *Law & Order* episodes started coming back in a jumble. Everything Ezekiel knew about law enforcement and crime came from those shows, but they were like the air he breathed growing up, and he couldn't tell them apart except that there were the ones with Jerry Orbach and the ones without him.

He knew this, though. If there was ever a time for backup with more skills than a high school freshman, it was now.

Shank apparently thought so, too. He led the way back to the car. He did not use the dispatch radio. Instead he used his mobile phone. "Because I didn't want this going out over the air," said Shank to whoever was listening. "And I didn't want it to be that loud right here. No sirens. Just four guys, two cars, the end of Old Ford Road. On the gravel, right to the river, the *very* end. We've got to get through a heavy door with a serious padlock that my tinsnips won't handle."

The other person said something but Ezekiel could hear that Shank cut him off. "Don't *think*, Sergeant Glee. Just do exactly what I said. Say it back to me right now."

Shank listened.

"If any part of this doesn't happen as ordered, you'll be up in Danville policing the mall, got it?"

Ezekiel couldn't tell if Glee got it or not, because Shank ended the call the moment he finished talking.

"I take it Glee had a better plan," said Ezekiel.

"Glee started telling me who was off tonight and who was on an assignment somewhere."

"So how long will it take them?" asked Ezekiel.

"The sober ones who have their pants on could be here in ten or fifteen minutes," said Shank.

"Isn't Glee going to just put out the call on the radio anyway?" asked Ezekiel. "And won't he just name her?"

Shank closed his eyes. "Shit," he murmured. He called the same number back again.

They talked for only a minute. "OK," said Shank when it was done. "He actually figured it out from the fact that I called him by telephone that he had to do the same when he was calling these guys in."

"Meanwhile do we stay here?"

"Got something else you need to do?" asked Shank. "A date with your non-girlfriend?"

"She's off doing something anyway," said Ezekiel.

"I thought she'd be sitting by the phone," said Shank.

"Phone's in her mother's purse and she doesn't know we've gone this far."

"So you can be discreet," said Shank.

"Didn't want to get her hopes up," said Ezekiel.

"That's a funny thing," said Shank. "The whole world runs on hope, and disappointment is one of the great constants of life, but we keep trying to shelter other people from disappointment by *hiding* from them stuff they ought to know."

"Like with the Delamares?"

"Come on, parents wanting to know where their missing daughter is are a different case. But how many stupid lies are told 'because I didn't want to disappoint you.' To which the answer is, 'If you told me what you were trying to do I might have cooperated and not been down at the church playing bingo when you came by the house.'"

"That sounds really specific," said Ezekiel.

"It wasn't. My mother lived for bingo at the church because that's where all her friends were and they could talk for hours while sort of listening to the numbers."

"So you grew up around gambling."

"Gambling and old women," said Shank. "Better than gangs and drive-bys."

"I wonder how many old women die in bingo games," said Ezekiel.

"That would be an interesting statistic, but I don't think they keep separate records of bingo game deaths. Maybe deaths in church buildings?"

"But that would include deaths from boredom," said Ezekiel, "so there'd be a lot of children in the mix."

That earned a kind of half-smile from Shank, which Ezekiel counted as a victory. Well, no, because it wasn't a contest. Maybe that half-smile counted as something like friendship. Ezekiel wouldn't know about that. All the experience he had of friendship was with Beth, and she was way funnier than he was, so he did all the laughing and grinning and, now and then, half-smiling.

It was getting pretty dark now. "Will they have flashlights?" asked Ezekiel.

"Standard squad car equipment," said Shank.

"With fresh batteries?"

"If they can't get it to light, they deserve to fall on their faces."

Ezekiel didn't say, Renee doesn't deserve to be rescued by clowns who can't see in the dark.

"The batteries will have enough juice," said Shank. "We really do keep to a calendar with equipment maintenance. Flashlight batteries get changed out every three months. More often if needed."

"You must use them a lot."

"Police work really picks up when the sun goes down."

"I didn't really notice when I was there, but I don't remember a lot of guys in suits at the police station. Everybody was in uniform."

"Not a lot of need for plain clothes in a town this size."

"So are you, like, the only detective?"

"I'm on loan from the Eden PD."

"Why would Eden have a detective on the force when Downy doesn't?"

"Eden's the largest city in Rockingham County."

"That's like being the biggest piece of fluff on a dandelion."

"Yeah, but it really matters if you happen to be a dandelion fluff. Are you really a snob about small towns?"

"I didn't choose this place," said Ezekiel. "I was brung."

"So your natural habitat is what, Atlanta?"

"I don't want to live in a city so big they have to cinch it in with a beltway," said Ezekiel. "Just a place that has a bookstore and a Baskin-Robbins."

"Pretty demanding. You're kind of a spoiled brat, you know."

"Or a library with books printed after the Copyright Act of 1978."

"Knowing you, I'm betting there really was a copyright act in 1978."

"Wouldn't be funny otherwise," said Ezekiel.

"Oh," said Shank. "Didn't know it was funny."

"It wasn't. Not to you. Just to me."

"So you were making fun of me for not knowing that there was a copyright act in 1978?"

"I wasn't making fun of you," said Ezekiel.

"Oh, right."

"It wasn't *about* you," said Ezekiel. "It was about how out-of-date all our library books and textbooks are here in Downy. In the high school library. I mean 'media center.' What if I'd said, 'A library that doesn't include Piltdown Man in their books about human evolution'?"

"So you have friends at school?"

"Only one," said Ezekiel.

"Is she as much of a loon as you?"

"Much more so. I aspire to be as loony."

"When I was a kid, if somebody said, 'I aspire to be' anything at all, he'd've gotten beat up after school."

"They leave me alone because I'm the famous thief."

"Ah, protected by your criminal record."

"I guess maybe," said Ezekiel. "When everybody shuns you all the time, every day, it doesn't feel like protection."

"What does it feel like?"

"Hatred," said Ezekiel.

"Oh, no, Ezekiel," said Shank. "Nobody can really hate you till they get to know you."

That hit Ezekiel like running into a wall. *Maybe* Shank was teasing, but were they good enough friends for that? Ezekiel checked—no little smile.

Shank caught him looking and then suddenly his face changed. "No, no, I said that wrong. I didn't mean *you*. Not you *specifically*. I meant the 'you' like 'everybody.' People, you know? Nobody can really hate a person till you get to know him. Not *you*."

Ezekiel was relieved enough that he didn't want to keep making Shank squirm over his wording. "So *me* they can hate without knowing me?" he asked.

Shank gave him a full smile at that. "Nobody hates you, Ezekiel, because nobody knows you. The people who do know you think you're kind of amazing. Scary smart, and then there's all the finding."

"You say 'people who know me' as if there was anybody besides my dad."

"Your mom thought you were amazing. Your dad says."

"Yeah, she did," said Ezekiel. "*She* was amazing."

"And Beth—would she be your friend if she didn't think so?"

"Beth has ulterior motives but sure, she likes me OK."

Silence for about a minute, which, Ezekiel knew, was a long, long time if it came in the middle of a conversation. Ezekiel looked toward the top of the road to see if somebody was coming.

"And *I* know damn well that you're amazing," said Shank.

Suddenly the road got bleary. Ezekiel tried not to wipe tears out of his eyes but he had to *see*, so he wiped a sleeve across his face and it kind of helped clear his vision.

"*Are* you my friend?" asked Ezekiel softly.

So softly that maybe Shank didn't hear him. But Ezekiel sure as hell wasn't going to say it again.

"It's taking me a minute to answer," said Shank, "because I think you mean that word seriously, and there's a lot of promising that goes along with it. So I had to think, am I up to that standard?"

"It isn't a high standard, Lieutenant Shank," said Ezekiel.

"The hell it isn't," said Shank. "It means that I trust you and you can trust me. It means that if something goes wrong for you I help as much as I can. It means that if you're not where you're expected, I look for you. It means that if good stuff happens I'm happy for you. It means that no matter what you say to me I still care about you. It means that when nobody else will tell you shit that you have to know, even if you'll hate hearing it, I'm the one to say it."

"Oh," said Ezekiel.

"The whole list is way longer than that," said Shank. "But maybe that isn't what you meant."

"No, it's what I meant," said Ezekiel. "But while you were saying it I realized that I'm a lousy friend to Beth."

"Why?"

"I went by her house earlier because yeah, I was going to tell her about stuff, but she didn't answer her door. I thought maybe she was mad about something so I yelled an apology. The thing is, if Beth was mad she'd come out and scream at me, she wouldn't give me the silent treatment."

"That's the kind of thing a friend would know," said Shank.

"I thought, maybe she and her mom are out doing something. But the car was in the driveway."

"Only one car?"

"Only one driver," said Ezekiel. "And the air conditioner wasn't running."

"Today wasn't *that* hot," said Shank. "A lot of people don't run their A/C in the fall."

"Hot enough," said Ezekiel, "when you consider that all the windows were closed tight."

"So did you try the door?"

"No," said Ezekiel. "Because Beth gets really strange if I even *see* into her house. She never lets me in. I stepped in one time and she had me out the door again before I could even look around. I mean I *did* look around because I wondered what's the big deal, and everything looked fine. Clean, you know, neat, tidy, stuff that could never be said about *our* house cause my dad's a butcher, not a janitor, and I'm the laziest kid alive."

Shank grinned at that.

"So like you said, if you're not where you're expected, a friend looks for you. And I didn't."

"Sounds to me like you looked as closely as she allowed."

"And she and her mom were probably on a walk, having lunch in a park, something perfectly ordinary. Babysitting for a neighbor. Something close enough they wouldn't need a car."

"Makes sense."

"We're Americans," said Ezekiel. "*Nothing* is close enough we don't need a car."

"You're a good friend," said Shank. "Because it sounds like you went all the way around the house, you were very observant, and you respected her rule about not looking into her house even when she wasn't there to yell at you about it."

"So maybe I'm a semi-good friend."

Headlights appeared at the top of the road. Ezekiel wondered if it was cops or the kidnapper coming back to the hideout.

"Why would there be a mine shaft here so close to the river?" asked Ezekiel. "Never heard about any mining operation here."

"Maybe they were digging for nightcrawlers," said Shank. "Or growing mushrooms."

"You don't pour concrete for that," said Ezekiel.

"I kind of knew about this place, though I've never actually been here. Something about how there was a tunnel or a cave during the Underground Railroad—a lot of Quakers around here, this whole area had a lot of runaway slaves coming through."

"Did slaves pour concrete?"

"Slavery ended a long time ago. But the cave was still there and maybe the concrete was poured when this was a stash during Prohibition. And in the seventies it was used for a while to warehouse weed for local distribution. Till twenty years ago or so. That's when the county put up that heavy door. This strip of the river is actually a historic site. So it's on our maps."

"But it doesn't get patrolled."

"Like you said," replied Shank. "Downy doesn't have its own detective, and we don't have manpower to check on historic sites that haven't been improved."

"Heavy door in a concrete cave entrance doesn't count as 'improvement'?"

"'Improvement' means picnic tables, a waste receptacle, parking spaces, and a toilet."

Ezekiel waved an arm to indicate the whole area. "It all looks like a toilet to the bears and me."

The car pulled up. There was another one coming behind it.

"She's thirsty," said Ezekiel.

"What?" asked Shank.

"Renee. She's really thirsty. I hope somebody has a bottle of water."

"I'll ask." Shank went over to meet the cops as they got out of the car. That was a good move because Ezekiel didn't want to hear a lot of questions about him. This way Shank could deal with the whole you-have-a-child-with-you and the we're-here-because-of-a-psychic? and isn't-this-kid-a-known-thief-and-a-liar? brouhaha without getting under Ezekiel's skin.

After the second car arrived, somebody apparently had a stash of water bottles because a couple of them were carrying water when they all came over to where Ezekiel waited by Shank's car. "Did *he* tell you she was thirsty?" asked one of them, indicating Ezekiel.

"If she's here, she's a prisoner and who knows how long she's been left alone," said Shank. "Just make sure that's not the bottle you pee in when you're too lazy to get out of the car to take a piss in a restroom."

There followed a quick-moving game of one-upmanship as each policeman made more jokes at the expense of the cop who had asked about Ezekiel. Without understanding most of the jokes, Ezekiel got the idea that the jokes were getting more and more obscene—especially the ones from the woman cop—until Shank finally asked, "Is this how you talk in front of children?"

The response was simultaneous:

"You started it."

"He's a guy, he probably talks worse with his friends."

"He might as well get used to it, he'll have a job someday."

"I thought you told us we definitely did *not* have a child with us tonight." This last was from the same cop who asked if Ezekiel had told Shank that Renee was thirsty.

Ezekiel learned something from this. First, cops got as nervous and scared as anybody when they were about to do something that might turn out awful, and they reacted by joking about it. Second, Shank was definitely an outsider in this group. They could all tease each other, quite offensively, but nobody took offense. While everything Shank said was taken with a bit of resentment. Protectiveness. He was potentially perilous to them.

Maybe that was always true with officers.

The cops organized themselves easily—the woman seemed to outrank the men, except for Shank, who left it to them, the local team, to deal with the details. In only a few minutes they were moving along, flashlights pointed only downward. All the flashlights had plenty of battery power. One of the men carried two separate bolt-cutting tools, and one of his cutters looked seriously heavy. Wouldn't want to walk to school carrying *that*, thought Ezekiel.

"I probably don't need to ask," said the woman cop to Shank, "but I'm sure you have a warrant somewhere on your person."

"If we were going into the house up yonder," said Shank, "then that might matter. But this is public land, a historic monument. Underground Railroad, the old ferry and ford. Government property and the government gave me permission to go inside anything on this land."

"When did they give you that?" asked one of the men.

"When they gave me this badge," said Shank.

When they got to the door they were absolutely silent. They all knew someone might be inside.

From the size of the padlock, the guy with the boltcutters apparently judged that he only need the smaller one. Shank thought otherwise, and wordlessly stopped him and pointed to the big one. The guy rolled his eyes but obeyed. The monster boltcutter went through the shaft of the lock like a hot knife through butter. Another guy was holding the lock itself so it didn't fall to the ground, and the woman cop took the dangling u-shaped shaft silently out of the hasp.

Finally it was time to forget about silence, because nobody expected the door to open quietly. All the guns came out, except for the guy would would actually pull the door open, and the cops arranged themselves so that one sweep of automatic fire wouldn't take them all down. One of them held his gun with only one hand, while holding a flashlight with the other. Ezekiel thought: That makes him the obvious target if there *is* a shooter inside.

The door was quieter than Ezekiel expected—somebody had oiled it—but it was still far from silent. It didn't matter. There was no light inside the cave, and no gunshots emanated from it.

When the door stood wide, Shank took the flashlight from the cop holding it and walked in—bravely, thought Ezekiel—shining the light around. Ezekiel waited until all the cops who were going in had done so—two of them were apparently assigned to guard the door from the outside. When Ezekiel went inside he already knew the obvious: Renee was not there by the door.

The walls of the cave were only poured concrete for about eight feet back from the door frame. Obviously it wasn't the place Ezekiel had seen. But his sense of where Renee was already told him to head into the tunnel on the right.

"Have these tunnels been reinforced or braced in any way?" asked the woman quietly. "I grew up in coal country and this isn't a safe tunnel."

"There *are* no safe tunnels in Carolina dirt," said Shank. "But we're going this way."

"Because the kid said so," asked the skeptical cop. Or, as Ezekiel called him, The Sane One.

"Go on outside and wait," said Shank, "if you're not willing to give this a chance."

"No, I'm in. Sorry." The man took his place right behind Shank.

Shank kept a tight grip on Ezekiel's wrist as the two of them led the way down the tunnel. With his other hand, Shank held a light. When Ezekiel tried to tug his hand free, Shank only gripped more tightly. "If the roof of this tunnel collapses," he said softly, "I want to know right where to find your body."

A couple of guys behind them chuckled.

"Not so tight," whispered Ezekiel.

Shank loosened his grip.

Nothing went wrong during their walk down the tunnel. Nothing lurched out at them from some cavity in the wall. No booby-traps like in an Indiana Jones movie. But that didn't keep it from being scary and creepy. More flashlights came on behind them, so Ezekiel figured the cops were creeped out about being underground, too. Ezekiel remembered a book he had once read about digging the Chunnel. It said something like, Our last common ancestor with the chimpanzee was a tree dweller, and there are no burrowing primates, so going underground is an unnatural act for humans.

How could somebody have poured cement walls this far into the tunnel? No cement truck could get through here, though none of the adults had to stoop at all, so the tunnel was high enough for people. From wheelbarrow-mixed cement you couldn't get a smooth continuous pour of concrete to make walls like Ezekiel had seen. Yet even as he wondered if this venture was a complete bust, he felt it even more strongly.

Karen.

That again! What was that even *about*?

They turned a corner and there was another door.

The guy with the boltcutters had left them at the outside door, and for a moment it looked as if they'd have to wait here for someone to go all the way back. But then the woman tried the door—a normal-sized one, this time—and they found that the padlock hadn't been fully closed. It came right open and so did the door and there was the girl.

She needed the water before she could even speak.

Ezekiel backed out of the room into the darkness outside, as the woman gave commands to the others. Then he could hear her asking the girl, "Is there anybody else in here?" Either the girl shook her head or she shrugged or she made no kind of reply, but the questioning stopped and the big guy who didn't bring the boltcutter into the cave carried her out. Others led the way with lights, until only the woman officer and Shank and Ezekiel were left.

"Hospital under guard," she was answering Shank when Ezekiel came back into the room.

"She's young, she may never tell us much," said Shank.

The woman nodded. "Got to catch up with the others or they'll tie each other's shoes together." As she was leaving she paused only to grip Ezekiel's shoulder lightly. "You did good tonight," she said.

"Minnie," Shank said. "Just so you know. There was no child with us tonight. We were acting on a phone tip."

Her name immediately became "Mouse" in Ezekiel's mind.

"I'll tell everybody else," said Mouse.

"And if anybody suggests that he knew where she was because he was in on it, use deadly force."

"Agreed," said Mouse. Then she was gone.

Ezekiel looked around the room, then reached for Shank's flashlight and shone it around. "How could I see this if there isn't a light in here?"

Shank fumbled with something and then there was a lot of light from a bare bulb hanging from the ceiling.

There was a ceiling. This room had been finished.

"I wonder where the power comes from," said Ezekiel.

"From straight above us," said Shank. "The way I figure it, we're directly under that house. And when we explore this more tomorrow, I'm betting that there's another way to this room that doesn't involve the outer door we came through."

"A route that would have needed a warrant," suggested Ezekiel.

"Possibly," said Shank. "Or just a, you know, manhole or something. Like a storm cellar. We'll find out. People in that house might not know a thing. Or they might be the perps and they already skedaddled."

"Or one of them might come down here to check things out and when she's gone, *then* they skedaddle."

"I notice you're saying 'them,'" said Shank.

"Could one guy do all this?"

"If all this includes the concrete pour, then no," said Shank. "But I think this wall is pretty old. Decades old. Maybe it was meant to be a fallout shelter or something. As for the rest of this ..." He indicated the rest of Renee's cell. "One guy or one woman could do it, sure."

"If she came in another way, what was with the bike tracks we saw outside?"

"He might not have known there was another way when he started. Maybe there *wasn't* another way and he dug his own back door, I don't know. It's a long way to carry stuff even with a bike."

"Were there tire tracks on the floor of the cave?" asked Ezekiel.

"Let's look on the way out."

Ezekiel started for the door, but Shank didn't come. Ezekiel stopped and turned back.

"Was this exactly how you saw it?" asked Shank.

Ezekiel looked around more carefully. It helped to have so much light.

"The torn-up Build-a-Bears," said Ezekiel.

"Somebody cleaned up," said Shank. "Maybe the lesson was learned?"

"Or maybe I saw what Renee *wished* she had done. I don't know how subjective the stuff I see might be. I'm not seeing what their eyes actually see, I don't think. Maybe I'm just seeing how it looks to them, or how they want me to see it. Or how they want to see it. I mean, till now it never mattered. I'd flash on the owner's house or car or something. Wherever they lived, wherever they were. And I'd know how to get there. It never mattered what I actually saw."

"Still doesn't," said Shank. "You won't be testifying because you were never in here."

"Thank you for that."

"I'm not omnipotent. Somebody else might talk and if they do, I can't stop a judge from granting a defense lawyer's motion and demand that we produce you to testify. But I *can* promise you that if that looks possible, you and your dad will have plenty of time to make yourselves scarce."

"Sort of anti-witness-protection?"

"Yeah, like that," said Shank.

"It'll hurt your career."

"My career for the last three months has been finding that little girl," said Shank. "You found her for us. She's going home."

"And you found me," said Ezekiel.

"You weren't exactly eager."

"I didn't see how I could help. I had to work on it. Think about it."

"But you worked and you thought," said Shank. "And you came through for her."

"Never would have happened if you hadn't walked away when I asked you to, that day on the way to school."

"Well, there you go. Pushy wasn't going to work with you, so all I could hope for was that you'd somehow decide to trust me. When Glee told me you were outside, that you had come to the station to talk to me, I almost wet myself."

"I don't know how our conversation would have gone if you had."

"I'm an old man," said Shank. "I wet myself all the time. The secret is, Depends."

"You're younger than my father," said Ezekiel.

"Rogaine and hair dye," said Shank. "Tell your dad, it'll do wonders."

They headed on out through the long tunnel. They didn't see anybody on the way out. When they got to Shank's car nobody else was there.

Everybody's off doing their job, thought Ezekiel.

And then: I did my job, too.

12

The next day was Sunday, and to Ezekiel's surprise Dad was up early and dressed in his suit. He was also standing in Ezekiel's bedroom doorway.

"You look like a man who means to go to church," said Ezekiel.

"I am such a man today," said Father.

"And you have the crazy idea that I might want to get up and go with you."

"I also had the crazy idea that you might want to say 'thank God' in a house of God. Because you made such fast progress. From knowing nothing to finding the girl in a single day."

"It's just my finding thing, and finally learning something about it."

"Beth helps you by saving stuff you told her to throw away. You figure out how to trick your finding-sense into locating the owner of those bears."

"Actually, that was you," said Ezekiel.

"My point exactly. Why did I key in on those bears? You were right there and you didn't realize you hadn't touched them. I only had your description to go on, so why did *I* think about whether you did or didn't touch them?"

"People think of things, Dad."

"Sometimes they do, sometimes they don't. Yesterday, you and Beth and I and pretty much everyone thought of the exact things they needed to think of."

"And I'm glad," said Ezekiel. "Also sleepy."

"You can sleep in church," said Father. "It's a sign that you're growing up, if you sleep in church."

Ezekiel laughed a little, but said, "I didn't think you actually believed in … well …"

"I've told you before that I believe in God."

"No, I knew *that*," said Ezekiel. "I just didn't think that you believed he, like, *did* anything."

"I spent a long time being enraged with God for not saving your mother. But then I realized that it was my whole family there on the sidewalk, my wife *and* my only child. I thought about what had been saved for me instead of what had been taken."

"So you're *grateful?*"

"Every time I see you or hear you or argue with you, I thank God that you were spared. And today, the parents of that little girl, and the girl herself, too, I think—they're thanking God. I'm thanking God. Now get out of bed. Even if you haven't grown up enough to have your own faith, trust in mine and go to church with me."

Ezekiel realized Father was really serious about this. "Dad, I can thank God here, can't I? I mean, he's not, like, trapped in the church."

"You can say the words. I want you to *show* your gratitude by moving your body from one place to another place. I don't often say this, Ezekiel, but I'm saying it now. Even if you have no better reason, please do this for me."

Ezekiel thought of a couple of clever retorts but he stopped himself from saying them because he realized that Dad was right—he almost never asked Ezekiel to do anything just because Dad wanted him to. Ezekiel knew that other kids often heard reasons like "because I said so," but he couldn't recall those words ever coming from Father's mouth. And even now, Dad was asking him, saying please, not ordering him to do it. Ezekiel could defy him and stay in bed. But what would be the point? It's not as if Ezekiel would sleep after this.

So he threw back the covers and stood up beside the bed. "Is the sun up?"

"It's eight o'clock. If you open the curtains on your east-facing window, you'll get independent verification."

"But church doesn't start till ten," said Ezekiel.

"After yesterday I thought you'd want to shower. I allowed an extra ten minutes for you to find appropriate clothes."

"What clothes are appropriate?"

"You may or may not be tall enough to look respectable in one of my old suits," said Dad.

For the first time Ezekiel really thought about how tall he was getting. Not as tall as Dad yet, but … not all that much shorter, either.

"I used to be thinner," said Dad. "Not as thin as you, but then, I often ate actual food when I was young."

"I'm skinny like Mom," said Ezekiel. "Can't help heredity."

"If you can't wear a suit of mine, then your nicest school clothes. From your closet. Nothing from off the floor."

So Father knew that Ezekiel often chose his day's clothing by finding whatever was on the floor that didn't actually smell. Of course, Ezekiel had several times thought of the fact that the shirts must smell *like him*, and since he was constantly smelling his own body, the shirts might stink but with an odor that Ezekiel was completely oblivious to.

What if wearing an actual grown-up suit looked cool?

"I'll shower," said Ezekiel, "and then let's see what you've got. If it can make me look like an adult instead of a kid playing dress-up, I'll be fine with it."

"I don't wear a suit very often," said Dad. "Basically, going to church and applying for a loan. So the old suits are in pretty good condition. Not old enough to look retro, but dull enough that they'll never go out of date."

"When have I ever cared about fashion?" asked Ezekiel.

"You've never *said* you care, but you also knew we couldn't afford 'fashion' even if you *did* care. I was just saying."

"Thanks," said Ezekiel.

"And you better take a long shower, son."

"I'm trying to think why," said Ezekiel.

Dad reached down and started pulling the bedding off Ezekiel's bed. "Because you walked in a cave, which means you got covered with cave dust, and your sheets look like we could plant carrots."

They were pretty brown. "I should have showered last night," said Ezekiel.

"The sheets are washable. *You* are washable. Go wash *you*, and I'll put these sheets and your pillowcase in the washer. I'll vacuum your dirt trail out of the carpet this afternoon."

"I'll vacuum."

"Whatever," said Dad. "You saved a child's life yesterday. I give you a pass on the carpet. But if you really *want* to ..."

Father left the sentence unfinished as he left the room, his arms full of sheets.

Dad had been right about the long shower. Ezekiel washed himself thoroughly but as he dried himself, the towel got dirty so he got back in the shower and started over. The second towel stayed clean so he figured he was done.

All he had done was walk through the tunnel. He didn't crawl, or lean on the walls, or dig a hole; there wasn't an explosion to throw dust in the air. But apparently all those feet walking along the tunnel floor stirred up enough fine-grained dirt to get into his clothes and hair and onto his skin as if he had been digging a fort in the back yard.

Church was pretty much as Ezekiel remembered it from the last time he went, which was too many years ago for him to have any idea of the date. Easter? Christmas? Ezekiel didn't feel any closer to God, and even though enough people remembered him that he heard a lot of, "My how you've grown!" he didn't feel at home here. This had been Mom's place, and now apparently it was Dad's. But it wasn't Ezekiel's.

Do I have a place? he wondered as he looked at the people chatting and hugging and making plans, at the children running around on the lawns surrounding the church. Home, yes, of course, but that was just him and Dad and memories of Mom, it wasn't ... what was the word? ... convivial. A bunch of people who knew you when you showed up and where you fit right in and you were accepted for who you were.

Was GRUT his place? Maybe someday, but not yet. Besides, he couldn't just *go* there, because except at the appointed time, his group wasn't there. School wasn't his place—he didn't think it was *anybody's* place, least of all the teachers'—and showing up at the Food Lion meat department was pointless because most of the store employees didn't know him.

His "place" wasn't to be found geographically. It wasn't on a map or in an aerial photo of Downy. A person's place was made up of people who showed up somewhere regularly enough that you could also show up and count on at least some of them being there. And then you could talk to them and say whatever asinine thing came into your head and even if they ridiculed you for it they did it like friends. Ezekiel had seen it in movies, he had seen it on TV, he had even seen something like it in real places where people greeted each other and then just hung out but …

His "place," he realized, was wherever Beth was. They weren't lifelong friends, they didn't know any of each other's darkest secrets, but they knew *something* about each other, they cared what the other one was doing, and they could talk.

It was only yesterday morning when Ezekiel and Beth went out returning lost toys, but so much had happened that Beth didn't know about yet. Maybe that's why Ezekiel didn't feel any kind of presence-of-God at church—what he mostly felt was absence-of-Beth.

Maybe they were in Manhattan seeing a Broadway show. Beth had told him the whole story of *Dear Evan Hansen*, which she had read about on the internet and so maybe her mother got some time off and they went.

But a trip like that had to be planned. You had to buy tickets, get hotel reservations; Beth must have known and she would have mentioned it to him. Unless her mother set it all up as a surprise. In which case it was a good thing Beth went home when she did because it was a long drive to any airport that had flights to New York City.

And their car was in the driveway.

No, she would have told him if there was an expedition. Unless her mother was dating somebody and they went in *his* car. That could have happened, Beth's mother planning it with some guy in her life, maybe a guy from the bank, and …

"Dad, could we go past Beth's house after church?"

"It's already half-past church," said Dad. "I talked to everybody who seemed to have any interest in talking to *me*, and so I think now is an excellent time to get moving."

They stopped across the street from Beth's house and Dad looked at the place through the driver's-side window.

"I'll take your word that all the windows in the back are shut, too. And the air conditioning's off. And the car is definitely in the driveway. But you were only with her yesterday, what could happen to her?"

"Girl alone walking on the street—a thirteen-year-old who looks seven and probably isn't carrying mace—you're right, Dad, nothing could happen."

"If she didn't make it home, her mom would have called us to see if we knew where she was. But we got no call."

"Maybe her mom doesn't know about me."

"So let's go knock on the door," said Dad.

They did. Nobody came. Nobody came to the back door, either. "Look," said Dad, "everything's fine or we would have heard. Of course she told her mom about you because she let Beth go with you yesterday morning with a big bag of garbage, right?"

"Bag of treasures, you mean," said Ezekiel. "To somebody."

"Like I said," Dad answered. Then he stopped and sniffed.

"What," said Ezekiel. "Smell something?"

"You don't?" asked Dad. "Something must have died in their crawl space."

"I don't smell anything."

"I'm kind of keen on the smell of rot," said Dad. "I have to be, cause if there's rot we can't sell the meat. Something died here, but a long time ago. It's like the memory of a smell."

"So … it rotted to nothing."

"The rats and roaches did their work, maybe. But slower than usual, so the smell got rank and then it faded. Smells fade, but for people with sensitive noses they never quite fade away to nothing."

"Is it a blessing or a curse that you can smell so well?" asked Ezekiel. He was thinking of Skunk at GRUT. He wondered if Dad could smell *past* the countersmells that Skunk generated. "I've been to her house twice, and walked all around it yesterday afternoon, and I never smelled anything," said Ezekiel.

"I smell a lot of things I wish I didn't smell." But he didn't seem to be remembering anything particularly disgusting. Instead he went into a reverie, and Ezekiel realized: Maybe Dad can smell traces of Mom in our house, after all these years. Maybe it makes him sad. Wistful. Something he wished he didn't feel.

"Let's go," said Dad. "They'll get back when they get back, and maybe she'll call and explain where she was when you were busy saving lives and bringing children home."

They got to the house to find a message from Lieutenant Shank on the machine. "I know it's Sunday but I'm going to be visiting the Delamares because Renee is home and I've got to find out what I can about the kidnappers. When I made the appointment the Delamares asked if you'd be there and I said, Do you want him to be, and it was pretty clear they wanted to see you a lot more than they wanted to see me. So call me when you hear this or I'll stop by about one or one-thirty." He said his number and Ezekiel looked at the clock and Dad said, "If he's already on his way, your return call won't matter, but if he's waiting for your call, then maybe he should receive it."

The doorbell rang.

"I bet he watched us arrive," said Ezekiel.

"Sneaky sneaky," said Dad, quoting some movie though Ezekiel couldn't remember which one.

Shank came in and he and Dad talked for a while about pretty much nothing, the way polite grownups did. That was better than what kids at school did, which was talk loudly about whatever was wrong with the weird kid. Though come to think of it, Shank and Dad were talking about the weird kid, weren't they? Phrases like "proud of him" and "smart kid" and "showed no fear" and "that's because he's an idiot."

Ezekiel was thinking about whether he should stay in the suit or change into regular clothes. Would it look stupid for him to be wearing a suit? Did it really fit well enough or was it obvious he was in his dad's hand-me-downs? But this *was* Sunday so it wasn't weird to be in Sunday clothes, and meeting Renee was kind of a solemn occasion and Shank wouldn't want to wait for him to change.

"Have you decided?" asked Shank.

"What?" asked Ezekiel.

"Whatever you were deciding," said Shank.

"He isn't sure whether to keep the suit on or change," said Dad.

That was weird. How could either of them know what was going through his mind?

"Suit looks good," said Shank. "Most kids your age don't even try."

Usually something like that from an adult would make Ezekiel insist on changing clothes, but he didn't feel that way about praise from Shank. Shank wouldn't lie to him.

"Doesn't fit, really," said Ezekiel.

"Neither do your other clothes so what the hell," said Shank. Then he looked at Dad. "Sorry."

"These days, 'what the hell' barely feels like cursing," said Dad.

"You want to come?" Shank asked Dad.

"Was I invited?"

"Well, I kind of think that's what I just did," said Shank.

"I mean did the Delamares invite me."

"I know what you meant," said Shank, "and no. But if Ezekiel's going, you have a right to accompany your minor child."

"I'll save meeting the Delamares till some other time," said Dad. "This belongs to you and Ezekiel."

Shank didn't insist and Ezekiel led the way to the door.

On the way to the Delamares' house, Ezekiel was too nervous to talk about anything intelligent. Fortunately, Shank wasn't tense at all—maybe he returned kidnap victims to their families all the time?—so he kept up a stream of talk about nothing, really. Weather, the hurricane down in Texas, which Carolina beaches were best, what in the world you actually do when you take a vacation in the mountains—"Do you just hike around in the woods to provide a buffet for mosquitoes and ticks?"—and it was sometimes amusing but it was always Shank talking and not Ezekiel and he was fine with that.

Mrs. Delamare greeted them at the door and it was kind of awkward. She stepped out and hugged Shank like a long-lost relative, weeping all over his shoulder, and then she turned to Ezekiel and maybe he gave off some kind of body language that said Don't Hug Me, because she held out a hand and then clasped it in both of hers—a Hand Hug, he decided he'd call it when he told Beth about it later—and she still wept and said nothing.

Through all of this she effectively blocked the door until her husband said, from inside, "Come on, Evie, let them come inside at least." She laughed in embarrassment and ushered them in and there in the living room sat Renee, surrounded by cushions like some newly discovered Dalai Lama.

Ezekiel felt even more shy around her than he usually did with strangers, but Mrs. Delamare drew him toward her. "Renee, darling, this is the boy who found you."

Renee looked up at him with grave eyes and said, "What took you so long?"

Mrs. Delamare laughed nervously but, oddly enough, it put Ezekiel at ease. He sat down on the other, unpillowed end of the sofa and said, "I didn't know how to look for you until yesterday, but then it went pretty fast. We didn't, like, wait for some committee to approve the project."

Mr. Delamare laughed now, but Renee kept looking at Ezekiel with those big eyes. "I kept wishing for a finder," she said.

"Until yesterday, I never found a person. I only found the *things* that people lost. So I'm new at this. I'm glad I finally figured it out."

Renee nodded gravely. "I think the woman didn't want to be mean," said Renee. "But she was scary all the same. I think she was crazy."

The mention of a female kidnapper made the adults alert and still. Though Shank didn't tense up like the Delamares did. He talked in a perfectly normal, relaxed tone when he said, "So was it a woman who took you there?"

Renee still looked only at Ezekiel. "No," she said. "It was a man who came onto the porch. I didn't see the woman till I woke up in the grey room."

She seemed to be quite calm.

"She seemed nice at first when I was crying because I didn't like the place and I wanted to go home and she asked me what I missed and I said Mom and Dad and my two bears and then later she brought me two Build-a-Bears but they were all wrong and I tore them to pieces because by then I didn't like her anymore."

"Did you ever hear the man and the woman say each other's names?" asked Shank quietly.

Renee shook her head. And then her face began to work at trying not to cry. "She made me call her Mommy," she said, and then she did cry, reaching for her mother.

Ezekiel got up off the couch so there'd be room for Mrs. Delamare to sit. Mr. Delamare went to stand on the other side of her and Ezekiel was thinking, Being a dad kind of sucks, because he loves his daughter and he missed her but now that she's back, it's the mommy that she reaches for.

As long as there's a mommy at all, thought Ezekiel. I *only* had my dad, so if I did any reaching it was for him. Except maybe not. Maybe I was reaching for Mom the whole time and he was as helpless as Mr. Delamare because he couldn't help me find her.

He had no reason to be identifying with Renee, thought Ezekiel, because she was able to come home to both parents, so she was OK now. But then, she had it worse because for Ezekiel, it was wham, car hits Mom, Mom flies through the air and then lies there in a shape no human should ever be in and he knew right then that she would never come back, not even as a cripple. Just like that, he knew where things stood, but Renee had weeks and weeks of having some crazy woman force her to call her Mommy and Ezekiel never had that kind of pain.

It made him grateful that Father, however lonely he might have been, never brought home a stepmother who would try to take Mom's place. Ezekiel didn't know if this had been a sacrifice for Ezekiel's sake or if Dad simply never met a woman he was interested in. It's not as if Dad talked about it. It's not as if Ezekiel asked.

Shank stood there for a long while, watching Renee cry and her parents comfort her, and then he sat down in an armchair and indicated for Ezekiel to sit in the overstuffed chair. Apparently they were going to wait this out. Because of course Shank had more questions and Renee hadn't really told them much of anything yet. Male kidnapper who actually took Renee, female who acted out a mothering fantasy on a captive child.

At least Shank had some kind of context to fit this in. Maybe he was thinking, OK it's not *this* type of kidnapping, it's *that* kind. Ezekiel tried to think of any of Dad's shows—*Criminal Minds* seemed to be the one that dealt with kidnapping stuff, only then it was always about crazy people who liked to torture their …

That was a bad thing to think about, when he was looking at this little girl. Safe *now*, but what if the guy had tortured her for a week and then killed her? Ezekiel wouldn't have been able to find even Renee's dead body then, because if she was dead she wouldn't have owned the bears anymore so his micropower would have been useless.

So whatever else she did, the crazy woman might have been the reason Renee was still alive. Maybe she kept the man from hurting Renee. As long as Renee was calling the crazy woman Mommy, maybe the guy couldn't bring himself to torture her. Maybe he was afraid Crazy Woman would go completely off the deep end.

Or maybe Shank was so disciplined he never went off on television-based flights of fancy. Just the facts. No guessing.

The tumult grew quieter. Except for a couple of hiccup-like sobs Renee stopped crying. Mr. Delamare stood with his hand on his daughter's head and told Shank, "Maybe this can wait till later?"

"I wish," said Shank. "We've got to have something to go on. A man and a woman—that's more than we had. Mothering fantasies getting acted out, that might help. And no names, that's a disappointment but if I could just ask a few more questions."

Mr. Delamare turned to his daughter, bent down. "Can Mr. Shank ask you some questions? I know you haven't known him long, but he's the detective who never gave up on finding you. We've come to trust him and I hope you can trust him, too."

"I thought it was Ezekiel who found me," said Renee.

"It was," said Shank.

"Lieutenant Shank found Ezekiel," said Mrs. Delamare, "so that Ezekiel would know that we needed him to find *you*."

Renee nodded. "You're not very old but you're older than me," she said to Ezekiel.

"I'm fourteen," said Ezekiel. "Ninth grade."

"I'm supposed to be in first grade only they wouldn't let me go to school."

Ezekiel wanted to say something flip and awful, like, "Lucky you," but he just nodded. "I bet you already know how to read, though," he said.

"I could read when I was four," said Renee.

"She read *Alice in Wonderland* to herself," said Mrs. Delamare. "I wasn't sure if she really understood it, but no matter what I asked, she knew. She knew the story better than I did."

Yes, yes, we're so proud of your smart little girl, thought Ezekiel. But Shank needs some answers …

Ezekiel glanced at Shank, but he was leaning back a little, not sitting on the edge of his seat waiting to speak. He knew the interrogation business. He knew when to press and when to let people talk themselves into talking. Ezekiel had no business trying to guess what his agenda was.

"I've never read it," Ezekiel said. "Nobody ever assigned it in school and I'm not much for talking rabbits."

"It's not like Peter Rabbit," said Renee. "It's not *cute*. It's kind of scary. There was a cake with a sign that said EAT ME and she did and she got huge and when she cried it almost drowned the place because her tears were so big. Like she cried an ocean."

Ezekiel saw a connection at once. "Did you cry an ocean?" he asked her.

Renee shook her head. "I saved my crying for later," she said. "It made that woman angry when I cried. She wanted me to pretend to be happy with her."

"We all pretend to be happy sometimes," said Ezekiel.

Renee nodded. But Ezekiel could see that her eyes were heavy-lidded. "Are you sleepy?" asked Ezekiel.

Renee nodded.

Mr. Delamare looked at Shank with a helpless shrug. What can we do? he seemed to be asking. Can we let the child sleep?

"Renee," said Shank, "did you see any other children?"

Renee shook her head.

"Did they mention any other children?" Shank asked.

Renee cocked her head a little to one side and seemed to be trying to remember.

Ezekiel thought he saw where this was going and he thought he could maybe help while also pursuing something that was still bothering him about the whole experience of trying to find her. "Maybe they said something about a girl named Karen?"

Shank stiffened. Without looking at him Ezekiel knew that he was annoyed. So maybe Ezekiel was wrong to ask.

No, *definitely* he was wrong. Because after just a couple of moments, Renee looked right at him with frightened eyes and she began to tremble. A real full-body shake like somebody who was out in the winter air too long.

"That's what she called me," said Renee. "I told her my real name but she always called me Karen and told me never to forget that Karen was my real name, my birth name. 'It's what I called you the whole time you were in my tummy,' she said."

Her voice was really scared. "I'm not Karen, am I, Mommy? I was never in that woman's tummy, was I?"

"That was a horrible lie she told you," said Mr. Delamare. "Your name has never been Karen. I wish Ezekiel hadn't said that name."

Again a burst of tears, but Ezekiel took it in stride because he was busy wondering why it was *Mr.* Delamare and not his wife who reassured Renee. Mrs. Delamare just sat there, kind of frozen, until she gathered her daughter into her arms as she sobbed again, this time harder than before.

Shank rose to his feet. "We've done all that I think is possible for today," he said. "You do understand that I must come back again. And please don't *you* try to interrogate her. Remember anything she says, but don't ask her about it. She'll tell you what she can bear to tell you. Leave the probing questions to the heartless professional. She doesn't need that from her parents."

The Delamares agreed as Ezekiel followed Shank to the door. Shank gestured for them to stay with Renee. "I know how doorknobs work," said Shank.

The crying stopped and Ezekiel heard the girl say his name. He stopped and faced her.

"Will you come back, too?" she asked him.

"If you want," said Ezekiel. Then he looked at the parents because he realized they might prefer if he didn't. After all, he was the one who said "Karen" and triggered the latest round of crying.

But the Delamares both nodded to him with little half-smiles.

"I can only come when Lieutenant Shank here gives me a ride, but sure," said Ezekiel. "I'm too young to drive."

"You're my age plus my age, plus two," said Renee. "Six and six is twelve, and you're fourteen."

"See? You're already ahead of first grade in arithmetic," said Ezekiel.

She gave him a wan little smile and then Ezekiel felt Shank's hand on his shoulder, gently but firmly guiding him the rest of the way to the door.

Before they even got to the car, Ezekiel started apologizing. "I had no business pursuing stuff that isn't even relevant to the investigation," he said, and then Shank interrupted him.

"Wait till we're in the car before you start recapping the interrogation," said Shank.

So Ezekiel waited. He wondered fleetingly if he should sit in back now, since he was obviously incompetent to be treated as a partner.

"I would never have thought of bringing up that Karen business," said Shank. "That was pure genius."

"It made her cry," said Shank.

"She'll be crying about this for the rest of her life," said Shank. "But in between, she has to tell us things or these bastards are going to get away with it."

"Why was it genius to ask about Karen?"

"Because it *didn't* come out of nowhere. You had no idea why the name kept coming to you but look at it, kid! That was the name *they called her*. So while they had her in their possession, it *was* her name. And that's why you thought of it. The name was attached to her."

"So yeah, I guess that's great that my micropower didn't completely malfunction, but—"

"The name 'Karen' wasn't an accident. It means something to the woman who took care of her or she wouldn't have chosen it. And maybe the woman was crazy, maybe it was part of her fantasy that she carried Renee in her womb, but maybe it wasn't."

Shank pulled the car over. They were only around the corner from the Delamares' house. Shank pulled out his mobile and hit a speed-dial number, just one digit.

From the ensuing conversation it was clear that he had called Mr. Delamare's cell, and he asked Delamare to get away from his wife and daughter to a place where they couldn't hear the conversation. Only then did Shank ask his big question.

"Was Renee born through some kind of surrogacy situation?"

Apparently Mr. Delamare took it personally for some reason, because he was talking loud enough for Ezekiel to hear snatches of what he said. Shank didn't even try to calm him down until Delamare said something about "real daughter" and then Shank quietly said, "Of course she's your real daughter, and there's no reason at all that you should have told me, ever, that there was a surrogate involved. It wasn't relevant, it wouldn't have changed the way we investigated. It only became relevant *now* because it sounds to me like this kidnapper was a surrogate mother."

Apparently this calmed Delamare down but also frightened him.

"No, no," said Shank. "I don't think this crazy woman was necessarily the surrogate mother who actually gave birth to Renee. That's pretty unlikely. But somehow she *knew* Renee was a surrogate birth. So maybe this woman was also a surrogate. Maybe she got so attached to the baby she was carrying that she changed her mind about giving it up, only the legal work was tight and she couldn't change her mind or somebody convinced her that she couldn't or maybe the baby was simply taken. They advise surrogates *not* to name the unborn baby because it only makes it harder, but for some reason this woman called the baby Karen and that's the name she gave to Renee."

More from Mr. Delamare that Ezekiel couldn't make out.

Shank, however, was loud and clear. "You're absolutely right, this is pure speculation. But it's speculation that gives me some phone calls I can make and some things I can look up and *maybe* one of those avenues of inquiry will lead somewhere. That's why I needed to know, and I appreciate your telling me."

Another string of information from Delamare.

"Of course we'll check the actual surrogate," said Shank. "And yes, it'll make my job much easier if you simply tell me her name and contact information. It's not a breach of contract for you to tell me information that will allow us to clear this woman as a suspect."

Mr. Delamare was looking for a paper. He found it. Meanwhile Shank had pulled out a pocket notecard wallet so he could write down the address. It was awkward and Ezekiel reached over and took pen and card and Shank repeated the address info for Ezekiel to write it down.

Ezekiel thought that was the end of it, but no. Shank had one more question. "Just for information, Mr. Delamare, so *don't* read anything into this. I need to know the biologicals. Was Renee conceived *in vitro* using reproductive material from both you and Mrs. Delamare? Or was it the surrogate mother's own egg?"

That one was apparently hard for Delamare to bring himself to answer. But finally he did, and then the call was over.

"Which was it?" asked Ezekiel when the call was cut off.

"I am *so* not used to having a civilian involved, and it's strictly against protocol for me to tell you anything."

"I'm not a civilian," said Ezekiel. "I'm the investigator who found the girl and I'm the one who had the name Karen. If we're not colleagues then—"

"The surrogate supplied the egg. She was artificially inseminated with Mr. Delamare's sperm. So you can see that the surrogate really was the biological mother."

"You're not ruling out their actual surrogate at all, are you," said Ezekiel.

"As soon as I drop you off at home," said Shank, "I'll be taking a few other detectives with me to find and interview this woman."

"So I'm not invited."

"There may be some shooting," said Shank. "You're not firearm-qualified, before you tell me you're a southern boy so you know your way around a gun."

"Never held one in my hands."

"If she comes with us peacefully, then it'll be astonishingly boring. If she tries to flee or fight, then it'll be dangerous. But most likely she won't be there, because she'll already be six states away."

Ezekiel could see how that might be the likeliest outcome.

"So if she's the one who did it, is your assignment here finished?" asked Ezekiel.

"This has all been an enormous sidetrack, is how it looks right now. My actual assignment was to track down a gang—we think it's a gang—that kidnaps young girls. Because of various evidence we had already linked the kidnappers with Alamance or Rockingham County, North Carolina, so here I came. But that is *not* the group that took Renee."

"How do you know?" asked Ezekiel. "You didn't even ask about—"

"How old are you really, Ezekiel?" asked Shank. "Just how much information are you ready to hear? What do you know about the evil in this world?"

"I read *Rise and Fall of the Third Reich*," said Ezekiel. "I know something about pure evil."

Shank seemed to weigh this, and then plunged in. "The girls these guys kidnap show up right away on child-pornography websites, the ugliest stuff. It gets uglier and uglier and then they get killed on camera. We estimate the whole process takes a week, and then the girl is dead."

Ezekiel didn't even know what to picture. This sounded as evil as the pure evil of the Nazis.

"So that isn't what happened to Renee," said Ezekiel, trying to reassure himself. No wonder Shank wouldn't let go of this case. No wonder he was so relieved when Ezekiel told him that Renee was almost certainly alive.

"I never told the Delamares about this kidnapping ring because—"

"Because it would make them insane with worry," said Ezekiel.

"We haven't told anybody. Girls have been taken from nine different states, and if word got out the whole country would be in a panic, which wouldn't make anybody safer at all, but meanwhile we'd have the media hounding us. Also, it would flood the child-porn websites with traffic. We'd be giving them free advertising."

"Can't you shut down sites like that?"

"It's a game of Whack-a-Mole. You kill one site, six others pop up and then we have to go searching for them."

"So you leave them in operation? Showing this kind of thing?"

"We monitor everybody who hits the site, track them back to the actual person, and arrest his sorry ass," said Shank. "Then we shut down the site and start searching for the pop-up replacements. It keeps a lot of FBI personnel employed, and sometimes I think we might be doing some good. Most child porn is made by people who have persuaded themselves that they love children and would never harm them, though of course the very act of filming them causes definite, deep, and lifelong harm. Most sites would refuse to post the videos in which the child dies. Even the ones that run it are probably told that it's all just Hollywood stuff, CGI, no child was actually harmed in the making of this shitty video."

"But you know it's real."

"We've found most of the bodies. They aren't really trying to hide them. Autopsies showed that they died in the manner shown on camera."

Ezekiel felt a shudder run through his body. Maybe he wasn't old enough to know about any of this. Saving a kidnapped girl, sure. But now to think what he might have been saving her from. . . . "If you haven't told the media, why are you—"

"You're a colleague, right?" said Shank. "And because you've proven to me that you know how and when to keep your mouth shut."

"Except for blurting out the name Karen," said Ezekiel.

"That wasn't a blurt," said Shank. "That was good instinct. The name and her reaction to it may be the key to finding the people who took her. Even if they aren't the gang I'm mainly looking for." "How does knowing the name help?" asked Ezekiel. "It's not like it'll be on any birth certificate."

"Ah, but I have hopes. This woman chose the name for a reason. Maybe a sibling that died as a baby. Maybe her mother, who ran off when she was little. Maybe a child of her own that she gave up for adoption. So as we go through lists of known surrogates, we'll cross-reference them with the name Karen and maybe that'll help us find someone to concentrate our efforts on. Narrow it down."

"But maybe she just likes the name," said Ezekiel.

"True," said Shank. "Or maybe it's also her own damn name and we nail her right away."

They were at Ezekiel's house again. Before getting out, Ezekiel said,

"You said I could keep my mouth shut, and I can. But Beth keeps her mouth shut even better than me and she's been part of this. When she gets back from wherever she is right now, can I tell her?"

Shank closed his eyes. "I don't know her," he said. "Bureau rules would say, Not a word to her. But then, Bureau rules would tell me not to give *you* any of the information I just shared. And not to take you with me to any interrogations like I just did."

"So you're already risking your career."

"But trust is trust," said Shank. "She's smart, and she helped you learn how to use your micropower to accomplish what you did, right?"

"To say the least."

"So she's a colleague," said Shank. "Use your judgment, and remember that if you're wrong and she blabs and it gets to the media, it helps the bad guys and it puts my career down the toilet."

"And it would make her and me ridiculously famous and completely ruin our lives," said Ezekiel. "I'll decide what else to tell her when I see how she reacts to the story of finding Renee."

"Just let me know what you decided and what you did, OK?"

"Yes, sir," said Ezekiel.

"Was that a sarcastic 'yes sir'?"

"It usually is, but not this time, sir," said Ezekiel. "You're treating me with respect and I'm returning it."

Ezekiel got out of the car and went into the house. He saw from the window that Shank was still sitting there, making phone calls before he drove away. He kept reading off the card where Ezekiel had written down the address of the surrogate. So whatever was going to happen, it would happen tonight.

Will he call me to tell me how it went? What he learned?

Maybe tomorrow. Maybe he'll call tomorrow.

Ezekiel hadn't asked about telling Dad everything, because it didn't cross his mind *not* to tell him, but if Shank didn't know from the start that Ezekiel would tell his father, then Shank was too dumb to be a Fed.

13

Beth still wasn't back from wherever she had gone, or maybe she arrived late and slept in. She wasn't at the corner where they usually met. Ezekiel waited for a couple of minutes. He thought of walking on down to her house and checking with her mom, but no, she was either sleeping late herself, or she had already left for work. Managing a branch of a bank meant long hours and they started early, Beth had told him, so ... Ezekiel headed on to school

It took way longer without Beth, even though Ezekiel strode freely and covered ground faster. All the lost objects kept yammering at him.

At school there was nobody talking about how the police found the little kidnapped girl. Ezekiel had not checked for the story in the paper—was it possible that there wasn't a story about it at all?—and if Dad saw one he didn't leave it out for Ezekiel to find.

And anyway, since when did high schoolers talk about the news? It would take a presidential assassination or some hot guy quitting his ultra-famous pop group to raise a stir at school.

It was the first time Ezekiel realized that even though he preferred to be left alone, like, always, he also had some kind of deep craving for people to know that he had used his weirdness to do something good. Something *important*, something that even grownups couldn't do without him.

Even guys in the CIA get medals for amazing achievements, Ezekiel reflected, and even though they don't get any publicity, their fellow spies know what they did. In this situation, Shank was the only official person who had a clue—and Ezekiel didn't regret that because he would have had a lot of people, mostly cops, questioning him to find out how he *really* knew where Renee was and who the other kidnappers were. Because they'd start with the assumption that he was one of them or at least knew who they were.

Micropowers could be cool, sure, but whenever you used them in any obvious way, like leading the cops to the place where a kidnap victim was stashed, it made other people, especially stupid people, feel threatened because their picture of how the world worked was officially out of order.

As Ezekiel had these thoughts, another part of his brain was saying, Look at you, so vain about your micropower. Hero Boy who saves kidnap victims *weeks* after they were originally scheduled to be killed. And now you're judging "stupid people" who feel threatened by your micropower, only since almost nobody knows about it, and everybody who *does* know thinks it's cool, how did you arrive at this conclusion? Watching X-Men movies? Starting to identify with Magneto, are you, Finder Boy? *They* scare people because their powers, besides being fictional, are also super.

Who's going to be scared after watching you find stuff on the road or in vacant lots or in the woods? Oh, wow, look. Oooh, aaah! Finder Boy has found another lost scrunchy! Hurry, there's a girl somewhere with *loose hair.* You must locate her and give her back her filthy road-dirt-covered scrunchy! See how she weeps with gratitude?

So after his disappointment at the completely predictable lack of attention the finding of Renee Delamare had among high school students, Ezekiel was able to talk himself back into his normal mood of resentful loneliness, only this time with an added layer of self-condemnation for having expected things to be otherwise.

And it's not as if Beth would have made him feel better. She would have ridiculed him for his vanity all the way to school this morning. That might even have helped because then he wouldn't have had that unconscious expectation of having people talk about the crime he helped solve, the child he helped rescue, so he could bask in his anonymous glory. Beth kept him from the worst of his own stupidity.

What if she and her mother had actually *gone*? What if they moved to some other state, no forwarding address? What if Mrs. Sorenson, Bank Manager, was a big-time embezzler and one of their vaults was empty like in *Ocean's Whatever?* What if she was driving a Ryder Truck full of cash all the way to the end of the world, which Ezekiel figured was likely to be Nunavut. Or Nauru. Except American money wouldn't be worth much there.

"Mr. Bliss," asked the P.E. teacher. "Do you have any idea what the other kids are doing right now?"

Ezekiel looked around and saw that they were on the ground doing boy pushups and girl pushups, depending.

"I was holding out for the crunches," said Ezekiel.

The P.E. teacher gave him a look of withering scorn and Ezekiel got down and started doing slow pushups.

"Faster, Mr. Bliss," said the P.E. teacher.

Ezekiel did a flurry of rapid pushups and then made a show of collapsing on the gym floor, gasping for breath.

"Are we a little out of shape, Mr. Bliss? Have you been eating too much pre-Halloween candy from your family's stash?"

That got a laugh from some of the other kids, but mostly they ignored the scene because in order to be interested enough to watch, they had to care about somebody involved in it.

The school day ended and Ezekiel walked home alone. Just like he did from middle school last year, and he had thought that he preferred it that way. But all the things he would have said to Beth came into his head and there was no way he could give vent to them without looking like a homeless schizophrenic or a pretentious dude with a cellphone earplug.

He thought of walking to her house yet again. But he felt pathetic doing it—had he really become *this* dependent on her only a couple of months into the school year? He stopped on the corner and looked down the street. Couldn't quite see. He walked a few steps, a few more, until he could see that the Sorensons' car was right where it had been. Nothing new to see, move along.

Ezekiel hadn't been able to concentrate in class so he had some unfinished work to do. He hated homework—Dad had shown him on the internet where there were lots of studies that proved that homework made no difference at all in student performance. However, he could also imagine Dad saying, But Ezekiel, this isn't homework, this is classwork that you failed to finish. There aren't any studies showing that uncompleted classwork might as well be ignored.

Besides, Ezekiel had nothing better to do. Renee had been found. All the other children kidnapped by these monsters were dead, so he couldn't find them even if Shank asked him to try.

I may have already done the most important thing in my life.

That realization staggered him. Maybe adults felt that way all the time. Maybe everybody had that moment when they knew that nothing else they ever did would matter quite as much.

He could hear Beth's voice saying, And isn't that a lot better than *never* doing anything that matters at all?

His house sounded empty to him. His shoes were loud on the wooden floors that Father had laid down to replace the crummy carpet when Ezekiel was still a baby. He tried to imagine being a toddler and then a little kid with only carpet to play on. Anything you built with blocks would fall over. Toy cars would constantly get snagged and you couldn't roll them because when you let go they'd just stop. But wooden floors had turned the main floor of the house into a child's paradise.

But an empty one, when Ezekiel was there alone.

Then he realized why it creeped him out today, of all days. Renee had been playing in *her* child's paradise and somebody came and opened the door and took her out of it. Would she ever feel safe again?

Would Ezekiel?

There was no law that said fourteen-year-old boys who were getting as tall as their fathers couldn't be kidnapped, too.

Well, actually, there *were* laws against kidnapping anybody, but there was no natural law of boychild immunity. I'm not much safer than Renee was. If somebody came to the door right now and did a huff-and-puff-and-blow-your-house-down routine, was Ezekiel prepared to defend himself? "Better go away or I'll refuse to give you any of your stuff I happen to find!" Micropowers didn't make you a hero, they didn't even raise you to the level of general competence.

He finished the classwork and thought about eating something. That would have been fine, but he not only wasn't hungry, the thought of eating made him feel kind of sick.

What is this churning in my gut? Am I getting sympathetic post-traumatic stress disorder because of what Renee went through? Or because of what she *might* have gone through if it had been a different set of kidnappers?

I don't even know her. Now that she's safe, why would I stress out about her?

An idea came to the back of his mind. Maybe I'm getting this sick feeling because Beth is gone and I don't know when she's coming back. Maybe this is what they're talking about in those stupid books that are all about love, people pining away for someone missing. Dad made him read some of them—he called them classics, and he said, "If you're planning to be able to make some woman happy someday, Ezekiel, maybe you should have some idea of what they care about and how they think."

But nobody felt like *puking* in those books, just because their dearest darling was away for a few days. They wrote long stupid letters and composed ridiculous poetry and fought duels, but they didn't pump their guts into a toilet bowl.

Which Ezekiel promptly did, as fast as he could get into the bathroom, because just thinking about puking made him feel even pukier.

He really hated vomiting. Not that anybody loved it, he knew, but feeling that acid burn in his mouth, in his throat, up into his nose—it was vile.

I shouldn't have eaten school lunch.

I didn't eat school lunch today, he remembered. So what, exactly, am I throwing up?

He rinsed his mouth out. It wasn't enough so he brushed his teeth. Then he wanted to throw away the toothbrush but replacing it would be an unnecessary expense. So he washed it with dish soap in the kitchen sink and then rinsed it thoroughly and laid it in the drainer to get dry.

Was it something I ate yesterday, and this is a really delayed case of food poisoning? Or is it a sampling of Renee's PTSD? Or am I truly some lovesick loser, pining for Beth to come back and say rude things to me? She looks like a six-year-old, for heaven's sake. If by some ridiculous fluke I actually had feelings for her, I'd look like some kind of ...

I'd look like the kind of guy who likes little girls.

Beth *looks* like the age group that Renee is in. The predators who were kidnapping young girls wouldn't know, looking at her, that she wasn't one of their target prey.

Ridiculous. If Beth was missing, her mother would have called the police by now. There wouldn't be this *silence*.

Beth is safe. I'm safe. Renee is safe ... now.

So why didn't he *feel* safe?

There was a knock at the door. No doorbell, just a strong knock. Ezekiel went to answer it and half-expected to find the door already opening when he got there, the way Renee must have seen her abductor getting past whatever fastener kept that porch closed up.

It was Shank.

Ezekiel cursed himself for a coward, and opened the door.

"Your dad's not home yet?"

"His shift is just ending and it takes him a while to wash up and drive home," said Ezekiel.

"I thought you might want to know where things stand on finding Renee's fake mommy."

"Did you find her?"

"Pretty sure we did," said Shank. "But only her, not the guy who did the actual abducting."

"Well, can you get her to tell you who he is?"

"I doubt it," said Shank, "because she's dead."

Ezekiel hadn't been expecting that. "Did she resist arrest?"

"We weren't going to arrest her, we were going to talk to her. Find out if she had an alibi. Like I told you, the surrogate really was Renee's biological mother. We had to eliminate her as a suspect before we tried to broaden the search. We went to her house last night but nobody was there and we didn't have a warrant, you don't break into somebody's house until you're a lot more certain of their involvement in a crime than we were."

"But you went back?"

"Today. This morning. Because we set some guys to watch the house and she never came back, and by then we had found out that yes indeed, she had a sister named Karen who died as a baby, and that gave us enough to get a judge to tell us we were close to a warrant and all that, but talk to her first, and so we went there and now, in daylight, we could see through some breaks in the curtain and somebody was lying on the floor of the kitchen with a knife or *something* that glinted like metal close by, and that gave us a reason to go in. She was dead on the kitchen floor, stabbed with the big kitchen knife that she probably picked up to try to defend herself. All the blood was hers, though, and so were all the prints, so maybe the medical examiner will say it was some other knife."

"So she wasn't just dead, she was murdered."

"We thought about it but we ruled out suicide because very few suicides stab themselves a half dozen times in the heart. She was dead long before the last blow was struck."

"You paint a pretty picture," said Ezekiel.

"There's nothing pretty about it. But I thought you ought to know."

"Which thing? That the woman who made Renee call her Mommy is dead? Or that the guy who kidnapped Renee and probably killed Fake Mommy is still out there and you don't have any idea who he is?"

"Kind of both things."

"Let me guess. He was probably watching the tunnel entrance from across the river when we went in, or maybe she was watching and she told him, so he's seen *me* as the person who was leading the way. Was it obvious I was leading the way?"

"I followed you there the first time, so, yeah. Pretty clear. But it definitely wasn't her watching the tunnel."

"Already dead?"

"She wasn't killed because we found Renee. I think she was killed because she was the only thing keeping Renee alive and the guy—or his boss, or his customers—they were tired of waiting while she acted out her fantasy. Maybe they told her she'd had her fun but it was over, and she started planning to kidnap Renee from the kidnappers and run off to keep her safe."

"OK, now you're just making crap up."

"Not really. There were two suitcases packed. One full of Fake Mommy's stuff, and one full of age-inappropriate children's clothing. Maybe it was some of her dead sister Karen's things that she'd been saving, I don't know. They would never have fit Renee, but she packed a suitcase for a child and if they found it, she was doomed."

"So you're saying that maybe Renee's abduction was tied to that ring of child-killers after all."

"Maybe. More than maybe. She and the guy who took Renee from the porch, they might have been partners, doing the kidnappings in order to supply the sicko who makes the films. Maybe the kidnapper told the film guys he had a girl for them, and they were starting to say, Bring her in *now*, you've dithered long enough. This isn't completely made up, either, because two witnesses of earlier kidnappings told us about what looked like a handoff—one at a highway rest area, one at a McDonald's, both in other states, but the people doing the kidnapping are probably *not* the people making the movies."

Ezekiel was seeing the story now. "So Fake Mommy says, 'Why do they get all the fun, let me have my little girl for a while,' only she wouldn't let go when the game had to end."

"A house of cards, that's all we've got, but we have to have *some* theory. We're trying to figure out if she had any relatives, some connection with the abductor, because if he didn't feel some kind of obligation to her, why would he let her play house with such valuable merchandise?"

Ezekiel shuddered. "You can *call* her that?"

"That's how *they* think of her," said Shank. "I've known enough of these predators, the ones who do it for money as well as their sick perversions. Once she's taken, they've got to get her in front of the cameras because the longer they take, the more chance there is of us catching them."

"So leaving the dead body there in her kitchen for you to find wasn't smart, right?"

"The abductor isn't exactly clever. If he's the one who's done all the kidnappings in the sequence, he takes opportunities as they come up. They were all abductions in busy places. A mall, a couple of parks, kids walking home from school. He happens to see a child who fits the desired profile and grabs her, then takes her out of state to the rendezvous point and hands her off. He only has her for a few hours."

"Except Renee."

"That's why I thought she wasn't part of the pattern. But I'm thinking that Fake Mommy—"

"Don't you know her real name by now?"

"Yes, I do," said Shank. "But you don't."

Ezekiel nodded.

"Fake Mommy says to him, I know a girl, I gave birth to her, I go and watch her play on the screened-in back porch sometimes. It's just a screen door, it's nothing, she's alone back there for hours sometimes, nobody can see. I'll show you where she is if you let me have a couple of weeks with her before you turn her over to *them*."

"You've got this written inside your head like a movie," said Ezekiel.

"That's how I work. If I don't have a script, then nothing goes right. I have to have a sense of who they are."

"Like you had a script for the day you asked me to help?"

"Oh, yeah. About five different scripts, but you didn't ever say your lines right."

"Not ever?"

"Not once."

"So we're not actually safer, is what you're saying," said Ezekiel.

"Well, actually, *you* are, you *and* Renee and her family. Remember that this predator goes for the easy grab, the random one, just somebody walking along the street or through a park or coming out of a birthday party or shopping with her mom. So without the motivation of Fake Mommy wanting her little girl back, he's going to stay far away from Renee. And you."

"But he's not the boss."

"I have no idea how much he told the people he works for. Maybe all he said was, I've got one. So as long as he brings them *somebody* by the deadline, they'll never know it wasn't the one he told them about six weeks ago. He's been stalling, he *killed* his partner—or his girlfriend, or his cousin, or whatever she was—and now he's desperate to meet the deadline. I keep expecting to hear of some other little girl disappearing."

"A substitute for Renee."

"Unless I'm completely off about this and I could be."

By now a voice was almost screaming inside Ezekiel's head. "Lieutenant Shank," he said, "my friend Beth disappeared."

"She's in high school."

"They skipped her up a couple of grades. She's in tenth but she isn't quite fourteen yet."

"Way too old for them."

"You've seen her, Lieutenant Shank. If you just saw her on the street, how old would you think she was?"

"Wouldn't her parents have reported her missing?"

"Her dad's long gone, but her mother manages the branch of Haw River Bank here in Downy."

"Well then, that's where we start. First thing tomorrow, as soon as the bank opens, I'll go in and talk to her mom and make sure everything's OK with Beth."

"And then you'll have a good laugh about the crazy kid who goes into a panic when he doesn't see Beth for a couple of days."

"People have routines in their lives and she stopped following hers. Of course you got concerned, especially with all this other craziness."

"When she walked home on Saturday she was alone, and it doesn't matter whether it was a 'good' or 'bad' neighborhood, right?"

"Actually, the 'good' neighborhoods usually have fewer people out on the street, so … fewer witnesses."

"Why is that?" asked Ezekiel.

"Cable TV, videogames, and air-conditioning," said Shank. It was a list he had enumerated before. "The poorer you are, the more likely you are to need to get out of the house just to stay sane. But people with air-conditioning, they don't go outside if they can help it, not in this climate."

"This time of year it's starting to get cooler."

"Not if you don't have air-conditioning. Still plenty hot indoors."

"They haven't been running their air-conditioning," said Ezekiel. "Beth and her mom. The car is just sitting there in the driveway and the windows are all shut tight and the air-conditioning isn't running."

Shank looked at him with more alertness. "OK, yeah, I can see how your being worried wasn't exactly irrational."

"If something happened to her because I didn't walk her home ..."

"You didn't abduct her."

"But like you said, these guys target somebody who happens to be in a place without witnesses and we had kind of a stupid disagreement about nothing and she just took off walking and made it clear she didn't need me to walk her home."

"And she probably didn't, she's probably fine."

"I keep telling myself, beach or mountains, that's where people in Carolina go to get away. Beach or mountains."

"Just not during the school year."

"Maybe they have a time-share. Maybe this is when they could get the place they wanted. It's not like Beth couldn't make up any schoolwork she missed. She's insanely smart. Well, she's smarter than me, anyway."

"And you're insanely smart."

"I'm good at school stuff and, yeah, I'll own that. I'm insane."

"Ezekiel, I'm really not a wait-till-morning kind of guy," said Shank. "I want to see that closed-up house and the driveway car that doesn't go anywhere."

* * *

Ezekiel left Dad a note about who he was with and where he was going because there was no reason to have *two* crazy people living in their house. Then Shank drove him to Beth's house and got out of the car. He didn't wait for Ezekiel to show him things—he knew how to approach a house where maybe something was wrong. He also made sure his weapon was accessible and when Ezekiel asked if he thought there were bad guys in the house,

Shank sort of laughed and said, "Bad guys would have that air-conditioning cranked to the max. *They* don't have to pay the bills. But … agents carry guns for a reason. You never know what might come up, especially when you're wandering around on unfamiliar turf near a mysteriously closed-up house with a fourteen-year-old as your only backup."

They went around the house, passing the compressor unit, which still wasn't going. Shank felt it. "Hasn't been working at all today," he said. They moved to the back door. Locked. Ezekiel hadn't dared to try it, but Shank apparently knew right where the edge of the law was. "If it had been forced open," said Shank, "then that's probable cause. And a sign that somebody might be in imminent danger."

But it was locked.

When they got to the slab of driveway where the car was parked, Shank walked around the car twice. He bent over to look at the tires. He tried the hood latch but it had to be opened from the inside first and the car doors were locked.

"What can you tell?" asked Ezekiel.

"Almost nothing," said Shank. "The things that go wrong with a car when it's parked for too long only show up when you try to drive it again. The only thing that I *might* see is that it looks like the tires have developed flat spots—look there, how much of the tire is in contact with the driveway."

"It's not a flat, none of them."

"But it might be out of round. I'm only eyeballing it though, and a real mechanic might laugh at me. Maybe I'm seeing what I'm looking for. Still, look at the dust and dirt on the car, in spite of the rain last week. Nobody loves this car."

"I don't love cars either," said Ezekiel.

"Careful who you say that to," said Shank. "There are guys who think that car-love is the only sure sign of manhood."

"Even if the car *has* been sitting here, I don't know what that means."

Shank shrugged. "Maybe it means they own two cars, this piece of crap that they never drive anywhere, and which they're too ignorant to know you have to drive every couple of weeks so things don't go bad, and then another, nicer car that they're in right now on some kind of wonderful family road trip."

"Never thought of two cars, because there's only one driver."

"Maybe they didn't get the turn-in value they expected so they figured they'd sell the old car later, only they haven't gotten around to it."

"You keep saying 'they' but it's just Beth and her mom, and Beth will probably never drive because she can't see over the dashboard."

"She, then. Mrs. Sorenson."

"Anyway, closed house, car that doesn't move," said Ezekiel. "What do you think?"

"That tomorrow I'm going to pay a visit to Mrs. Sorenson."

"When I ask if I can go along, you'll only say—"

"You'll be in school, that's what I'll say," said Shank.

"But you'll tell me, right?"

"Yes," said Shank.

"Good news or bad, you'll tell me."

Shank took a deep breath before answering. "I'll tell you what I can. What I think is right. Look, it'll be nothing, a perfectly simple explanation. Well, maybe not simple—maybe they're running away from killer debt and they're—*she's* letting the bank take back the house. But, you know, one where letting Beth walk home alone has nothing to do with her not coming to school today."

"Dad says it smells like something died," said Ezekiel.

"I don't smell it," said Shank. "In another life, I was a homicide detective and believe me, I know that smell."

"Ask him yourself," said Ezekiel, because Dad was walking across the street to join them. He must have read Ezekiel's note and decided to join the team.

Shank and Dad talked for a while and Dad explained about the smell. "Probably an animal in the crawl space," he said, "and it was a long time ago. Just the last traces, that's all I smell."

"I still don't smell it," said Shank, "but they say the sense of smell is the second thing to go when you start getting old."

Ezekiel wanted to ask him what the first thing was, but Dad gave

Ezekiel a glance that told him that he really had nothing to contribute to this conversation.

"I barely smell it," said Dad, "so maybe it was so long ago that it was before the Sorensons moved here."

"Maybe that's why they got a price they could afford," said Shank.

"Why, do you know something about the price of the house?" asked Ezekiel.

"It's a big deal when a single mother is able to buy a house," said Shank. "Divorce usually leaves everybody poorer, and the woman is usually a lot poorer than the man. So, good for Mrs. Sorenson."

"I don't know whether you've got a family to get home to," said Dad, "but Ezekiel does. Our dinner reservation's at six-thirty and if we don't get moving we'll be late."

Shank looked surprised. "There's a restaurant around here that's worth making a reservation at?"

"A few."

"Where are you eating?" asked Shank.

"Hoping for an invitation? Because you're welcome to come, as long as you pay your own check."

"No, no, just curious," said Shank.

"Burger King," said Dad.

"They take reservations?"

"I always have reservations when I eat at Burger King," said Dad. "But the shakes are worth it, as long as the burgers don't kill you outright."

14

Dad put the car in gear and they pulled away from the Sorenson house.

"Dad," said Ezekiel. "I'm seriously worried about Beth."

"Me too," said Dad. "That house is seriously wrong."

"Something besides the smell?"

"Everything," said Dad. "Closed up like that, the car not moving for a long, long time. Are you sure Beth was really living there?"

"Yes, I came to the door a few days ago, she was there. Inside. She practically used a battering ram to push me back *out* of the house, but she was inside it."

"So she didn't want you coming in."

"Like, she's insane about it," said Ezekiel. "In my opinion."

"Something wrong with that house."

"But there's nothing we can do," said Ezekiel.

"Really?" asked Dad.

They were parked in front of their own house now, but Dad didn't get out of the car. Ezekiel wanted to ask him what he was doing but he knew perfectly well that Dad was deciding something. And Ezekiel's offering any kind of opinion wouldn't hurry the process at all. Ezekiel knew better than to stare at his father, either. He just sat there looking over the dashboard at the neighborhood. Thinking: I am already tall enough to drive. And Beth probably never will be.

"Well, hell's bells," said Father. He put the car in gear and started going again. Then he made a series of turns that amounted to a U-turn. They'd been gone maybe twenty minutes when they pulled back onto the street where Beth lived.

"What are we doing, Dad?" asked Ezekiel.

"Will you look at that," said Father.

Ezekiel looked. Shank's car was still in front of the Sorenson house. "Shank isn't gone," said Ezekiel.

"Shank thinks there's something wrong here, too." Father brought the car to a stop, this time nose to nose with Shank's car. Then he unbuckled and got out. "You stay here."

Ezekiel closed the door. From the outside. "In a pig's eye," said Ezekiel.

"That's disrespectful," said Father.

"You're going in, aren't you?" asked Ezekiel.

"I am if Shank is," said Father.

"Because butchers are all automatically licensed detectives?"

"My son's best friend might be in that house, or she might not. I'm not sure which would be worse, but my son has a right to know."

"Your son has a right to be there."

"Not a right, just a wish," said Dad.

"Exactly as much right and authority as you," said Ezekiel.

"Son, when are you going to learn? Felons on death row have more rights than children."

Father didn't even go up to the front door. He led Ezekiel around the back. The door was standing open.

"Well look," said Father. "An apparent burglary in progress."

"It doesn't look broken into," said Ezekiel. "I think Shank had a key. I think he has a warrant."

Shank was walking down the stairs. He came into the kitchen, where Ezekiel and his father were standing.

"Let's have a sit-down here in the kitchen," said Shank.

Ezekiel wasn't having it. "Is Beth here? Alive or dead, man, you have to tell me."

"She's not here," said Shank. "No sign of her being abducted, either. Just … not here."

"Then why are we sitting down in the kitchen?" asked Ezekiel.

"First do what I told you to do," said Shank, "because at the moment you're giving me lip and ignoring the instructions of a police officer at a possible crime scene."

Ezekiel sat down. Father was already sitting.

Shank also sat down.

"What crime?" asked Father.

"Possible crime. Our local crime scene investigators aren't capable of dealing with what I found. So I'm waiting here until we get bigger guns in here."

"What did you find?" asked Father.

Shank took a deep breath. "Beth's mother is dead," he said.

Father said nothing.

"Murdered?" asked Ezekiel softly.

"I don't know," said Shank. "That's why nobody, and I mean *nobody*, is going into that room until the crime scene people—*my* crime scene people—get here."

"How can you not know?" asked Ezekiel. "Is there some kind of wound? A bottle of pills? What?"

"If there was a wound, anybody could do the crime scene. If there were pills spilled on the floor from an open container—or an open container with *no* pills—then I'd say 'probable suicide.'"

Father rested his hand on Ezekiel's forearm, brought his arm down to the table very gently but firmly. "You're tolerating us here inside the house."

"I didn't believe for a second that you were really leaving for real," said Shank. "Why do you think I left the door open?"

"You had a key?" asked Ezekiel.

"Tomorrow I would have gotten a key from the real estate agent who sold them the house. It's quite possibly illegal, but there are real estate agents who keep a copy of the key to every house they've sold, in case the owner gets locked out and thinks to call their agent. So I was going to show her the warrant and suggest that she might help me get in without damaging the door."

Ezekiel was getting impatient with the hypothetical. "But you *didn't* wait till tomorrow and you *didn't* talk to the agent—"

"I did on the phone," said Shank. "And she told me that Mrs. Sorenson has a small fake rock with a key hidden inside, among the bushes near the southwest corner of the house."

"Very nice," said Father. "No warrant, then?"

"I have a lovely warrant, all legal and everything," said Shank.

"And what was the basis of your warrant?"

"Everything Ezekiel saw," said Shank. "And what you smelled, Mr. Bliss. I keep a fax machine in the car and a judge on call with the task force, so I have the warrant on paper, in case there was somebody inside to challenge the legality of my entry."

"We must have been gone longer than I thought," said Ezekiel.

"When the lives of children are at stake," said Shank, "the wheels of justice sometimes have a little zip to them. But it's hurry up and wait, because we've got a little time before my people get here. And before the locals send me someone to guard the crime scene."

"*Possible* crime scene," said Ezekiel. "What about Beth?"

"Not here," said Shank.

"Patience," said Father. "You can see he's dying to tell us what he found out, and I, for one, am dying to hear."

"First indication was when I called the bank," said Lieutenant Shank.

"It's closed by now," said Father.

"The police have the *real* telephone numbers, so we don't get the answering machines that kick in after business hours."

"So was she there?" asked Ezekiel.

"I talked to the current manager. Mrs. Sorenson *had* been the manager of the Downy branch of Haw River Bank. Until last May."

"She was fired?"

"No," said Shank. "There would have been no reason for it. Everybody was happy with the way she was managing the branch, it was looking to be profitable under her leadership, and so it came as a complete shock when one day she simply didn't show up. Didn't answer her landline, didn't answer her cell. Next day, still no show. Her second-in-command came by the house, no answer to the doorbell or to a knock on the back door."

"Embezzling?" asked Father.

"First thing they suspected," said Shank, "but nobody was surprised when a quick forensic audit showed that there was absolutely nothing amiss. In fact, she herself had put in safeguards to make sure *no*body could jimmy the books and slip out with cash. So … clean as can be. No crime. Just a manager who one day flaked out and didn't show up."

"Only her car was still in the driveway," said Father.

Again Ezekiel thought, Dad's got a mind for this. Maybe butchers *are* automatically deputized.

"Exactly," said Shank. "They even filed a missing person on her after a few days. She deserved her privacy, yes, but what if she had been abducted? Injured? The problem was, the one cop who came to talk to them found out that Mrs. Sorenson had a thirteen-year-old daughter and asked why she didn't answer the door or the phone."

Good question, thought Ezekiel.

"I talked to that officer and *he* did his job. He went to the school and talked to Betty—that's her legal name on the school records—and *she* said everything was fine with her mom, she just wasn't working at the bank anymore. And he said, Why didn't she notify them? And she said, Mom left them a letter of resignation and she said she was sorry she gave them no advance notice but she didn't know until it happened that she was going to get this opportunity."

"What opportunity?" asked Ezekiel.

"You know, son," said Father, "chances are excellent that until you interrupted, that was exactly what Lieutenant Shank was going to tell us next."

"It was," said Shank. "But Ezekiel isn't a trained interrogator, so he doesn't know that a good interrogator lets the subject keep talking because you get way more information that way."

Ezekiel put his hand over his own mouth.

"Betty told the officer that it was online work and she didn't exactly understand it, but her mom loved the work and it paid better. The officer said, why doesn't she answer the phone or the door? And Betty rolled her eyes—I'm quoting him here—and said, 'Man, she's *working*.'"

There was enough of a pause that Ezekiel felt justified in saying, "Beth told *me* that her mom was manager of the Downy branch of Haw River Bank."

"Present tense," said Shank.

"Definitely not her previous job, it was her current job. When she said that in September."

"Because if she said that her mom was working at home," said Shank, "then you would have expected to meet her sometime. Or, you know, *any* time you came over."

"She wouldn't let me come over," said Ezekiel. "I told you."

"How long has her mother been dead?" asked Dad.

"That's what the crime scene team is for," said Shank, "but judging from the condition of the body, there's nothing to contradict the idea that she died sometime between the close of work on the last day she went in, and the morning of the first day she *didn't* come in."

Ezekiel tried to let that sink in. "The whole time I've known Beth, her mother was dead?"

Shank nodded.

"And her mother's body was *upstairs*?" Ezekiel started to rise to his feet.

Again Father caught his arm, guided him back to a sitting position at the table.

"Beth—I'll use *your* name for her now," said Shank. "Beth was resourceful. She must have found her mother's body in the morning and then thought pretty carefully about what to do. She knew that the law would never let a thirteen-year-old live by herself, and because her dad is a flaming ... frankfurter, let's say ..."

Ezekiel thought of supplying a better word, but kept his mouth shut.

"She figured he wouldn't want custody and probably wouldn't get it. *If* we could find him, which I have two FBI people working on right now because there's a faint chance that Beth is missing because he did step up and come get her."

Ezekiel thought of that as a hopeful idea, which was therefore completely unlikely to be true.

Shank went on. "So I checked on the financials—another of the things that the Bureau can access far more easily than a very small local police department—and here's how Beth has been surviving without a car. She knew her mother's PIN so she could get cash four hundred bucks at a time. She *didn't* use the ATM at the Haw River bank because she didn't want people there asking her about her mother, I guess. Besides, the bank is a long walk from here, and the nearest ATM may charge a fee, but there are no questions."

"Without a paycheck," said Father, "that wasn't going to last long."

"What Beth may not have known until her mother died is that her mother's grandmother was very, very rich. Oil money. When Beth's mother was born, grandma settled an oil well on her. When she came of age, Beth's mother began to get the dividends. Until then, they had all flowed into a trust fund. Mrs. Sorenson named Beth—well, Betty—the recipient of all those saved-up funds. Beth probably *doesn't* know how many hundreds of thousands of dollars are in that trust fund, and it wouldn't have helped her if she knew because she can't access it till she's eighteen."

"The dividend checks?" asked Father.

"One of them had arrived by mail a few days before her mother died. When Beth went through all the envelopes on the kitchen desk—right over there—she must have discovered it, because she *mailed* that check with a deposit slip for the same checking account as her mother's ATM card. Her mother had a for deposit only rubber stamp so Beth didn't even have to fake her signature. You can see that so far Beth hasn't done anything illegal except failing to report a death."

Ezekiel already respected Beth's intelligence, but her mother was dead and Beth managed to think through all this stuff and act on it.

"Beth used the ATM to get cash, only now she had essentially unlimited funds. Until she began to realize just how much had to be paid out every month. House payment. No car payment—she owns it outright—but utilities, the yard guy, the housekeeper, groceries, insurance premiums—health and life, almost as big as the house payment."

"She kept paying the premiums on her mother's life insurance policy?" asked Father.

"Either she doesn't know how insurance works, or she was afraid that if she let coverage lapse there might be a fight about it when she finally filed a claim. She'd have to prove *when* her mother died and she wasn't sure she could do that. So ... better to keep paying."

"She wrote checks from that account and mailed them," said Father.

"She also sent emails from her mother's address—again, she must have known the password—to the yard guys and the housekeeper. Very polite letters. I sat there thinking, this is a *child* writing this?"

"It wasn't," said Ezekiel. "It was Beth."

"All right, a cool-headed genius child who knew how to sound like an adult. Like a bank manager. Exactly the right letter to make it so that the yard guys would come only once every three weeks to mow the lawns, and they would receive payment by mail and they should *never* knock on the door. And the housekeeper was dismissed with a five-hundred-dollar severance check and thanks for her good service, and she could simply throw away the house key because they'd be moving soon anyway."

"Had to keep the lawns mowed," said Father.

"If she ever thought of mowing them herself," said Ezekiel, "she would've noticed that she isn't big enough to push a mower."

Shank smiled wanly. "I'm sure she knew that. So her life consisted of walking to school—her mother used to drive her and Beth couldn't arrange to get herself put on the bus list without a phone call, which was out of the question."

"And besides, she was eager to walk with *me*," said Ezekiel.

"I don't know if that was part of her plan to start with, but it's worked out pretty well, hasn't it?" said Shank.

"But how could she live in a house with the smell of death in it?" asked Father. "Why wasn't it on all her clothes?"

"When I went up there, all the rooms were normal, doors open, beds made, except one, the master bedroom. Closed tight. Locked—easy to pick, like most interior doors, but still. Beth wasn't going in there. And she must have anticipated the smell of a rotting corpse, because she stuffed wet paper towels tightly under the door. I mean, she must have tamped them in with a ruler or something, adding new layers of wet towels every day for a long time, so the odor barrier was complete. When I opened the door, I had to shoulder it, and the dried paper towels were like cement, extending continuously a couple of feet into the room."

Ezekiel wanted to cry and he wanted to scream. Cry because he couldn't believe how painful all of this must have been, how sad and lonely Beth must have been. And scream because he never had a clue about the deep pain in Beth's life.

No, he *did* have a clue, because Beth never let him in. But how was that a clue, actually? Was he supposed to think, She won't let me in her house, ergo her mother must be *dead* in there?

"You couldn't have known," said Shank. "And she *did* trust you, but come on, you know that you *would* have told your father, and Mr. Bliss, you know that you couldn't have let it go. You would have told the authorities."

"Yes and yes," said Father.

"This was a matter of life and death to her," said Shank. "That's how I see it, anyway. Her mother was dead. She didn't want to get put into foster care because who was going to embrace a thirteen-year-old who looks like a seven-year-old? And how could she remain in the same school, or even the same city? She wanted to be in control of her life. She didn't want strangers to have authority over her. So she walked to the grocery store, walked all the way to Walmart to buy school clothes, four hundred dollars at a time."

"Those aren't Walmart clothes."

"She paid cash, I have no records on this. She bought them somewhere, and wherever it was, she walked there."

"She's a fast walker for her height," said Ezekiel.

"My guess is that most weeks, she probably walked a half-marathon, just keeping food in the house."

Father said, "She turned off the air-conditioning to save money. But why leave the house closed up tight like this? Even on a day as cool as this, it's hot and stuffy in here."

"Maybe when she was actually home, she opened windows. But maybe not. Her countermeasures at her mother's bedroom door worked perfectly—I don't smell anything up there. Maybe you can, Mr. Bliss, but she kept the smell contained."

"Except I caught a residual smell outside," said Father.

"I think the bedroom windows or the master bathroom window weren't completely airtight," said Shank, "and there was no way she could seal them tighter. She might not have opened the windows because she didn't want to have to breathe in the outside air that might be carrying the smell of her mother's corpse decaying. And we don't know when she turned off the air-conditioning. It might not have been till school started or till the weather cooled down."

"She still had to sleep in the same house with her mother's body," said Ezekiel.

"But not the same floor," said Shank. "I saw the room that must have been hers, but there was dust on the coverlet, dust on everything. Unused in months. She was sleeping on the couch down here on the main level. Another reason she wouldn't want you coming inside. Questions would come up if you saw the couch sheeted and pillowed for sleeping."

"I'm proud of her and sad for her at the same time," said Ezekiel. "But I'm also scared for her because I know how she feels about her father and she would *not* go with him if he was trying to lead her out of a burning building."

Shank nodded. "I take your assessment very seriously. But there's no sign of forced entry here. If Beth was taken, she was not taken from this house."

"No," said Ezekiel. "She was probably taken when I let her walk home alone on Saturday. You know what I think? I think that Renee's kidnapper had already killed the woman who called her Karen and he'd decided to let Renee die of dehydration or whatever because he wasn't going back. I think he decided to fill his contract with a substitute girl."

Father and Shank looked at him with real concern.

"Son, do you have any particular reason to think that?"

"Dad, no, I don't have any, like, *information* about her, it's not my micropower. I'm just thinking, the guy drives around looking for unescorted six-year-old girls, or maybe he's not even looking yet, but he doesn't know what he's going to do because he doesn't want to be seen going into those tunnels. So he happens to see a girl just the right size walking along the street—and remember, Beth doesn't have any signs of dwarfism, she's proportionate—so he sees her from the back, she looks like six or seven, he takes her."

"In broad daylight," said Shank skeptically.

"What time of day was it when he took Renee?" asked Ezekiel.

"None of the standard tricks would work on a girl Beth's age," said Shank. "'Help me find my kitten.' 'Would you like to come to my daughter's birthday party? Most of her friends didn't show up and she's kind of sad.' 'Your mom's in the hospital, they sent me to get you.' 'Your house burned down, I'm a neighbor from up the street, the fire marshal sent me to get you.'"

"Those actually work?" asked Ezekiel.

"On six-year-olds," said Shank. "They don't know how the world works yet. Most of the time it never crosses their mind that somebody would lie about things like that."

"It crosses Beth's mind all the time."

"So maybe he tried one of those and she started to run so he snags her and stuffs her in his car," said Shank.

"And nobody sees," said Father.

"Do *you* sit in your living room looking out onto the street to see if everybody out there is behaving properly? Especially since there's *nobody* out there most of the time?" said Shank.

Father nodded. "Or maybe he just starts out by drugging her, so there's no conversation, no attempt to run away."

"That's possible," said Shank.

"Only he kidnapped the wrong kid," said Ezekiel.

"He wouldn't know that," said Shank.

"He'd know it pretty quick," said Ezekiel. "She may be short, but she's starting to grow boobs."

"So you were looking," said Father.

"Come on, Dad. I wasn't *staring* but I'd have to be brain-dead or completely not-male to miss that."

Shank shook his head. "All right, suppose you're right—and I hope you are *not*—what does this guy do when he finds out that his substitute girl is really a nubile thirteen-year-old?"

Ezekiel wasn't sure what "nubile" meant because it hadn't come up, but he could guess.

"What does he do," said Shank, relentlessly, "if he finds out that her value in the child-porn market is exactly zero?"

"And now he doesn't have a female accomplice to take care of her," said Father.

"Or maybe he thought he did," said Ezekiel. "What if the Karen woman says, You can't have my Karen, so he goes looking for a substitute and he comes home with Beth, and it's the *woman* who discovers that she's not … suitable?"

"I think we've moved beyond things that my son should be thinking about," said Father.

"He was going to think about them anyway," said Shank. "I've come to have a lot of regard for your son. He isn't afraid to face the truth."

"Doesn't mean that hearing all of *this* will do him any good," said Father.

"I've heard it now," said Ezekiel, "and yes, I'm going to be thinking about nothing but this because what else explains her disappearance? She's a careful person, there's no reason for her to disappear just when our study of my stupid micropower was getting interesting. Just like her mom, Beth is *not* somebody who flakes out. So somebody took her."

"And you're thinking that there's only one known kidnapper working in the area," said Shank.

"Detective Shank, is Beth already dead?" said Ezekiel.

"I don't know," said Shank. "I hope not. I hope there's still time. That's what I was afraid of with Renee, that there was still time to save her life but my incompetence was going to get her killed. That's why I was so desperate that I asked this kid who had a record of 'finding' things."

"It's not going to work this time," said Ezekiel. "Beth's mother isn't *lost* to her, she's dead. I don't think Beth has some treasured stuffed animal, that's not her style. What do I do, handle her schoolbooks and see if I get a vibe?"

Shank looked at him like he was thinking, Duh.

Ezekiel stood up and this time Father didn't stop him. "Do you know where her backpack is?"

"Don't go near the stairs," said Shank. "I don't think she *ever* went up there once she stopped stuffing wet paper towels under the door."

It didn't take long to find the backpack, but when Ezekiel dumped everything out on the kitchen table, there was nothing really personal there. Even in the notebooks, there were no doodles, no art. Just meticulous class notes, outlined and organized for study. Ezekiel held each item for five or six seconds each. Normally that would be plenty of time to get *something* about the owner's location, but ... nothing.

Just like with Renee's other toys. She didn't care about them, so not having them with her didn't bother her. It was the Build-a-Bears that Renee missed, so those were the lost objects that clued him in on her whereabouts. If Beth cared about something she owned, Ezekiel never saw a sign of it.

"I don't know what kinds of things girls care about," said Ezekiel. "Maybe some book? Are there books—"

Shank was already leading the way to a set of shelves in the TV room. A separate TV room *and* three bedrooms upstairs. Mrs. Sorenson must have made a lot more money than Dad, thought Ezekiel. Not to mention the royalties from an oil well. Not to mention a huge trust fund for Beth.

Was he really *envying* Beth? For what, her *money*? With her mother dead and Beth herself maybe—probably—kidnapped by people who had no use for her and had a history of killing the girls they took?

But he sat there with Father and Shank—Shank handing him book after book, and Father putting them in neat stacks on the coffee table to be reshelved later. Ezekiel held each book for a brief while. Which of these books did Beth love?

The children's books were on the bottom shelf and Ezekiel thought, she might have fond memories of these, she might have read them with her mother, or listened while her mother read them to her. They must mean *something* to Beth or surely they would have donated them to a library or Goodwill or thrown them out.

Nothing from *Goodnight Moon*. Nothing from the *Frog and Toad* books. Ditto with the *Don't Let the Pigeon* books and *Moo! Baa! La La La*.

"Well, maybe this is a good sign," said Shank.

"What, that she no longer cared about the books she read with her mother?" asked Ezekiel, despairing.

"This one was lying across the top of the children's books, like somebody had actually read it. And it didn't have dust on it."

Shank handed him *Charlotte's Web*.

"You think she read it recently?" asked Father.

Ezekiel held up a hand. There *was* something. Very faint. Almost nothing. Maybe like what Father smelled outside, the very faintest whiff.

"I think she's alive," said Ezekiel.

"You think but you don't know?"

"No location, nothing like that. No images like I got from the Build-a-Bear. Just … what do I call it? A sense that the owner of this book *exists*."

"So you don't get anything from items lost by people who since died."

"I don't know if I've ever found anything whose owner was dead," said Ezekiel. "But I every time I got a feeling about something, the owner was alive."

Father stood there with his hands in his pockets, slouching exactly the way he told Ezekiel not to. "Son," he said, "you get vibes from lost scrunchies."

"I know, it makes me insane. Like it did with Renee's other things before the Build-a-Bears. Why can I find scrunchies that the owners don't even care about, when I can't get anything from an owner who desperately needs me to find her?"

"Still working out the rules of your micropower," said Shank.

"It's one of the things I was going to talk to Beth about. When I told her about Renee. The only idea I came up with on my own was, maybe there's a difference between things the owner actually lost, like a scrunchie coming out of her hair, and something that was stolen from her. Or something *she* was stolen *from*. She knows exactly where these books are, where her backpack is. Just because she can't lay hands on them doesn't mean they're lost."

"But something she really loves, something she wants *right now*," said Shank.

"*That's* the one that would have a strong connection. Maybe. But … what does this mean, that I feel like she's alive? Maybe she wishes she could read this again? Maybe *Charlotte's Web* means more to her because at the end, Charlotte becomes a mother and then she dies, leaving all her friends behind?"

"Or all of the above," said Shank.

"I don't see anything else down here that belonged to Beth except her clothes," said Father. "Here and in the laundry room."

"She's not going to miss her *clothes*," said Ezekiel. "She hates them all because she has to buy them in the children's department."

"But she had them close to her body," said Shank. "This is police work. We have to be thorough."

Ezckiel felt embarrassed to be handling Beth's clothing, especially her underwear, whether it was in the small group of dirty clothes or the damp ones in the washer that she was probably going to change over as soon as she got home. He recognized all the outfits because he had seen her wear them, but the underwear and the one bra on a drying rack were all new to him and he felt like he was doing something unfair and intrusive.

"It's to try to save her life," said Shank. "If it works, do you think she's going to mind?"

"My plan," said Ezekiel, "is that if either of you ever tells her that I touched her bra and her …"

Shank provided the word Ezekiel didn't want to say. "Panties."

"I'm going to kill myself," said Ezekiel. "Am I clear?"

"Solemn oath," said Father.

"Such a temptation," said Shank, "but no, I'll be as discreet as an FBI agent."

When they had looked all through the downstairs and even out in the car—apparently Shank had taken a class in breaking into cars—they sat at the kitchen table and reviewed. "Beth managed to live for five months all by herself," said Shank, "and nothing in this house is so connected to her that it shows her to you the way you got a view of the place where Renee was being held."

"Except that I think I'm sure that she's alive," said Ezekiel.

"Well, FBI protocols won't prevent me from acting on the assumption that she's alive," said Shank. "I don't have to mention your involvement in order to speak of Betty Sorenson as if I'm sure that she's alive somewhere."

Ezekiel understood. Shank needed to keep himself off of his colleague's crazy meters. Some of them knew he had used Ezekiel to find Renee. But he couldn't let them think he was relying on Ezekiel now for *all* his cases. Especially because Ezekiel was proving himself to be unreliable on this, the most important case ever. To Ezekiel himself, anyway.

"We're actually getting close to the point where I'm going to have to start explaining to cops and agents and crime scene guys why I brought a civilian father and son into a dead house," said Shank.

"Time for us to go," said Father.

"Burger King calls," said Shank.

"Not to me it doesn't," said Ezekiel. "Like I can eat now."

"But you will," said Father.

"What can I do now?" Ezekiel asked Shank. "I can't just go home and forget about Beth."

"Not forget," said Shank. "But I let you search this house because I didn't want you to worry about missing something that might have helped you. I don't want you to have some crazy compulsion to come *back* here."

"Doesn't mean I won't wonder if I missed something."

"I don't want you to be thinking *back*," said Shank. "When does your micropower group meet?"

"Wednesday."

"Let me call Dr. Withunga and see if she's got another micropower group you can meet with tomorrow."

"*They* won't know what to do."

"Ezekiel," said Shank. "You know what bad detectives do? They think they know that somebody won't have any useful information and so they don't bother to interview them. Most of the time, they were right, that person had nothing. But bad detectives will never know that."

"So why do *you* know that?" asked Ezekiel.

"Cause I'm the agent the bureau sends in to clean up after their sorry asses, and *I* go interview all those can't-possibly-know-anything-useful witnesses. And most of them are worthless. But you know another statistic? *Every* cleanup case that I managed to resolve, it was because of information or some idea that got triggered on one of those interviews. Many of them remain unsolved because that's the nature of crime investigation, especially when some previous agent has spent six months screwing it up before I even get there. You're probably right that whatever micropower group you visit, they won't *know* anything. But maybe, because they have micropowers of their own, they'll *ask* you something that makes you think of something that makes you think of something *else* that you can do and *maybe* that will help us come closer to finding Beth before …"

Ezekiel didn't need to have him spell out what that "before" was about. He didn't *want* him to say it out loud. Before they kill her for being older than she had seemed to the abductor. Or kill her because they figured out how to use her anyway, maybe to appeal to a different audience of sickos. Or …

He was making himself think of all the things that Shank had refrained from saying.

"Making yourself a nervous wreck about this won't help Beth," said Father.

"Neither will my standing around breathing and eating and sleeping," said Ezekiel. "But I'm going to keep doing those things so I can stay alive, and then try to think of some way I can help *her* stay alive."

"If we don't find her in time," said Shank, "you will absolutely know that you did everything you could. Your micropower helped save one girl. That was good. But your talent isn't a superpower. It's small and limited. And Beth's situation might just be outside those limits. That's not your fault, and it wasn't your choice."

"I'll tell myself that if the time comes," said Ezekiel. "But you're not a therapist and I don't need counseling about how to deal with her death, not until she's actually dead. Is it OK if we make that a rule in our future conversations?"

"If you take *Charlotte's Web* with you," said Shank, "will you know by holding it whether she's still alive?"

"I don't know," said Ezekiel. "That impression faded while I was holding it the first time. I don't know if I'll ever feel it again no matter whether she's alive or not. But I'll take it if that wouldn't mess up the crime scene."

"I think it's going to turn out that this house *isn't* a crime scene. It's just a last-known-address."

"So it's OK for me to steal a book?"

"Borrow a book, with police supervision."

Ezekiel and his father left the house through the back door and when they drove away, none of the other cops were yet on the scene. Slow response time, thought Ezekiel, but then, maybe Shank didn't call it in as an emergency. It's not like EMTs would have a chance to revive Mrs. Sorenson, and Shank might not have told the Bureau yet that this was connected to a possible kidnapping. Ezekiel didn't know how the FBI worked, or what Shank did.

"It was very kind of him to let us into this investigation," said Father as they drove. "He didn't have to."

Ezekiel thought, Yes he did. Because he knows that there's something wrong and it's probably a kidnapping. But unless they got something from the site of the Karen woman's murder, they've got nothing to go on, trying to find this abductor, beyond what they already had from previous cases. Not even a description of the guy, because he didn't think Renee was going to be able to come up with one anytime soon.

That's what Shank is going to do, though. He's going to press the Delamares to let him question Renee more. He's going to tell them that there's a little girl missing, taken by the same kidnapper. He's going to pressure and manipulate them, and then he's going to question Renee, and Renee's going to cry, she may even scream, and the parents will try to stop him, they'll demand that he leave her alone, and meanwhile they're going to be filming Beth being forced to do filthy terrible things and then they're going to kill her on camera and put it out on the internet. And when Renee grows up and realizes that because she was unable to cooperate with the investigation, another girl died, it's going to torture her the rest of her life.

"This is such a lose-lose situation," said Ezekiel.

"We don't know that yet," said Father.

"We don't know it isn't."

"You aren't done thinking yet," said Father. "You haven't used everybody and everything that might help you."

"Like what?" asked Ezekiel. "Like who?"

"If I knew, I'd tell you," said Father.

"So here we are," said Ezekiel. "My friend is going to die. My only friend. I'm such a selfish bastard that what I'm worried about is me, what I'm going to lose."

"Love is a complicated business," said Father. "For every time I felt sorry for you about losing your mother, I've felt sorry for myself five times over. Don't beat yourself up because your brain thinks about you more than about other people. The selfishness of the human brain is how our species has survived."

"You always told me we survive by cooperation," said Ezekiel.

"Didn't say our motives were pure, did I?" asked Father. "So. Burger King? Or poached eggs on toast at home?"

"Have you learned how to poach an egg?" asked Ezekiel.

"I'll have you know that when your mom and I were dating, I'm the one who poached the eggs."

"Wow. You really were a cheap date," said Ezekiel.

"She fell in love with my frugality," said Father.

15

Dr. Withunga looked over the group as if taking a silent roll call. Ezekiel wished that she would recite that roll call out loud, since he only knew a few of these people.

"This isn't my show," said Dr. Withunga.

Well, it sure isn't mine, either, thought Ezekiel. I didn't ask for a micropower convention, I just asked if she could think of a way for the group to help him.

"The group," he had asked on the phone. To him that meant the ones he had met in his sessions, the ones who had met Beth, not every micropot she knew of in Virginia and the Carolinas.

"It's your show," she said to them all. "One of our members needs our help in a big way, with an unknown but urgent deadline. I invited you here so you might be able to suggest something he could do, or something you could do to help him, or ..."

"Or critical mass?" asked Jannis, alias College Girl.

Critical mass had to do with assembling enough fissionable material to trigger a nuclear chain reaction. But Ezekiel immediately leapt to how that idea might apply here. What if micropowers nurtured each other, or fed off of each other? What if you assembled enough micropots—micropotents, the name they were starting to call themselves and each other—and everybody got stronger?

It wasn't as if Ezekiel's finding power had gotten stronger from attending the smaller meetings for a few weeks, but apparently that wasn't critical mass.

Or maybe, who's to say, maybe it was because of that group strengthening that he was able to get such an unusually clear vision of where Karen was? No, Renee, not Karen ... but why had that name come so clearly to his mind so early on? Before Shank actually told him anything about the missing girl?

If he was getting strengthened right now by being here, Ezekiel wasn't feeling it.

He briefly wondered what Dr. Withunga had told Risotto, the principal—Mr. Rizzo—and whether he knew the meeting was all about Ezekiel and Beth, probably the two weirdest students at Downy High School.

"That's not even a theory yet," said Withunga. "Barely a hypothesis. More like speculation. What if bringing a bunch of micropotents together strengthens us all?"

"And if it does," said Skunk, "how long do the effects last after we disperse?"

"I think it's time for Ezekiel Blast to tell us his story," said Withunga. "Two, stories, really. I'd start with Karen, if I were you, Ezekiel."

So Ezekiel stood up, went to the lectern, leaned close to the mike. "This doesn't go anywhere else in the school, does it?" he asked.

"It goes to the amp and speaker built into the lectern," said Withunga. "But we all need to hear you because anything you say might trigger an idea in someone else."

"I find things," said Ezekiel. "And I know where they belong. Who they belong to. And it's hard for me to ignore them. So it got me in trouble with the police when I was younger, because they thought I stole stuff and then pretended that I found it."

A lot of them nodded. Maybe their micropowers had been misunderstood, too.

"Anyway, a cop, a detective, was looking for a kidnapped girl—at least they were hoping she was still a kidnapped girl, and not a dead body." Saying it right out loud made Ezekiel realize just how bold it was, that

Shank had trusted in Ezekiel's micropower enough that he didn't flat-out despair of ever finding Renee alive.

"So he came to you, help me help me, yadda yadda," said a bored-looking kid in the front row; or maybe not a kid, since he had enough beard growth that he might be in college or even older.

Ezekiel didn't like the heckling, but he also didn't want to get distracted.

"I had never found a person before, because in a sense people never get lost," said Ezekiel. "And I'd never looked for anything on purpose. So I didn't want to try. But then I started coming to GRUT and my friend Beth encouraged me to test my limits, you know, like Dr. Withunga says we should, and we realized last Saturday that I got a lot more information from lost objects than I had ever realized. So I went to the missing girl's house and when I put my hands on her favorite toys—a couple of stuffed bears that she would be missing more than any other objects—I saw where she was."

"A map?" asked Dahlia, preempting Bored Boy.

"I wish," said Ezekiel. "I saw the room where she was being held. Concrete walls, a bed, a heavy door. And I also knew how to get there. Not a map but just—turn here, turn there. And within an hour, we found her and the police took her home."

There was a murmur from the group, and also some laughter.

The laughter flustered him, and Withunga leaned in to the mike. "What's funny?" she demanded from the group.

A girl off to one side said, "It isn't funny, it's—I mean, these are micropowers we have, right? But his micropower let him actually save somebody."

Dahlia also stood. "I can only make people yawn," she said. "Still working on how that might rescue somebody."

"So she's safe now," said Bored Boy. "Why are we here?"

"My friend who helped me. Beth."

And then Ezekiel paused, thinking: What do they need to know? What's relevant? Surely not that her mother died and she lived in the same house with the corpse since May. What, though?

"She might have been taken by the same ring of kidnappers," said Dr. Withunga, leaning in again. Ezekiel was grateful. That cut right to the chase.

"So find her favorite toy," said Bored Boy.

In a regular classroom, a teacher would have shut him down by now. But then Ezekiel remembered that Withunga had told him, We have to let them talk, you don't know who's going to have the critical idea.

"Again," said Ezekiel, "I wish. She's older, almost fourteen, and when the cops and I went through her house, nothing popped as her favorite anything. Handling a copy of Charlotte's Web got me the idea that she was still alive. But that's about it."

To Ezekiel's surprise, as he recounted these bare facts, he found himself getting emotional, and his voice quavered a little and he could feel his face flush and his nose and sinuses thicken as if he were about to cry. What was that about? How would it help for him to get all teary-eyed?

It wouldn't. Cool it, he told himself.

"We don't know her," said Bored Boy. And this time he wasn't just heckling—several other people murmured their agreement. "How can we tell you anything that you don't already know?"

"I don't know," said Ezekiel. "Was it the little girl's Build-a-Bears that, like, magically told me about her? Or was it the connection, how much she loved those bears, how much they were part of her life?"

"What about her parents?" asked Jannis.

"I tried touching them, the way I touch found objects," said Ezekiel. "But that was worthless. I've never gotten anything from people."

Again Dr. Withunga intervened. "There may be a confusion of pronouns here. Jannis, were you asking about the parents of the little girl they found, or the parents of Ezekiel's friend that we're hoping to find now?"

"I mean, both," said Jannis.

"Beth's parents are both … out of the picture," said Ezekiel. True of the dad, but … well, being dead puts you out of the picture, too, probably.

"So you're saying, people can't be lost, right?" asked Bored Boy.

"You always know where you are, right?"

Several people said, "I wish" or "hardly ever," and there were some chuckles.

"No, I mean, you're right here. You never have to go looking for yourself, do you? You might have to go in search of, like, your car in the parking lot or your parents in whatever store they went to in the mall, but you're not lost."

"So that little girl," said Jannis. "To her, she wasn't lost, but … she hadn't lost her parents?"

"I don't know. Touching them didn't help, so … maybe not. Maybe not in her mind. I don't know how this works. It's not as if a scrunchy or a squirt gun knows who owns it but when I find one on the street, it still tells me—or at least I sense—who owned it. Owns it."

"Please don't bring back my lost scrunchies," said a girl.

Some guy near her muttered something and a bunch of people around him laughed.

Withunga again took the mike. "Please say that louder so we can all hear," she said. "You might have been making a joke, but we have no idea which suggestions might help somebody think of something."

"It wasn't a suggestion," said the boy, looking embarrassed.

The girl who said not to bring back her scrunchies stood up. "He said, 'She means her panties,' which was actually funny, but inaccurate."

Another boy muttered—loud enough to be heard—"Cause she doesn't wear any."

This time, though, no laughter at all. "Thus we cross the line from humor to harassment. It's hard to know where that line ever is. But now let's think about these ideas. Yes, Ezekiel finds a lot of scrunchies. Hardly ever any underwear, because people might lose them, but probably not on a public street." A few chuckles from the group. "We still don't know if people can be lost, but we do know that Ezekiel doesn't find lost people, he finds the people who own the lost things that he finds. Is that right, Ezekiel?"

"That's how it looks," he said. "I kind of tricked my micropower into finding the little girl because she had lost a couple of things that mattered a lot to her, so by touching those things I could sense who and where she was. As the owner. But I know Beth pretty well, and she pretty much doesn't give a rat's … petoot about anything she owns. No blankey, no teddy bear, nothing she cuddles up with at night or tells all her secrets to."

"Or you just haven't found it yet," said Dahlia.

"I know her pretty well," said Ezekiel again. "She's not a cuddly person. Maybe in her mind she doesn't own anything."

"Or maybe, in your mind," said Mitch,—Spider Guy—"you only think you know her that well."

That was true. That was a real point. "You're right," said Ezekiel. "I might not know her half so well as I think I do. So I shouldn't be rejecting any ideas because I think I know better."

Withunga didn't come to the mike this time, perhaps because she was mostly talking to Ezekiel. "But you still know her better than anyone else."

"I'm willing to bet," said Ezekiel, "that I know her better than anybody alive. But that still doesn't mean that I know her."

Then a boy from the back of the room stood up. "This Beth—is she, like, really small? Are you talking about Bitty Betty?"

Ezekiel instantly filled with rage toward this boy. "So are you one of the bullies who made her life hell?"

"Hell no," said the boy. "I just heard about her. The name I heard was Bitty Betty and if that's offensive I'm sorry, and I'm glad you call her Beth, OK? Nobody here is going to persecute anybody for being weird, all right?"

Loud murmurs of assent.

"Sorry," said Ezekiel. "I just know how much it hurt her to be called names like that. She insisted that I call her Beth, and so that's how I think of her. But yes. She's a proportionate dwarf, so she looks like a perfectly normal seven- or eight-year-old, at first glance, anyway. How many of you have actually seen her or even talked to her?"

"How many have seen her?" asked Withunga.

About a half-dozen hands went up.

"What was her micropower?" asked Bored Boy, seeming to be interested for the first time.

Ezekiel shook his head. "Maybe she didn't have one. She only came to GRUT to keep me company."

"Cause you were scared to come alone?" asked Bored Boy. The contempt in his voice was palpable.

Instead of getting angry, Ezekiel just said, "Damn straight."

"We all were, starting out," said Mitch. "It's not like any of us didn't have plenty of experience hiding our micropowers, and it takes a while to build up trust."

"But you trusted Beth," said Jannis.

"I did," said Ezekiel. "I do. I didn't want her to be my friend, I didn't think I wanted friends at all. But it turns out that I did, and even if I didn't, she was going to be my friend so I might as well go along."

"Maybe her micropower is getting her way," said Skunk.

"That would be a superpower," said Dahlia.

"Maybe her micropower is making people talk with her when they think they don't want to," said Ezekiel.

Bored Boy spoke sneeringly again. "Maybe the only thing she lost was you. Except wait, it's you that loves her."

That knocked everybody back a little, it was so rude but also kind of interesting.

It took Ezekiel a moment to think of a response, but the room stayed silent while he did. "I don't know, but maybe you're right. I mean, yes, I'm really dependent on her. We don't 'cuddle,' so I'm not her teddy bear. But she's the only living human that I actually tell things to, except my Dad. And I'm pretty sure that I'm the only living human she tells her stuff to, at least since she decided we were walking to school together every day, back in the second week of school."

"So touch yourself and find out where she is," said Bored Boy. "Bet you have plenty of practice."

There were a couple of nervous giggles. Withunga stood squarely in front of the microphone now. "That was out of line, as you knew it was," she said to Bored Boy. "You're only here as a courtesy, Aaron."

So Bored Boy had a name.

"I'm here because you're my ride home, since you took away my car."

No, Bored Boy was her son.

"Ezekiel, why don't you go sit down."

The only empty seat on the front row was either way at the end, or right beside Aaron the Bored Boy. Ezekiel would rather have sat as far from the jerk as he could, but this was Be Brave for Beth Day, and so he plunked himself down beside Aaron.

Instead of looking annoyed at Ezekiel, Aaron was just looking at his feet, which were stretched out in front of him.

"I want you all to give this some thought. We've had the suggestion that Ezekiel may be the thing or person that Beth values most, the thing she misses most. That's a good idea, but what can we do with that? We also have other possibilities, don't we? Whatever you think of, float it with the people sitting near you. And remember brainstorming rules. No matter how lame or crazy an idea is, we never contradict it, we never say no. We think of how things might work if the idea was true. Right?"

Several people said "right" out loud, but obviously everybody had heard this before—except Ezekiel, probably because he hadn't been a member very long and so there had never been a brainstorming session since he started.

"What do I do?" asked Ezekiel.

"Same as everybody," said Withunga. "Nobody on Earth knows what the limits of your micropower might be, but you have the most experience with it, so talk to people, see where their ideas take you."

The people to one side of Ezekiel were already talking to each other—they clearly knew each other. Ezekiel's only candidate for conversation was Aaron, and since his mother's lecture, he had sat there like stone, staring at his feet.

"Any ideas?" asked Ezekiel.

"I don't have any of your amazing magical powers," said Aaron.

"Pretty funny, though," said Ezekiel.

"Didn't see you laughing."

"I'm worried about my friend," said Ezekiel. "The guys who have her, they might be a gang of … kidnappers, whose victims end up dead by the end of the week."

The word "dead" seemed to bring him to life a little. "I don't have anything you've got. Micropowers or friends."

"I only have one of each. And one parent."

"I officially have two," said Aaron. "And if I had a micropower, I might matter to at least one of them."

"Maybe your micropower is seeing what's funny."

"Maybe my micropower is throwing up when you try to be fake-nice with me."

"Let's see," said Ezekiel. "I can be much nicer."

Aaron made a suggestion that didn't sound nice at all.

"Is there a plan B or is that all you've got?" asked Ezekiel, trying to increase the amount of false cheeriness in his tone.

"If I didn't have to sit here I'd be so gone by now. Any chance you can shut up and leave me alone?"

"Exactly what I kept saying to Beth that first day when she insisted on walking to school with me."

"But she wouldn't go away?"

"Nor would she shut up, however kindly or sternly I suggested it."

"Why didn't you kick her to the curb? Trip her? Roll her on her back so she couldn't flip over and get up?"

Everything Aaron said made Ezekiel want to hit him. But he tried to respond to Aaron's ideas, not his deeply offensive tone. "Maybe I could have ditched her," said Ezekiel, thinking back. "I mean, I have long legs. I'm no athlete, but I could have outrun her."

"Yeah, tall guy like you running away from the shortest kid in the school. Your proudest day."

"But since I don't give a rat's ass what anybody at school thinks of me—"

"Except Beth," said Aaron.

"Yeah."

"So what did she say that made you not run away from her?" asked Aaron. He said it with an impatient sing-song tone, as if he was trying to hurry Ezekiel along in a story that was boring him.

Ezekiel didn't challenge him. Because thinking back over his relationship with Beth might make something click. Talking about it with a decidedly hostile audience might help him see things differently, too.

"She saw how all the other kids thought I was a thief, so they avoided me completely. Like crossing the street if I was overtaking them, or slowing down if they were overtaking me. To her it looked like I was in some invisible bubble. So basically she announced that she was going to avoid the bullies by walking to school inside my shunning bubble."

"Your what?" asked Aaron.

"Shunning bubble. The space everybody left around me."

"Hell, it's got a name. I've got one of those."

"Not really," said Ezekiel. "More like the opposite. Still a shunning bubble, but it's you shunning everybody else."

"Whatever," said Aaron. "It isn't working with you."

"Remember what I said about rats and their asses?"

"For a guy who doesn't care about them, you sure keep bringing them up."

"She was asking for my protection," said Ezekiel.

"And it made you feel big and strong."

"It made me feel like there was something she needed that I had and could share."

"Made you feel wanted."

"Needed."

"So your being a complete leper, that was actually what attracted her."

"Unclean, unclean," Ezekiel intoned.

"And from then on, she owned you," said Aaron.

"Not really. Not like—you know, slavery. Couldn't sell me, couldn't make me do stuff—"

"Sounds like she could make you do whatever she wanted."

Ezekiel didn't like the implications of that, but he could see how it would look that way to a cynical angry jerk like Aaron.

No, no. Calm down, Ezekiel told himself. It looks that way to Aaron because that's how it is. Was. Is. She did kind of own me. I wanted to get away at first, but then she really owned me and I stopped even wanting to escape. To the point where Dad thinks I'm half in love with her, and I keep thinking, this is friendship, this is having a sister, this is … yeah, admit it to yourself, this is love.

"You think it's love," said Aaron. "Or friendship, or loyalty, but look how she owns you even now. What do you think she wants most in all the world right now?"

"Me?"

"Man, you're a self-centered prick," said Aaron. "No, she wants to be safe, she wants to get away from her kidnappers. But she only owns one thing in this whole world—isn't that what you said?—only one possession she cares about, and that's you. For the past couple of months she's told you what to do, all the time, and you do it. So right now, can you think of anything else but saving her? Can you get her out of your head for a single second?"

Ezekiel couldn't answer. Because there was no answer.

"You've got the owner calling out to the thing she owns, and you're too blind to realize that it's her. Maybe if you pay attention, she'll tell you where she is, like that girl's bears told you where she was."

"So you were really listening," said Ezekiel.

"I always listen. Maybe you haven't noticed, but we primates can't close our ear holes. What I don't is care."

"I'm the Build-a-Bear," said Ezekiel, "so I'm getting her message, her … information … without touching any object at all."

"I don't know," said Aaron. "Are you? You're the Miracle Max here."

It sounded like a Princess Bride reference, so almost by instinct, because of years of quoting movies with his dad, Ezekiel said, softly, "Wuv, twue wuv."

"Maybe you'll find her when she's only mostly dead," said Aaron. He probably meant to be cruel, but Princess Bride references meant that he had watched the movie and cared about it enough to remember tags from it, and that meant that Aaron was probably a decent human being, somewhere deep inside.

But as Aaron had pointed out, all Ezekiel could think about right now was Beth.

And instead of trying to think about what she owned, how he could find her, he closed his eyes and tried to think about Beth's information.

Only that wasn't how it worked, wasn't how it had ever worked. The information just came to him. He couldn't reach for it, he couldn't …

And then, all of a sudden, he could feel himself falling.

No, not falling, just … getting dragged out, getting dragged off, he was going to fall—

He leapt up, jumped forward, threw himself across the top of the lectern from the audience side, clung to the lip of it, then struggled to pull the weight of his body up and over the lectern. There was a part of his brain that registered what he was doing, because his eyes were open and he could see that he was tall enough that he didn't need to hang from the lectern at all, he could easily reach across the top to the other side of it. But instead there was no strength in his legs, his legs were useless, they couldn't grip anything, least of all the floor, so the only way he could keep from falling was to get over the lip of this thing, get his body's weight up and onto it and if he didn't he would fall and die just like … just like …

He got up onto the lectern, the weight of his body now fully balanced there. Not falling anymore. It had taken all his strength, he could feel how raw and painful his muscles were, he could see how the skin had been scraped and abraded on his arms from the struggle, from trying to grip the rough concrete of the floor …

And then the panic and the sense of falling were gone and he was just one lone idiotic boy lying prone atop a lectern that was wobbling from his exertions to get on top of it. He also saw that there were no abrasions on his arms because he was wearing a long-sleeved shirt.

"Are you all right?" asked Dr. Withunga.

"You mean, besides suddenly jumping up and acting like a loon?" asked Ezekiel.

"No, I'm taking your actions as some kind of message, some kind of link to Beth, am I guessing right?" asked Dr. Withunga.

"Or he had a fit," said Aaron.

"Aaron, you're really not—"

"No, he did help," said Ezekiel, interrupting Withunga. "He really helped."

Aaron looked surprised but he didn't argue.

"I was talking to Aaron here and he had the weird idea that Beth's most valued possession was me, and then he made a case for the fact that she really did own me. And she did. Whatever ownership is, she owned me as much as anybody ever has, so, like Aaron said, maybe I already have the information about where she is linked to me, the way that little girl's bears did. Is this making any sense?"

A few murmurs. Dahlia said, "You're the bear." A few people turned back to their interrupted conversations.

"Just another minute, OK?" asked Ezekiel. "I sat here trying to sense some kind of message or information or, you know, anything, and then I was falling, getting dragged out of a … off of a … I don't know what. It was rough concrete, and I knew if I couldn't get myself up and over the edge, I'd fall and I'd die. Splat. I was thinking of 'splat' like … like … like maybe somebody else had just fallen. That's what I was doing, acting out trying not to fall off a … ledge? A roof? I don't know but I knew it was really high up and I was getting all scraped up from the concrete floor but then I got myself up and onto the—"

"That's the part we saw," said Dr. Withunga. "Do you think it came from her?"

"I don't know if it was a memory or if it was happening right that moment. Maybe I just opened myself up to it because of what Aaron said."

"So I'm the hero," said Aaron dryly.

"Maybe this was something real, in which case, yeah," said Ezekiel. "Not that I know any more about where she is than I did before."

"But she was going to fall from some rough concrete surface," said Withunga, "and then she managed to climb back on and she didn't fall."

"I don't know if it was real," said Ezekiel.

"Did it feel real?" asked Mitch.

"Felt real enough that I scrambled up onto this lectern like a raccoon trying not to fall off the roof."

"Let's be scientific about this for a moment," said Dr. Withunga. "We don't know if this happened because you opened yourself up after Aaron said whatever he said, or maybe because you were here with a critical mass of other micropotents—"

"Excuse me, Dr. Withunga," said Ezekiel. "We don't know if anything really happened at all. I got a crazy impulse, like a panic attack, and I knew stuff but none of it was true, at least not right here in this room. So yeah, maybe I was, like, channeling Beth's memory or maybe even something she was doing right then, maybe she's in a high place and she almost fell, I don't know, but you know what I don't feel like doing?"

"Being scientific about it," said Dr. Withunga.

"Damn straight," said Aaron. Maybe he knew he was echoing what Ezekiel had said near the beginning of this meeting, maybe not. Maybe Aaron was just sick of his mother trying to be scientific about stuff. That was between them. If you weren't a jerk, Aaron Withunga, you'd know how unspeakably lucky you are to have a mother, because some people in this room, in this town, in this world are fresh out of mothers.

But then his thoughts about Dr. Withunga and her son faded to nothing. Neither of them owned him the way Beth did, so they were not his concern. What mattered to him was that maybe his little "fit" meant that Beth was being confined high up in a tower or on top of some structure and she almost fell and he felt her panic. But she made it—or at least that was how it felt. Only maybe only he made it, and the intense panic faded because while he was wriggling on top of the lectern, Beth had fallen to her death.

No, not possible, because she still owns me. I still feel owned. I belong to Beth Sorenson so she can't be dead. It wasn't Charlotte's Web that told me that, it was my own mind, my heart, my liver, my spleen, whatever part of me it is that receives messages or feelings or whatever from my owner.

No, not my owner, that was just a temporary idea. From my friend. Maybe that's what it means to be friends, real friends. You own each other a little. You feel responsible. Protective. You care if your friend is in danger.

"You're going to go looking for her," said Dr. Withunga.

"I'm going to call the detective I've been working with."

"Makes sense," said Dr. Withunga. "But maybe you want to take at least a few micropotents with you? In case the critical mass thing is true?"

"You won't all fit in his car," said Ezekiel, "and I think if all of you drove separately it would look like a funeral procession or an invasion and whoever's holding her captive might be alerted."

"Take a couple, anyway. Two or three," said Dr. Withunga. A whole bunch of hands shot up.

"What if it's dangerous?" asked Ezekiel. "Since this thing started, there's already been one murder."

Most of the hands went back down.

"You didn't mention that."

"I should really go, but ..." Ezekiel looked at the hands that were still up.

Every single one of them was from his original GRUT meeting group. If he was only going to pick two, who would they be? Who could he put in danger like this? Whose micropower might be useful?

None of them, so far as he knew. But maybe something from Skunk, something from Mitch. Stinks and spiders. That's the ticket.

Ezekiel took a moment to remember Skunk's real name. "Lanny," he said. "And Mitch. Are you sure you want to?"

"Of course he takes boys," said Dahlia.

"Because making bad guys yawn is so helpful," said Jannis, jabbing at Dahlia for the lameness of her micropower.

"Why not?" said Dahlia, playing along. "Maybe I can weaponize it. Can you aim a gun when you're yawning like a sleepy cheetah?"

"If you don't all mind squeezing into the back seat, you come too, Dahlia," said Ezekiel. "And all of you—thank you. Thanks for being part of, you know, the critical mass." He looked at Aaron, who wasn't looking at Ezekiel at all. Since he wasn't looking, Ezekiel stepped to him and held out a hand. "Thanks for—"

"I was an asshole," said Aaron.

"Like I was saying," said Ezekiel. "Thanks for being such a chatty asshole."

Aaron grinned and took his offered hand. Instead of shaking hands, though, Aaron gripped him and used him as leverage to stand up. Only then did Ezekiel notice that one of Aaron's legs was about an inch shorter than the other. He was wearing ordinary shoes, though, so he leaned to one side.

Aaron saw him notice, saw him look down at his feet. Ezekiel met Aaron's gaze and saw defiance there.

"So I guess you can only go around the mountain in one direction," said Ezekiel.

Aaron rolled his eyes. "The mountain goat joke," he said.

"It was the only one that seemed to fit."

"Silence would have been fine," said Aaron.

"No it wouldn't," said Ezekiel. "You were daring me to say something.

You sure as hell wouldn't have believed me if I pretended not to notice."

"I'm not a micropot," said Aaron, "I'm just a pot."

"Don't call the kettle black," said Ezekiel. "Want to come with us?"

"Four of us in the back of a cop car?" asked Aaron. "I don't think so."

"Thanks for talking to me," said Ezekiel, and then he headed toward the door, Lanny, Mitch, and Dahlia close behind.

"I thought you were going to call the detective," said Dahlia.

"I don't have a phone," said Ezekiel.

"Lost it?" asked Mitch.

"No juice?" asked Skunk.

"I'm just poor," said Ezekiel.

"I didn't know anybody was that poor," said Mitch.

"Now you know," said Ezekiel.

Dahlia handed him her phone. The number pad was already visible on the bottom of the screen. Ezekiel entered Shank's number and pressed the little green telephone handset symbol. As if anybody had a phone shaped like that anymore.

16

Ezekiel Blast was surprised that Dr. Withunga made no effort to include herself in the expedition. When Lieutenant Shank pulled up in front of the school, Dr. Withunga hurried away as if she was afraid of getting sucked into the vortex of people churning around Shank's little Ford SUV.

"The EcoSport can actually fit three across the back seat?" asked Dahlia.

"Three skinny people who don't mind touching each other," said Mitch.

"Any room left over for spiders?" asked Skunk.

"Just make it smell nice," said Dahlia.

Shank looked at Ezekiel as he closed the front passenger door. "I don't want any spiders in here," said Shank.

"Too late," said Mitch.

"He sees all the spiders and other arachnids," said Ezekiel to Shank. "But since they're pretty much everywhere ..."

"I don't see them," said Mitch. "I just know where they are."

"Please tell me there are no spiders in this car," said Shank.

"There are no spiders in this car," said Mitch.

To Ezekiel, Shank said, "He's lying, isn't he?"

"Probably," said Ezekiel, "but it's a kind lie, don't you think?"

"And this car doesn't stink, by the way," said Shank.

Dahlia laughed. "Well, not now that Lanny's in here."

Shank and Ezekiel both yawned. It was the first time Dahlia had used her micropower on him and now Ezekiel understood what it meant to really yawn. A huge hippopotamus yawn. A catch-a-foul-ball yawn. It made his jaw joints ache when it finally ended. And his eyes were filled with tears.

"That was Dahlia," said Ezekiel.

"Are you all through showing off?" asked Shank as he dried his eyes with a small towel he kept draped over the gear shift.

"I think they just wanted you to respect them," said Ezekiel.

"If a spider crawls on me," said Shank, "I'm crashing this car. Not a threat, just a prediction."

"What I know about Beth's location," said Ezekiel, "is that she's high up in a structure where there's at least one open side, no railing, no outside wall, rough concrete floor, and a single door that's locked."

"I don't know of any such place in Downy," said Shank. "Or in Rockingham County. Or Alamance County."

"I'm thinking maybe Greensboro," said Ezekiel.

"New construction?" asked Shank.

"Maybe." But Ezekiel hadn't gotten any feel of newness. Whatever that meant.

"Let's just head for Greensboro and drive around till you tell me to make a turn," said Shank.

"This is pretty vague," said Dahlia.

"Google Maps may not be able to do much with 'tall unfinished buildings with open sides,'" said Mitch.

"You guys are with me," said Ezekiel, "so that maybe my micropower will be stronger and when we get closer to the place—"

"If we're getting closer to it," said Skunk.

"Then maybe I'll be more sensitive to whatever information I'm getting."

"What's the lost thing that you figured out Beth cared about most?" asked Shank.

Ezekiel hated to answer. But he didn't have to.

"Ezekiel," said Dahlia.

A moment's silence.

"Oh, you were answering me," said Shank. "I thought you were talking to Ezekiel."

"He's apparently the toy she loves most," said Dahlia.

"Toy," said Ezekiel.

"I know, right?" said Skunk. "Like Tom Hanks said in Big, 'What's fun about that?'"

The banter went on in the back seat. Ezekiel wasn't part of it. Why should he be? He had only joined the group a few weeks ago, while the three of them had been together for a year or so. And they were all older than Ezekiel by a couple of years at least. Plus the guys were probably kind of showing off for Dahlia, racking up cleverness points while teasing her and each other. Ezekiel envied them their easiness with each other. Had he ever been that way with anyone? Before the thief thing started, did he have friends? Not like this. Little kids didn't have this kind of friendship, because they didn't know enough, they didn't even have enough language to carry on a mostly verbal camaraderie.

Why am I thinking about them? I'm out here to look for Beth. These guys are only along because they're supposed to lend me some kind of greater strength or reception or acuity or something. Instead they were a distraction. Not that it would help him if they tried to offer suggestions. What were they supposed to do? "Should we turn here, Ezekiel? What about here?" Might as well be "Are we there yet?" over and over again.

Maybe three wasn't enough for critical mass anyway.

"Guys, we're supposed to be helping look for Beth," said Dahlia.

"Is she a spider?" asked Skunk. "If not, then Mitch can't help."

"Even if she had a particular smell, Lanny would only neutralize it," said Mitch.

"We could at least be quiet so Ezekiel can concentrate," said Dahlia.

So they fell silent.

That was so much worse. It was like having somebody behind you in line, saying nothing, but pressuring you all the same by their mere presence. Silence like this could be so heavy.

Ezekiel didn't know how long it went on. He was about to say something. He didn't know what. Maybe, "Try being normal," or "This was a stupid idea and I'm sorry I wasted your time." But they were only on Highway 29, not all that close to Greensboro yet. If Greensboro was right.

Was this the right direction? He certainly didn't have any feeling like it was the wrong way.

A flicker of something. Like a voice in the silence. Then a man's voice, muffled, not loud in the first place, and on the other side of a wall: "The key won't go in. Are you sure this is even the right one?"

Another man's voice: "He was supposed to meet us here. Let's just wait."

Maybe there would have been more, but somebody in the back seat—Mitch, probably—said, "He's asleep."

"No he isn't," said Shank.

How would he know? wondered Ezekiel.

"Is this even the right way?" asked Dahlia.

"He'll tell us if it isn't," said Shank. "By the way, that silence thing, that was a good idea."

They got the hint and fell silent again.

But the voices didn't come back.

Where are you, Beth? Ezekiel reached out to her the only way he could think of, talking to her inside his head. I need to see you.

Over and over again, the same messages.

And then a firm "no."

What? This didn't really have a voice, it was more like the idea of negation. Did it come from Beth? What was she saying no to? No, don't look for me? No, I won't tell you where I am? No, I don't want you to see me?

Are you all right? Ezekiel asked her silently. Can you even hear me, or sense my words, or read my invisible text messages? I have no idea how this would feel on your end, if "this" is even a thing. Maybe it's all in my head.

No, not all in my head. I found Renee. And those voices, those men, that was clear. Clearer than ever. Maybe there really was something to that critical mass thing. Maybe the three micropots in the back seat were helping just by being there. Or maybe not. Maybe nothing was helping.

Stop thinking about yourself, Ezekiel. Stop thinking about the process. Just reach out for Beth.

He didn't get that wave of negation again, but he also didn't get any voices. He pictured two men outside a door, a heavy door that they couldn't just kick in, holding a key that wouldn't fit in the door. In the lock. Not a simple knob lock, but a dead bolt, because with a beveled knob lock they could open it with a credit card, couldn't they?

They weren't burglars or one of them would have suggested picking the lock.

They were the buyers, that's what they were. They made sick, evil videos to put online and they had come for Beth. Only for some reason the guy who kidnapped her wasn't there. And their key didn't work. And Beth couldn't open the door from her side, either, or she would have been long gone before they got there and so he wouldn't have been able to hear them. Beth had to be there or Ezekiel couldn't have heard them.

Talk to me, Beth.

No, don't talk. Keep silent just like you're doing. Make them wonder whether you're even in there.

Ezekiel thought of a room with a rough concrete floor. An open wall where the floor ended in a multi-story drop-off, where Beth had nearly fallen. Ezekiel could remember how hard his muscles had to work to hang on and not slide off the edge. How rough and painful the friction with the floor had been, how it hurt when he pulled his body across the floor, dragging his legs out of the abyss and onto the level surface.

No, when *she* did those things. He felt it, he even acted it out on the lectern, but *she* had done it for real.

Are you in pain, Beth? Are you bleeding? Scraped up by the rough concrete, your arms, your stomach, torn up and stinging with the pain of a hundred abrasion injuries?

I'm coming. We're coming. Shank is coming, an actual detective with a gun.

One detective, against two men. Were they armed? And if the kidnapper

came, that would be three men. How would Shank do against three oppo-
nents? If they were armed, he'd be outgunned. Plus, good guys couldn't just
come in with pistol blazing. Shank would have to wait, assess the threat.

And it sure wouldn't help him to have four teenagers creeping along
behind him. Just more targets for the bad guys' bullets.

"We're going to need more cops," said Ezekiel.

"You're getting something?" asked Shank.

"There are two men outside her door. Their key doesn't work, they
can't get in. They're waiting for the kidnapper, I think. Maybe he changed
the lock or something."

"Didn't want them to be able to pick up the merchandise without
paying him first, probably," said Shank. "Not a lot of trust among
criminals."

"How are you getting this?" asked Lanny. "I mean, that was pretty
specific, when you still don't even know where it is."

"Or do you know?" asked Dahlia.

"I think we're going the right way, or at least not the wrong way," said
Ezekiel. "And I heard them talking, that's all. Key won't go in. Wait for
'him' to come, 'he' was supposed to meet them there."

"What about Beth?" asked Mitch. "Is she saying anything? Why are
they talking to you, and she can't?"

"They aren't talking to me," said Ezekiel. "I'm hearing what Beth's
hearing. Nobody knows I'm there."

"You're not there," said Dahlia. "You're here."

"I know," said Ezekiel. "I'm not much of a finder of lost people."

"You're the lost person, remember," said Dahlia. "You're the lost object.
Beth is the owner. You're just trying to return yourself to her."

Right, thought Ezekiel. He had to keep this whole thing inside that
frame. He was bringing himself back to Beth, like the Build-a-Bears to
Renee. Here's the thing you lost. This belongs to you, and you didn't know
where it is, but it's right here, heading for you. Wherever you are.

"Take the Wendover exit," said Ezekiel. "Westbound."

"OK," said Shank. "That's pretty specific. Do you have a map in your
mind now?"

"No," said Ezekiel. "I just got a sense that we needed to go near Brassfield. Dad and I go to cheap movies there sometimes. I got the idea that we'd pass it on the way."

"So … Wendover westbound," said Shank. "Then Battleground out to New Garden?"

"And left on New Garden. But it isn't there, it's past there. We'll keep going, but I got the feeling we'd pass Brassfield on our right."

"Well, that's the route, then. So far."

"We used to go to Pie Works before the movie," said Ezekiel. "But it's closed now."

Shank said nothing.

"Now I'm hungry," said Dahlia.

"Can we stop and eat something?" asked Mitch. "It's dinnertime. We're missing dinner."

"You're not missing anything yet," said Shank. "Rush hour is only just starting. Your parents wouldn't be serving dinner yet."

"Like anybody at our house ever cooks anything," said Lanny.

"So, Rice Krispies for every meal?" asked Shank.

Silently, Ezekiel answered, What happened to all the silence I was supposed to have? To help me think? Just because I got a couple of things doesn't mean that I can deal with distraction now.

Especially because Ezekiel was hungry, too.

No. No, he wasn't hungry. Beth was hungry. And thirsty. Raging thirst. So dry.

Hadn't they provided anything for her?

Why should they? They didn't expect to keep her there long.

"If we pass a McDonald's or Booger King can we stop and get something?" asked Mitch.

Ezekiel wanted to scream, Do you think this is some kind of outing? But he kept silent. He didn't need to make them angry with him. If they had some kind of micropotential bond, anger might break it, and what good would that do for Beth?

There was more chat, more complaint, more banter about who was hungriest and who was a big baby with no self-control, they couldn't stop for food because Mitch didn't have his really big bib and he'd spill food all over himself. Until Shank turned the car left at Westridge and pulled into the McDonald's.

"I'm not treating," said Shank.

"This isn't police business?"

"Not unless I'm arresting you," said Shank. "Anything you want to confess?"

"I got nothing," said Mitch.

"A conscience pure as snow," said Shank.

"I mean I got no money."

"I'll treat," said Dahlia, sounding more put out than generous.

"Me too?" asked Lanny.

"Are you broke? Are you even hungry?"

"Well if he's eating, and this is dinner, then yeah, I'll eat," said Lanny.

"But you don't have any money?"

"I've got money," said Lanny.

"Then what's the problem?" asked Dahlia.

"I was just asking, like, if you're treating him, are you treating everybody?"

"Pay for yourself like a man, Lanny," said Shank.

And Ezekiel thought: What would it be like to have enough money that you could just stop at McDonald's and not even have to think about it. Enough money to treat somebody else.

And then he thought: When I'm thinking about McDonald's and money and treating people to dinner, I'm not thinking about Beth. If I eat a Big Mac, will it help Beth not to be hungry? I can't believe Shank would stop like this.

Unless McDonald's is just a diversion while he calls for backup. But if he calls somebody in Downy or Eden, they'll take as long to get here as we took. So it'll be local Greensboro cops. And what'll he tell them? I got a kid here who heard voices. Two men talking about how their key won't open a door. And then he has a strong impression that there's a little girl who's very hungry and thirsty.

No, he's not calling for backup.

I should call for backup, thought Ezekiel. I should get there to Beth and do whatever I can do for her. Not alone—alone what could I possibly do? But with Dad. He's my backup, not Shank, not these other teenage micropots.

"Out of the car," said Shank. "We're going inside, you can see the line at the driveup, this'll be faster."

"Not if all the workers are taking care of the driveup," said Dahlia.

"You used to work at a McDonald's?" asked Mitch.

"Not 'used to.' I work at a McDonald's. Which is why it's kind of disgusting that I'm using my hard-earned wages to buy McDonald's food for you."

"I'll pay you back," said Mitch. "I'm not poor, I just don't have money with me."

"That makes you poor," said Lanny. "Do you earn your own money, like Dahlia? I didn't think so. So it's your parents who are not poor, and you're just going to beg some money from them to pay her back."

"I'm not going to beg," said Mitch. "I'll tell them I borrowed the money from a friend and they'll give me what I need to pay her back."

"So, poor with parents. The usual condition of children," said Lanny.

Ezekiel had followed the other kids into McDonald's and they were waiting for a cashier to come to a register so they could order. Shank had stayed in the car so maybe he was calling somebody. But why? He didn't even know where they were going yet, because Ezekiel didn't know.

"Can I borrow your phone?" Ezekiel asked Dahlia.

Wordlessly she handed it to him.

"Everybody's borrowing everything from Dahlia," said Lanny. "Poor Dahlia."

"Rich Dahlia," said Mitch. "Poor Mitch. Right, Lanny?"

Ezekiel stepped outside McDonald's to make his call. He couldn't see Shank's car because he had parked on the Battleground Avenue side of the place.

Dad was still at Food Lion and he happened to be the one who picked up the phone in the meat department. "Dad, I'm in Greensboro, we're looking for Beth."

"You think she's there?"

"I know she is, and I'm close. Shank drove us and we've got three other kids with micropowers with us, only they stopped for McDonald's and it's making me insane. I'm pretty sure there's two bad guys waiting outside the door where Beth is locked in. They can't get in cause their key doesn't work, but Dad, these are the ones who'll kill her if they can."

"What can I do?" asked Dad.

"I'm not going to wait for these guys, I'm done with them, they keep distracting me and they're eating and Beth is hungry and thirsty and my being mad at them isn't helping me concentrate on her."

"Then get out of there."

"And walk?"

"I'll leave work right now. I can do it, Garry and Wim are here to cover the meat department."

"It's a long drive, Dad," said Ezekiel apologetically.

"Where will I find you?"

"I'm not going to walk on Battleground, Shank would just catch up with me and I'd be right back where I am now. I'm going to walk down Westridge to Friendly and then west on Friendly. I'm pretty sure that'll get me as close as going on New Garden the way I was going to. It's farther south, it's kind of a lot farther south, so … if I'm walking, I can concentrate better."

"What if I don't get there before you need to turn off of Friendly?"

"I just won't do that. Besides, it's a couple of miles on foot. You'll be here before then."

"Beth will be OK while I'm driving down there?"

"I don't know, Dad. I just know that I'm the one who has to find her and Shank can't get help from any of the local cops because, come on, this whole thing is crazy and borderline magical and if somebody told me the story he has to tell them, I'd lock him up in the loony bin."

"You and me both, but that's the world we live in," said Dad.

"It's the world I live in, but thanks for coming along. I'll see you in about a half hour."

"Less than that," said Dad. "See you."

Ezekiel stood there with Dahlia's phone. He didn't want to go back inside and give it to her because then they'd wonder where he was going when he left again. So he pushed the phone down into his pocket and figured he'd give it back to her later. Then he strode off to the south, out of the McDonald's parking lot, past the restaurant and then down Westridge.

Sitting in the car, he hadn't had to look at anything, he could close his eyes and concentrate on whatever might be coming to him from Beth. Now he had to watch his step because there were cars and traffic and he couldn't help Beth if he stepped in front of a car during rush hour. At first, cutting through the parking lot and making turns took a lot of his concentration and he thought, this was a bad decision, would I even notice if Beth was trying to show me something?

But then he was on the sidewalk farther down Westridge and he could think again. Beth, talk to me, he said silently. Let me know what you're hearing, let me know what you see. What you need right now. Help me find you.

Here's what he did know, with every step. He was going the right direction. He wasn't drifting anymore, hoping to see something that could be the building where she was. Nothing close by was tall enough, strange enough. Just a bunch of houses with trees all around them. But he was getting closer.

17

Ezekiel Blast was right at the point where he had to turn off of Friendly, get farther south, down past Market. But he told Father that he would stay on Friendly. So he should stop right here and wait.

Only he couldn't. He felt something pulling him on, pushing him. Holding still wasn't even an option.

He didn't even know where this road led. Off to the left, it looked like a tiny residential road that was going nowhere. He couldn't go any farther west on Friendly Avenue, because that would take him farther from Beth, but he couldn't take this turn, because he needed Father, and not just because the car would be faster.

Why didn't I wait and do this in the car with Shank? What can Father do that Shank couldn't do better? What if we get there and the bad guys have her, they hold her right at the edge and threaten to push her off? Shank would know what to do. What can Father and I do?

More than I could do alone, that's for sure.

Was there some kind of plan behind this? Was Ezekiel being guided? Or was it just something in the universe that bent him toward this? None of it made sense in the real world. It might be a micropower but it was big enough to overwhelm one skinny stupid kid named Ezekiel Blast.

Ezekiel Bliss. The name he had when Mother was alive. Maybe that's the kid who's being led or pushed or whatever it is.

Ezekiel couldn't hold still. He walked a little way into the side street, then circled back across somebody's lawn and got himself back to Friendly Avenue. He looked to the east—Father has to be coming from the east—but none of the cars was Dad's, and he headed down the side street, went a little farther this time.

He thought about Beth. Thought about how during their entire friendship, Beth had been living in the same house with her dead mother, fending off all inquiries, handling everything that got thrown at her. I lost my mother, but is it even comparable? I still had Dad with me, I didn't have to worry about money, about maintaining my independence. And in the midst of that, she saw my shunning bubble and decided, "I want me some of that."

So I'm the half-orphan kid with a sad tale because my mommy died, and then Beth takes me under her wing—because that's what she did, she adopted me like a pet in a shelter—and even though she's suffered bigger losses, even though she's living a weirder life, she heals me.

And now all she needs from me is a simple thing like saving her life and here I am hung up at this corner, having ditched the cop who might have been really useful, and I'm waiting for my dad, whose main skill is knowing how to chop up meat in ways that will induce housewives and guys who grill to buy this piece of beef or that pile of chicken or this string of pork sausages and I don't see how his skills are any more useful than mine, which means useless, but I also know that I have so much more of a chance to help Beth if Dad's with me, and Dad, where are you, when will you get …

A couple of toots on a car horn made him almost jump out of his clothes. Ezekiel turned around that there was Dad, the car window lowered. "This is how you stay on Friendly?"

"This is how you get here before I have to turn?"

"I never said I could do it that fast. You just don't know how fast you walk."

By now Ezekiel was in the passenger seat. "When this road ends, take a left."

"So you know where she is?"

"I know which way to go and thank you for coming, I'm so ... crazy right now."

"Oh, so you were in need of a crazier person to make you feel relatively sane?" asked Dad.

"Yes, but it isn't working," said Ezekiel.

"Here's what's working. We're heading for Market Street and I still have plenty of gas even if she's in Asheboro."

"She isn't," said Ezekiel. "She's really close. But what if the bad guys are there?"

"Then that's good. Because we'll go back and find a phone—"

"I just don't know if we're in Jaws, when by the time you know you're in trouble it's already too late."

"We're not in Jaws. No boat, no water. And definitely no shark experts here."

"But that's how scared I am, Dad. I'm just shaking. Like I'm freezing cold."

"It's going to be a chilly night, maybe under forty. It really is getting cold."

"I'm afraid we're going to find her and she'll be ..."

"Everybody dies, Ezekiel. And if she's dead when we get there, you didn't cause it. You did everything you could."

"I ditched Shank and the kids from GRUT and—"

"You did what felt right. You have to trust your micropower."

"But I don't know what comes from the micropower and what's just the product of my own pathetic thinking." Then Ezekiel told him about the big GRUT meeting. About what he heard, about climbing the lectern, about the pain he knew Beth had felt.

"This just comes to you," Father said softly.

"The theory is that I got so much clarity because all those other micropots were there." Then, before his father could ask, he added, "Micropotents. People with micropowers."

The road narrowed, then veered to the right. It looked like it was heading off into the nowhere of rural Guilford County.

"Any turns coming up?" Father asked.

"This one," said Ezekiel. "Left."

"This doesn't look like much of a road. No stripes, just oil and gravel, not asphalt—"

"This is the turn."

Dad turned the car and they road along a roller-coaster road, the kind that goes steeply up and even more steeply down. Ordinarily they'd have fun with a road like this, going up one slope fast enough that they'd be a little weightless at the top. And Dad was driving that way, but there was nothing fun about it. Ezekiel wanted the road to level out so they could just go.

Then they came up another slope and reached the crest and Ezekiel saw it, the tower that he knew she was in.

"What is that, even?" asked Father.

"And does this road go there?"

"Well, we're going there, even if we have to ditch the car," said Dad. "There aren't any other cars here in this … do I call it a parking lot? Or somebody's weed garden?"

"That tower doesn't look finished at all, but somebody poured a whole lot of concrete."

The parking lot—that's what it was, because there were a few faded stripes still visible—ended at a one-story building that stood between them and the tower. No road led back to it. So was it part of this low building? The two buildings made no architectural sense together.

"It's like a five-story fire escape for a one-story building," said Dad.

"What was it supposed to be?" asked Ezekiel.

"Look in that window, plain as day," said Dad.

The window he was pointing at looked like a schoolroom window—extremely faded kindergarten art attached to the glass.

"It's like a school that died five years ago and nobody even bothered to take anything out of it," said Dad.

"I can't believe it hasn't been totally vandalized."

"Because to vandalize it, you have to know it's there and get to it somehow. You don't just happen to get here."

"It's the tower, not this abandoned school," said Ezekiel.

"This is when we stop talking out loud and pretend that maybe somebody really dangerous is up there," said Father. "And I'm in charge. Yes, yes, you have all the information, I get that. But if I say no, then stop, and if I say go, then haul ass, laddie."

Ezekiel was already walking through the high weeds around the side of the school. Father caught up and now he walked with a hand on Ezekiel's shoulder. Not to restrain him, he wasn't pulling or pushing. He was just … connected.

Ezekiel led the way, though he didn't know where he was going except that Beth had to be up in that tower. As the sun was sinking in the west, the tower was almost dazzlingly bright. But on the west side there were no openings or gaps that could have been the place where Beth nearly fell, and where Ezekiel had shared her experience of painfully clawing her way back up to safety.

Still, that didn't mean that the entrance to the tower wouldn't be on the same side as the school—in fact, anything else would make no sense at all. But unfortunately it made even more sense: the tower was joined to the school by a windowless passageway that offered no outside door at all.

"Maybe around back," said Father.

"Or maybe we have to go back and come in through the school," said Ezekiel. "I don't see any kind of path around this side, anyway."

"Depends on how many trips they've made along here," said Father. "This ground is dry, but the vegetation isn't brittle. Everything would spring back if they've only walked here a few times."

They reached the back corner of the tower and now they saw that on all the floors above the ground floor, the tower was completely open. No exterior wall at all.

"I can't imagine this was going to be part of the school," said Father softly. "This tower is just the elevator shaft and the fire stairs, plus a landing zone on each story. I don't know if the rest was going to be apartments or offices, but this is such a weird arrangement."

"I can't believe they just left it open like this."

"Bare concrete, weather won't hurt it," said Father. "But how do you get in?"

"Through the school," said Ezekiel.

"Or the south side?" asked Father.

Ezekiel took a step toward going around the back, but then he felt enormous resistance. What was this, his micropower warning him of some danger? Or Beth not wanting him to go that way? "Let's go to the front," said Ezekiel.

So instead of circling behind the tower, they retraced their steps to the front.

The door of the school was locked, and showed no signs of having been forced. "Maybe they have a key," said Father.

"So these guys, one of them owned this place?" said Ezekiel.

"Or he was an employee with a key, or the friend of an employee, or the guy who stole the key from the home of the owner, or is really good at picking locks," said Father.

"I guess having it be the owner would make Shank's job too easy," said Ezekiel.

"No, the universe couldn't stand for that," said Father.

They walked around the south side of the building this time, and now there was a path. In fact, there was a concrete walkway leading to that enclosed passage between the school and the tower, and on this side of the passage, there was a double door. Even though the knob on the door didn't turn, pulling on it met no resistance at all; Father pulled the one side of the door wide open, and it stayed open.

"Convenient," said Ezekiel.

Father put his finger to his lips, and then said in a much lower voice, "We've been careless so far, talking out loud and saying whatever's on our minds."

Ezekiel took this as a good reminder that whoever put Beth in this place—if she was in fact here—was not nice and might be very dangerous.

"Do we go call Shank now?" asked Ezekiel, very softly.

"Do we know for sure that Beth is here?"

"Almost for sure," said Ezekiel. "Yes, I'm sure. But am I sure enough to get Shank to risk his job calling in other cops because some psychic said—"

"Are you a psychic?" Dad interrupted.

"I sure don't think so," said Ezekiel, speaking softly but also slowly, so he could be understood. "But the Greensboro cops aren't going to be interested in the distinction."

Father stepped through the door into the dark interior. It was colder inside than outside, which made sense, because this inner space didn't get any sunlight or air from outside. To Ezekiel it also meant: Beth must be really cold.

Father looked for a lightswitch, found it, flipped it. Nothing happened.

"Do you have a flashlight?" asked Father.

Ezekiel shook his head, then realized Dad probably couldn't see him. "No," he said softly.

"Then it's a good thing I keep a little LED flashlight on my key ring," said Father. He switched it on. Tiny, but it was enough light to see the boarded-off elevator opening and the concrete stairs leading upward. Now Dad had to lead the way, with Ezekiel keeping his hand on his father's shoulder. It was kind of a stretch, what with Ezekiel being a step below him the whole way, but he was surprised and pleased that he was tall enough now to keep up.

At the end of the first double flight of stairs, there was a heavy windowless metal door. Not locked. Father shone the flashlight beam around. "I'm surprised there isn't a bunch of discarded drug paraphernalia here," he said.

"Kind of out-of-the-way," said Ezekiel. "Most crack dens are more conveniently located, aren't they?"

"Not an expert on crack dens," said Dad. "You?"

"Also not an expert," said Ezekiel. "I'll take the AP Drug Culture class next year."

"Please tell me and God that you're joking," said Father.

"People like me never understand what's going on in Advanced Math. Could be Advanced Meth for all I know."

Second floor. Unlocked door, the room looking a little webby but apparently the wind blew out any serious dust. Ditto with the third floor and the fourth floor.

No sign of human habitation, visitation, or existence until they reached the top of the last flight of stairs. The fifth-floor door was locked.

And when Father shone the light directly on the locking mechanism, it was obvious that it was a new deadbolt, installed much more recently than the original hardware.

"Is she in there?" asked Father softly.

A voice came from the other side of the door. "I can hear you," she said.

"Beth," said Ezekiel, louder now. "Are you all right?"

"Define 'all right,'" she said.

"I know you almost fell out," said Ezekiel. "Thank God you pulled yourself back inside."

"I'm freezing cold and I can't get the door open. Mr. Pigface deliberately broke the key in the lock and now it can't be opened from either side."

Ezekiel thought back over the conversation he had overheard. "They're coming back to drill out the lock," he said.

"I know," said Beth.

"My dad's here," said Ezekiel.

"I know," said Beth. "Hi, Ezekiel's Dad. I'm not sure if I should call you Mr. Bliss or Mr. ..."

Ezekiel knew that Beth wasn't sure whether Dad knew that Ezekiel called himself by the last name Blast.

"We're going to go and call the cops. Lieutenant Shank," said Ezekiel.

"No!" Beth's voice sounded panicky for the first time.

"It's not like we can get the door open," said Father.

"When they come back they're going to ... They'll have a camera, a Steadicam, and they'll ..."

"Then we have to hurry to call the cops," said Father.

"If they're here with me when the cops come, they'll kill me. They know I'm old enough to testify in court."

Father shook his head. "They won't dare kill you, Beth," he said. "Your dead body would testify against them even more than you could accuse them alive."

"Thanks for the encouragement," said Beth. "Please please don't leave me alone. I'm begging here. When they find that I'm alone and the guy they left with me is gone I don't know what they'll do."

"Then we've got to get you out of there," said Father.

"How?" asked Beth.

"The open side of the room you're in," said Father. "If you crawl backward out that opening, and dangle your legs down, I can grab you and haul you in on the floor below this. That door is unlocked."

"That's insane," said Ezekiel. "She can't do that."

"I can do it," said Beth. "I've got no choice."

"You can't do it, Dad. It's the sheer physics of the thing. Suppose her legs are dangling, barely in reach. You're just as likely to fall out trying to reach her as you are to be able to haul her in. And once she's halfway out again, I don't know if she can change her mind and climb back up."

"I'm glad you're thinking things through," said Father. "So now that you've seen these problems, how do we fix them?"

Somehow Dad had known that Ezekiel would already be thinking of solutions. "I can stand behind you, holding you by the waist of your pants. I can help keep you from teetering too far."

"Sounds good, let's do it," said Father.

But Ezekiel kept picturing the operation as they clattered down the stairs to the floor below. As Father opened the door into the open room, Ezekiel had already thought of the next problem, just as bad as the fear of Dad falling while trying to reach Beth.

"The only way you can grab her will be with your fists around her ankles, right?" said Ezekiel.

Father kept his hand on the south wall as he walked carefully to the edge. "Damn but it's a long way down."

"As soon as she stops holding on to floor above, her body will fall. Then your grip on her ankles won't be enough. She'll bend at the knees, and—"

"I'll fall backward," said Father. "I'll let my own weight haul her in."

"And you'll land on me, right behind you," said Ezekiel, "so your head won't hit the concrete floor. But Dad, her head will hit it. Nothing you do can stop her head from smacking into the concrete, either right on the edge there or on the floor inside."

"But she won't fall all the way to the ground outside," said Dad.

"How is a one-story drop where you land on your head on concrete any better than a five-story drop where you land on weeds?"

"I think her odds are better this way," said Dad.

"Survival isn't that great if it's survival without a working brain," said Ezekiel.

Apparently she could hear them on the floor above, because now she said, "I'm for survival," she said, "and then we'll see what surgery and rehab can do about my brain."

Ezekiel tried to think back—had he received anything visual about Beth's location?

"Did they give you any kind of mattress to lie on?" asked Ezekiel.

"A piece-of-crap playpen mattress, about two inches thick," said Beth.

"Does it bend or fold?"

"That's the only thing it does," said Beth.

"If you can get that mattress down to us we can lay it on the floor where your head would land and maybe that can save you a lot of damage."

"This mattress is like putting down aluminum foil as a trampoline," said Beth.

"Is it really, or would it help?" asked Father.

A pause. And then a cheap plastic mattress, about two inches thick, appeared near the top of the wall on the south side.

"I can't hold this forever," Beth said.

Father kept one hand on the wall and reached with his left hand for the mattress.

"No," said Ezekiel. "We do this the way we're going to do it." Ezekiel took hold of Father's belt and leaned back, holding him firmly, while Father let go of the wall and reached for the mattress with both hands. He got it easily and then he stepped back into the room, almost tripping on Ezekiel.

"You were supposed to fall backward," said Ezekiel.

"I didn't have to, the mattress was light," said Father, and then, before Ezekiel could argue, Father added, "How many times do you think I can fall on my ass on concrete in the same day, Ezekiel?"

"You're going to fall on your butt on me," said Ezekiel.

"You think you can do that twice?" asked Father. "OK, Beth, let's do this."

No feet dangled over the edge. Beth's voice came again. "I'm pretty much naked," she said.

It took Ezekiel a moment to process that. This was a matter of staying alive, and she was worried about modesty? "What's 'pretty much'?" he asked.

"Flimsy doll clothes," said Beth. "Not even a sheet over the mattress. I'm cold."

"How did you survive last night?" asked Father. "It was in the thirties."

"I wasn't here last night," said Beth.

"We won't look," said Ezekiel. "Just enough for Dad to grab your ankles and then we'll cover you up." Ezekiel was already taking off his shirt.

Father looked at him, took Ezekiel's shirt, and then began taking off his own. Father was wearing a t-shirt underneath; Ezekiel had nothing.

"You walked all that way with only one layer of cloth?" Father asked.

"I was exercising, and it wasn't that cold with the sun shining," said Ezekiel. It was cold now, though.

Loudly enough for Beth to hear, Father said, "We're ready to cover you as soon as we've got you safely inside on this level."

There was a faint sound but Ezekiel was pretty sure he knew what it was. "A car just pulled into the parking lot out front," he said.

"Are you ready?" asked Beth. "Because I'm doing this, and I'm not going to be talking while I do it. Get my ankles as soon as you can reach them and tell me when to let go up here."

Ezekiel felt a sick dread. He had thought all he had to do was find her. This was crazy stuff. But they had to do it, and it had to work. It had nothing to do with having a micropower. It was all physics plus physical strength and dexterity.

Father had already laid out the mattress so it cantilevered past the edge of the floor by about four inches. That way, if Beth's head was still outside the room when she hit the floor, she wouldn't have her skull crushed against the concrete edge. Of course, she could still have her neck broken, or Father's grip could fail and she could simply plummet five stories, or her momentum could drag Father out of Ezekiel's grasp and he'd have lost his father and his friend.

Beth's bare feet and ankles became visible. She was much higher up than the mattress had been. Father had to stand on tiptoe to reach her, and for the first time Ezekiel could feel himself holding some of Father's weight. If I weren't holding him, thought Ezekiel, he'd already be falling. He's only able to reach so high because he trusts my hold on him. Ezekiel tightened his grip even more, as he bent his kneels a little and lowered his body to increase his backward momentum as a balance to Father's weight.

This meant Ezekiel couldn't see what was going on. All he could see was Father's back.

"I've got you!" Father said loudly to Beth.

And I've got you, Ezekiel answered him silently.

Then Father fell backward and Ezekiel fell backward and Father's torso and head landed heavily on Ezekiel's belly and chest exactly as Ezekiel's butt and back hit the floor. Because Ezekiel had already been poised so low, his head barely hit the floor at all.

With the air knocked out of him, Ezekiel couldn't shout or say or even whisper the thing he had to ask: Did it work? Is Beth all right?

"Here, kid," said Father. "Get this shirt on. We aren't looking. Ezekiel, face the wall."

Ezekiel turned his face to the wall and he could hear Beth's bare feet padding around a little.

He had his breath back by the time Beth said, "OK, you can get up now."

Well, that was easier said than done. Ezekiel couldn't do anything until Father's weight was off of him. Dad wasn't a heavyset man, but he had massive shoulders and muscle weighed a lot.

Dad rolled off of him and got up on all fours, then stood. Ezekiel rolled over. Beth was wearing Dad's shirt, buttoned up and with the sleeves rolled up. He could see his own shirt's sleeve emerging at the wrists and at the neck. Dad's shirttail actually touched the floor, Beth was so small.

"Thank you," said Beth. "For finding me, and for … this …"

"Thanks for having the courage to do it," said Father.

"I think we should be really quiet now," said Ezekiel. There were footsteps on the stairway far below them.

Now that he could look around, he saw that there was a scrap of lacy-looking cloth on the floor. Beth saw him look at it; she picked it up and dropped it over the edge. Ezekiel realized that must have been the "doll clothes" the kidnappers had given her to wear. She took it off before she put on our shirts. As if those doll clothes had been the chains of her captivity.

Father strode to the door and closed it quietly. Then he indicated for Beth and Ezekiel to sit against the wall. Father whispered, "They probably won't come in here. So we sit tight."

"What if they do?" murmured Ezekiel.

"Then we fight like hell," whispered Father.

Beth was trembling.

"Don't be scared," whispered Ezekiel.

Beth rolled her eyes at him.

"She's freezing," murmured Father. "Body heat, Ezekiel."

Like I have any extra body heat to spare!

Father sat down on the other side of Beth and put his arm around her shoulder. Then he grabbed Ezekiel by the neck with that same hand and drew him closer, so that Beth was pretty much in a Bliss sandwich, between father and son. She was really, really shivering, and her teeth were rattling. Ezekiel realized: If she had spent a night in that space upstairs, open to the cold air, she would have died. For all he knew, she still might die of hypothermia.

For that matter, shirtless as he was, so might he. If the guys spent a few hours trying to get into the upstairs room past the broken lock, he might be shivering as bad as Beth.

Body heat, Father had said. That would help Ezekiel, too. So he turned to face Beth, wrapped both his arms around her, and held tight. It really did make him warmer.

"Loosen up," Beth whispered. "I still need to breathe."

But it was then, twisting his body to face Beth, that Ezekiel felt that there was something in his pocket. It took a couple of moments and then he remembered. Dahlia's phone. He had a cellphone with him.

He pulled his arm away from Beth and dug into his pocket and came out with it, brandishing it where Father could see.

Father took it from his hand and set the phone on the concrete floor. Of course, with those feet plodding up the stairs just outside the door, this was not a good moment to make a phone call.

But he could send a text to Lieutenant Shank. Ezekiel picked up the phone and started entering Shank's number as they listened to the noise of men carrying heavy loads clumping up the stairs.

18

Father had to enter the actual text message to Shank, because only Father, who had driven the route, could explain how to find the unmarked road that this abandoned school was on. And Father, who had never owned a cell phone, as far as Ezekiel knew, was not exactly adept at entering text. Dahlia apparently had auto-correct and type-ahead set at some incredibly high level, so that Father kept being bothered by irrelevant text appearing in the blank space where he was trying to write. And it's not as if Ezekiel could help.

Apparently, though she owned no mobile phone, Beth did understand something about how this stuff worked. "Just keep typing," she whispered. "The wrong words disappear."

Oh, thought Ezekiel. Who knew?

Like, everybody, he could imagine Dahlia answering.

Father finished the message and then sat there, looking baffled. Beth took the phone from his hand and pushed whatever you had to push to make the message go.

Father looked nonplussed. "Did you erase it?" he whispered.

Beth shook her head. "I sent it." Then she showed him where his message now appeared higher up on the screen.

Then Beth quickly slid her finger downward from the top of the screen, pushed some imaginary button, got a new screen, then made it go away. Father looked at her quizzically.

"I muted it," whispered Beth. "In case it makes a sound when a message is received."

Almost immediately, a single word appeared on the message screen: "Coming."

Father grabbed the phone and typed again. "Hiding but easy to find," he wrote. "Bad guys top floor. No lights no sirens."

No answer from Shank. But then, with any luck he was driving and on the phone with the Greensboro police or the Guilford County sheriff's department—Ezekiel couldn't make an intelligent guess about the jurisdiction of this place—and besides, Shank had a brain.

The whiny sound of a power drill came from upstairs. The noise was pretty loud even through a heavy closed door. Father whispered, "If we're lucky, they won't have any lubricant and they'll burn out the bit."

Ezekiel wondered how his father would know that. How many locks had he drilled out in his life?

"And if there's a pin or a ball bearing to block them, it won't work anyway," Father added.

"Does that help us?"

"The longer they're drilling, the more—"

Father stopped cold, interrupted by a sudden silence upstairs. He put his hand over his own mouth. No more talking.

But Ezekiel could finish the sentence: The more time for Shank and the cops to arrive.

The drilling started up again.

"They were oiling the bit," whispered Father, and then he covered his own mouth again.

When in his life had Father learned about drilling out locks?

It felt like forever, but it wasn't really that long before the drilling stopped and a different noise began. Metallic.

"It's still not opening," they heard a man say upstairs. He was talking loudly, presumably because he was frustrated or angry.

"There's still the regular latch," said another male voice.

Were they the same voices Ezekiel had heard when he was getting information about Beth back with Dr. Withunga? His memory for voices wasn't good enough to even make a guess. Especially when the voices were muffled by closed doors. Both times.

The drilling sound began again.

The next time there was a lull: "Can't we just take it off the hinges?"

"Can you see that the door opens inward?" the other man answered scornfully. "The hinges are on the other side. If we could reach the hinges, we wouldn't be drilling locks."

More whining from the drill.

The next lull: "Why hasn't he said anything?"

"Is there anything useful that he could say, after breaking the key in the lock? If he broke it."

"Why is she so quiet?"

"Because she's not a little kid," said the scornful one. "She knows when it doesn't work to whine."

Ezekiel felt Beth shudder under his arm.

Father put his free hand on Beth's arm. "Getting warmer at all?" he asked in a whisper. As if he thought her shudder was merely a shiver from the cold.

Two more rounds of drilling, and then a sharp crack like a gunshot. Ezekiel couldn't prevent his startle reflex, and Beth also jerked. But Father was unperturbed. "They broke the bit," he whispered.

For the moment, the men were so busy cursing and blaming—"You could have put my eye out!"; "You didn't want safety goggles"—that it was safe to whisper, there where Ezekiel and Father and Beth were hiding.

It was Beth who reached down and picked up the phone, then showed the texting space, where Shank had written: "We're here. Stay hidden. Live ammo."

"Did you ever see if those guys had a gun?" whispered Father.

"I never saw anybody but Pigface," whispered Beth. "He used needles."

For a moment Ezekiel flashed on the image of a man wielding a giant needle like a switchblade. Then he realized that she meant the guy drugged her.

A very faint deedle-deedle sound upstairs.

"Ringtone," whispered Beth.

The men spoke quietly now, but in a moment they were clattering down the stairs. Toward where Ezekiel, Beth, and Dad were hiding. Ezekiel could feel the others stiffen their posture, getting ready to leap to their feet for a fight.

Then the steps continued on down the stairs.

Father picked up the phone. "How do I place an actual phone call to Shank?"

Beth pushed twice in different spots on the face of the smartphone and handed it back to Father.

Yep. Except as a landing pad for Father's head and a shirt-hanger for Beth's new wardrobe, I'm pretty useless here, thought Ezekiel.

"Shank?" Father said. "They're running. Heading down the stairs. The only door is on the south side of the corridor connecting the tower with the school."

Shank said a couple of short statements that Ezekiel couldn't understand.

"We're supposed to sit tight," said Father, "and I'm supposed to stay on the line."

"Dahlia's going to be pissed that we're running down her battery," said Ezekiel.

Beth gave a short, whispered bark of laughter. One of her best kinds of laugh.

The bad guys were leaving, the cops were here, Ezekiel and Dad and Beth weren't going to have to fight, they weren't going to die.

So now it was time for Ezekiel to remember what mattered most. Beth was alive. He had found Beth. He had her back.

Or, come to think of it, she had him back. This only worked when Ezekiel started thinking of himself as her most valued possession, recently lost. It was himself that he was returning to her.

But it felt like he was getting her back.

He'd better not say either thing to Beth. That he was her favorite possession? Oh, that would go over so well.

But if she asked how he managed to find her, he wasn't going to lie. If she mocked him for it, then it would still be good to have her back, mocking him.

With these thoughts his eyes filled with tears. But with his arm around Beth's waist—when had he moved his arm to her waist from her shoulder?—there'd be no subtle way for him to wipe his eyes.

Oh. Not a problem. Beth had buried her face in her hands and now she was crying. Not like a baby. Not a fussy cry. Deep sobs of relief. More than relief. Something else.

"All right," said Father. "There are some things we have to say now, before the cops find us. Are you up to it?"

Ezekiel almost answered but he realized in time that Father was speaking to Beth.

Beth nodded. "First thing," she said—and her voice was steady, if maybe a tiny bit hoarse. "If you look over the edge, Pigface is lying about three feet from the tower. After I got back in, I watched him for fifteen minutes or so and he never twitched."

"Ezekiel, can you crawl to the edge—and I mean crawl, no standing, I've had enough terror for one day. Crawl to the edge and make sure he didn't come to and wander off."

Ezekiel did not want to go anywhere near the edge, but he was closest and Father still had things to say to Beth. They continued talking while Ezekiel crawled.

"Just tell the police the truth. Did you push him?"

"Yes," said Beth.

"You don't have to prove that he was threatening you at that moment. Anything you did while unlawfully being held prisoner is self-defense. I'm not a lawyer but I know that much of the law. So just tell them the truth."

"I always do," said Beth.

"Shank found your mother's body," said Father. "We know how you managed, financially. Plus you have proven yourself to be a brilliant liar. You value your independence but the authorities are not going to let you continue alone in that house. You do understand that."

Ezekiel looked over the edge. It was near sunset and the body was in the darkest shadow, but there was still plenty of light to see that yes, the kidnapper's body was still there. And he could see that there was no possibility that his spinal cord was attached to his brain anymore.

Which was a moot point because the man's head had landed on a pile of cinderblocks and much of his brain was now a lumpy smear.

"He's there and he's dead twice over," said Ezekiel.

"The only way he could have moved," said Beth, "was if his name was Lazarus and Jesus stopped by."

"His name is Humpty," said Ezekiel, "and the king didn't bother sending any horses or men."

Father went on as if they hadn't said anything. "I'm prepared to offer you my guardianship. I don't know how Child Protective Services works or how guardianships are assigned. We're not relatives of yours but I think this little adventure may give them a good reason to consider me for the job. Your money would be put in a trust that I couldn't touch without the consent of the court—I'd insist on it, because once your house sells you'll have kind of a lot of money."

Beth shook her head.

"There's only the problem that I'm not married," said Father, "and, you know, this teenage boy lives in my house."

"There's a third problem," said Beth. "You've seen me barely dressed."

"I was looking at the wall and Father was between us the whole time. So I saw you wearing Dad's and my shirts. Whereas you saw me bare-chested. If you can call what I have an actual chest."

Father chimed in. "We were saving your life, Beth. Nobody took pictures, mental or otherwise. Give us some credit here."

Beth sobbed again.

"No decisions today," said Father. "I'm going to offer guardianship and I'm going to pay for my own lawyer to fight for you. Sooner or later you're going to realize that I'm your best offer. You don't have to pretend to be happy about it. If you don't want me in that role in your life, just tell the court and they'll make other arrangements."

"Like foster care?" asked Beth. "If I thought that was a good idea I'd have reported Mom's death."

"There are horror stories," said Father, "but most of the time, foster care seems to work pretty well. If things get bad we'll make damn sure they get better."

Ezekiel could see two men running across the vast vacant field of grass and brush and sapling trees, and a bunch of cops in uniforms and suits running after them, some waving pistols. Except for the one near one side, kneeling with a big honking rifle with a scope. One of the men fell to the ground. Had the sniper fired his rifle? The fallen man hopped right back up so maybe he just tripped. The other guy didn't turn back to help him. In moments the cops who were chasing them caught the one who had tripped. The other one got away into the trees.

Ezekiel could barely make out, through the trees, that there was a car waiting there. He could see when the runner got to it, and the car took off so quickly that there was no way the guy had gotten in and started it. More like he barely had time to dive into the back seat. So there was some kind of road there, and a getaway driver, with the engine running. Shank would want to know that. He could imagine having to say, over and over, "I couldn't see the license plates, it was three hundred yards away behind trees, and even with half the leaves gone I'm lucky I could tell that it was a sedan and not an SUV or a pickup truck or something else." And then he could imagine the cops accusing him of lying, accusing him of being in on the conspiracy or how else could he have known to come all the way to Greensboro, to this godforsaken abandoned building that nobody knew about, in order to find the kidnappers' lair?

Father wanted Beth to come live with them. Ezekiel's first thought was: I never asked for a sister. Don't I get a vote?

Underneath that, but a lot bigger and deeper, was another feeling: Father better not adopt her. I don't want Beth to be my sister. I want her to stay my friend.

And then, the shallowest thought of all: Now we can walk the whole way to school together.

The police must have worried that there was still someone else, some other bad guy, because they came up the stairs so quietly that Ezekiel didn't hear anything until the doorknob turned and the door slowly came open. Ezekiel froze in place, leaning up on one elbow near the edge of the room. Father slowly turned to face the door. Beth looked down and in front of her, as terrified as Ezekiel had ever seen anyone look.

It was Shank. There were two uniformed officers with him. Apparently this place was inside Greensboro city limits, because they were police, not Guilford County sheriff's deputies.

"Who needs medical attention?" asked one of the uniforms.

"We all need blankets," said Father. "And Beth has serious ventral abrasions that need to be attended to."

Beth bowed her head, looking dejected.

It took a moment for Ezekiel to realize that Beth hadn't mentioned those abrasions, so she probably thought this meant Father had lied when he said he didn't see her before she was wearing their shirts. But Father couldn't explain, in front of the cops, that he knew about the abrasions from what Ezekiel had told him about how painful it had been when he was going through Beth's experience of clawing back up into the room. Ezekiel would just have to explain later.

"There's also a body outside on the ground directly below this room," said Father. "When Beth was confined on the floor above, she was able to push one of her captors over the edge. If she hadn't done that, Ezekiel and I wouldn't have been able to get her down from there into this room before the other conspirators came back."

"'Ventral abrasions'?" asked Shank.

"Are you a medical professional?" asked a uniform.

"I'm a butcher at Food Lion," said Father, "but I didn't think it was right to say that she had scraped up her brisket."

Shank couldn't keep a smile from playing across his lips.

"She's alive," said Shank, "and even though you and Ezekiel are possibly the stupidest human beings alive—especially Ezekiel, for ditching me and coming on ahead with a grocery-store butcher as his bodyguard—you did good work here. Was this cot mattress here already?"

"Beth passed it down to us before she crawled over the edge," said Father.

One of the uniforms was flabbergasted. "You let a six-year-old kid climb over the edge and—"

"She's fourteen," said Shank. "A little small for her age, that's all."

"Heart of a lion," said Father.

There was so much pride in his voice. It was almost awe.

And Ezekiel realized Father was right. Beth had the heart of a lion. No whimpering about how she was scared she might fall. She knew it was her best shot and so she did what it took. He remembered her saying that if there was head trauma, she'd count on surgery and rehab, because at least she'd be alive. Would he have been that cool under the circumstances?

And when she crawled out backward over the edge, counting on a man she had barely met to catch hold of her ankles and pull her to safety without dropping her, she was reinflaming the injuries she suffered when Pigface almost pulled her over the edge with him. But she didn't complain about the pain, not before, not during, not after.

She isn't a lion, she's a dragon.

"I'd rather have the wings of a pegasus," said Beth. "Way more useful when you're trapped in a tower."

Shank gave her the courtesy of a laugh. So did Father. So did the cops.

But Ezekiel couldn't laugh. He was busy looking out over the field to where the other cops were examining everything with flashlights as they led off the perp they had caught. Not that he could see anything, with his eyes swimming. But he sure wasn't going to show these cops that he was crying. Not over this short tenth-grade girl who had taken possession of his life.

"Can you walk down by yourself?" asked Shank.

Beth's answer was a firm nod, but by then two EMTs were entering the room, handing blankets to Father and Ezekiel, and wrapping Beth up like a swaddled baby.

"This isn't a Christmas pageant and I'm not the baby Jesus," she said testily. So they unswaddled her enough that she could move her arms. They also insisted—demanded—that she lie down on the stretcher a couple more EMTs had brought up the stairs.

"I think I can handle the stairs better walking than you can handle them with a stretcher," she said.

"Then you think wrong," said the boss of the EMTs. "Because we practice running up and down stairs like this and we never drop anybody or let them roll off."

"Run?" she asked.

"Don't worry, we won't run while—"

"You'd better," she said. "That sounds like fun."

Ezekiel could hear them take the stairs pretty quickly. Not actually running, but fast enough that he could hear Beth laughing as they went.

"She's in good hands," said Shank, when he was alone with Father and Ezekiel. "Now we have to come up with a good reason why you knew to come to this tower."

"I don't suppose anybody would believe that we were just driving by," said Father.

"We knew to come here," said Ezekiel, "because I have a micropower. I can return lost things to their owners. As crazy as that sounds, it has the virtue of being true, so I can't get caught in a contradiction."

Shank regarded him steadily. "You know that the Greensboro police have jurisdiction here, and they aren't used to you."

"Meaning they don't have a six-inch file on me and a long history of thinking I'm a thief and a liar," said Ezekiel. "And they've got an FBI agent to affirm that you've seen me do this and you know I had nothing to do with the kidnapping."

Shank shook his head. "I thought I made it clear. Nobody knows I'm with the Bureau—I'm here undercover."

"You went undercover as a cop?" asked Father, incredulous.

"I went undercover," said Shank, "because the guy we picked up out in the field there is on the force in Downy."

"You knew he was—"

"We believed that the buck kept stopping in Downy, North Carolina, and somebody on the job was running interference for these bastards. The State Bureau of Investigation wanted to send in a team to conduct a big open investigation, but kidnapping is a federal crime and I bigfooted them into getting out of my way and helping me create my cover."

"So you're not coming out of your cover yet?" asked Father.

"One of them got away," said Shank.

"In a sedan," said Ezekiel. "It was already running and had a driver in it."

"Big sedan? Little one?"

"Not a Mini or a Fiat," said Ezekiel, "but not a Cadillac, either. Just …
in the middle. Like an Accord."

"Don't write 'Accord,' in your report," said Father. "Because if it turns
out not to be an Accord, they'll accuse Ezekiel of lying to help them get
away, and if it is an Accord, they'll claim that he must be in on it because
there's no way he could have identified the make of the car through those
trees."

Shank nodded gravely. "I'm not an idiot but you were right to warn
me. You've been dealing with officious pinheads for a long time."

Father tried to placate him. "Not that you're an officious—"

"Oh, I am most definitely an officious pinhead—when it's useful," said
Shank. "I teach the course in Officious Pinheadery at Quantico. How do
you think I bigfooted my way through the NCSBI? But besides being a good
kid who doesn't deserve any more shit, Ezekiel is also a valuable resource
that I don't want to alienate any further than my coppish predecessors have
already done."

"So he's nothing to you but a potential asset," said Father, though it
was clear from his tone that he didn't believe it.

"That's my story and I'm sticking to it," said Shank. Then he grinned
at Ezekiel. "Thank God this girl had you in her life. Not to mention Renee
Delamare."

"Everybody who has Ezekiel in their lives is lucky," said Father. Then
he held open his arms and it was a good thing because Ezekiel started
crying so hard he needed Father to hold him or he'd probably fall off the
edge of the room in his teary blindness.

It was tears of relief, after so much tension. Tears over Beth. But he
also knew that it was tears because his father was proud of him, and Shank
was proud of him. He had actually achieved something worth doing, for
the first time in his life, and the only men who mattered to him knew that
he had done it. Something he'd thought would never happen as long as
he lived.

"I do have one more thing I need to resolve," said Shank, when
Ezekiel's crying turned into silent clinging to his father's embrace. "A little

matter of a stolen phone. And don't bother telling me that you just found it, Ezekiel, because I saw Dahlia hand it to you and then you walked away."

"Borrowed and not returned yet," said Ezekiel, his voice muffled in Father's blanket.

"Returned now," said Father, handing the phone to Shank.

"I'll persuade Dahlia not to call it stolen. In fact, I'll praise her so much for helping the investigation by lending Ezekiel her phone that she won't dare tell anybody that she didn't actually give you permission to take it away from McDonald's."

"She'll make me yawn all the way through the next GRUT session," said Ezekiel.

"That yawning thing. I told her not to get in the way, but with her normal respect for adult authority, I think she yawned that one guy into tripping."

"But not the other?" asked Father.

"Maybe at that distance she can only do one guy at a time," said Ezekiel. "If she weaponized her yawn, then that's cool. Way more useful than—"

"The micropowers are all useful for something," said Father. "Nobody's micropower's more useful than yours, Ezekiel."

"These micropowers," said Shank. "I wonder if I have one. I wonder if everybody does, only we think the stuff we're doing just happens by chance."

"I know I don't have one," said Father.

"Sense of smell," said Ezekiel.

"Nobody else could smell death outside Beth's house," said Shank.

"Maybe your micropower," said Father, "is to look at a case where everybody was sure a kid was lying about finding stuff, and still consider the possibility that he might be telling the truth."

"Seeing what nobody else wants to see," said Ezekiel. "That's almost, like, a superpower."

"Just common sense and solid investigative procedure," said Shank. "Let's get you both looked at by doctors."

Ezekiel wanted to say, I wonder what Beth's micropower is. But then he thought maybe he knew, and it would be better if he didn't out her to adults. Even the good guys.

"We weren't injured," said Father, "and we need to get to our car so we can drive home, put on shirts, and eat some dinner."

"I'll take your statements tomorrow," said Shank, conceding the point.

"And can you make sure that Ezekiel and I aren't mentioned in the media? At all? You were acting on an anonymous tip when you came here, right?"

"I'll do what I can to promote that story," said Shank. "I don't control the Greensboro police, but most of them are fathers, and they're used to protecting the identities of victims and witnesses."

"You'll ask them to do that for me and Ezekiel, then?"

"I already did. But I still have to take your statements. At your house, not at the Downy police station. It's going to be in some turmoil tomorrow."

Shank left.

Ezekiel and Father stood alone in the open-ended room. Father looked him up and down.

"I know, I'm way too skinny," said Ezekiel.

"I was thinking that you've reached the stature of a man," said Father. "Let's get out of here."

19

Ezekiel Blast sat across from Ms. Banerjee. He had turned the chair sideways and the office was so small that with the back of his chair rocked back to lean against her bookshelves, his feet could press against the door.

"Your father called in this morning to tell us you had a very difficult night and you were here today against his better judgment."

"He worries," said Ezekiel. He knew perfectly well that she wanted to find out what happened, and he wasn't going to tell her.

"Well," said Banshee, "I applaud your dedication, coming to school when your father wanted you to stay home." She took in his non-response. "I'm glad you value your schoolwork so highly."

"If you were glad I value my schoolwork, you might have shown it by leaving me in class."

"I might have," said Banshee. "But I didn't."

"Have you come up with a new career path for me?" asked Ezekiel.

"I might, if you told me more about the kinds of things that keep you up all night."

"Except when I'm making prank calls and toilet-papering people's houses, I generally fall asleep by ten-thirty."

Banshee sighed. "I'm not trying to do therapy, and I'm not going to tell anybody about what I learn in this session."

"You can't do therapy because you're not licensed to, so doctor-patient privilege doesn't apply. You could be compelled to repeat anything I told you."

"But I won't repeat it."

"I know you won't."

"Because you're not going to tell me anything," said Banshee.

"I'm going to tell you lots of things," said Ezekiel. "I'll answer any question that your job description entitles you to ask."

"Well, that's a very broad category," said Banshee.

Ezekiel quoted from memory: "'Professional School Counselors create nurturing relationships with students that enhance academic achievement and personal success as globally productive citizens in the twenty-first century.'"

"That's a very small part of a very long document," said Banshee.

"Dad made me memorize some key passages, back when my elementary school counselor was trying to probe my psyche to find out why I kept stealing things."

"So that you could politely defy them by citing the relevant rules," said Banshee.

"Are you trying to find out what I did last night in order to 'choose professional development activities that foster your own professional growth'?"

"Part of my role is to advocate for students, of which category you are a specimen."

"I'm more than a specimen. I'm exemplary," said Ezekiel. "Judging from my grades and my obedience to tedious commands that I leave class in order to joust with clowns."

Banshee had to take a breath before replying. He was getting to her. Soon she would either blow up or dismiss him to go back to class.

"If we're jousting, that was your choice, not mine."

"I know," said Ezekiel. "You chose for me to capitulate completely to your curiosity, regardless of how much I do not want to talk about this subject. Or any subject. With you."

"Do you remember that I'm the reason you found out about Dr. Withunga's program? Haven't your sessions with Dr. Withunga gone well?"

"The refreshments leave something to be desired."

"Like what?" asked Banshee.

"Refreshments," said Ezekiel.

"Poor lad, they don't feed you enough?"

"They don't feed me at all. Neither do you. Would it kill you to keep a bowl of fun-size candy bars on your desk?"

"It might," said Banshee, "because I'd end up eating them myself, causing me to blow up like a balloon, contract type-two diabetes, and die fat with my legs amputated."

"That is some fierce imagination," said Ezekiel. "I hope you're seeing somebody about that."

"I foresee the negative consequences of my likely decisions, and act in such a way as to avoid having the chance to make bad choices," said Banshee.

"In that case, I assume you will recognize that I, too, foresee the negative consequences of the decision to talk to you about anything important to me, and therefore I will 'act in such a way as to avoid' those consequences."

"I'm not your enemy," said Banshee.

"You're not my friend," said Ezekiel.

"Something happened last night because Dr. Withunga called to see if you were in school."

"It's sweet of her to care," said Ezekiel. He pulled his legs back under him and rose to his feet.

"Ezekiel Bliss," she said. "What did you find?"

"I didn't find anything," said Ezekiel.

"I know about micropowers. I know about …"

Ezekiel grinned at her.

"Why are you laughing at me? If I put you in contact with a scientist, why shouldn't I find out something about how the research is going?"

"You pay taxes, and yet the government never calls you up to tell you how it's doing, money-wise."

"Ezekiel, I just want to know if you're making any improvement. If the sessions are enhancing your micropower."

"Do you have a micropower yourself, Ms. Banerjee?

"You mean, do I have a vested interest in this question?" she replied. "Yes, I do."

"What's your micropower?" asked Ezekiel.

"I'm not going to talk about it with you."

"Turnabout is not fair play?" asked Ezekiel.

Banshee closed her eyes. "You'll ridicule it."

"Better a little ridicule than to get dragged down to the police station while they try to get you to confess to things you didn't do."

"Here it is, then, Ezekiel Bliss. My superpower is that no matter how I drive, no matter how many slowdowns there are on the road, when I reach my destination I come to a complete stop exactly when the tune on the radio comes to an end."

Ezekiel considered this for a moment. "Do you get any choice about which song it is?"

"I don't think so," said Banshee. "But it's almost always Elton John."

"Lucky you. It could have been the Jeopardy! theme."

"I've never been able to think of any way that this micropower could be of any possible use."

"Well, considering that I only just heard about it, I'm certainly not going to come up with any way to help you. Ms. Banerjee, may I go back to class now?"

"First, call me by the name you really use for me."

"I call you Ms Banerjee. How is that not real?"

"The name you call me in your own mind."

"Restricted area," said Ezekiel. "Authorized personnel only."

"Go back to class," said Banshee.

For some reason Ezekiel wasn't happy with this petty victory. What did he gain by winning?

"I call you Banshee, but in a friendly, accepting way."

"I'll try to imagine a universe in which that is possible," said Banshee.

"If I flunk my physics exam it's your fault for taking me out of class."

"I took you out of history."

"I've been here so long that the hour turned." Ezekiel got up to leave.

"Did you succeed in finding him?" she asked.

"Finding who?"

"Whomever you were looking for."

"I think you've got me confused with a detective. Or a grammar nazi. Or perhaps a prying twit who never took to heart the old adage about curious cats getting one of their lives snipped."

"How would it hurt you to just tell me if you found him?" she asked.

Ezekiel had a retort ready, but it occurred to him that as long as he didn't give her any information that the media would care about, he could be candid about some things.

What would a decent person do? he asked himself. And even if I figure that out, am I a decent person? Why should I be decent in the way I treat school officials?

Because Banshee really did help me when she got me into GRUT with Dr. Withunga.

"The person who was found last night," said Ezekiel, "was not a him."

"Do I assume that it was, therefore, a her?"

"Don't push your luck here, Banshee," he said aloud. Because why not use the name to her face, now that she knew what it was?

"Banshee," she said with a sigh. "I wonder if I still have time to make myself a costume."

"Do you go out trick-or-treating?"

"I dress up to answer the door and give out candy," said Banshee.

Ezekiel smiled at the idea of her passing out candy while dressed as a banshee. "Nobody knows what banshees look like."

"If they existed, one of them, at least, would look exactly like me."

"Good one," said Ezekiel. "It's much easier to put up with an unfortunate nickname if you accept it and embrace it."

And then he slipped out the door and closed it behind him. An empty gesture, walking out. He kind of liked Banshee. She had done him no harm and always treated him with respect. Why should he act as if he disdained her, when in fact he was beginning to trust her?

He wondered how Beth would have coped with rumors and curiosity about the rescue among the faculty and staff. Or if she was already dealing with much worse at the hospital, among the cops, and with people from Child Protective Services.

The only thing he wanted right now was to talk to Beth, find out what she was thinking, tell her about his own experience in finding Renee, in finding Beth herself. What if they plunked her into foster care and she no longer lived in this neighborhood? Wherever they put her, she would be alone the way that Ezekiel was alone at school today.

Besides worrying about Beth, and about himself-and-Beth, what kept coming back into his mind all afternoon was a question he should have asked Banshee and didn't: How did she know he was looking for a person? How could anything that happened yesterday already be known to her, without anything getting into the media?

Finally, as he was putting things away in his locker so he didn't have to haul them home, he realized: Banshee wasn't asking about his search for Beth. She wouldn't have heard anything about that. She was asking about the search for Renee Delamare, and that came about because at some point Shank probably talked to her about a missing "child," gender unspecified, and it was almost certainly from that conversation, and at Shank's urging, that Banshee connected Ezekiel with GRUT. So, when it came to rescuing Rapunzel from the tower last night, Banshee knew less than nothing.

That came to Ezekiel as a great relief. He remembered that last Monday, when he was fresh from finding Renee, school had been a let-down because nobody knew that he had done something productive with his micropower. The sane part of him knew that it would harm Renee and her family if everybody knew what happened, yet another part of him hungered for "validation from his community," as Beth would have put it.

Not that Downy Soft High School was in any sense his community. Without Beth, he didn't really know anybody and nobody knew him. They still shunned him because of his reputation as a thief. Nothing had happened, as far as the other students were concerned, to end his leperhood. He didn't need them to give him three cheers or a medal or even an extra dessert at lunch.

What he needed was Beth.

* * *

When Father got home from work that evening, Ezekiel greeted him with a question. "Do you think we should attempt another rescue?"

"I thought the ogres were all in custody," said Father.

"Is Beth still being 'observed' at the hospital?" asked Ezekiel. "Is she being grilled like a steak at the police station? I know what that's like."

"They don't suspect Beth of anything," said Father. "She'll have a very different experience."

"What if the prosecutor decides she has to testify anyway, and they're going to keep her in protective custody until the trial?"

"Instead of speculating," said Father, "would you like to hear what I found out today, when I talked to our lawyer?"

"We have a lawyer?"

"We do now," said Father. "A family law specialist, who I'm paying by dipping into your college fund. He laid out all the possibilities for me. Concerning Beth. I think you'll be relieved to know that in all likelihood, we will not be granted custody of Beth."

"It would have made walking to school more convenient," said Ezekiel.

"But you're not sure you wanted her as a sister," said Father. "Don't deny it, you'd be crazy not to wonder what it would do to our regular, organized life of bliss."

"Bliss," said Ezekiel. "I see what you did there."

"People call this the House of Bliss, don't they?" asked Father. "But without a family connection—a blood connection—they'd be quite uncomfortable putting Beth into a house with a teenage boy."

"Oh, like suddenly I'm dangerous?"

"Not dangerous," said Father. "In fact, they worry about the danger you'd be in. What if Beth got angry and accused you of making some kind of advance, something that made her feel unsafe?"

"I'd never," said Ezekiel, blushing.

"Exactly," said Father. "They want to protect her because of the damage already done by being kidnapped and exposed by those bastards, but they also remember the story of Potiphar's wife."

Ezekiel tried to remember a story about a potmaker's wife but …

"I can see that they must've taught that on a Sunday you weren't in church," said Father.

"Which would be almost all of them since Mother died," said Ezekiel.

"Potiphar was a great Egyptian general," said Father, "and Joseph, as a Hebrew slave, became a part of his household, and quickly rose to be among Potiphar's most trusted servants. But Potiphar's wife got the hots for him and when her husband was out inspecting the troops, she suggested to Joseph that they might do a little hanky. Or panky, the book of Genesis isn't clear. Joseph said no. She tore his cloak and began to scream that Joseph tried to rape her."

"Since Beth was probably driven mad by her experience, naturally she would accuse me," said Ezekiel. "Unless I was also driven mad and actually tried to interfere with her."

"Interfere?"

"I've read some of your English mysteries and police procedurals."

"Agatha Christie? Ruth Rendell?"

"Poirot, Marple, Wexford, Rumpole," said Ezekiel. "Who remembers authors' names?"

"So for Beth's and my mutual protection we can't be hospitable and take her into our house," said Ezekiel. "And since I'm her only known friend on Earth, and she's a total orphan, that means that wherever they put her, she'll be among strangers."

"That's what my lawyer said."

"Did you shoot the messenger?"

"No, he's still going to earn out his retainer. Because I asked for him to petition the court to bestow custody of the wee lassie on a family that lives near enough that we can remain a part of her life. Preferably, a home where she and you could continue to walk to and from school together. The lawyer pointed out that we had no standing. I pointed out that we both risked our lives to save her, she clearly matters to us, and we also have her trust, and why doesn't somebody ask her and see if she really wants to be cut off from you."

"It sounds like you were really eloquent."

"I wasn't. But it's the lawyer who gets paid for eloquence, not me."

"So saving an orphan's life doesn't give you legal standing to interfere in her custody, unless you hire an eloquent mouthpiece," said Ezekiel.

"I asked the question that I knew would be foremost in your mind."

"Can we visit her in the hospital?" asked Ezekiel.

"He's earning some of his fee by finding that out."

"I'm betting that he won't get permission from the hospital," said Ezekiel.

"He won't even ask the hospital. They don't make policy, they just follow rules. He also isn't going directly to Child Protective Services because their natural disposition is to assume that we want to get our greedy, poverty-stricken hands on her wealth."

"You're the person they can trust most with her money," said Ezekiel.

"Well, I'm not as safe as you, because I'm not sure you understand what money even is," said Father.

"The little thin ones are dimes, and they're one-tenth as worthless as pennies," said Ezekiel.

"Going to high school is really paying off for you."

"They're going to ask the police," said Ezekiel. "Because over the years, they've come to love us."

"The Downy Police Department is completely out of this because of the fact that the guy that was arrested worked there and the investigators haven't yet figured out how far the conspiracy reached. So it's the Greensboro Police Department that has Beth right now, and Guilford County Child Protective Services, plus the FBI, because Shank called me to tell me that he had come out of cover and the FBI was … he called it 'bigfooting'? … the whole case. So he has a lot of influence over the Greensboro Police right now because it's really his case and they were just assisting him."

"Man," said Ezekiel. "A mere kidnapping with intent to kill on camera, and they're making a federal case out of it."

"I wondered if you wanted to join me in seeing Beth at the hospital, where she's still recovering from exposure and massive abrasions plus two huge bruises shaped like my hands on her ankles, and a concussion on the back of her head from landing on concrete with only a very, very thin mattress to protect her."

"Let's go," said Ezekiel.

"Just so you know the plan," said Father, "I thought we'd ask her if she wanted us to smuggle in a meal for her, and then we'll go get the food and sneak it into her room, and then eat with her."

"If she wants to," said Ezekiel. "If she isn't still creeped out by the fact that we saw her so weak and vulnerable."

"Don't bring that up," said Father. "We never saw her weak. We saw her incredibly brave and then completely exhausted."

Ezekiel didn't even bother to answer. Did Father think his only child was a complete idiot?

Well, why wouldn't he?

They drove to the hospital and everything went according to plan, until she asked for takeout from The Meatball Shop on Stanton Street in Manhattan. "Best food I've ever eaten," she said. "And that time we went to New York, Mom took me to a bunch of equally fancy places."

"Fanciness equal to that of a meatball restaurant," said Father. "Ground beef. When there are steaks and roasts and lobsters and fishes to be had."

"They had chicken meatballs and pork meatballs, too," said Beth.

"Concussion, Dad," Ezekiel explained. "Let's go to Firehouse Subs and tell her we got her meatball sandwich from The Meatball Shop."

"I'll figure it out," said Beth.

"We'll tell you that you're hallucinating the Firehouse Sub bag and wrapper," said Ezekiel. "You'll never know the difference."

"We know how much you trust us now," said Father, "seeing as how we caught you when you tried to jump off the top floor."

"Not how it happened," said Beth. "My grip on reality is still firm."

It was good to be back with Beth. Firehouse Subs turned out to be OK with her. Ezekiel wasn't even surprised when Beth refused either of the meatball sandwiches they brought and instead chose the smoked turkey sub that Father had ordered for himself.

"Not a meatball?" asked Father.

"After you've had the best, you lose your taste for the pretty good," said Beth. "Besides, my favorite from The Meatball Shop was the veggie meatball."

At this, Father, a career carnivore, made gagging noises. Or hairball noises—Ezekiel knew that Dad made the same noise to represent both.

They didn't talk about the rescue in the tower beyond those few joking references—Ezekiel never even called her Rapunzel. Instead, Ezekiel and Father told her the story of finding Renee Delamare, which Beth had never had a chance to hear, on account of having been kidnapped before Ezekiel had touched Renee's Build-a-Bears, let alone found the girl.

"She gets the cave," said Beth. "I get the tower."

"Neither one of them easy to find," said Father, "without a very resourceful guy with a micropower."

"I figure you did as much to find Renee as I did," said Ezekiel, "on account of you pushing me and helping me and just talking things through with me last Saturday."

"So you forgive me for not throwing away that one bag of lost items?"

"I forgive and thank you for making me take those lost toys back to their owners so I remembered what it felt like to get … information. Guidance."

"GPS," said Father.

"So, what did I own that guided you? What was my Build-a-Bear?" asked Beth.

It took Ezekiel a moment to realize the only possible answer, and then he turned red and couldn't even stammer because he was pretty sure that she'd hate hearing him appoint himself as her most prized possession.

"It was Ezekiel himself," said Father, who apparently had no such qualms. "We realized—he realized—that your most valuable possession, which you had lost, the one that you would miss the most, was himself."

Beth looked at Ezekiel with no expression. "We have a bit of a lofty impression of ourself, do we?" she finally asked.

"It was between me and Charlotte's Web," said Ezekiel. "But you never walked Charlotte's Web to and from school, or ate lunch with it, or attended GRUT sessions with it, or refused to go away when it ordered you to."

"And that worked."

"Maybe it only worked like Dumbo's feather," said Ezekiel, "but when I thought of my task as being to return me to you rather than to try and find you, I started getting strong impressions. That's when I felt you dangling off that concrete ledge and struggling with all your strength to crawl back on."

That was the first time they really broached the subject of what Beth had been through. She closed her eyes.

"I know that I didn't actually have the same experience," said Ezekiel, "but I felt some glimmer of your fear. Your desperation. Not really a glimmer—it was pretty intense. I threw myself into struggling with you, by pulling myself up onto a lectern from the high side."

Beth kept her eyes closed.

"I shouldn't have mentioned it," said Ezekiel.

"I wasn't going to make it," said Beth. "I was slipping faster than I could claw my way onto the concrete. The surface was rough and I was ripping my hands and my belly on it and I clawed three nails right off my fingers—well, not completely, but they were so separated that the doctors took them off." Beth held up both hands and waggled her fingers to show the three whose tips were encased in gauze. "They tell me they'll eventually grow back," she said.

"I'm so sorry you went through that," said Father.

"I was slipping," she said. "All my strength wasn't enough to get me back up onto the ledge. And then … it was enough."

"Adrenalin," said Father.

"Or Ezekiel," said Beth. "Because I didn't have the strength to try any harder than I already had, and that was failing, and then suddenly without my finding any more strength, my hands held and I was able to worm my way up and I was safe. Or at least I was safe from falling, for the time being."

"And you think what I did might have … what, added to your efforts?"

"It felt like when you stand on your mom's feet and she kind of dances you around the room and you feel weightless, or at least lighter."

Ezekiel could only nod. It was his dad's feet that he had stood on to do that, but maybe Mom had done it too when he was too young to remember.

"I'm sorry," said Beth. "I didn't mean to mention your mom."

"And I'm so sorry about your mom," said Ezekiel. "I can't believe I spent weeks bemoaning how I was an orphan because my mother was killed right in front of me and all the time, you were dealing with the same thing, only worse, because you didn't have my dad, so you had to cope with everything on your own."

Beth's eyes were closed again.

"Enough about that," said Dad. "Let's just say that everybody in this room has been through some tough and scary … things, but here we are, breathing and talking and being, you know, people."

Beth's eyes opened. "Thanks for the sandwich," she said. "And mostly thanks for the Miss Vicki's jalapeño potato chips. They aren't big on empty calories here in the hospital, except in the form of Jell-O."

"If I helped you get back up onto the ledge," said Ezekiel, "I'm glad. And if I didn't help you at all, I'm still glad that you got back up onto the ledge. And I'm also glad that however it happened, the kidnapper who took you and who took Renee made that five-story drop and broke his head open on cinderblocks. That was the ugliest and most beautiful thing I've ever seen. Because some guys can't be left alive by decent people. That's just how it is, even if you're, like, anti-death-penalty."

"Which I'm not, as of Saturday," said Beth.

"Enough," said Dad. "She's tired. She just ate a turkey sandwich even though she kept casting covetous eyes on your meatballs, and turkey's tryptophans are making her sleepy."

"Plus I have serious brain damage," said Beth, "so I'm hallucinating that my only friend and his father brought me a Firehouse Sub in the hospital. Please take all the garbage that says Firehouse with you so the nurses don't yell at me."

"They're going to yell at you anyway," said Father. "Just thank them politely and smile at them when they're done chewing you out, and they'll tell everybody what a model patient you are."

"Thanks for offering to take me into your home," said Beth. "Even though it can't happen—Shank told me earlier—it meant a lot that you invited me. Now get out because I need to either sleep or cry and I don't want you here while I do either."

"I think she forgot to brush and floss," said Ezekiel loudly as he followed Father out of the room.

"Jalapeño works like fluoride," Father answered, and then the door was closed and they headed out through the labyrinth of Moses Cone Hospital until they got to the parking lot and searched for their car.

"Is the car lost?" asked Father. "Isn't this your specialty?"

"I don't find things I'm looking for," said Ezekiel. "I simply know who owns the lost things that I happen to find. And there it is, right there. It belongs to us. Well, you."

"It belongs to the bank," said Father, "but not for much longer. I'm going to use the money we would have spent on Beth's food and bedding and stuff to make extra car payments."

"You are a prudent man, Father," said Ezekiel. "But now that we know Beth's favorite was a vegetarian meatball, will you still let me be friends with her?"

Father made a show of shuddering, then backed the car out of its parking place.

20

Ezekiel Blast felt like a hero coming home, until he actually walked into the room where his regular GRUT group was already assembled.

"Too cool to arrive on time anymore, eh?" asked Mitch, though he smiled when he said it.

"I'm not even going to ask in what foul place on your person you carried my phone when you were 'borrowing' it," said Dahlia.

"Thanks for asking," said Ezekiel. "I kept it in my front pants pocket, until I needed to use it to wipe my butt."

Jannis rolled her eyes. "How did I get trapped back in seventh grade?"

"Ninth," said Ezekiel. "What's wrong with this picture? Why are you ragging on me? Isn't this what GRUT is for, to help us improve our skills and increase our knowledge about micropowers? So, thanks for assembling the supergroup, Dr. Withunga, and thanks to those who came with me even if you didn't like my taking your phone, because I got clearer images than I've ever had before, and in case you were wondering, my dad and I found her, got her out of the room she was trapped in, and Beth is doing fine. Having the phone saved our lives, by the way, so I'm sorry for stealing but I'm glad I had the phone."

"Come on, Zekey boy," said Skunk. "They're just poking you because they're, like, jealous. Your thing is looking more like a superpower every day."

"It's a micropower, just like yours," said Ezekiel.

"Except my ability to purify the air hasn't ever saved anybody's life," said Skunk.

"Lieutenant Shank said that Dahlia might have yawned one of the bad guys till he tripped and they caught him."

Dahlia scoffed at that. "He tripped. We don't know if I made him yawn or if yawning made him trip."

"It's Shank's theory that people who are at maximum yawn can't run through a meadow at twilight, not without tripping," said Ezekiel. "So, good work."

Dahlia shook her head. "If I could really weaponize this thing I'd be an only child, long since."

"It's more like confusing the enemy, not hurting anybody," said Ezekiel. "If he hadn't been running away, then he would have stood there yawning as the police arrested him, so he'd look bored. If you don't care whether you yawned him into submission, fine, but I thought we might work on discovering just what your range is, because what if you could harmlessly disable a perp who's trying to get away?"

"Ride along with the cops, Dahlia," said Mitch. "If somebody gets hostile and pulls a gun on them, or even tries to swing at them, maybe you could yawn them right onto the ground."

"So far I use it to avoid horrible dates," said Dahlia. "If a guy starts to ask me out, he suddenly yawns so wide he can't finish a sentence."

"You don't date?" asked Jannis.

"Sorry, I only yawnify guys I don't want to have ask me out," said Dahlia. "If they can't ask, I can't say no, so it saves their fragile egos in case they, like, grow up to found Microsoft or Google. Then they'll remember me as the girl they almost asked out in high school."

"Always thinking ahead," said Mitch. "That's why I'm always kind to my spiders, so that in case I get caught in a Shrink Ray and I'm being attacked by savage giant ants, my spiders can come and rescue me."

Dr. Withunga finally decided to intervene. "Have we had our fun, boys and girls?" she asked. "Because this really is an important day for all of us. What did we learn from Ezekiel's rescue of Beth?"

"Love conquers all," said Jannis.

"When we all get together," said Skunk, "we all get stronger."

"If you climb over a lectern like you thought it was Mount Midoriyama, it makes God happy," said Aaron.

Aaron, Withunga's son. He had never come to a regular GRUT session before, and, true to form, he was making his debut by sitting low in a chair at the back, so Ezekiel hadn't noticed him till now.

Ezekiel nodded gravely at him, and Aaron gave him a look that might have had a hint of a smile somewhere in it.

"Thinking and testing and practicing, they really help," said Ezekiel. "I spent so many years hiding from my ability to find things that it didn't develop into anything. Beth worked with me for just one day, one morning, and we learned stuff that I had never known. It just helps to have somebody doing it with you."

"Like having somebody spot you at the gym," said Skunk.

"Like you've ever been inside a gym," said Jannis.

"The best-smelling gym in the whole world," said Skunk. "It about wore me out before I left."

"I don't expect you all to be friends," said Dr. Withunga. "But allies, now. Why not allies? Why not strengthen each other?"

"Here come the Mops, like a bat out of hell, someone gets in our way, someone don't feel so well," sang Dahlia.

"West Side Story, girl," said Jannis, giving her an air fistbump. "Bernstein and Sondheim."

"I adapted the lyric," said Dahlia. "I wish writing lyrics were my micropower."

"Maybe it is," began Aaron, "and people only yawn because ..."

It sounded like he was heading for a real zinger, but he didn't get to finish because he started yawning like a post-prandial lion.

"Tonsils are in fine shape," reported Jannis, half-rising as if she were looking down Aaron's throat, though he was across the room.

"We don't use our micropowers against each other," said Dr. Withunga. "That was rule number one."

"I was using it to protect everybody," said Dahlia. "What's he doing here? He's not a member of GRUT."

"He's Dr. Withunga's son," said Skunk.

"So this is day care now?" asked Dahlia.

"Aaron has a micropower," said Dr. Withunga, "and after our supergroup session he decided to attend one of our meetings. Since you routinely taunt other people, Dahlia, I would think you'd be able to take it without retaliation. So why shouldn't I suspend you from GRUT for making Aaron yawn?"

"If he's a member then I'm sorry," said Dahlia. "How could I know?"

"Because he's here," said Dr. Withunga. "I don't invite observers."

"What about Beth?" asked Dahlia defiantly. "She was here for however many meetings, and that was only because she was joined at the hip with Ezekiel."

"Beth also has a micropower," said Dr. Withunga.

"She never said so," said Mitch.

"She doesn't know," said Dr. Withunga.

"So you discovered micropower radar?" asked Skunk.

"What do you think Aaron's micropower is?" asked Dr. Withunga.

Everyone turned to look at him. He was still recovering from his yawn, pressing his hands against the place right in front of his ears where the jaw joint had opened way too wide.

"He tells you who has micropowers?" asked Ezekiel.

"He's been doing it since he was about five," said Dr. Withunga. "Like you, Ezekiel, he manifested early. Because of what he saw in people—who has micropowers and who doesn't—I started researching micropotency and here we are."

"Did he identify us all?" asked Skunk.

Dr. Withunga nodded. "Even if you came here by another route, he verified you."

"I never met him till the other day," said Ezekiel.

"He was in the corridor the first time you got called in to see Ms. Banerjee," said Dr. Withunga. "You wouldn't have been invited if he hadn't passed you."

"Well, what good is it if he can't tell people what their micropower is?"

"I don't think I ever said he couldn't," said Dr. Withunga. "But even if he can, it's better for people to find their micropower by self-examination. He told me that I had a micropower long before I realized that I was aware of the navel configuration of everybody around me. I've been working on it since, which is why I can now detect the umbilical morphology of people I didn't even know were there. I learned that by playing hide-and-seek with Aaron."

"She's such a cheater," mumbled Aaron.

"That was back when he was cute and nice. He'll be nice again someday, I think," added Dr. Withunga.

"But he can kiss 'cute' good-bye," said Dahlia.

Aaron might have retorted, but since he was still rubbing joints that were sore from the last yawn, he thought better of it.

"You do understand that you're a bully, Dahlia," said Ezekiel. "Being mean to people who can't strike back."

Dahlia glared at him, but Ezekiel did not yawn.

"What we need to do today," said Dr. Withunga, "is listen to Ezekiel's account of everything significant that happened during his search for Beth. Nothing about the actual rescue is relevant to us," she added, "because your micropower was used only to locate her. After that, it was whatever wits and strength you and your father and Beth could muster, right?"

Ezekiel shook his head. "It was whatever my father could muster, and Beth herself. I was like the dimwitted cousin who barely knows what's going on."

"I doubt it," said Dr. Withunga, "but start at the beginning. Start, perhaps, by telling us about last Saturday morning when you and Beth worked on returning lost toys to their owners."

"After that can I go?" asked Dahlia. "Because I was there for most of it."

"There for some of it," said Dr. Withunga, "but oblivious to everything that Ezekiel was thinking and doing and sensing. And you definitely weren't there when Ezekiel and Beth were working out how his micropower works. Be patient, Dahlia. Listening to this will benefit everybody, if you listen with care and intelligence."

Then Dr. Withunga's hand flipped upward, immediately silencing whatever witless comment anyone might have been about to make concerning Dahlia and the necessity of listening with intelligence. That gesture was the signal that they were no longer in teasing mode, they were working now, and everybody settled down.

* * *

Ezekiel Blast got back to Downy in the van, having spoken very little to the driver. Ezekiel wasn't sure who the man worked for. Dr. Withunga's university? The Downy school system? The van had North Carolina plates, but not government ones. But that meant nothing—just like ships with Liberian registry or corporations officially doing business in Delaware, it was merely a matter of convenience what state's plates were on the car. Was the driver with the FBI, like Shank? This must be the worst assignment ever, chauffeuring a snotnose high school freshman to and from what amounted to a therapy session in Virginia. But maybe that's how you got entrusted with bigger jobs—by flawlessly executing the scutwork assignments you were given when you were new in the Bureau.

All of this was speculation, because if he started asking the driver questions, either the driver would continue to say nothing, which would be awkward and embarrassing to Ezekiel, or the driver would become chatty, and would think that answering Ezekiel's questions entitled him to ask questions of his own. And since Ezekiel wasn't interested in providing answers, and wasn't really all that interested in finding out the secret agony of a van driver's life, silence turned out to be the best option during the entire drive.

As always, Father had supper ready. Because Dr. Withunga was scrupulous about ending on time, and because the van driver adhered rigidly to speed limits, Ezekiel got home from GRUT sessions at exactly the same time each week.

"I don't need to set the timer on the oven," said Father, "because you walk into the house exactly when the filets are supposed to come out."

The pan in the oven contained meat, and it smelled terrific, but it bore no resemblance to filet mignon.

"I see you chose not to wrap them in bacon this time," said Ezekiel.

"Why should a pig die so I can eat beef?" asked Father. "And if it's a good beef, the bacon is only an unfortunate distraction."

Ezekiel could almost have recited it along with him, not because Father was tedious about repeating it, but because it was simply true. In fact, it might have been Ezekiel who said it first, back when he started getting his own opinions about what meat did and did not need. And Father tried to respect Ezekiel's preferences, except when Ezekiel decided back last spring that ketchup was a perfectly reasonable variant on steak sauce. Father replied that a little red wagon was a perfectly reasonable variant on the landing gear of a 747. Ketchup continued to be reserved for french fries.

They were halfway through the meal—and Ezekiel made it a point to eat his peas and broccoli first, to prove he was grown up enough to not make a fight about every stupid thing—when the doorbell rang. It was fully dark outside, and the porch light was off, so whoever had come wasn't good at estimating how welcome their visit was going to be.

Ezekiel opened the door and it was Beth.

He stepped back, and Beth came into the house and then followed the smells into the kitchen.

"One more steak is ready, unless you like blood in your meat," said Father.

"After slurping my fill of Jell-O?" asked Beth. "You overestimate my capacity."

But to Ezekiel, it was surprising that she would even have a capacity. Always thin, her days in captivity had rendered her emaciated-looking, though that was probably just dehydration. Though the hospital had probably spent a lot of effort on trying to get her rehydrated. Maybe almost getting killed and killing a guy yourself was a weight loss program that could really catch on.

"Well, sit down anyway and keep company with us," said Father.

"I'm sorry, sir," said Beth. "I can't stay."

"Then I'm puzzled as to why you came."

"I need to take a walk with Ezekiel," said Beth.

Ezekiel immediately imagined himself walking along a sidewalk, hand in hand with Beth, swinging their arms and counting cadence like soldiers in training.

"I'm willing to wager," said Father, "that you have a destination in mind."

"Not terribly far," said Beth, "but we have to be sure to get there before everybody's in bed."

"It's only eight o'clock."

"There's a child involved," said Beth.

Ezekiel realized. "You want to meet Renee."

"I have something to offer her," said Beth.

Father chimed in. "If I drive you most of the way, you have time to eat some of the cookies I made today."

"Instead of that," said Beth, "could you put them on a tray and cover them in cling wrap so I can take them as a house gift when I drop in?"

"If you don't want my cookies, why do you think they would?" asked Father.

Beth just tilted her head a little.

"It's not about whether they want cookies or like cookies or like my cookies," said Father.

"Then what is it about?" asked Ezekiel.

"Not coming empty-handed to a house of fear and pain," said Beth.

"But it isn't anymore," said Ezekiel. "Renee is home."

The other two just looked at the table, letting Ezekiel's words hang there.

"Well, I'm definitely through eating, since this non-conversation is taking away my appetite," said Ezekiel. "I take it we're walking?"

"Only if you want to walk around the mean streets of Downy late at night," said Father. "My offer to give you a drive is still on the table."

"It's kind of a long walk to Delamares' place," said Ezekiel.

"Still a wimp," said Beth.

"Did you walk here?" asked Ezekiel. "And if so, where were you walking from? Moses Cone Hospital?"

"I'm a determined walker," said Beth, "but I'm not actually insane."

"Shank drove you," said Ezekiel.

"And I didn't even have to sit in the back like a perp or a governor," said Beth.

"I like your juxtaposition of categories," said Father.

"If I know Shank, that means he's still out there and he could drive us to Delamares'," said Ezekiel.

"I offered first," said Father.

"And I have to take back what I just said," Ezekiel added. "Shank would not want to drive us to Delamares' house, because he would prefer to follow us unobserved."

"He is a stealthy man," said Father.

"When he thinks people need backup," said Beth, "he likes to stay where backup belongs."

"In the back," said Ezekiel. The two of them laughed together.

"I'm beginning to understand this friendship," said Father.

"Are you?" asked Beth.

"You do understand that thinking like Ezekiel is not generally regarded as a sign of mental health," said Father.

"Then it's a good thing that it's Ezekiel who's beginning to think like me," said Beth.

* * *

Father dropped them a block from the Delamare house so that there'd be no visible sign that they hadn't walked the whole way. And also, he said, so that he could see if Shank made himself visible at some point.

"Maybe he's not following us," said Ezekiel. Then he and Beth laughed that same dry chuckle.

"Dr. Withunga would know where his belly button is," said Beth.

"Let's go see if Renee is still awake," said Ezekiel.

"Let's see if Renee has been able to sleep for the past few days," said Beth.

Which made Ezekiel wonder if she was extrapolating from her own experience. Maybe Beth was also having trouble sleeping.

That one block was a longer walk than Ezekiel had expected, and the night wasn't as cold as he had thought it would be when he chose the jacket to put on.

"Let's walk around the block another time. I'm not sweaty enough," said Ezekiel, as they stepped up onto the porch.

"You're sweaty enough to meet my requirements," said Beth.

"I'm not sweaty enough to have walked from my house."

"We're not visiting Sherlock Holmes, Ezekiel," she said. "They won't be looking for clues." She pressed the doorbell.

Mr. Delamare recognized Ezekiel at once, and Ezekiel introduced Beth. Immediately Beth took over the conversation. "I was hoping your daughter would still be awake," said Beth.

"Yes, she is," said Mr. Delamare. "But she isn't exactly receiving visitors these days."

Beth nodded gravely. "I know the feeling. But since I was recently kidnapped by the same goon that took her, I think I'm the only person on Earth who actually knows something about what she went through."

By now Mrs. Delamare was beside her husband in the doorway. "Walter," she said, "these aren't trick-or-treaters, they're guests."

"We weren't invited," said Beth, "and Mr. Delamare is being appropriately careful about your daughter's feelings."

"What do you plan to say to her?" asked Mr. Delamare.

"I don't have a plan," said Beth. "But I think I can reassure her."

"Do you think we haven't tried?" asked Mr. Delamare.

"You don't sound like any child I've ever talked with before," said Mrs. Delamare.

"She's fourteen," said Ezekiel. "She's a little small for her age."

"You look like someone I'd expect to show up if Renee were having a birthday party."

"I'm more than twice her age," said Beth, "and I'm in tenth grade, because they figured that since I already look as if I skipped five or six grades, I might as well skip a couple more and study things that are more in line with my abilities."

Ezekiel couldn't figure out how Beth was doing this, because nothing about her actual words seemed particularly reassuring, yet the Delamares had calmed down and seemed to be amused by her words, or maybe her tone. She was winning them over.

Is this her micropower? Ezekiel wondered. Because somehow that first day when I kept telling her to go away, she kept right on walking with me and talking to me and I kept right on allowing her to stay beside me. If she wants somebody to do something, then as long as she keeps talking, they want to do it.

She could probably buy cigarettes and beer without showing i.d., if she just kept talking long enough. Which may explain why she was able to keep people from coming over to check on her mom.

"We've kept you two out here long enough," said Mrs. Delamare, gently pushing her husband aside. "Walter is careful and he's protective, but I think we both believed Detective Shank when he told us you'd do no harm by talking to our daughter tonight."

"I mean no harm," said Beth. "But I'm obviously going to make her think back on what happened to her, and if she's anything like me, she might well cry."

Ezekiel tried to imagine Beth crying.

Then he remembered that he didn't have to imagine it. He could remember it.

The Delamares ushered them into the same living room where Ezekiel had sat before, when he first visited them. When the Delamares left the room to get their daughter, Ezekiel turned to Beth. "The introductions are made. Are you sure you want me here?"

"I can't do this without you," said Beth, and Ezekiel realized that she, too, hated thinking back on what had happened.

Beth had placed herself on one end of the couch, and sure enough, when Renee came in she walked straight for the other end—apparently her regular place—and plunked herself down, with one leg tucked up under her. There were no Build-a-Bears in evidence. Maybe they lived in her room now. Or maybe they were on the porch. Or maybe the Delamares had put them in a safe deposit box at the bank so that the next time Renee was kidnapped, there'd be no chance of the kidnappers dragging the bears along.

"Did your parents tell you about me?" Beth asked her, almost immediately.

Renee didn't say anything.

Beth waited patiently.

Mr. Delamare broke first. "Honey, she asked you a—"

"It's all right," said Beth. "She doesn't have to talk. Because I'm just going to tell her something very simple."

Renee didn't look at her. It was plain that simple or not, she didn't want to hear it.

"Just so you know that I really did go through the same experience, I can tell you that the drug they gave us made all the food taste like licking a bicycle tire."

Renee nodded and then kind of smiled. Not because the memory was funny, but because Beth had put it in such a colorful way.

"Ezekiel saved us both by finding us," said Beth. "He got your bears to tell him where you were. And he got my favorite book, Charlotte's Web, to help find me."

Ezekiel rather liked this way of spinning the story. It wasn't any magical talent on Ezekiel's part—the bears had simply told him what only they could have known. And she wasn't even lying, not really.

And then he realized that this was her exact micropower: People trusted her. People believed her.

Renee still looked skeptical, but she shrugged and sat a little farther back on the couch.

"I just wanted you to know," said Beth, "that the bad guys are never going to come after you again."

Renee seemed to shrink deeper into herself.

"They arrested the most important guy," said Beth, "but the guy who actually took us and injected us with that needle—he's not going to hurt anybody ever again."

Renee looked at her with tears in her eyes—Ezekiel could see them glistening.

"Because he's dead," said Beth. "I saw him dead. Ezekiel saw him dead. His days of kidnapping little girls are over."

Renee just looked at her. Beth said nothing more. Renee said nothing. Mr. and Mrs. Delamare were standing there wringing their hands.

Beth glanced at Ezekiel, and as surely as if they had rehearsed it, Ezekiel spoke up. "He was as dead as a guy can be," said Ezekiel. "Completely dead."

A moment. Another moment. And then Renee burst into tears, huge sobs wracking her body, pulling up her bathrobe to cover her face, each sob making her gasp in air and then cry it back out so loudly that it was almost screaming.

Mrs. Delamare ran to her, sat between Renee and Beth on the couch, and tried to gather her daughter in her arms.

But Renee ducked out from under her embrace and slid off onto the floor and ran over to Beth and flung herself on top of her. "You killed him!" she screeched, and then it became clear that somehow her crying had turned into, or had always been, laughter. Or maybe it was both. It was an emotion so powerful it couldn't be contained. "He's dead! He's dead!" Renee cried.

Ezekiel was thinking, Beth didn't say that she had killed the guy, but Renee somehow knew it.

"Sure is," said Beth. "You're safe."

Mr. Delamare was crying, tears coming right down his cheeks, but he wasn't covering his face at all, because he couldn't take his eyes off his little girl.

And Mrs. Delamare was crying, too, and like her husband she didn't cover her face. Nor did she dab at her eyes in order to preserve her makeup.

These people know the moment of catharsis when it comes, thought Ezekiel. They know what it means to have somebody kill the bogeyman, the monster under the bed, the troll that invades back porches and steals away little children. Ding dong, the son-of-a-bitch is dead.

Somehow, there in her hospital room, or maybe talking to Shank, or maybe just waking up after a nightmare of her own, Beth had realized that she had one gift to give Renee, and she got Shank to bring her to the Bliss family so she could drag Ezekiel along as her witness. She planned this and she carried it out flawlessly and he was in awe of her all over again.

Ezekiel thought about how Beth had pushed the guy. He tried to imagine the physics of it, the way he had when he imagined Father grabbing Beth as she dangled her legs over the side. If Beth had run and pushed the guy with her arms, then if she fell after him it would have been head first and she couldn't possibly have caught herself. So she must have done a flying leap, pushing him with her feet.

And because she hit him feet-first, that put the whole upper half of her body inside the room, so that even though her legs went over the edge, she could claw with her hands, her arms, her fingernails, and keep from falling long enough for Ezekiel to mimic her actions, add his strength to her strength, his grip on the lectern to her grip on the concrete floor, until he could pull himself up over the edge of the lectern, until she had pulled herself back up inside her prison cell.

Beth didn't need to tell that story because Renee already had enough fears and nightmares. She didn't need to have Beth add to the total.

That story would remain Beth's own nightmare. Nobody could take that one away because nobody could kill gravity, and it was gravity that had tried to tug her down from the tower and break her open on those cinderblocks below.

Beth reached out and took Renee by the shoulders. They looked at each other eye to eye, both of them standing now in front of the couch, and Beth gravely said to her, "Renee, I know you've been having bad dreams."

Renee nodded.

"Maybe they'll go away now that you know Pigface is dead."

Renee echoed the name with loathing. "Pigface."

"That's what I call him, in my mind," said Beth. "But maybe we should think of him as Humpty-Dumpty, because he's broken like an egg, and nobody can put him together again. If you have a dream about him, you just reach into that dream and turn him into Humpty-Dumpty, lying there in pieces that nobody can fix."

This was close enough to the vivid memory of a broken skull that Ezekiel carried in his head that he was afraid it would be disturbing. But Renee thought it was funny—she was already laughing at the image. The two girls were smiling together.

266 | ORSON SCOTT CARD

"You're the boss of your dreams," said Beth. "From now on, if you don't want to be afraid of Pigface, you just break his head like an egg."

The words she didn't say rang in Ezekiel's mind: Break his head like an egg, because that's how I killed him.

I killed him. That was something Beth was carrying around inside her. No matter how justified, how brave, how vital it was, Beth had deliberately pushed a man over a five-story drop. Almost died herself in the process, but she had calculatedly taken the life of another person.

And Ezekiel was fine with it. Renee was way more than fine with it.

But was Beth really fine with it?

No way to guess the answer to that. Beth probably didn't even know the answer. Ezekiel knew that if he asked, she'd ridicule him for even wondering and she'd reassure him that she was so fine with that.

But Ezekiel knew that Dad wasn't even fine with killing meat animals. He had started out in a slaughterhouse. He only told that story once. No, wait. It was Mother who had told the story, when Ezekiel was barely old enough to understand it. Father had the job of killing the steers at the slaughterhouse. One at a time they come up the ramp to his position and he kills them and they flop over and slide down to where the process of skinning and gutting them begins, other guys turning them from a once-living body into a side of beef.

"He just had to quit doing it," said Mother. "Your father is too tender-hearted for a job like that. There's something terrible about killing a living thing, you see. Even though you have to do it, even though human beings have always had to kill animals to get meat, your father isn't the kind of man who can look a creature in the eye, a creature that's breathing, with a beating heart, not understanding what's happening, not even afraid, or at least not as afraid as it ought to be—your father isn't the kind of man who can kill that creature. He did it for a whole week because we had a little baby and he had to earn a living. But by the end of that week, he had talked his way into a job in the meat department at Food Lion and sure, he cuts up sides of beef all day and helps people choose what they need and tells them how to cook it and yes, his hands are covered with blood, or at least his apron is, and his gloves are. But he does not kill the steer because that's too much of a burden for him to carry."

That whole memory flashed through Ezekiel's mind in a moment, and he realized that this was why he knew that Beth was not actually all right, because it was still a grave matter to take another life, even the life of a deeply evil man.

But Beth had not told that story tonight, not to the Delamares, not to their frightened little girl. Renee somehow understood a glimpse of it, but Beth hadn't given her the whole picture. The kicking, the falling, nearly dying herself, but then seeing the man sprawled there, neck broken, skull spilling out brains and blood.

"I'm the boss of my dreams," said Renee. Beth was making her repeat it. "Nobody can scare me in my dreams because I'll turn their heads into eggs and blow them all up!"

"You're going to have one really messy dream kitchen," said Beth. "All that blown-up egg everywhere. That's your real nightmare, kid. Because somebody's going to have to clean that all up."

"Your dream father will take care of that," said Mr. Delamare. "You just turn your back and walk right out of the room, and I'll clean up all the exploded eggs."

Ezekiel could see a spark of resentment alight in Mrs. Delamare's face—how dare Walter make himself a hero in Renee's future dreams?

But before that spark could turn into a flame, Ezekiel did what he could to put it out. "That's what fathers are for," said Ezekiel. "I know all about what mothers are for because when my mother died, there was nobody who could really do those things. But I was lucky I still had my father. Because fathers can come into your nightmares and make everything better."

"Does your father do that for you?" asked Renee.

"I don't have many nightmares now," said Ezekiel, "but yes, that's what he always did. And not even in my dreams. When I woke up he was really there, a real man who lived in my house. And you know the best thing? Even though my mother was dead, she was still there in some of my dreams, in the good ones, she was there to put her arms around me

268 | ORSON SCOTT CARD

and tell me that she loves me and she's proud of me and I'm doing just fine. Only your mother is real. She's really here when you wake up, just like your dad."

And that did it. That put out that spark of resentment in Mrs. Delamare's face.

It didn't do much for Ezekiel's face, because he had never told anybody about his dreams of his mother, and even though he hadn't really told the Delamares any details, Ezekiel had thought of those memories and dreams and just like always, they made him cry.

I've been doing way too much crying these past few days, thought Ezekiel. If I'd known that I'd end up crying like this, I don't know if I would have come with Beth on this expedition.

Yes I would, he answered himself. I would have come no matter what, because Beth asked me to.

There wasn't much more talk. Mrs. Delamare suggested that it was way past Renee's bedtime and shouldn't they go and say her prayers and get her last drink of water and go to bed?

As Mrs. Delamare led Renee out of the room, she turned and beckoned to Beth. "I think Beth wants to see your room, don't you, Beth? Don't you want her to see your room?"

Well, duh. So Beth trotted after Renee and Mrs. Delamare, so Ezekiel was alone with Mr. Delamare.

And without even thinking, Ezekiel started talking. "That girl," he said, "that Beth, she has a hard enough life being so small for her age, but it's a lot worse. Her father walked out on them when she was really young, she barely remembers him. And then her mother died this past May, and Beth was determined not to go into foster care, so she hid out and used her mother's ATM card and paid all the bills and basically became her own mom, walking everywhere to do grocery shopping and buy school clothes and whatever it took. It wasn't until she was kidnapped and we rescued her that anybody realized that she was all alone in the world."

It all came out in a rush, and he deliberately left out any mention of Beth's mother's body desiccating in the master bedroom, because it wasn't part of the picture he wanted to paint.

"My dad offered to take her in, and she was all for it, and so was I, but Child Protective Services had a problem with putting her into a home with a single father and a teenage boy, especially since I'm kind of twice her size, so even though Beth and I knew nothing would go wrong, Child Protective Services has rules for a reason, because stuff does go wrong sometimes, so now they're going to find a different foster home for Beth. Only it's hard because she's so small, and for somebody who looks like she's maybe seven years old she has such a smart mouth on her because she's, you know, a teenager. She's a good person, she's absolutely responsible because you don't keep all the bills paid for six months if you think life is all fun and games, but I don't know how they're ever going to find a home for her."

Mr. Delamare gazed steadily at Ezekiel. "Is this why you came over here tonight?"

"I came because Beth told me to, because she needed me as a witness. I really saw the dead body, so I told the truth when she needed me to. I'm telling you now about Beth because while I was watching her with your daughter, it occurred to me that I once heard that you and Mrs. Delamare wanted more children than just one."

"One is fine," said Mr. Delamare.

"And even though Renee will almost certainly become much taller than Beth as time goes by, Beth will be off to college anyway in a couple of years. And don't worry about the expense, Beth's grades and Beth's brain will get her a full-ride scholarship somewhere. It's just a matter of keeping her out of foster care while she finishes school. Maybe keeping her in this part of town, so she doesn't change schools. And lest you imagine that I'm saying this out of the goodness of my heart, my motive is totally selfish, because I'm not only Beth's only friend at school, she's my only friend, and if I can't walk to school with her in the morning and have lunch with her and then walk her safely home after school, I won't have a life. So I'm looking out for myself, here."

"I'm not sure we live within walking distance of Downy High School," said Mr. Delamare.

"You've never seen how Beth walks," said Ezekiel. "And when her house sells she'll have enough money to finance her college education anyway, she just needs somebody trustworthy to sign off on things for her because she won't be eighteen for another four years."

"So it won't cost me anything, ever," said Mr. Delaware, "and it's really to help you out and not for her at all, because you don't love this friend of yours, you just need her to stave off loneliness, and she really doesn't want to go into foster care so she'll be very well-behaved, and she can take care of herself completely so the only thing we need to do is sign things for her and give her a legal address and a bed. Have I understood this?"

Ezekiel got the irony in "you don't love this friend of yours," but he wasn't about to quibble because, yes, Mr. Delamare understood the whole situation. "I've got nothing to add," said Ezekiel.

"So here's the thing you weren't taking into account," said Mr. Delamare. "When I saw what Beth did for my little girl tonight, I loved her more than I've ever loved anyone except my wife and my daughter, and I promised myself right then and there that if Beth ever needed anything from me, she'd have it, and if she just wanted something from me, she'd have it, because you know what? Now I understand all those fairy tales, where the king says, 'And for your reward you can have anything you want, even up to half my kingdom.'"

"Oh," said Ezekiel. "So you didn't need me to—"

"I needed you to tell me Beth's situation, yes, I did need that. But you didn't have to sell me. I have eyes; I know her life was hard before she lost her mom, and it's harder now, and she went through the same thing my daughter did. But that young woman already owns me, heart and soul."

Then Mr. Delamare stood up, so Ezekiel stood up also. Mr. Delamare stuck out his hand. Ezekiel took it. It wasn't a handshake. It was a grip.

"And Beth isn't the only one I feel that way about," said Mr. Delamare. "Just so we're clear about that. Because I know who brought my little girl back home to me."

"Yeah, but I don't need anything."

"Someday maybe you will," said Mr. Delamare. "And when I'm through having my lawyers chat with Child Protective Services, I'm betting that there are going to be some icy mornings this winter when you'll be glad when I show up in front of your house with Beth in the car, to give the two of you a ride to school."

"If there's actual snow or ice," said Ezekiel, "they close the schools." But because Mr. Delamare was still gripping him, Ezekiel nodded and said, "Thank you."

Mr. Delamare let go of his hand.

Mrs. Delamare came back into the room. "Walter, I'm not sure what to do. Renee asked Beth to lie down beside her and then she asked her to get under the covers and now she's fallen asleep with such a grip on Beth's hand that I'm not sure but what she'll cut off the poor girl's circulation."

Mr. Delamare turned to Ezekiel. "So who do I call to tell them Beth is spending the night with us?"

"I don't know," said Ezekiel. "Except Shank. He's the one who brought her to my house. And we're pretty sure he followed when Dad drove us to a place about a block from here."

"Bet he's still close," said Mr. Delamare.

"Sir," said Ezekiel. "Just one ... just one thing."

Mr. and Mrs. Delamare waited. Ezekiel had no idea how this was going to go over, but it had to be said.

"Beth isn't some kind of service animal. She doesn't exist just to meet Renee's needs. She's this incredible person and I want her to be happy the way you want Renee to be happy and I just had to say it because she isn't just another Build-a-Bear. She needs to be in a home where she's regarded as another daughter, almost an adult, and—"

Mrs. Delamare put her palm against Ezekiel's cheek. "Oh, how I wish I had had a friend like you, growing up. Yes, we do understand that we're not acquiring Beth like a plush toy to keep our daughter happy." She looked at her husband. "I'm guessing that you've had a conversation?"

"She's an orphan and Child Protective Services doesn't have a clue what to do with her."

"I think we'll qualify as foster parents," said Mrs. Delamare.

Ezekiel nodded gravely.

"My daughter doesn't need a toy or a service animal," said Mrs. Delamare. "She needs a friend who might just turn into a sister. Is that good enough, Ezekiel?"

"It is," said Ezekiel.

"And if Beth is here, I expect that you and your father will be here, too, from time to time."

"That would be nice," said Ezekiel.

"And if your dad brings us a perfect cut of meat now and then, I make a mean osso bucco and you will weep over my pot roast."

"No exaggeration," said Mr. Delamare.

"And my name is Eva. Evie."

"And I'm Walter," said Mr. Delamare.

"My parents are kind of old-fashioned," said Ezekiel. "They didn't insist on my saying 'sir' and 'ma'am' all the time, but they never let me call adults by their first names, even when they insist."

"That's fine," said Mr. Delamare. "But the day will come when you're a full-fledged adult and on that day, my name is Walter. Am I clear?"

Ezekiel nodded. But he couldn't help wondering how long gratitude and respect would last. Everything fades and goes away. But while you have it, be glad of it.

Apparently Mr. Delamare had been locating Shank's number on his mobile phone, because now he lifted it to his ear. "You anywhere close?" he asked the phone. "I thought so. I've got one kid who needs a ride home to his father, and another who has been roped into staying the night. Kind of a slumber party." He listened for another moment, and Ezekiel saw headlights pulling up in front of the house.

"Fastest Uber driver on earth," said Mr. Delamare into the phone.

Ezekiel wanted to say good-bye to Beth. He wanted to be the one to tell her what had just happened. And if she didn't like the idea, he wanted her to be able to yell at him for meddling.

But it would be better if the Delamares made the offer themselves. Beth could handle the situation. She could handle anything.

Out in the car, as soon as Ezekiel pulled the door shut, Shank said, "It takes about four minutes to get to your house, and I'm going to hear the whole story, so you'd better talk fast."

"Better idea," said Ezekiel. "Come on inside and I'll tell you and my dad at the same time."

21

The next day at school, Ezekiel Blast let it slip that he thought the cafeteria food tasted fine.

"You make fun of it just like all the other kids," said Beth.

"No, I make fun of it much more effectively, cleverly, and memorably than all the other kids."

"So it's a competition thing."

"They only give out participation trophies," said Ezekiel. "You can't win, you can't lose. You just have to eat the cafeteria food and say what comes to mind."

"I see why I can't make fun of it," said Beth. "I don't eat it."

"I've watched you eat here practically every day," said Ezekiel.

"I hope you enjoyed the show. I try to chew with mastery and confidence," said Beth, "and I almost never let a thin trickle of drool seep out onto my chin."

"Cool that you gave a Yelp review to your own mouth," said Ezekiel.

"If I don't, who will?"

"What about your nightmares?" asked Ezekiel. "Have they stopped?"

Beth didn't bat an eye about the abrupt change of subject. "Until my nightmares wake you up at night, they're pretty much none of your business."

"You were so good with Renee," said Ezekiel. "You knew what she needed."

"What about your nightmares, Ezekiel Blast?" asked Beth. "As long as we're tourists in Prying Personal Question Land."

"My only nightmare was seeing my mother hit by a car," said Ezekiel. "I don't have that one very often anymore."

"I don't have nightmares," said Beth. "But the tradeoff is, I don't dream at all."

"Everybody dreams."

"If I do, I don't remember it, which is the same as not having it."

They ate in silence for a minute or so.

"Aren't you eating cafeteria food right now?" asked Ezekiel. "You said you don't eat it."

"I cram it into my mouth, chew, and swallow. I don't eat this swill. This isn't eating."

"Beth," said Ezekiel. "How did you get through it? How did you keep your head?"

She raised her eyebrows. "What makes you think you have the right to—"

"You're the girl who forced this friendship on me," said Ezekiel, "and I was truthful with you about everything. I understand why you were keeping secrets because you didn't know if you could trust me, but you were never actually honest with me."

"Now you know, I'm a liar and a secret keeper," said Beth. "You can drop me as your friend if you want to."

"No I can't," said Ezekiel. "I don't want to, and I can't because—"

She interrupted him. "It was you that got me through it," she said. "Something you said when we were trying to figure out what it means to be lost. You said no person is ever really lost because you always know how to find yourself, because you're always right there."

"It's just an old stupid t-shirt slogan," said Ezekiel. "'Wherever you go, there you are.'"

"And a sign on the map in the mall," said Beth. "'You are here.'"

"How did that help?" asked Ezekiel.

"There I was, drugged for a while, tied up for a while, and then I ended up in this Game-of-Thrones prison where if you take one step too many you fall over the edge. And I could have made myself panic by trying to figure out how to get from where I was to somewhere better. Or trying to guess whether you'd be able to find me, because I didn't know that you had finally nailed it in your search for the little girl."

"Still didn't help that much in searching for you, because you apparently don't love any of your material possessions."

"I complain about my body," said Beth, "but I'm actually quite fond of it and I want to continue owning it and using it for a long time to come."

"So there you were."

"But that's exactly right. There I was. Not lost, but unfree. So instead of thinking about how much I needed rescue, I thought, how can I keep this bastard from doing any of the things he keeps threatening to do, or threatening that his bosses were going to do."

Ezekiel nodded. "So you just kept your mind on the problem at hand."

"The trouble was that my plan required Pigface to stand right at the edge of the floor with his back to me."

"So you maneuvered him to do that."

"Basically I asked him to do it."

"And when he stood there, you couldn't dither."

"Should I, shouldn't I, what if it doesn't work, what if it does, I thought of all of it in about a half a second and then I said to myself, Do it, it's your only chance. And because I'm so obedient, I did it."

"Man, that is what you do. It's better than a micropower. You don't just think of stuff, you do it. You decide that you want to walk to school in my shunning bubble, and—"

"Why are you doing this?" asked Beth. "You keep talking about stuff that happened weeks ago. And even the stuff that happened a couple of days ago—why?"

"Because those are the things that changed us," said Ezekiel. "Changed me, anyway. And your mother dying, that sure changed your life."

"My problem wasn't that it was a change," said Beth. "I go into Mom's room because she wasn't answering and she didn't come downstairs and she was lying there and I couldn't wake her up and I thought, Maybe she's dead. So I tried to take her pulse and then I used a mirror in front of her nose and then I just had to deal with it. Here I am now, and what's going to happen if I call nine-one-one, or if I call the police, or if I run crying into the street, or if I call the bank. I didn't like any of the things that I could think of happening, so then I thought, what can I do to keep people from finding out that Mom's dead and I'm alone. And I did those things."

"You did things that you never thought of doing."

"Of course," said Beth. "Nobody expects their mother to suddenly be dead on her bed."

"So your whole life changed."

"Look, Ezekiel Blast, the past is like gum stuck to the bottom of your shoe. When bad stuff first happens, it's like when the gum is sticking to everything—the road, the sidewalk. And you can't wear that shoe into the house because it will get all involved in the carpet and the bathroom rug, but when you try to scrape it off on the edge of the sidewalk or the edge of the porch, or you try to rub it off in the grass, it won't come off. So you have to just live with it. You walk along, your foot trying to stick with every step, but gradually as the gum gets dirtier and dries out more and more, it loses its stickiness. And eventually, without ever actually removing it, you forget the gum is there. Except maybe on a hot day the gum gets soft and a little sticky again, and you think, Oh, yeah, gum on my shoe."

Ezekiel tried to relate this to the past. "So my mom stayed dead," said Ezekiel, "but I kept going on with the business of living and the more I lived, the more time that passed by, the less it hurt. Never stopped hurting, but it stopped consuming my thoughts every minute I was awake and asleep."

"You got by."

"Gum on my shoe. My mother became gum on—"

"Your mother is always your mother. She is never gum, not on your shoe or anywhere else."

"I'm not an idiot, I get that."

"You keep bragging about not being an idiot," said Beth, "but you only say it right after you prove that you are."

"Ironic, isn't it?" said Ezekiel.

"Listen," said Beth, "I spent the first day after my mother died trying to think of everything I was going to need. Money, the yard guys, everything that was going to come up. Groceries. The fact that I cannot even imagine driving any vehicle bigger than a tricycle. What passwords would I need to get online? What software did she use? And then the body started to stink and I realized that this would be a dead giveaway, I've read the stories, 'Body found when neighbors noticed the smell,' so I spent a week jamming wet paper towels under the door and running the air conditioner full blast till I nearly froze to death in that house. And twice I had to open the door after all and go in that room because there was something I needed from her closet or wherever she kept it and yes, I did find everything I was looking for, because my mother is a careful woman and she had every password written down in a place where no burglar would ever think of looking, and I had to outthink that hypothetical burglar and find it."

"And you did," said Ezekiel.

"And then I had to push more wet paper towels under the door."

"I can't believe you kept your head together."

"I had to," said Beth. "It was that or invite Child Protective Services to dispose of *my* body."

"You hadn't even met me yet, so it wasn't my idea about people never being lost because you're right there."

"You put it in words. I knew you were right because that's what it was like that first week. I'm alone in my house with a dead body, and my mother will never be able to shop for groceries or pay her bills again, so here's what I've got to do. I made a list and kept adding to it and man, parents do a boatload of stuff all the time that kids never know about."

Ezekiel thought of his father, doing two parents-worth of jobs, so Ezekiel would never have to think about it.

"And then that royalty check arrived from the oil well—I did not have a clue that Mom owned an oil well—and I realized I could deposit it by endorsing it with her rubber stamp—that was my second trip into her bedroom and then resealing the door again—and so I didn't even have to fake her signature. Emails! No signatures! I never actually forged anything."

"I don't know if I could have done anything like what you did."

"You don't know what you can do until you have to do it," said Beth.

"But you didn't have to. Back in May you could have just let the world do to you whatever it does to undersized thirteen-year-old orphans."

"I made a choice and then I made it work for a while," said Beth. "That's all we can ever do about anything. But one thing for damn sure, Ezekiel Blast. I wasn't going to let the big thick wad of supersticky gum on my shoe trip me up or slow me down."

Ezekiel shook his head ruefully. "I've spent half my life chewing on that gum and sticking it on the bottom of my shoe myself. Not my mother's dying, that worked out just the way you said, passage of time and all that. I'm talking about all the accusations that I'm a thief, all the rumors and stories, all the suspicion, all the meanness of the other kids at school, all the parents who ordered their kids not to invite the thief to their birthday party if the kid even thought of inviting me at all."

"So that was your shunning bubble," said Beth. "Because yes, they were jerks, but you let the gum stick you to the sidewalk and all you could do was pivot in place."

"I can imagine you going up to one of the walking dead and saying, 'Do you believe I'm a thief? Have you heard that I steal stuff? Well let me ask you, have I ever taken anything of yours? Have I ever stolen something from anybody you know? From anybody at school?'"

Beth smiled. "Yeah, that's exactly what I would have done."

"And it would have worked," said Ezekiel. "But it never crossed my mind because I was ashamed."

"Innocent and yet ashamed," said Beth.

"When people treat you like you're guilty, then you feel the shame just as if you were. Shame is what other people force on you. I didn't imagine it."

Beth nodded. "I lied about the food. Cafeteria food tastes pretty good. And you know why? Because I didn't have to make a mile-and-a-half round trip to Food Lion in order to buy the ingredients."

"So you think that the food they serve here actually had ingredients?" said Ezekiel.

"What, you think they just conjure it out of primordial ooze?"

"I would think that, only it would be unfair to the ooze."

"Ezekiel, I don't want to live in the past. I don't want to keep scraping and scraping at the gum. I want to figure out what my micropower is, since Dr. Wingummy thinks I have one."

"I think your micropower is getting people to listen to you and believe what you tell them," said Ezekiel. "I think that's why you were able to get everybody to believe you about why your mom wasn't there."

"Who knows?" answered Beth. "I've got a new life starting up. But this half of my life, my post-mother life, it really began with you. When we became partners in crime—though of course you didn't know you were abetting my fraud—when I stopped being so alone, that was the most important thing. And if that hadn't happened, you wouldn't have been there to find me. Or whatever you did. Return your precious lost self to me."

"On the other hand, if I hadn't ticked you off so you walked home alone that Saturday, you wouldn't have needed rescuing."

"Ezekiel," said Beth, "everybody needs rescuing. You rescued me on that sidewalk on the way to school, and I rescued you, too, right?"

"Lonely people need rescuing, anyway."

"There's nothing but lonely people in this world," said Beth. "Even people who think they're not lonely, they're aching with loneliness or the fear of being lonely. So we saved each other every day for the past couple of months. And even though I have a little sister with whom I can trade outfits, in case I want to dress like a six-year-old, and the Delamares seem like decent people, it's still you. My partner in crime."

"No honor among thieves," said Ezekiel.

"There is if I say there is," said Beth.

"I'll try to live up to that," said Ezekiel.

"Lunch is over," said Beth.

"I didn't hear no stinkin' bell," said Ezekiel.

The bell sounded.

"Come on," said Ezekiel. "It's fine that you refuse to live in the past, but please don't live in the future, either. That just confuses me."

Beth gave him her bratty grin and carried her tray to the garbage can to dump her lunch litter. Ezekiel watched her go and tried, successfully, to keep the lump out of his throat. She almost died. She could have been lost to him forever. That didn't mean she wasn't still annoying.

He'd have to ask Dad about this. Did Mom ever annoy him? Can you be really close to somebody and still they drive you crazy?

Ezekiel was pretty sure the answer was yes. He wouldn't even have to ask.

He stood by the garbage can after he dumped his trash, watching other people clear their trays and head for class. And he thought: Out of all this crowd, she picked me. The coolest person in school chose me to be her friend and slapped me silly until I finally consented to it. I hope I'm never stupid enough to forget how completely that changed my life for the better.